Chalet in the Sky

Chalet in the Sky

by
Albert Robida

translated by
Brian Stableford

A Black Coat Press Book

Visit our website at www.blackcoatpress.com

ISBN 978-1-935558-87-3. First Printing. March 2011. Published by Black Coat Press, an imprint of Hollywood Comics.com, LLC, P.O. Box 17270, Encino, CA 91416. All rights reserved.
Printed in the United States of America.

TABLE OF CONTENTS

Introduction

This is the third volume of translations from the works of Albert Robida that I have published through Black Coat Press, the earlier volumes being *The Clock of the Centuries* (2008), which also included "Yesterday Now" (ISBN 9781934543139) and *The Adventures of Saturnin Farandoul* (2009) (ISBN 9781934543610). The latter volume featured a translation of Robida's first novel, originally issued as a part-work in 1879, while the former featured a novel originally published in 1902 and a short story first published in 1890. The two works translated in the present volume, "Un Potache en 1950" (1917; here translated as "A Schoolboy in 1950") and *Un Chalet dans les airs* (1925; here translated as "Chalet in the Sky") belong to a later phase in his work, the latter being his last published novel.

By the time he wrote these two stories, Robida had witnessed considerable changes in the marketplace in which he worked as a writer and illustrator. Although a boom in the publication of popular magazines in the 1890s had added considerable scope to his opportunities, it had also signaled a future shrinkage of those opportunities as photographic illustration began slowly but inexorably to replace hand-drawn illustrations in the more upmarket periodicals. This trend added to the corrosive effect of the tailing off of the boom in the first decade of the 20th century, and it decisive interruption by the outbreak of the Great War in 1914. It is not surprising, therefore, that a gradually-increasing proportion of Robida's work, not only in magazines, but in his own self-illustrated books, was aimed at younger readers, where the tradition of illustration, especially of the comedic variety favored by Robida, was more robustly maintained.

There were, however, other reasons why the nature and inclination of Robida's futuristic illustrations shifted quite markedly after the turn of the century. Having become famous for his pioneering work in futuristic imagery in the early 1880s, when he published the extravagant serial publication *Le Vingtième siècle* (1882-83; revised 1895; tr. as *The Twentieth Century*), and the his garish depiction of *La Guerre au Vingtième siècle* (1883; book version with different text 1887; tr. as "War in the Twentieth Century"), he found himself somewhat typecast, continually asked to add further tranches to the account of life in 1950, elaborately described in the former work and frequently commissioned to illustrate futuristic essays and novels by other writers. In particular, he was often asked to illustrate future war novels, which became increasingly popular in France after 1890—something that must have irritated him somewhat, given that he was a pacifist who had intended his luridly satirical depiction of 20th century warfare as an awful warning, while many popular writers of future war stories were excited, sometimes lasciviously so, by the possibilities of large-scale destruction. As a freelance illustrator, he was presumably reluctant to turn down work, but such tasks as illustrating Pierre Giffard's long-running part-work *La Guerre infernale* (1908) must have caused him to wonder whether he was any longer on the side of the angels, or whether he might actually be contributing to the enthusiastic expectation of a new war fought with airships, submarines and high explosives.

Once the Great War had actually broken out, of course, the marketplace for the depiction of futuristic weaponry—especially its satirical depiction—became very problematic indeed, and depictions of the future in general feel somewhat out of fashion as the urgent vicissitudes of the present monopolized attention. There was, however, an exception to this rule in publication for younger readers, where a requirement a recognized to insulate children somewhat from the worst horrors of the war, and to maintain their morale in a fashion distinctly different from the German-demonizing strategies of adult propaganda. By 1917, the pacifist Robida presumably felt in dire need of some kind of psychological release from the horrors of the war, and one can easily imagine how he came to be attracted by the prospect of returning to the world of 1950 in the milieu of a school, where no thought need be paid, or could be paid, to matters of large-scale international conflict and the possible means of its promulgation.

"Un Potache en 1950" will undoubtedly seem far less exotic to English readers than it would have done to its original audience because it is, to a large extent, a parody of something with which they are inevitably far more familiar: the English public school story. It is important to remember, while reading Robida's satire, that no such genre existed in France. Although there are certainly some French novels of the late 19th and early 20th centuries set partly or wholly in schools, there was no distinct publishing category of that sort, or anything remotely akin to the deluge of such works published in England. Indeed, the readers of *Mon Journal*, the children's periodical in which "Un Potache en 1950" was first serialized, would have been far more familiar with English stories of that type in translation than with similar works originated in their own language. They would, however, have known perfectly well what it was that Robida was mocking.

Although the roots of the English public school story can be traced back to Thomas Hughes' *Tom Brown's Schooldays* (1857), or even to Charles Dickens' several accounts of the horrors of English school life, the school story was not formularized and established as a genre until the late 1880s, when it was pioneered by Talbot Baines Reed. Its nostalgic mythos had, however, been satirized in advance by F. Anstey's *Vice Versa* (1882), which set out to disprove the common but blatantly absurd axiom that schooldays are the best days of one's life—an axiom to which the school story offers broad and determined, if not entirely unqualified, support. The genre made such rapid and spectacular progress in the nation's literary heart that it attracted writers of the status of Rudyard Kipling, in *Stalky & Co.* (1899) and P. G. Wodehouse, in *Mike* (1909), and the notion that England's officer class were in serious training for imperial responsibility—including the attendant warfare—on the playing-fields of its public schools became

9

enshrined in such mawkish masterpieces of bad verse as Henry Newbolt's "Vitaï Lampada" (1897).[1]

Equally importantly, in terms of the parody featured in "Un Potache en 1950," was the spectacular rise of the girl's school story, pioneered by L. T. Meade, but brought to a strange kind of perfection by Angela Brazil in the long series of novels she launched in 1906. Having displayed his feminist credentials flamboyantly in *Le Vingtième Siècle*, Robida was only too willing to incorporate similar elements into his account of the rival single-sex school of Chambourcy and Villennes. His anti-racist credentials may not seem to the modern reader to be entirely convincing, but one only has to compare his account of the African Alfred Koufra with the many contemporary accounts of the sons of Indian maharajahs arriving at English public schools—of which Robedia's subplot is an obvious parody—to see that he was at least a little way ahead of his time, and a long way ahead of such jingoistic writers of English "boys' books" as G. A. Henty.

Looking at the genre from outside, with a comedic sensibility, Robida was presumably more acutely conscious than its earnest writers of the fact that the school story was a subspecies of Utopian fantasy, reflecting a perverse yearning for a kind of innocence that had no more real existence than any other imaginary Golden Age. He obviously understood, too, that it was by no means lacking in charm on that account—indeed, quite the reverse.

There is a curious sense in which some of the futuristic technology that Robida had integrated into his image of 1950 at the outset—especially the miscellaneous aircraft—fitted into that mythos very comfortably, adding an entirely appropriate element of décor. Had other writers taken notice of what he was doing—although no English writer was likely to take

---

[1] The chorus line of which is "Play up! Play up! And play the game!" Its extravagant use as an instrument of propaganda during the Great War would have ensured that Robida was familiar with it.

kindly to having the piss taken out of him (or her) by a Frenchman—it might not have been necessary to announce the death of the genre half a century before J. K. Rowling revealed that all that was required for its triumphant resurrection was a powerful inoculation of fantasy. The uses made of such communicative technology as the "telephonoscope" in the school life of Robida's 1950 are somewhat less apt, and more obviously played for amiable laughs—a slightly ironic observation, in view of the fact that such technologies have since made much greater strides in actuality than personalized air transport. On the whole, however, the modern reader will have no difficulty slotting as comfortably into the life of the "open air" school of Chambourcy as into the life of Hogwarts Academy, nor in appreciating the equally strong links that bind it to the obsolete but unforgotten mythology of the English school story

The determined lightness, intense insulation and curious quasi-familiarity of the world within the text of "Un Potache en 1950" cannot, however, conceal the fact that its Utopian ideals are tarnished, if not frankly deceptive. The disasters featured in the novel are the results of accidental breakdown rather than malice, but that only serves to make their threat seem more ominous, especially in combination with the story's visit to England, and the discovery there of the continuing thrust of the Industrial revolution. Like all Robida's other accounts of life in 1950, his school story is not as optimistic as it seemingly wants or tries to be. If the story has a moral—and it does not try overly hard to avoid displaying one—it is that technology, in the end, is a treacherous crutch, on which it is unwise to rely too heavily, no matter how ingenious one might be in its sophistication and deployment. Robida meant that very sincerely, no matter how jokily he repeatedly integrated the lesson into his plot

Robida showed little inclination to return to the world mapped out in *Le Vingtième siècle* after publishing "Un Potache en 1950," partly because he had exhausted the inspirational seam and partly because it had become out-dated, especially by the hideous lessons of the Great War. After producing a scorching dramatization of those lessons in *L'Ingénieur von Satanas* (1918), he did attempt a relatively modest revision, in an unreprinted serial aimed at an adult audience, "En 1965" [In 1965] (1920), but it was probably too unadventurous in its scope at make much appeal, as well as badly-timed, and its relative failure must have demonstrated to him that the marketplace was not only no longer sympathetic to such endeavors, but was becoming actively hostile to them. It is not surprising that he reverted to gentler imaginative fare for a while, but nor is it surprising that he did not give up. He evidently thought it worthwhile to move his imagery forward into a more distant future, in order to update his vision more extravagantly, although he also thought it politic to do so in a book aimed at younger readers rather than the audience for which *Le Vingtième Siècle* had been written.

There is a certain propriety in the fact that Robida's most adventurous futuristic work, in terms of its temporal reach, should be his last—his swan song, in effect—and that it should have been planned as a book for children in much the same vein as "Un Potache en 1950." That propriety did not, alas, prevent it from proved unmarketable in its intended context—it was not serialized in a juvenile periodical, as he presumably hoped that it might be—as a result of its inability to refrain from touching on adult themes with a distinctively adult sarcasm.

It cannot be claimed that *Un Chalet dans les airs* is one of Robida's best works—its quality does not come remotely close to that of the works of his literary prime—but that is understandable, given that Robida was nearly 80 by the time it was published, and within a year of his death. It is a patchy text, whose frequent trivial repetitions and petty contradictions suggest that he might have kept forgetting what he had written, but it also a remarkable text in several ways. Most importantly, in displaying the extrapolation of his ideas into a further future, it reveals their underlying thrust more explicitly than ever before. It also makes a more obvious, and conspicuously more plaintive, display of the particular kind of nostalgia that he set out in such a lovingly tongue-in-cheek fashion in "Un Potache en 1950." It is quite possible that the narrative is a patchwork, recovering and absorbing at last one item of work that he had written at a considerably earlier date—the account of the fall of Astra—but it does have a certain overall coherency in the way it carefully extrapolates the fundamental themes of "Un Potache en 1950." It presents a more expansive account of future transportation, a far more horrific image of a polluted and hyperactive industrial city of the future—New York instead of London—and allows its young protagonists to indulge in the big game hunting that remains out of reach in the earlier story, albeit with a distinct preference for the camera over the machine-gun.

In a sense, the later story complements the earlier one, whose plot was confined by the school year, in featuring a kind of endless vacation, in which work and study, although notionally going on, are conscientiously avoided to the greatest possible extent. *Un Chalet dans les airs* contrasts very sharply with "Un Potache en 1950" in one respect, however; in the earlier story, Chambourcy and Paris sit contentedly side by side; however Utopian the "open air school" might be, it is not out of place in the mundane world of which it is a part; it is an appropriate institution for its place and time. The whole point about the "aerovilla" of *Un Chalet dans les airs*, however, is that it does not and cannot fit into the world where modern road-works writ large are undertaking a complete resurfacing of the globe, whose crust has been exploited to the point of exhaustion. It is the characters' escape-mechanism from that project, and their intention to return home once they have enjoyed a brief vacation, becomes less convincing with every page that is turned. They really are in full flight from a civilization that has become literally intolerable in its ambition and methods, and the only real question facing them is whether they can possibly find anywhere else to go that is not either a sham (like the Caucasian Archipelago) or in the process of being co-opted (like Astra).

There is no "if" at all about the question of whether *Un Chalet dans les airs* has a moral; it does, and how—and whether one can accept that moral wholeheartedly or not, it is certainly shaped with conviction and a certain flourish: a distinctive panache that Robida had at the very beginning of his career, and never entirely lost, even as senility began to get a grip on him. As swan songs go, *Un Chalet dans les airs* is far from trivial; it is both fascinating and admirable, despite its minor flaws. "Un Potache en 1950" provides a useful and appropriate prologue to it, so the two stories will hopefully make up a satisfactory volume.

The version of "Un Potache en 1950" used for translation was the reprint issued in 1994 by Apex in its Periodica collection, which is a facsimile of the *Mon Journal* serial. The version of *Un Chalet dans les airs* was the photographic reproduction of the first edition available on the Bibliothéque Nationale's invaluable website, *gallica*.

Brian Stableford

A SCHOOLBOY IN 1950

I. The Arrival of a Newcomer

On the morning of September 15, 1950, Gustave Turbille, the son of the well-known businessman, was in the
process of packing his bags in order to return to the open air
school of Chambourcy, looking to see whether he had forgotten any of his kit for tennis, football, golf, hydroplaning, mo-
tor-boating and so on, and whether his rackets, hockey-sticks,
skates, notebooks, phonodisks and other important accessories
were all present and correct. His sister Colette was doing the
same in the next room, for her return to the girls' open air
school at Villennes.[2]

A telephone call from his father summoned the boy ur-
gently. The elevator took two seconds to go up to the 12th
floor of the comfortable town house, where the large bay windows of Monsieur Turbille's study, next to the aero platform,
overlooked the stirring horizon of the immense city of Paris.

"Gustave," said Monsieur Turbille, who seemed to be in
a hurry, "you're a serious boy—14-1/2, aren't you? Yes?
Good... Going back to school today, eh? All ready? Good...

---

[2] There never was a significant school at Chambourcy, nor at
the nearby town of Villennes-sur-Seine; the choice of location
might have been influenced by the fact that a deserted village
near Chambourcy became the site, after the 1789 revolution,
of the "desert of Retz," a Romantic garden featuring several
impressive follies.

First you're going to the Gare du Sud-Ouest for the 10:25 a.m. tube from Bordeaux, to meet young Alfred Koufra, from Villeneuve-sur-Oubangui in the Congo…same age as you, going into the third form with you. I'm his sponsor…too busy to take care of him today, so I'm leaving it to you; take delivery, and you can go on to school together."

"All right," Gustave replied, slightly surprised. "I'll go—but how will I recognize Alfred Koufra?"

"It's agreed with his family that you'll put our index finger to your nose like *this* as the voyagers arrive; Alfred Koufra will do the same… A handshake, you become acquainted, he gets into an aeroclette with you,[3] and at 10:45, you're in Chambourcy. Understood?"

"Yes, Papa."

Gustave Turbille went back downstairs, tightened a few buckles on his suitcases, ran to embrace his mother and sister and went back up to the 12th floor, to the flight platform, where his aeroclette was waiting for him.

It was a bright, clear September morning. From the heights of the Saint-Cloud district, the immense city was neatly outlined, with its successive levels, its monuments and its steeples, the curves of the Seine, the local aerial embarkation-platforms, and the long lines of tubes crossing vast spaces beneath arcades before plunging towards all the points of the horizon. The tubes, which had replaced the slow and cumbersome old railways everywhere, transported travelers at 1200 kilometers an hour—even more for the expresses of the major lines.

Above the thousand details of the earthly panorama there was the landscape of the sky, a picturesque particularity unknown to our ancestors, animated by dense, noisy traffic,

---

[3] It is not obvious from the text at this point, but Robida's illustrations make it clear that an *aeroclette* is a small helicopter; Gustave's is subsequently referred to as a *helicoclette*, although there is also a descriptive passage that lists the two terms separately, as if they were distinct.

swarming with vehicles of every sort: aerocabs, aeroteufs, heavy airships, large Post Office aeronefs, or slender motoclettes, light birds of the air, spiraling up into the blue and flying at all heights. And the customary music of the heavens hummed and vibrated, like the sound of huge perpetual organpipes intercut with rapid whistling murmurs.

Gustave did not pay much attention to these details. He started his engine and, in five or six minutes, without hurrying, found himself at the Bordeaux Tube. At exactly 10:25 a.m., he heard the muffled whistling of the approaching train, still some distance away, in the tube. A slight quiver of the metallic framework of the station, a siren-blast, and the train was there! Then the balcony of the arrival hall was suddenly flooded by a hectic crowd, and the elevators slid through their shafts, bringing the passengers down.

Gustave leaned on the barrier meditatively, with one finger applied to his nose, according to his father's instruction, in order that he might be recognized. The passengers filed past him, perhaps a trifle stunned by the rapidity of the means of transport, which launched them through the immense tube like a projectile, without jolts or jerks.

Among the passengers, he distinguished from afar a tall boy of approximately his own age, who was coming forward very gravely, also holding his index-finger to his nose, looking around.

Oh—he's black! thought Gustave, surprised. *Not difficult to recognize, so there was no need of such complex instructions. An African from the Congo—good. But what language shall we speak?*

Gustave had already prepared his first sentence, in a confused mixture of Esperanto, Volapük, Ido, blue language and five or six other so-called universal languages.[4]

---

[4] International languages were much in vogue in the decades prior to the Great War; Volapük was devised by Johannn Martin Schleyer in 1879, Esperanto by L. L. Zamenhof in 1889, and Bolak, also known as "blue language," by Leon Bollack in

The black youth had seen Gustave; he smiled broadly and put more pressure on his nose as he came forward.

"*Toi passir par ici,*" Gustave called, waving his arms. "*Moi t'attendir, y a bon...as-tu bagages besef?*"[5]

The boy seemed nonplussed and stopped, getting in the way of impatient passengers. Gustave multiplied his gestures and reverted to his improvised Esperanto.

"I beg your pardon, Monsieur?" said the black youth, in surprise.

"Good—you speak French. How are you? I'm Gustave Turbille; Papa is your sponsor, you know."

"So this is Paris, then! Oh, it's more beautiful than Villeneuve. I'm Alfred Koufra. Papa is a notary in Villeneuve-sur-Oubangui. Almost two days from the Congo to Bordeaux, and the tube has given me a slight headache...the one at Villeneuve is an old model, and runs so slowly..."

"You'll be getting straight into an aeroclette, my dear chap—we're going to school right away; we need to be there to meet friends...your luggage? Good, you have the ticket—your bags will be over there, behind us."

Gustave tapped the black youth on the shoulder; the latter was staring at the landscape, wide-eyed.

"You still seem bewildered," said Gustave. "Well, this is Paris. You haven't seen anything like it? So it doesn't resemble Villeneuve? Over there is the Seine—not as impressive as the Oubangui, perhaps? There are no baobabs here, you know. And now that you've had five minutes of contemplation, let's go."

"Beautiful!" proffered young Koufra, as they walked on.

"Of course! Come on—to the garage, quickly!"

1899; Ido (Robida has *Ito*) was a revised version of Esperanto (its name means "offspring), which made its debut in 1907.

[5] This is actually calculatedly-botched "trading French" rather than a compound of the universal languages cited above; as the addressee is supposed to find it incomprehensible, there seems little point in "translating" it into pidgin English.

In the midst of aerial vehicles of every sort—aeroclettes, helicoclettes and others—somewhat tangled up on the terrace, the comings and goings of pilots and passengers, and the mind-numbing tumult of take-offs, Gustave moved entirely at his ease, but the black youth seemed slightly anxious.

"You'll get used to it! People are still rather rustic in the Congo, it seems? Don't overplay the innocent newcomer in front of the lads, though... Here's my little aero; get in behind me and you'll see how we eat up the countryside!" He pointed to his machine, the very latest model, both elegant and comfortable, perfectly safe, which could hold three people in a light cabin fitted with much-reduced flexible wings.

"And it's you who...you who drive it...?"

"I've known how for a long time! You don't drive aeros or motoclettes in Villeneuve, then?"

"Rarely...not all alone..."

Gustave shrugged his shoulders. "Child! Perhaps you drive hydros? With your rivers and lakes, the Oubangui, the Congo, the Zambezi...the hydro-sport must be very good there. Do you do that?"

"Not much."

"Oh, I've got an idea! Buckle up—I'm taking off. Are we all right? Smooth, isn't it, old chap? Don't you feel as if you're gliding? It doesn't skim the clouds, at least, like those cabs—those aeros for hire over on the right. Is that all right? We're going to set a course over the forest of Saint-Germain, that blue patch on the horizon...the school is beyond it, not far... I told you I had an idea; this is it: Papa is your sponsor in Paris, so your father must be my sponsor in the Congo! Oh, it's a good idea: in the Easter vacation, I want to go big game hunting in Africa with you! Very chic! I seem to remember that you said your father was...what?"

"A notary."

"A notary—that won't do. Look, there's no need to tell the other boys that he's a notary. Naturally, he's a little...colored...too, your father? Well, let me handle it. At school, I'll say that you're the son of a powerful African monarch that my father met out there while building his power stations at the Zambezi falls; that will set you up at school. It's agreed, then?"

II. The Return.
Sensational Introduction to the Schoolfriends.

As they drew nearer to the school, Gustave moderated his helicoclette's speed in order to show off the countryside to his young friend from the Congo, who was still slightly stunned by the journey.

"Do you see all that greenery to the right? That's the forest of Saint-German. Over there...Chambourcy School takes up all of that large area between the forest and the Seine. We'll make a circuit around it before going in, in order that you can get a look at it. Not bad, our school—first rate, you know!"

"Good teachers?" asked Alfred Koufra.

"And how! All renowned for 50 or 60 years..."

"Oh!" said Koufra, surprised. "They're very old, then?"

"And a golf course! Excellent—the best of all of those I've played in school and college competitions. Don't forget—you're the son of an African monarch. That will set you up, I tell you."

"Yes, yes..."

"Here are the school buildings, the Headmaster's house, the open-air auditoria, the study-arbors, the halls for rainy days, the garages...the football-ground directly beneath us, the velodrome for the little boys...the broad path over there is the peripatetics' walkway...[6]

---

[6] The term *péripatéticiens* [peripatetics] has a double-meaning in France; although derived from the "peripatetic" school of Greek philosophy, the word is also used to refer to street-walkers of a more vulgar sort. Obviously, Gustave is applying

"Further away, that inlet of the Seine is our yachting harbor; the boats, yachts, canoes and kayaks aren't here yet; you'll see them in a few days! Those other buildings over there on the left are my sister Colette's school at Villennes... It's not bad, is it, our landscape? Now you know, let's make a suitable entrance...but don't forget—a king's son!"

By means of a clever descending maneuver, Gustave Turbille gained entry to the school. With the graceful motion of a bird allowing itself to glide, his helicoclette settled gently to the ground, alongside other aerial vehicles of various forms, which had also brought pupils.

Joyful shouts welcomed him; meeting again after the scattering of the vacation, everyone had a great deal to say to one another; handshakes were exchanged, along with claps on the shoulder and bursts of laughter.

"Not everyone arrives by aero," Gustave said to his companion, "some come by road on motocyclettes...it's a little outdated, the motocyclette, good for distant colonies or old codgers, but it lacks chic here. Ah! Here's some friends from the third form. Hello, Béguinot, are you well? Hello, Lavigne! Hello, Mathis!"

The arriving boys were forming up in little groups in front of the vast entrance to the grounds; boys were seeking one another out, loudly giving one another their news. With every passing minute, more aeroclettes appeared in the sky. Their occupants were recognized from afar and they were greeted with waving arms.

A few blasts of a siren behind the trees were heard.

"The school bell!" said Gustave. "Bah! We have time...come on, my dear Koufra, I'll introduce you to my friends in the third form... My friend Pignerol, day boy, a brilliant student, an especially good swimmer...comes from

---

the former meaning to his teachers, and Robida would not expect his readers to think otherwise, although he would be well aware that they would notice the *double entendre.*

Orléans every morning by aeroclette and goes back at 5 p.m…"

"The long way round if the weather's fine," said Pignerol.

"Other good friends: Rodolphe Boulard, our heavyweight boxing champion, and Marcel Labrouscade, our poetry champion—good old Labrouscade, the most celebrated *littérateur* in Chambourcy, who will one day deign to take an armchair in the Académie…"

Koufra bowed deeply.

"Tony Lubin, also a half-boarder, the valiant, elegant and distinguished tennis champion of Chambourcy…comes from Châlons-sur-Marne every day in his aero…"

"Not today," said Tony Lubin. "Hired machine—I crashed my aero in the mountains a fortnight ago. Can you imagine…"

"Hey!" said Gustave. "I didn't notice—you're arm's in a cast?"

"Yes," said Tony Lubin, gloriously. "A landing accident in the mountains, near the Vosges! My dear chap, I nearly impaled myself in a fir-tree—a huge devil of a fir-tree that reached for me malevolently with its pointed branches…oh, the brigand! I only just avoided it; I only got a few grazes…and I think even those have healed!"

Tony Lubin withdrew his arm from the sling and swung it gently. "Yes, it's OK!"

Gustave burst out laughing. "A mere bruise, such as we all get," he said. "You wanted to arrive with your arm in a sling as a tease!"

"Word of honor!" said Tony Lubin, "A squall, a gust of wind, and I only escaped being impaled thanks to my presence of mind and skill…"

"Exceptional, of course," said Gustave.

"And my aero remained hanging in the tree! The family was furious, you know—an 8000-franc machine. But as you'll see next week, its successor is the very latest thing, with all of this year's improvements. What about you—good holiday?"

"Sea bathing in Constantinople, like every year."

"Me," said Béguinot, "Cap Nord in August, stayed with my aunt in Pithiviers in September...that was even colder. Cap Nord, old chaps, cruising the fjords, quite wonderful!"

"I know! I was taken there when I was small. Now, I only dream about hunting—hunting big game!"

"Big game? Brrr! Where's that? Lower down the Seine, for giant ferocious hares and monstrous wild boar?"

"No, my friend, no—better than that, I assure you...and on that note, I'll continue the introductions. My good friends, a new boy for the third form, my good friend Koufra, who comes from a little further away than Pithiviers, and can't go home every evening. Papa is his sponsor in Paris; we came together: my good friend Koufra, from the Oubangui, eldest son and future successor of a Congo monarch!"

Gustave leaned toward Béguinot and whispered something in his ear, of which Alfred Koufra only heard a part: "An African potentate, my dear chap, a fine fellow—I'll say no more...Papa told me about him. You know—you've read the tales of the great explorers...well, it's still the same out there, old chap! Then again, it's very curious; one day..."

"My boys," Gustave continued, aloud, "my friend Koufra is a good lad...but I must say that my holiday on the beaches of the Bosphorus and the casinos of the Archipelago were dull—Papa's idea; he wanted me to brush up on my Greek history! I had hoped for something else, in the home of Koufra's father, but—just between us, he was busy; a revolt to put down...shhh!—it's been put off until the next vacation. Koufra and I are flying off to his father's, and then it's off into the bush, after big game!"

An admiring circle had formed around Koufra, who was slightly embarrassed. Gustave Turbille's introduction had been a success.

The siren continued its appeals. The pupils condescended to pass through the school gates while still chatting, very slowly. Late-comers were still landing, leaving their aeroclettes to the mechanics.

"Come on, gentlemen!" said an earnest individual in a black frock-coat standing by the gate. "May I remind you that you're 20 minutes late!"

A hum in the sky, slight at first but quickly amplified, caused young Koufra to raise his head. A cigar-shaped airship, nimbler and more elegant in its movements than the vulgar transporters of the minor lines, was advancing rapidly in the direction of the school.

"It's our omnibus," said Gustave. "Every morning, it goes to Paris to pick up the day boys who don't come alone— first the little ones, then the others. There are some who don't have their flying permits, you know, or have even had them taken away because of some excessive awkwardness…"

The dirigible touched down. On its envelope, between two large rosettes in the school colors, pink and green, were the words:

Chambourcy: First Class Open Air School

The passengers disembarked, welcomed by other pupils in a rather noisy fashion, in spite of the appeals for calm uttered by the earnest individual at the entrance.

"Come on, come on, gentlemen—the vacation is over. The school year has begun, let's be serious!"

"Who's that?" asked Koufra of his friend Gustave.

"Monsieur Virgile Radoux, the third's form-master. We're on very good terms—I'll recommend you to him. It will be all right—you'll see! He's a bit old-fashioned, but it's good to see the old-timers—an outmoded and superannuated generation, with very curious ideas, sometimes funny, but quite interesting. We call that doing psychological archeology. Don't look at me with those astonished eyes; what I've just told you is profound, but it's suggested by experience— experience that you can't have acquired in your distant land, naturally… Bah! Just three months of school and you'll have caught me up!"

Rolling his eyes admiringly, Koufra made a gesture of protest full of modesty.

"Leave it to me! When we're chasing rhinoceroses in your country, I'll be a novice and you can crush me with your scorn! How many rhinoceroses have you killed?"

Koufra was about to reply that he had never seen any large animals in the already-industrialized vicinity of Villeneuve-sur-Oubangui, but Gustave had already changed the subject. "He's a poet, you know!"

"Who is?"

"Monsieur Virgile Radoux, our form-master; that explains which he seems a bit grumpy sometimes, between two rhymes that don't quite seem to work, but a good fellow all the same. I'll introduce you to him."

Monsieur Virgile Radoux, the form-master, is a tall, thin man; his face is framed by a short, yellowing beard, his tilted-back hat reveals a premature baldness, and he is incessantly replacing on his nose a pince-nez that persists in falling off again. He comes forward, chatting to a few older boys, veteran sixth-formers and prospective science students at the École Polytechnique.

"Monsieur, here's a new boy…"

"Ah! Very good!" the form-master replied. "Let's see— I'll wager that you're the pupil from the Congo we've been expecting! I've guessed it, haven't I? I'm a physiognomist…"

"Dead right, Monsieur," Gustave replied. "This is him, Alfred Koufra of the Oubangui; he's come a long way, from Central Africa."

"Well, Koufra, you're going into the third form. Do you have your scholarly record?"

"Villeneuve College," said Koufra, timidly, handing a little book to the form-master.

"Let's see," said Monsieur Radoux, leafing rapidly through the booklet. "*French language, good. French composition, good. English…Math, adequate. Physics and Chemistry, adequate. Geometry, almost adequate. Latin, good. Greek, good. Latin composition, good…* The comments now: *Intelligent student, but still unserious… Much too frivolous… Little talent for Mathematics… Sometimes inattentive… Well-*

intentioned, but too easily-distracted… Progress in Classics… Insufficient progress… Serious progress… Almost satisfactory term… Hope for more sustained attention next year… Good! I know you now, Koufra—you're good at Classics…"

"If you like, Monsieur. Papa puts great store in Latin; he makes me work on it at home. Papa writes very good Latin verses, Monsieur…ouch!"

Gustave Turbille had given him a violent dig with his elbow. While the form-master was studying the notes, Gustave had been giving his friends some further information about the newcomer.

"Young Koufra is really someone, old chaps. His father is a king in the Oubangui, the most absolute monarch there is, a potentate in the old African mode, but broadly open to modern ideas…"

What Koufra had confided to the form-master troubled Gustave slightly—an African king who wrote Latin verses!—but he quickly collected himself. "Open to European ideas, you see," he said, "even our old superstitions!"

They arrived at the school buildings.

"Back in custody!" said Gustave. "Now, the inaugural lunch, and soon back to class! A consolatory glass of champagne, before tomorrow's abundance! Then you'll have the Minister of Public Education's speech…"

"What, he's here!"

"Of course! You'll see! To welcome us and solemnize the start of term."

*III. In which Turbille reveals himself as an innovator
and an enemy of old routines.*

In the refectory, which was rather noisy when the time for champagne arrived, a stern voice suddenly demanded silence.

"It's the Minister," Gustave whispered.

Koufra looked around, searching behind the other tables. There was no one there but the pupils, Monsieur Radoux and the other form-masters.

"The Minister's here? Where? He's put himself out for us?"

"It's his custom at the start of the school year—but don't look for him under the table," said Gustave, laughing with his neighbors. "The Minister is in front of you…"

On a small table amid the larger ones, elevated above the crockery and baskets of bread, was the horn of a large phonograph; that was what had spoken.

Koufra was about to get up, respectfully, but Gustave tugged at his jacket.

The phonograph coughed, as if it were clearing its voice.

"Young people," it proclaimed, "now that you are resuming your studies, the Minister of Public Education will perform his duty, offering you official encouragement and reminding you of the importance…immense fields of science…preparatory work…brilliant careers…"

In spite of the Minister's fine voice, Koufra could only grasp these fragments of sentences, for the conversations of his neighbors was continuing mutedly, and Gustave undertook to furnish him with explanations.

"Yes, my dear chap, at Chambourcy, as at all the other schools in France at this moment, we have the ministerial speech…"

"And to alternate with regular and fecund studies, also count on the government, which has prepared for you, over the school year, a program of distractions as broad and attractive as possible... And now, to work, young people!"

The peroration was greeted with an *ah!* of satisfaction; glasses of champagne were raised in the Minister's honor, and the inaugural lunch concluded as noisily as it had begun.

During the half-hour break before work began, Gustave showed his friend around the school.

"We need to go up to the top floor quickly, my boy! Five minutes with me, and you'll know the classrooms, the lecture theatres, the laboratories, the large cinema, the sports halls, the famous pupils, our champions, our teachers...very chic, the teachers!"

"Papa told me that—the best teachers..."

"Certainly. Muscle and brain! Educational sport, very important at Chambourcy. So, as you'll see, for boxing, we have the foremost pupil of the famous..."

"No, what about the other teachers?"

"You'll see—all very chic, I tell you, the teachers!"

He took a list of courses from his pocket. They were, indeed, all celebrity university graduates, whose renown had reached as far as the Congo. Monsieur Koufra senior had quoted them to his son with pride.

Having gone over the entire school and rapidly met all of Gustave's friends, Alfred Koufra waited, a trifle intimidated, for the first class. He sat between Gustave and his friend Bouloche, the hope of the school for the long jump.

All the pupils were holding their pencils and pens at the ready. And the teacher? He had not arrived. On the chair in front of the blackboard, Monsieur Virgile Radoux was arranging papers, on which irregular lines of handwriting could be distinguished.

"Sonnets and ballads!" Gustave whispered in Koufra's ear. "After the lesson, I'll ask him for the favor of a few morsels..."

"But where's the professor?"

"Here he is!"

Virgile Radoux had just flicked the switch of a phonograph. At first, the preliminary murmurs of a distant voice were heard, but it soon took on an impressive gravity. It was the professor. At the same time, he appeared beside the blackboard—or, rather, his cinematographic image trembled, then came into focus, on the screen of a telephonoscope behind the phonograph. It was a sufficiently imposing physiognomy: a man with a vast bald forehead and a beautiful black beard, whose authoritarian gaze surveyed the pupils ranged before him.

Although that gaze seemed to settle particularly on him, Koufra no longer felt as intimidated. After some initial hesitation, his pen-holder moved quite regularly, and by the time the lesson was well under way, he was covering the pages of his notebook briskly. He had made a good beginning at the school! To think that he had been so fearful of his first days, the annoyances and difficulties! But now, everything had fallen into place admirably!

Beside him, Gustave yawned occasionally. Koufra noticed that he was not taking notes. Behind a little notebook that he was holding up, he was operating a bizarre little machine, totally unknown in the backward college of Villeneuve-sur-Oubangui. What was it? He would find out after the lesson.

When the professor had finished, the Headmaster—or, rather, his image—passed through the rooms by telephonoscope to say a few words to the pupils; then, before further study, they had two hours of recreation in optional courses: various kinds of sports; gymnastics, fencing, etc.

"What were you doing with your machine, then?" Koufra asked, as soon as they had left the lecture-hall.

"I was experimenting with a method of my own for lectures. Taking notes by hand is very old-fashioned—I might even say infantile and barbaric. My method constitutes an immense progress, and it seems to me to be working very well. I'm simply recording the course on phono disks."

"Oh!" said Koufra.

"It's done automatically; I have the complete course instead of mere lecture notes, like you—and, moreover, time to reflect and think. I might even absent myself, if the formmaster has no objection. Can you see the advantages?"

Koufra expressed his admiration with expressive nods of the head.

"Yes," said Gustave, negligently, "it's not a stroke of genius—it's quite simple, but it was necessary to think of it! Personally, my boy, I don't rest content with what I find hardly functional—all the material and paraphernalia of civilization. I immediately think about improving it...I'm a man of progress! And now, let's rest the intellect—a session on the parallel bars, perhaps? A little football?"

Gustave, who was filling out and very fit, observed the inferiority of his companion on the sports field sadly. What, no stronger than that? No good at all at fencing, barely passable in gymnastics, worse than mediocre at football, no good at the high jump or the long jump...what about swimming and yachting?"

"Not too bad at swimming," said Alfred Koufra.

The siren, which has replaced the antiquated bell in modern schools, recalled them to the study halls. The pupils went back in, leaping over bushes and jostling one another somewhat in the grounds.

They set to work, in that first study period, with only moderate enthusiasm, the good times of the vacation still being so close. Books and various items of apparatus were spread out on the tables; then the tap-tap of typewriters began quietly in one corner of the room, and slowly spread to make itself heard everywhere. All the machines were tapping away except Koufra's.

The latter, with his head in his hands, was trying to concentrate in order to read over his notes. His mind was still elsewhere; everything in this vast school was too new to him; he felt that he needed to catch his breath. Eventually, his machine was at work like the others; Koufra was very zealous, and he intended to distinguish himself, for the honor of the

Oubangui. Gustave was working too, though grumbling somewhat.

When their assigned work was finished, the tap-tap dwindled away. Koufra's machine was the last to fall silent.

Gustave said *oof* and got to his feet. "What are we doing this evening?" he asked a friend.

"Tennis before dinner," the latter replied. "How's that?"

"Certainly! And after dinner?"

"Nothing organized yet—a little concert via the telephonoscope?"

"The weather's too good! After dinner, I propose a stroll along the Seine to inaugurate our nautical circle…agreed? Koufra—to the tennis court! Do you have a favorite racket?"

"No, I haven't brought…I didn't know…"

"One can forget one's books, old chap—there are always books around—but a racket! A racket that feels good in the hand! Anyway, I'll lend you one of mine…"

Does the tennis professor give his lectures over the telephonoscope too?" asked Koufra.

"No, it's Madame Luco, 20 years of success in all competitions! Be careful—don't be too much of a duffer; she gets angry. Beware of nasty reports! Let's go to tennis, and this evening, I promise you an idyllic time on the Seine; you'll see that I'm no oarsman, although I'll fearlessly take on any fifth- or sixth-former with a sail!"

IV. A Cinematic lecture by the great historian Trubert.

Gustave Turbille could take on anyone in a sailing boat or a rowing-boat; even so, he caused his friend Koufra to take a bath, four meters from the bank, on the return journey—and he knew how to swim! They only had the inconvenience of getting back in a hurry to put on dry clothes. But had their suitcases arrived? Yes! They were there; all was well. All things considered, the dip brought the first day of school to a pleasant conclusion.

In the room that he shared with his friend, Koufra went to sleep immediately, while Gustave was still giving him interesting details of life at school and the professors, and explaining his personal ideas regarding the authentic modernization of the University and desirable progressive changes.

The next day, 3A had a Latin class in the morning and history in the afternoon.

Koufra was able to observe a certain lack of enthusiasm in the Latin class; no one around him was talking about anything but the imminent history lecture; people were recalling the lectures of previous terms, discussing them so keenly that Koufra lost the thread of an author who was not that difficult. The history course must be very well-constructed, and the professor particularly remarkable, to arouse such interest in advance.

"Who is this history professor?" asked Koufra, as soon as he had emerged from his Latin translation.

"It's Trubert!"

"Trubert, the great historian?"

"The very same. I told you that Chambourcy was a first-rate school, and you shall see for yourself!"

At 2 p.m., when the siren whistled for history, the third form left the sports field without being asked, abandoning an exciting game of football. The history lesson was for the entire school; all the classes were gathered there. The venue was vast: an immense amphitheater in front of a large elevated stage, with the professor's chair in the middle, along with the telephonoscope screen.

"Why," said Koufra, "one might think…"

"The school's great cinema, naturally," Gustave replied. "The space is necessary for important events to unfold in their full amplitude, with mass-movements in their historical frame, great characteristic scenes, the reconstitutions of civilizations, with the individuals of the first rank around whom the centuries evolved… I'm talking like the school brochure, my boy, in order that you'll understand that history can't be taught in any other way. Pay attention—the lecture's about to begin!"

An electric bell had just sounded. The hubbub on the benches immediately ceased. All of the pupils leaned forward, their eyes attentive. A man appeared on the telephonoscope screen.

Koufra recognized the earnest face and long white hair of the famous historian Trubert. It really was the great man. "It's him," he whispered to Gustave. "I thought he'd been dead for at least five years?"

"What does that matter?" said Gustave, impatiently.

Koufra leafed rapidly through a book, read two lines of a footnote, and went on: "Yes, yes...it was nine years ago that..."

"As if that slight detail could prevent him giving his lecture...a lecture previously recorded on the phonograph. Shh! Shut up. He'll still be giving his lecture in 100 years' time, without any trouble, in the same voice...unless he's been outmoded and superseded by some other great man..."

The great historian Trubert spoke. An explanatory prologue. History aggregated and condensed, so to speak, in large characteristic tableaux, initially displaying the nature of civilizations and the life of peoples, summarizing in broad terms the march of events, their consequences and repercussions, modifications, progress and decadence.

"He talks the way you did just now," said Koufra.

"Yes, he anticipated my ideas," Gustave replied.

The great historian fell silent. The cinema lit up; a great city appeared: monuments, colonnades, triumphant arches, temples, statues, hills laden with white buildings amid majestic trees, aqueducts extending into the distance.

"Imperial Rome!" said Trubert.

The scene came to life. It was the Forum, with its circulating crowd: plebeians, merchants, slaves, patricians, senators passing in litters, soldiers, citizens of distant provinces, foreign ambassadors going to the imperial palace—all the types and faces of the Roman world.

Trubert explained.

The cinema flickered momentarily. The Forum disappeared; in its place, a severe semicircular hall appeared: the senate. Men in togas came in gravely and sat down on the benches: the senators. Then there was the palace of the Caesars; an ambassadorial reception; tributes from the kings of vanquished peoples...

There was whispering on the school benches. Nero was about to appear, A celebrated actor was expected in the great role. He was welcomed by discreet applause running from bench to bench.

"He's good as Nero, eh?" said Gustave. "Last year we had a first rate Julius Caesar—Chose, of the *Comédie Française*; very good! And Cleopatra too, the famous tragedienne of the *Cinema Mondial*. You don't know her?"

"Not yet," said Koufra, sadly. "It's always in the cinema, then—the history course?"

"How can you expect it to be done otherwise? In old books, it's dead history, whereas in the cinema, we live it. We don't have to learn it; it unfolds before our eyes, and we remember it effortlessly, since we've almost lived it. Once, in Papa's time, how much time was wasted engraving the sequence of events, the great periods, the dates and all that confused mess in one's head? With today's method, it's merely a matter of opening one's eyes tranquilly; it enters and classifies itself of its own accord; how much time is gained thus for other pursuits! Shh! Here's the circus now, a scene I've been waiting for!"

The great circus, with its tiers heaped with spectators, the imperial box, the Vestals, the patricians, the people, the petty merchants selling refreshments, and the gladiators filing out, raising their weapons to Caesar. A few combats. Various episodes...

There was more subdued applause when the great Trubert stopped talking.

"Obviously, it's hard to organize, a course like this," Gustave explained, "and the Public Education budget recognizes the fact. The scenery, the equipment, the costumes, the machinery…how expensive it all is! And the principal roles, and all the direction! It's a considerable initial layout for the for the ministry, but it will get it back over time; our public education films have been adopted by many foreign countries, and—a great economy—this is happening in all the schools in France, with the great historian Trubert…"

But Trubert had just faded out on the telephonoscope screen; today's lesson was over. What, already?

In the racket that ensued, the students were uttering admiring exclamations or discussing particular aspects of the lecture. They recalled the previous year's lecture; some plumped for Julius Caesar, superbly evoked by the tragedian Chose, others for today's Nero, so well-depicted in all his monstrous horror.

"I'm looking forward to the next lecture," Gustave declared," on the decadence and fall of Rome—the invasions the barbarians, when Alaric will appear, or something like that. I have the program in my schoolbag—you'll see…"

In the study-period they were still talking, to the detriment of the assigned work to be done. The typewriters clacked at a moderate rate. The form-master, Virgile Radoux, whose preferences were interrogated, grew impatient.

"Come on, come on—it's a history assignment that's demanded of you, not theater criticism. I once represented Nero in a sonnet…no, I won't read it to you today…later… Work! Work!"

"So, Monsieur," Koufra put in, timidly, "that lecture is already some years old?"

"Trubert's lecture, undoubtedly, but the film is very recent—two years of work in the staging…"

"Pardon me, but what about the other lectures by phono? The other professors? Those in physics and chemistry, French, Greek, English…all celebrities also, all of them as…"

"Alas, some of them quit the world some time ago, but they continue to profess…they persist! They remain at the University, my friend, and without wanting to criticize the superior authorities, I find that deplorable in some respects, for it inhibits progress considerably! One remains a form-master, in spite of all the degrees and diplomas one accumulates—it's deplorable! The chair of French Literature belongs to a famous critic of 40 years ago; I can scarcely hope... I console myself with poetry, but times are hard for poor poets!"

Koufra returned to his desk, pensively.

Many other astonishments awaited him.

V. *The Phonographic loudspeaker is unwell.*

The weather is fine. Gustave and a number of other pupils are both content and furious. It is vacation weather. Does it not stand to reason that the vacation should be resumed? But the pitiless University does not see it that way. Gustave foments agitation, primarily desirous of bringing the government and the ministry down a peg.

The Sun is shining as if it were August; Chambourcy becomes an open air school in truth. All the classes are held in the grounds.

On both sides of the main drive, arbors are established, framed with lindens or hedges trimmed, according to the regulations, by the students—fortunately with the help of a few gardeners. There are grassy banks; on the shady side, a few long trestle-tables are set up, with benches; in addition, the pupils have permission to bring deck-chairs and beach-loungers. There are even sybarites in the sixth-form who sway back and forth in rocking-chairs while listening to the professors.

In the filtered sunlight, in the open air refreshed by the breath of breezes passing through hedges and flowering bushes, one can work more agreeably, much better and more fruitfully than in the enclosed school-rooms.

Gustave invites Koufra to admire 3A's arbor, which is one of the most agreeable: a good situation, soft grass, a good view over the grounds. It is very comfortable there, lying on the grass.

In the shelter of a thick clump of bushes, beneath a tall pine tree, Monsieur Virgile Radoux has his little table and his armchair; he is happy, and privately repeats the verses of Virgil, his distant forefather and fellow Apollonian. Moreover, smoking is permitted; while quietly supervising his class, he is able to follow the little plume of blue smoke rising into the sky, bearing away his thoughts.

For the pupils, however, there is a slight shadow over this idyllic scene. It is the mathematics course—elementary math, but math all the same. It always seems rough and forbidding, at least to most of them. No cinema possible, nothing to alleviate the subject somewhat and facilitate its ingestion.

The arbors fill up with the quantity of tumult permitted in the grounds. Even the oldsters of the sixth form are seen playing leap-frog as they move toward their places, and a few others advance walking on their hands. Physical culture: the form-masters can only approve; relaxed minds can only be fresher for study as a result.

Gustave arrives late at a great gallop. He has gone to his room in search of a rather large package, which he is clutching to his heart.

"What's that you've got under your arm, Turbille?" asked Monsieur Radoux, snapping out of his reverie.

"It's a hammock, Monsieur. I ask your permission to hang it between these two linden trees."

"A hammock?" says Monsieur Radoux, reflectively. "But I don't think a hammock has been seen at the school, as yet…"

Turbille has already unwrapped his package and is preparing to hang the hammock. "I think, Monsieur, that if I'm comfortably installed, I shall only work harder in consequence—isn't that so?"

"Wait. The hammock is unanticipated; I shall have to refer it to the administration. I'll telephone the headmaster…"

Having finished hanging the hammock, Gustave sways back and forth in it serenely.

"Always good ideas, Turbille!" exclaims Tony Lubin. "That's what a truly maternal university ought to give us."

"Even for indoor classes," says Béguinot. "You'd see rapid progress!"

Monsieur Radoux comes back, shaking his head. "As I told you, Turbille, there's no provision for hammocks. We'll have to wait for ministerial authorization."

"Meanwhile, Monsieur," Gustave Turbille complains, "the grass has its defects. I must tell you that I have a horrible dread of rheumatic ailments. It seems to me that the grass did me no good last year…"

"Sit on a bench, if you wish, but wait for the minister's decision regarding the hammock."

Monsieur Radoux's attention is called away. A ball is circulating very visibly among the pupils, who have just stolen it from 3B in the neighboring bower.

Gustave takes advantage of the moment, goes to the professor's chair and spends a considerable time examining the phonograph at close range, doubtless to calm his bad mood—and he succeeds, for he comes back smiling.

Monsieur Virgile Radoux comes back. The school siren announces the beginning of the lesson. Monsieur Radoux switches on the phonograph's loudspeaker. The math professor appears on the screen of the telephonoscope beside the phono, making gestures in front of a blackboard, with a piece of chalk in his hand. His voice rises, clear and authoritarian, vibrant enough to make the leaves on the trees tremble as if in a strong breeze. The same voice is also heard, albeit muffled, in the neighboring arbors, where the ubiquitous professor is likewise giving his lecture to forms 3B, C and D.

Pens suspended over notebooks, the pupils sitting comfortably on the grass are all ears—but the pens are not writing and brows furrow in an effort of perception and comprehension.

"A little obscure…for me, at least," said Koufra, anxiously.

"A little too much!" declare his neighbors. "It's a truly difficult lesson—there's been a mistake; this must be the advanced math course!"

"Bah!" says Gustave. "Just wait—the meaning will become clearer. I'm picking up the thread, myself."

But the pens still remain inactive. Only Koufra, brimming over with determination, scribbles a few notes. The pupils writhe on the grass as if on a grill, those in rocking-chairs swaying furiously, doubtless to shake up their mulish brains.

A murmur went up. Monsieur Radoux finally perceived a certain agitation in his class. "What's wrong?" he demanded, taking advantage of a moment when the professor on the tele paused to draw a diagram on the blackboard.

"A little difficult, Monsieur. It's hard to grasp—yes, particularly hard!"

"Bah! You're not paying enough attention—I noticed that. You know that I don't like punishment, preferring to appeal to your conscience, but I insist that my class behaves well. Get on with it, conscientiously—I'll keep an eye on the inattentive ones. At school, sharpen your intellect, always be on the alert, ready for anything! You've got your entire life afterwards to be distracted…"

The phono loudspeaker resumed.

"No, it's not as obscure as all that," said Monsieur Radoux, going back to his table. "It's clear—crystal clear!"

"You don't say," said Gustave, nudging Koufra, who was scratching his head dolefully. "Don't be too hard on yourself—there's something…I tell you. If the lecture's a little hard to grasp, it's my fault; just now, as I was tyrannically forbidden to settle down to swallow it at my ease, I wanted at least to gain a little time…for me and everyone else…"

"How?"

"I retuned the phono to make it go faster—you know that I'm good with machines. Gaining time, no matter how, is always a victory. But I think…"

"What?"

"I was in a hurry; I must have mistaken the switch…"

"So?"

"So, the phono's out of order; it's doing the lecture backwards. If you were a little stronger in the subject you'd have realized it immediately. Which proves that I'm the most knowledgeable in the class, without making any effort!"

When they returned to their studies after two hours devoted to games and sports, all the pupils of 3A still had furrowed brows. They had taken few notes during the math lesson, and had brought away very vague ideas on the subject; the work would be hard.

Monsieur Virgile Radoux, when consulted, tried to offer a few explanations, and then declared that there would certainly be a lavish distribution of bad reports and extra work assignments.

The study period remained silent. No sound of typewriting broke the awkward silence. For half an hour, the whole of 3A looked alternately at the floor and the ceiling, without finding anything.

"Hang on, you simpletons," murmured Gustave. "You'll see what good work I'll do, myself. I'll consult my private tutor and pass the information on…"

"He has a private tutor!" sighed Koufra, who had a great many notes but could not find his way through the confusion.

Having gone up to his room, Gustave did not take long to return.

"Your tutor was busy?" said Koufra, sadly, his overburdened head drooping.

"No—here it is!" said Gustave, placing a minuscule phonograph on his fiend's desk. "A pocket tutor, my boy—a great advantage, never ill, much more comfortable. I've got the number of the course; it will repeat it to us quietly, but in the proper order this time…"

The work of the class at the end of the study-period consoled Monsieur Radoux for the disastrous beginning. All the pupils were sighing gratefully, the sky was bluer and life had become rosy again. "You know, Turbille," he said to Gustave, whose typewriter he had heard galloping at a remarkable speed, "you're a good pupil. In consideration of your zeal, while awaiting the minister's decision on the matter, with the headmaster's authorization, I shall tolerate your hammock in the open air classes."

"Thank you, Monsieur; my work will be all the better for it, you'll see!"

"I'm counting on it!" Rubbing his hands, Monsieur Radoux went on: "Today, even the dunces have distinguished themselves. Excellent work, the whole of 3A, although things didn't seem to be going well at first…"

"We were meditating, Monsieur, turning over the lesson in our brains before putting them in gear…"

Turbille was top of the class, naturally, but Alfred Koufra, who had lost his way while trying to utilize all his notes, found himself 46th out of 46.

I fear, thought Monsieur Radoux, *that that boy might be destined to become one of our most conspicuous duffers; I'll keep an eye on him!*

VI. Mademoiselle Yes Uncle, and her various vocations.

"Today," Gustave Turbille said to his friend Koufra one morning, "we're going to beat my sister Colette and the entire girls' school over there…"

"What?" said Koufra.

"Yes—you know that it's the agronomy lecture…"

"I know."

"Well, it's the same professor for Villennes School—I've already told you that, you weren't paying attention. Between Chambourcy and Villennes girls' school there's an era of 80 hectares, used by the two schools for the course in modern agronomy, given in both schools simultaneously by Professor Thomassin. An 80-hectare farm cultivated by us, old

41

chap, according to rigorously scientific methods—the very latest thing in truly modern agronomy. Colette was talking about it the other day to Valérie Mérindol. So, today, it's laboring, digging, autumn sowing, and full speed ahead the automotive plow!"[7]

Every Sunday, on returning from walks in Paris with his friend, Koufra met Gustave's sister Colette and her cousin Valérie Mérindol. Colette, who was a year younger than Gustave, and Cousin Valérie were in their fourth year at Villennes School, very near Chambourcy. They were boarders, and only came out on Sundays. Monsieur Turbille did not allow them to risk flying by themselves in an aeroclette as yet—an excess of pusillanimity, Gustave said—and it was the Villennes dirigible that took them back with the other boarders.

The lively and cheerful face and mannerisms of Colette Turbille—who was always in motion, her curly blonde hair always streaming behind her as if borne away by a crazy breeze ("Collette's flighty, not serious," Gustave claimed)—contrasted strangely with the physical appearance of young cousin Valérie, whose character, much more composed, seemed almost grave at first sight.

Monsieur and Madame Turbille imagine that their daughter Colette is a veritable bird, light and fluttering—and given to mockery, Gustave adds—but Valérie Mérindol has nothing birdlike about her. Tall and strong for 14, she possesses strongly-emphasized features, to which her black eyes and dark, markedly-arched eyebrows give a willful and determined expression. And yet, beneath that resolute appearance, she really is the gentlest and least combative girl in the world. Colette and Gustave are well aware of that. Colette tyrannizes

---

[7] I have translated Robida's *charrues automobiles* with literal clumsiness rather than employing the word "tractor" for the automotive component, because he could certainly have employed the word *tracteur* if he had wanted to, assuming that he wrote the story not far in advance of its publication in 1917, but chose not to do so.

her and Gustave, who initially nicknamed her *the black lamb*, now calls her *Mademoiselle Yes Uncle*.

Valérie Mérindol, the black lamb, is an orphan. She has four uncles—excellent, beloved uncles, who also cherish her a great deal and take a serious interest in her—but these four uncles, unfortunately, are scattered in different provinces, in the four corners of France, very busy with important projects and situations. When business affairs permit, they race by express tube from North, South, East or West to embrace their niece and check up on the progress of her education. They descend upon cousin Turbille or Villennes School, or even, most commonly—for their time is limited—embrace her[8] by telephonoscope, interrogating her and offering her advice.

As there are four of them, the tele is always going. Every day, at the school or in Monsieur Turbille's house, there is at least one uncle on the apparatus, making affectionate recommendations or long speeches. Valérie has to sort herself out; the school years are flying by; the time is coming when she will have to launch herself into a career; the decisive turning of her life is approaching. Each of the four uncles is deeply preoccupied with the matter, and every day, there are long sessions of advice for their niece, on the direction of her studies, with a view to an enjoyable and brilliant career.

Koufra has been brought up to date by Gustave. Every Sunday, moreover, he hears Valérie's replies to the telephonoscope, a constant refrain of: "Yes, Uncle...Yes, Uncle...Yes, Uncle!"

On the previous Sunday, when it rained and they were taking tea in Monsieur Turbille's house, with a few school friends, vaguely following a theatrical recital, the four uncles

---

[8] What the French mean by an "embrace," in this context, is the gesture of kissing someone on both cheeks, which has no similarly economical descriptive term in English. It is, therefore, necessary for the reader to imagine the various uncles blowing multiple kisses over the telephonoscope, addressed to poor Valérie's cheeks.

succeeded one another on the tele, in the room next to the drawing-room, and the refrain of "Yes, Uncle" had almost worried and slightly aggravated the slightly noisy company. The "Yes, Uncle" at the end of the fourth session seemed exceedingly plaintive.

"You see, my dear child, nothing is finer than the bar; there's no career more glittering than that of an advocate, for a young woman who shows a real inclination toward it, as you do…I would even say—so much the worse for your modesty—who possesses, like you, certain gifts of natural eloquence, which you will develop, of course, and very easily, with a little advice and a little work. It's superb, the bar! Think, therefore, of the defense of innocence accused and sometimes overwhelmed, the fight for the truth, causing the great breath of conviction to pass through souls, the vibrant court of assizes, the inflamed speech that snuffs out…no, I mean, the torrential eloquence that drowns accusations—false ones, of course—and confounds the vile accusers…"

"Yes, Uncle!"

"Or better still, the defense of great interests! A business advocate—that's even finer…"

"Yes, Uncle…"

"And the bar leads everywhere…Parliamentary tribunals…the ministry…imagine yourself, one day, an elected deputé…and then, who knows…?"

"Yes, Uncle."

"I'm glad to have discerned your vocation! The road is open, you have only to follow it. After school and advanced classical studies, the law, the great principles…and then one enters a solicitor's office for practical case-studies…that's the program, my dear child!"

"Yes, Uncle…"

"That's Uncle Georges," Gustave told his friend. "I know exactly what he's saying to Valérie. He's an engineer with important mining project in the North; he preaches in favor of the bar and wants his niece to be an advocate—isn't that so, *Maître* Valérie Mérindol?"

"Yes, Unc...yes, Gustave," said Valérie, coming back into the drawing-room.

There were scarcely ten minutes for the young woman to listen, in the midst of the laughter of the young company, to a series of popular tunes from Guatemala and Venezuela, before the bell of the tele in the next room rang again.

This time it was Uncle Lucien, an advocate at the Marseille bar, who was taking advantage of a moment of liberty to come and talk affectionately to his niece.

"Hello? Hello? Still well, little one? Good, delighted! Your aunt too...we embrace you from afar... Your aunt concurs entirely with my opinion, absolutely with my opinion... that's very rare, you know, and proves that I'm right on the subject of your career! You're right, and we're glad to see that your inclinations are taking you in that direction... *medicine*, an admirable career when one senses a vocation like yours! The curative art! To engage in a dogged battle against disease and suffering, every day! To soothe! To heal! It's fine and it's good! Your heart is already beating, full of ardor, at that thought! I can hear it from here...tick, tick!"

"Yes, Uncle."

"That's very good, my child! It will be necessary to work hard, but you're courageous. After school, medical chemistry, microbiological studies...do a great deal of natural science and chemistry at school in order to prepare yourself... *Au revoir*, well content—your aunt too, well content... We embrace you, Madame Physicienne. Keep going! Your aunt would already like to ask you for a consultation..."

"Yes, Uncle."

Another quarter of an hour of tranquility and laughter with Gustave and Colettes's friends, then a further ringing at the tele. It was Uncle Pierre who appeared on the telephone screen, smiling at his niece from afar—from Bordeaux, where he practices medicine.

"Oof!" he said. "It's me, between two visits—demanding invalids who think themselves doomed and disturb my for the most trivial matters. I can breathe for a minute, therefore, and take advantage of it to come and have a little chat. All is well? Yes, indeed: imperturbable health; my niece is constructed from reinforced concrete…solidity, resistance, very good: I'm glad to know it. And the work—that's going well too? Perfect—continue, my child, continue! By the way, the more I think about it, the more delighted I am with your resolution to prepare for a career in industrial science."

"Yes, Uncle."

"You see, these days, that's the only thing! Large-scale industry, vast enterprises, great works…you shall be an engineer! It's magnificent! The spirit of invention, intuition, a flair for great discoveries and their practical applications…for the development of general or individual wealth…it's superb! I'm glad to see your studies making good progress with a view to the École Centrale. That will be nice, eh, Madame Engineer! Hold on, I'm being called for a consultation…another invalid! Never quite for more than five minutes, damn it! I have recommendations to make to you, though…I embrace you, your aunt too…"

"Yes, Uncle…"

On the tele screen, Uncle Pierre's silhouette flickered and faded; the doctor hurried to his patient.

"Well?" Colette Turbille asked Valérie, when she reappeared in the circle, pale and slightly distressed. "That was your Uncle Pierre—have you confessed to him that the engineering profession definitely has no appeal for you?"

"Yes, Colette…that is to say, I didn't have time…my uncle was called away on an urgent case, you see…"

"Then he'll continue to sing the praises of practical science to you…the École Centrale…large-scale industry…"

"Yes, Uncle…yes, Colette…that is to say, no; the next time, I'll hasten to tell him that I'm not yet entirely decided."

Laughing, Gustave had just begun to imitate the speech of one of Valérie's Uncle's urging his niece to aim at the career of mortgage broker or registrar when Mademoiselle Yes Uncle was summoned to the telephone yet again by a strident ringing.

"Valérie's fourth uncle," said Colette.

Gustave and Koufra held the door ajar in order to watch the tele screen. It was, indeed, Uncle Florentin, a notary in the foremost office in Lille, another somewhat strong-minded man with an expansive manner, but very busy.

"Good day, my child... Still serious, I see; I'm delighted... I scarcely have time to embrace you and chat for a while... You're right, I approve; you'll succeed; you'll be a palaeographical archivist—your aunt is happy and proud in anticipation!"

"Yes, Uncle."

"It's admirable, the past reborn before your eyes, men of distant centuries reappearing, in their true context, in their true features! One ends up knowing them better than one's contemporaries. How I'd love that!"

"Yes, Uncle."

"And then, beneath the dust of ancient documents, parchments indecipherable for the layman, one discovers the true reasons, the real causes of great events, revolutions... it's fascinating! And the secrets of kings and queens, the mysteries of courts: one has the right to be indiscreet—it's fascinating! Study, work, prepare yourself! How I'd love to be in your shoes!"

"Yes, Uncle..."

Valérie was able to return to her friends. She sighed a little. Her uncles, who took such a paternal interest in her education and her future, were so good! She reproached herself for not having showed them enough affection, for not having asked them about their health, and that of her aunts, and the whole set of little cousins of both sexes.

"Well, that's the family council concluded," said Gustave. "Have you decided anything?"

"Well, Mademoiselle Yes Uncle," Colette added, "I'll wager that you haven't yet said anything, that you haven't yet revealed to your uncles that you're thinking of going into the diplomatic service?"

"Or that you want to be an astronomer?" said someone else.

"A stockbroker... a tax inspector... a veterinarian... captain of a long-haul vessel..."

"Yes, my children," said Gustave, "you have no suspicion of the resolution and obstinate determination of Mademoiselle Yes Uncle... Yes, yes, she does not deign to make the slightest objection to Uncle Lucien or Uncle Pierre, any more than to Uncle Georges or Uncle Florentin, because she refuses to argue, but the truth is that she has a secret vocation that she will unveil when the time is ripe—probably something extraordinary, perhaps even blameworthy. Then people can say what they want, but you'll see: nothing will make her yield!"

"Yes, Uncle...yes, Gustave!"

VII. An Automotive Plow Race
on the Agronomy Course.[9]

On returning to school on Monday morning, they were able to see that the weather was improving. It was not raining; a pleasant and gentle Sun displayed itself. The classes in practical agronomy at Chambourcy and Villennes were overflowing with merriment. At Chambourcy, they were rubbing their hands joyfully at the fine day in prospect.

"We have to organize an automotive trenching-plow race against Villennes," Gustave said. "I've mentioned the idea to Colette and she's already talked about it in whispers."

"Perhaps we ought to go over last year's course, in order to do a little revision in agronomy," suggested a few timorous pupils.

---

[9] Two of the multiple meanings if the French *cours* are in play here; it can refer to a racecourse as well as a course of lessons.

"Hang on, I'll put you through a rapid exam. Tell me what the differences are between cereals, leguminous vegetables and oleaginous plants? Are carrots cereals? Do rye and maize grow on trees? You know all that? Good, that's fine, you're all up to scratch. Monsieur Thomassin would be proud of you."

The pupils of Chambourcy got astride bicycles and motorcycles in order to reach the site of the course rapidly. A little cloud of dust on the road on the far side announced the arrival of the Villennes pupils.

Next to the absent-minded Monsieur Radoux, traveling at a moderate speed well behind the other pupils, was Marcel Labrouscade, the school's future great *littérateur*, who was discussing—or, rather, arguing about—poetry with the form-master. Labrouscade's literary opinions, which were very advanced, sometimes exasperated Monsieur Radoux, but as the school magazine—of which Labrouscade was the editor—occasionally published Monsieur Radoux's verses, signed with a pseudonym, they nevertheless had an understanding.

"I have the beginning of a little poem to communicate to you, my dear master," said Labrouscade. "It's inspired by the agronomy course. I'd like to bring Virgil up to date, for he isn't any longer, and in a few years, no one will understand him any longer…"

"Oh!" said Monsieur Radoux.

"Yes, yes—a Virgil in tune with the march of progress, do you see? That would be rather interesting. Listen to my little trial…

"The pensive agriculturalist, on his polyplow, dreams of importation;

"Watching over his engine, firm at the steering-wheel, he lets the clutch in or out.

"And the machine, pricking, forcing, piercing, rolling over the glebe 'tis furrowing,

"With its 12 pointed plowshares... "[10]

"What's that?"

"I told you—a fragment of a didactic poem inspired by today's course..."

"Those are lines of verse?"

"Short lines, only 20 feet...that's a concession to partisans of ancient rhythms, because of the age-old subject-matter. I hesitated between 20 feet, the double Alexandrine, and even 30 feet, which I find quite musical..."

Monsieur Radoux and the poet Labrouscade were delayed by their discussion; when they arrived on the terrain, the course was already under way.

On a concrete-covered area in the very center, near the buildings of a rectilinear model farm, which looked as if had been taken out of a box for an agricultural exhibition, the savant professor of modern agronomy, the engineer Thomassin, was speaking, with a roll of papers in his hand.

"...I repeat that I am not content! You have not lived up to the expectations of your professors; our farm at Chambourcy-Villennes has not yielded the expected practical results, permitting the partial remuneration of the capital invested... In spite of all the trouble that your professors have gone to, the balance-sheet is deplorable!"

The schoolboys of Chambourcy, lined up to the right and the schoolgirls of Villennes, grouped to the professor's left, tried to impose mournful expressions on their physiognomy. How, in spite of the ardor they had put into the work, and the prodigies of activity an intelligence they had deployed in the previous year, had the agricultural endeavors of Chambourcy and Villennes Schools, both in the first rank, turned out so badly?

---

[10] In order to keep these lines to the requisite 20 syllables I have had to abridge them slightly, English being slightly less economical than French in that respect.

Gustave Turbille affected authentic amazement. How? It was incomprehensible! There had not been any cataclysm, nor even any gross atmospheric perturbations.

"The figures are there, unfortunately!" the professor went on. "Quality of produce decidedly inferior, yield ridiculously mediocre, 80% below average! The administration, which has made considerable sacrifices for the practical organization of courses, expected that our cereal production might at least supply the flour required by the two schools…

"Well, it's a shame! A deficit of 75%. And our legumes, the importance of which was explained to you by the savant specialist professor—do you know the figure at which last year's production of our legumes was evaluated in Les Halles? You have no suspicion? Well, exactly 66.50 francs—just 66.50 francs! What a balance-sheet! How shameful! How offensive! But we won't rest on that; we shall pick ourselves up, we shall catch up! We must! Your honor is at stake; you will throw yourselves furiously into study and work; you will struggle zealously and competitively. Chambourcy will not allow itself to be outdone by Villennes, nor Villennes by Chambourcy!"

"Yes, yes, Monsieur! No, no! Yes, Monsieur!" cried the pupils to the right and the pupils to the left.

Gustave offered an example of stern resolution to Chambourcy, raising his hand toward the heavens as if he were taking an oath, as if he were swearing by Ceres, the ancient goddess of agriculture—for want of one more modern—and Colette did the same for Villennes.

"Yes, yes—we won't let ourselves be outdone in a little while with the trenching-plow and automatic digger," Gustave added, in a low voice, nudging his comrades.

"In his laboratory, the agricultural chemist meditates on,

"Compost and phosphates, analyzes and weighs…" Labrouscade wrote in his notebook. "Good! My poem's growing—better than our wheat! It's always the way…"

The eminent professor, after his severe exposé of the results of the previous year, so painful for the self-respect of the two schools, spoke for a further half an hour. It was a little preparatory theoretical summary before passing on to the practical course. He recalled preceding studies of the physical and chemical properties of the soil, which it was necessary to know for the purposes of crop rotation, and explained the different chemical operations comprising agriculture; he talked about selection, fertilization... Today, they were going to proceed with the initial operations: ploughing, clearing, sowing....

The students took notes, and the inspired Labrouscade immediately put the formulas into verses of 20 feet...or thereabouts.

In front of the wide-open machine-shed—in which one could admire rollers, harrowers, harvesters, automotive reapers of the most improved models, extremely complicated and refined instruments bristling with teeth, rakes, combs and plowshares of every shape and size, combined in all sorts of unexpected and extraordinary ways—the mechanics had brought out four large trenching-polyplows, admirable in their cleanliness and shininess, with an impressive and almost menacing appearance, like machines of war, all of them ready to hurtle forward to attack the work.

There were two for Chambourcy and two for Villennes; the pupils' ranks closed up in order to hear the explanations of their functioning given by the mechanics.

The explanations, trials and supplementary explanations took a good half-hour. Koufra scribbled notes furiously. Labrouscade penned fragments of verse, of which he only had to adjust the meter on going back inside. Gustave grew impatient, sometimes interrupting the mechanic in order to prove that he understood the mechanism well enough to start the plow moving without attachments or hoppers.

The professor designated two pupils per plow as drivers. Gustave Turbille had been the first to be chosen, naturally; the second Chambourcian machine was entrusted to the studious Koufra. For Villennes, Colette was also designated as a driver.

Monsieur Thomassin gave the signal. Gustave immediately started his engine. Koufra would have had difficulty doing the same on the second machine; his notes, when consulted, said nothing about that—fortunately, his acolyte, more knowledgeable about automobiles, took hold of the steering-wheel.

The Chambourcy pupils followed behind the machines, while the professor climbed on to a little belvedere, from the top of which he could follow their movements.

"Now comes the truly interesting moment!" Gustave shouted to his sister Colette, as he passed alongside her while turning round. "We'll meet again after the first turn!"

The two schools' plows set off, turning their backs to one another at first; when they reached the limits of their particular ground they were turn round and come back to the central path, where they would meet, only to depart again on a second furrow, and so for the entire field.

At the first turn, Gustave, standing up on his polyplow, called out to his sister Colette, who was concentrating hard on the steering-wheel for the sake of the elegance of her furrow-reversal. "Hey!" he cried. "What diggers we'd make! Here are furrows that one would have thought traced by ruler, but have been done by hand and eye! Personally, I prefer fantasy and well-executed flourishes…but beware of bad reports and deficits in the yield! All the same, this plowing doesn't seem to me to be sufficiently sportive; we'll give it a little interest, won't we? Let's go…flat out! I'll give you half a dozen furrows…"

The automotive plows accelerated; Colette's made an abrupt jump as it turned, earth flying up from beneath the blades.

"Look out—no tricks!" said Gustave. "Perfectly straight furrows!"

From his observatory, the professor was soon able to observe the acceleration of speed and a few irregular turns, which he initially attributed to an excess of determination on the part of pupils desirous of redeeming the faults of the previous year.

53

"Too much zeal!" he shouted, as the plows passed in front of him. "Slow down!"

"You can never have too much zeal!" shouted Gustave, when he was far enough away from the professor. "Giddy up, you old nag! Giddy up, my 25 fine horses! And up with Chambourcy! Hey, Villennians, this might shake you up more than tennis, don't you think?"

Indeed, it was becoming more exciting than tennis. As they got further away from the master's eye, the furrows were no longer designed in such a neatly—stupidly, Gustave said— rectilinear fashion; they affected curves unusual in banal plowing, sometimes cutting out artistic flourishes, like those the audacious Gustave liked so much, or even zigzagging in an incoherent fashion—especially on the Villennes side, when Colette was subject to distractions that were translated into hesitations of the steering-wheel.

What a race, in the end! The pupils of the two schools, on the central path, became very excited, amusing themselves madly and shouting encouragement to their respective teams at the top of their voices; it was already evident that Chambourcy would win, by ten or 12 furrows.

At each passage, Gustave offered Colette mocking consolations on Villennes' behalf; the racket of laughter and shouting increased to such an extent that Monsieur Thomassin's advice, criticisms an objurgations were lavished utterly in vain.

"Won—in an armchair!" said Gustave, jumping to the ground after the last furrow.

Koufra was also glad to get down; several times over he had thought that he might fall head-first from his perch in front of the terrible plowshares. Finally, no accident—and a win! Villennes, humiliated, bowed its head.

Monsieur Thomassin manifested his discontent. "Certainly," he said, "I can give credit to the pupils of Chambourcy in particular, but I disapprove of that inordinate speed. It's necessary to control one's ardor. At any rate, we shall catch up, I hope, with the sowing. Calm and deliberation in the movement!"

For greater safety, he placed a mechanic in each automotive sower. Gustave pleaded fatigue and ceded his place to Koufra. The sowing was therefore done in a less sportive but more regular fashion. Gustave found the rest of the operations dull, and that spoiled the day.

Among all the pupils of Chambourcy going back after the course, there was only the poet Labrouscade who was showing a little enthusiasm. He brought back 35 completed lines of his modernized Virgil—each of 20 feet—15 half-lines, and a few brand-new mechano-poetic ideas, plus a certain number of rare rhymes to mount in the first stanzas. He murmured his 35 complete lines to Monsieur Radoux while pedaling alongside him.

VIII. Poetry Champion and Editor-in-Chief of the Free Student.

Gustave's best friend at the school—after Koufra, of course—was the audacious inventor of rhymes Marcel Labrouscade, one of the glories of Chambourcy, a future great man, firmly determined to force his way into the Académie française before 30, and, in the meantime, the editor-in-chief of *The Free and Universal Student, Magazine of the Open Air School of Chambourcy*.

This magazine had commenced the publication of *The Amended Virgil*, but Labrouscade had had the chagrin of not seeing his *Modern Georgics* greeted with the enthusiasm he had expected to burst forth. Labrouscade, alas, had received a certain number of threats to cancel subscriptions, accompanied by critiques formulated with frank brutality. They subject was thought to be too classical and the poem soporific to a superlative degree.

One can disdain bad reviews, scorning them and abusing their authors—obtuse brains, obstinate or obliterated—and one can even offer a few rounds in the boxing ring to excessively virulent detractors, but cancelled subscriptions are more annoying. Labrouacade was gripped by melancholy, and interrupted the publication of his poem. To give a little animation to his journal and revive subscriptions, he launched into a polemic directed against the Villennes *School Magazine*.

This little war was ignited in connection with the course in modern agronomy, by pointed jokes and excessively lively mockery regarding the deplorable weakness of Villennes in all sports, up to and including mathematics. Labrouscade having offered some humiliating advice, as if to little debutants, Villennes retaliated, and its magazine, instead of replying to the sporting criticisms, indulged in a malicious parody of Labrouscade's poem, of which it published a pastiche in lines of 75 feet, signed by Mademoiselle Colette Turbille, the very own sister of his old comrade.

And the battle was joined!

That was not all. The editor of the *Free Student*, thus provoked, avid for combat and filled with righteous fury, still had another affair in hand.

He was in the grounds, in a deserted corner for which he had a particular fondness when he had to mediate, far from the football players, for some sensational number, and was mentally preparing a sharp riposte to Mademoiselle Colette, when his friend Gustave appeared unexpectedly, unaccustomedly grave and solemn.

"I have something important to say to you, Monsieur Labrouscade."

"I don't have time—you're distracting me…"

"You'll have to make time. You're going to follow me to the tele…"

"Eh? What? Why? What are you saying? What do you want from me?"

"Personally, as a friend, I don't want anything! I remain your friend. You can welcome me like a dog at a game of skit-

56

tles—it's all the same to me! You insult me, I insult you; as friends, that's unimportant…but as a second sent to you by an adversary, that's another thing, and I demand satisfaction!"

"Second? Adversary?"

"Yes, the second of my friend Koufra, who finds that he has been gravely insulted by you in the latest issue of the *Free Student*, and who has charged me with demanding reparation from you. Ah! You understand now…and I shall lead you to the tele, where Koufra's other second—for there are, of course, two of us—is awaiting us for…"

"Ah! All right, Koufra is annoyed because of the little item in the *Student*…but why at the tele? He couldn't come with you, this other second?"

"No, but we can arrange that by tele. I won't hide it from you that Koufra is furious and wants it to come to blows. It's serious, very serious! Above all, hush! Let's not make any noise. Let's go to the tele…"

"No need—I…"

"You'll issue an apology? These are our instructions: *apologize, or fight.*"

"Apologize? Dishonor the *Free Student*! Never! I'll appoint my seconds, who will arrange the details of the affair with you. Wait, here's Tony Lubin and Béguinot, two fine fellows—I'll put them in touch with you."

Tony Lubin and Béguinot were strolling along at a leisurely pace, glad to be idling in the Sun, with no suspicion of the drama that was in preparation. Labrouscade ran over to them and rapidly brought them up to date. From the energetic gestures accompanying his instructions, Gustave deduced that the affair would not sort itself out, and that they would be taking to the field.

Labrouscade's bellicose ardor was getting the upper hand of him; Gustave regretted that the time of the musketeers was passed; he would have loved to draw the sword too, like the seconds of yesteryear. The jealous Tony Lubin had permitted himself, during the agronomy course, to make jokes at his expense; this would have been an opportunity to ram them down his throat.

Having briefed his seconds, Lambrouscade put on a rather distracted air, and scribbled down a few verses, which sprang from his inflamed brain:

> *Let's go, my dear sir, swiftly, en garde!*
> *Let steel embrace steel!*
> *The blades collide, sparks fly—beware!*
> *Clink! Clank! Turn and wheel!*
> *Touché! Break! Strike and riposte, my dear!*
> *There you are—done deal!*[11]

Tony Lubin and Béguinot approached Gustave, their expressions grave. They bowed ceremoniously.

"Our friend Labrouscade has given us the mission of arranging this polite affair with you..."

"I hope," said Gustave, that the difference might be settled; my friend Koufra is a god fellow, he'll be content with a sincere apology, plain and complete, in the next issue of the *Student*..."

"Don't count on it," said Tony, dryly. "Our friend refuses any retraction, the slightest appearance of regret or apology."

"In that case...!"

"Yes, it remains for us to arrange the conditions of the duel."

"Would you care to come to the tele to join Koufra's other second, who isn't at the school..."

"Come on, it's almost time for the third form's open air class—let's call this other second."

---

[11] I have altered the word-meanings in this parodic verse slightly, though not its spirit or substance, in order to conserve the rhyme scheme, dutifully reproducing the original's deliberate inexactitude (Labrouscade rhymes *en garde* with *regarde* and *cher*, so "beware" and "dear" will surely do just as well).

When he was in front of the tele that the professor used, Gustave rang sharply.

"Villennes School—Mademoiselle Valérie Mérindol, please?"

"Ah!" said Labrouscade's seconds, who had been expecting to find that their adversary's other second was some master-at-arms or some known fencer. They raised no objection, however.

The tele bell rang and Mademoiselle Valérie Mérindol appeared on the screen. Her face displayed its habitual gravity, with little tremors that were undoubtedly not due to the tele. One does not have the opportunity every day to assist a friend as a second in a duel—which explained the excessively visible emotion. To dissimulate that weakness, Gustave started speaking immediately.

"Your client Labouscade published in the last issue of his magazine an article that my friend Koufra deems insulting to him. As I have told you, we require an apology or reparation. Look, it's a fake Frech assignment written in *sabir*,[12] which Labrouscade has had the audacity to sign with Koufra's name: *The Siege of Troy: French Assignment, a Classic Summarized and Abridged.*

"*Hector, besef brave à guerre, cassir et fracassir la cabèche à Patrocle, etc.; prendir tout the fourniment d'Achille. Y a bon, dit-il...* etc."

"Bah! A simple literary amusement, written without the intention of insulting or harming anyone," said Tony Lubin.

---

[12] *Sabir* is a common trade language employed in North-Africa and the Middle-East, but not in the Congo; the word is also used more generally in France to mean jargon tending towards gibberish. The offending piece, if the quoted section is typical, is actually written in polluted French strangely similar to the improvised dialect with which Gustave originally greeted Koufra. As before, I can see no point in translating it into bad English. (It is, of course, the beginning of a synopsis of the plot of the *Iliad*.)

"Monsieur Koufra is annoyed when he ought, on the contrary, to have been the first to laugh...we do not owe any apology to Monsieur Koufra."

"Our friend Koufra is punctilious in matters of honor; his African blood is boiling! He cannot accept a refusal of reparation—especially given that he is the son of a powerful monarch, a potentate of the profound and mysterious forests of wild Africa..." Gustave was about to expand on this theme, but he remembered that the ascendancy attributed by him to his friend was not entirely certain... He cut it short; in an affair as serious as this one, it was better to remain within the narrow bounds of reality. "You don't bring Monsieur Labrouscade's apologies, then?" he added.

"No."

"So be it. A fight, then—a fight!"

In the tele, Valérie raised her arms in the air.

"Our client is the offended party," Gustave went on. "He may claim the choice of weapons; however he has entrusted that to us. It only remains for us to discuss the conditions of the duel: the weapons, the location, the time..."

"Oh!" cried Valérie, in the tele. "Don't go too quickly. Is it really...?"

"Mademoiselle!" said Gustave, severely. "I have Koufra's instructions; let me speak. As I as saying, we have only to decide on the conditions and the weapons."

"Épées," proposed Béguinot.

"He refuses the épée—that's out of date. We require something Corsican. I've thought hard about an American duel, the two adversaries released into the grounds, armed with carbine, hatchets, etc. It would have been very exciting...but my client would have an advantage; he's a child of nature, accustomed to the virgin forest and its ambushes; he knows how to hide his approach and move secretly better than Labrouscade. No, no...no American duel..."

"What, then, if you're rejecting the épée and the carbine...?"

"I'm searching..."

"Let's all search!"

The discussion lasted for a long time. From time to time, Valérie uttered exclamations of fright and put her hands together. It required abrupt and severe glances on Gustave's part to recall her to dignity and prevent her from offering apologies to the insulter.

Finally, everything was arranged; Mademoiselle Valérie, sighing profoundly, disappeared from the tele screen as if she had vanished, and the seconds left to acquaint their clients with the results of their mission.

Labrouscade was still strolling, pencil in hand, gesticulating and miming his lines.

Title: *Honor is satisfied!*

The pistols loaded, the coxcombs assume their places,
Behind a tall tree, prudently, the seconds hide their faces,
And piff! paff! poof!
Double hit! Both fall flat on their faces: splat! oof!

He raised his head distractedly and said to his seconds: "It's going very well—perfect."

"What's perfect? We haven't yet told you the conditions of the duel…"

"I was talking about my next issue of the *Student*. It's going well. That's true, I'd put it out of my mind—my duel with Koufra. Well?"

"It's arranged. You gave us *carte blanche*; the adversary had the choice of weapons. There was a long discussion. Finally, everything has been arranged; you'll fight with lances.

"What? Lances?"

"Yes, old chap—it's very chic, the lance. It will give a luster to our old Chambourcy; the other schools will shrivel up with jealousy. And for a first duel—for it is your first…"

"Very nearly…I've had slightly animated boxing matches, but that doesn't really count. It's the first duel of my career as a journalist; I hope it won't be the last!"

"We're counting on it."

"With lances!"

"Yes. He's ferocious, you know, Koufra. His African blood is up! I believe that he'd rather have had a duel in the American style, with carbines, in the grounds, or perhaps with bows and poisoned arrows. Gustave mentioned that... We set aside fencing, at which you're strong, because Koufra is more familiar with the club and the *assegai*. Then after searching hard, Gustave thought of lances. We discussed it with one another, we reflected, and finally, we accepted. It's all set now: an initial report to be draw up, and you'll fight with lances..."

"But how? On horseback, like..."

"Not on horseback—that's outdated. In boats!"

"In boats?"

"Yes, on the Seine, in front of the Chambourcy jetty, each of the adversaries standing in the bow of a boat propelled by two vigorous oarsmen, the seconds in a third boat stationed in the middle of the arena..."

"The arena?"

"The liquid arena."

Labrouscade reflected momentarily. "That's all very well. I accept the lances, since it's been agreed, but the Seine is cold—autumn is here, and that doesn't suit me as well. I consent to everything, I accept the danger—but I don't want to risk catching a chill!"

"Don't worry, my friend; we've thought of that. Everything's arranged—the weapons, the place of combat, the hour...but not the day. For that, we'll await a return of the warm weather."

"That's perfect! Ah, you must give me your report so that I can publish it in the *Student*. All in all, Koufra will demonstrate that he's very chic in this affair; the *Student* will recognize that freely..."

IX. The Paris-Naples Tube Catastrophe.

The naval duel in preparation, featuring combat with lances, caused a great stir at Chambourcy School. It was the only topic of conversation; the thermometer and barometer were consulted every day, in the hope of seeing a return of the mild weather that would permit the two adversaries to resolve their quarrel. But the weather remained cold, and Labrouscade, who revealed that he was vulnerable to chills, no longer went out without a scarf.

He was not disposed to risk freezing; the *Student* had declared that its editor in chief did not want a duel to the death with influenza!

At Villennes School, too, the affair gave rise to considerable emotion. Even the oldest girls looked at Valérie Mérindol, as a second in an affair of honor, with a certain respect. Prayers were said for Koufra; it was hoped that the young black paladin would reckon with the editor of the *Free Student*, who never lost an opportunity to direct imbecilic gibes at the pupils of Villennes—the *Villennes*, as he put it, emphasizing the absurd pun,[13] which was as ridiculous as his poetry: his 1000-foot lines, which were so pretentious, although frightfully flat and denuded of all lyricism, as the *Villennes Gazette* never tired of pointing out.

The *Gazette* began printing weather forecasts every week, by courtesy of a pupil who was the daughter of a noted astronomer:

PROBABLE WEATHER
Sunshine, fine weather, heat wave.

---

[13] The pun is recognizable in English, even though the French *vilain* has a broader range of reference than the English "villain," and all that English has by way of a feminine variant corresponding to the French *vilaine* is the cumbersome and unnecessary "villainess."

Fight on!

Cooling of the temperature. Strong probability of unsettled weather. Rain. Wind.

Fight off!

Labrouscade did not fail to reply to these jokes with his finest penmanship, and the little war preoccupied the two schools, perhaps to the detriment of effective study.

One day, when the *Free Student* had taken note of the *Villennes Gazette*'s jokes in an exceedingly acerbic tone, the third form's study period was interrupted by a strident and uninterrupted ringing on the tele. It was Villennes that was calling in such an energetic fashion.

"Here we go," said Gustave, on seeing an arm appear on the tele, triumphantly shaking a copy of the *Gazette*. "Good. The situation is deteriorating, undoubtedly. Villennes is going call out all Chambourcy for a general battle! Hang on—no, it's my sister Colette. What's going on?"

On the tele, Colette Turbille continued to brandish the *Gazette*, speechless with laughter.

"Victory!" she said, finally. "Victory! In the great mixed school competition, it's Villennes that has the prize! The *Free Student* can announce it. The first ten in each class from the 15th on have won a week traveling in Italy. I'm included, along with Valérie, and your Chambourcy has nothing. *Au revoir*, I'm off to pack my suitcase."

"Bravo! Bravo! Congratulations! Bon voyage! We wouldn't have wanted to deprive you of it. Italy—pooh! That's very trite...too well-known!" Gustave and Labrouscade's exclamations were echoed by all the other pupils.

Colette had already disappeared.

Too well-known, yes—but a nice tour, well-guided, with all comforts and all possible charm—a week of blue sky, far from classes, studies and assignments!

In the afternoon, Colette reappeared on the tele to tell her brother that he departure was arranged for that very evening at 7:55 p.m., by the express Paris-Rome-Naples tube, stopping at

Milan to commence the classical tour the following morning in a private dirigible.

At 7:55 p.m., Gustave escorted his sister to the tube with the inseparable Koufra, and both of them, along with a certain number of brothers and parents, cheered the happy winners of the great mixed competition.

"A magnificent program," said Gustave. "Ascension of Vesuvius in a dirigible! Visit to Pompeii, floating 25 meters above the town—the best way—Sorrento, Capri, Ischia, Procida, then Rome, in the same fashion, without fatigue, joyfully, taking siestas, smoking cigarettes…"

"Cigarettes! The pupils of Villennes!" said the backward Koufra. "In the Congo, no one…"

"While traveling, it's allowed… And Florence, Venice, the lakes!" In a melancholy tone, Gustave added: "And in the meantime, we'll have a not-very-enjoyable week: chemistry, math, philosophy…and other daunting subjects. Oh, the lakes, the Borromean islands, Isola Bella…"

He sighed profoundly.

"Be brave," said Koufra.

"I am, old chap!"

The next day, in the middle of a philosophy study-period under the trees, Gustave—who was falling asleep, back-to-back with the somnolent Koufra—was awoken with a start by Monsieur Radoux, who arrived suddenly, in a state of alarm.

"Grave news for Villennes," he said, "Very grave! A terrible accident! A disaster! A catastrophe!"

"What?" asked Gustave, yawning. "Has the school next door collapsed?"

"No—if it were only that, we would fly to the aid of our neighbors. The school is solid. But out there, in the tube, in the depths of the tube, we can't do anything…except pray…"

Gustave leapt to his feet, leaving Koufra sprawling on the ground. "What? The tube?"

"The Paris-Naples express…accident, cause unknown… stuck and immobilized in the tube, in the Alpine tunnel, 12 kilometers from the entrance and 13 kilometers and a half from the exit. Catastrophe!"[14]

"Fatalities?"

"No, none. The telephone on the train is working... the catastrophe happened quite gently... The tube was flowing...suddenly, there was a jam, two minutes of friction with an ear-splitting grating, then a conclusive stop, almost without a shock...only a few heads bumped, when suitcases were dislodged from the luggage-racks. They were laughing in the tube!"

"Oof!" said Gutave, relieved. "I can breathe—it'll be all right."

"Yes, but, as I told you, the tube is stuck, screwed in...it can't move."

"They'll unjam it!"

"No—and this is the calamitous, the catastrophic aspect of the adventure: the engineers sent to help the train in distress encountered unforeseen difficulties. The work of freeing it will be laborious—it will take I don't know how many days... weeks... no one knows, they can't calculate it."

"We'll be patient..."

"That's easy for us—we have our four meals assured— but the passengers on the train..."

"What about the passengers on the train?"

"Yes—no food, and there are 845 of them in all, stuck for weeks, with no other communication with the external world than the telephone..."

---

[14] Transalpine tunnels were among the highest-profile engineering projects of the late 19th century. The Mont Cenis railway tunnel was the first to be completed in 1871, followed by the Gotthard tunnel in 1882 and the Simplon tunnel in 1906. The second-named was the most controversial because 200 men died in an accident during the construction (it was also the first to use compressed air to propel trains, perhaps providing the inspiration for Robida's tubes).

Abandoning the philosophy course, Gustave leapt on to his bicycle and flew off, followed by Koufra, followed in his turn by Labrouscade and a dozen others, as far as Villennes School, in order to try to obtain news.

Villennes was in turmoil, all classes suspended. People were weeping in the courtyards, running and colliding with one another in the corridors, while all the tele bells were ringing and the latest dispatches were being touted around. The Administration had no idea what to do to calm the pupils or reply to the tearful relatives.

Gustave sent the rest of the day running back and forth between the two schools. The few dispatches that came from the tube were not very reassuring. Finally, at about six p.m., as he was about to leave Villennes to go back to Paris, the Headmistress of Villennes opened her office window and called for silence.

A phonograph loudspeaker was brought to her, which she immediately activated.

"*Finally, the day is saved!*" howled the phonograph, with tremolos in its voice. "*The day is saved! All is well! The chief engineer of the Tubes has announced that they have succeeded in reaching…*" The phonograph repeated itself in a thunderous voice: "*Succeeded in reaching the train wedged in a tunnel… The day is saved! A conduit has been set up through which the trapped passengers will be able to receive their nourishment throughout the time necessary for the work of liberation. Everyone may be reassured! The chief engineer guarantees the rescue!*"

"Bravo! Hurrah! Bravo! Long live the chief engineer!"

The pupils and relatives embraced one another. Of course, they had known that there was nothing to worry about! Serious accidents never occurred in the tubes, save for rare exceptions that confirmed the rule; everything was always sorted out…

Gustave was able to return to Paris, where he found his father similarly reassured by personal information.

"I've seen the director of the Tubes himself. I'm not worried; everything is arranged; the passengers will merely have to be patient during the rather long-drawn-out work. But they won't be able to complain—they'll be cared for, the ventilation is fine, the temperature in the tube agreeable. They'll even be sent a Sorrento breeze, soft and perfumed, and their nourishment is assured, at Company expense, by means of a pipe, which they have taken a great deal of trouble to push through to the train. The Company has made arrangements; they're excellent—not very varied, necessarily, but excellent: soup, a perfect consommé always under pressure…"

"Nothing but soup?"

"Excellent consommé, I tell you—I've tasted it; the director's office sent me a sample. Delicious, my boy, delicious! All is well; it's only a matter of waiting for a few days, less than a week…it will go by quickly!"

Out there is the tube, the travelers were not taking things quite so philosophically. To begin with, they had been furious, thinking that the accident was going to delay their arrival in Milan and their dinner for an hour or two. After the anger came the annoyance, the anxiety, then the fear…the train had not started moving again! And suddenly, they learned the truth: the serious jam, immobilization while the work went on.

Terror! What about food?

There was nothing at all on the train, for there were no restaurant cars in the tubes. Nothing to eat!

Therefore???

The horror of the situation made everyone's hair stand on end.

The poor pupils from Villennes bitterly regretted having done so well in their competition, and started to cry.

Fortunately, the telephone was still working; it announced that a pipe had just been connected to the rear of the train, and that dinner would arrive by that route.

It was the Company's savior soup. The train's staff rapidly set about organizing the service. The passengers took tin cups and mugs from their luggage, formed an orderly queue, and the consommé was distributed along the length of the train.

It was found to be excellent. For soup, it was fine, but afterwards? After more soup, soup, and yet more soup for dessert!

Finally! Everyone felt weary after such great excitement. They lay down on the benches to sleep. The benches on the tube were not very comfortable for sleeping on.

It was a long night.

The next day, a telephone call from the Company announced breakfast. The work of liberation had begun; it might take a long time; the passengers were asked to be patient. To help them pass the time, the Company organized readings by telephonograph; the Paris newspapers would be read to them first, then they would have carefully-selected new novels by famous authors, and perhaps also lectures.

In addition to the Villennes pupils and all the other participants in the classical tour of Italy, there were a number of travelers on the express for whom the accident was extremely inconvenient: merchants, industrialists and bankers summoned to Italy on business. These urgent travelers protested violently, fulminating against the Company, and launched one telephone call after another to Paris, complaining about the inconvenience. Several of them had already started proceedings for damages and compensation, and were setting lawyers and advocates in motion.

Notebook of Mademoiselle Colette Turbille

"...Slept badly. Emotion. Dreamed that the tube ran amok and that our train, borne by compressed air, overshot Naples and plunged into the Mediterranean....

"Still eating breakfast while listening to the newspapers being read. Soup again—not very varied. A telephone call to protest. No response. Doubtless the Company doesn't want to interrupt the exceedingly interesting articles in the newspapers, which give dramatic details of our accident.

"I notice that every time these articles get to the work of liberation and its anticipated duration, the tele malfunctions.

"Midday. Lunch. Let's see the menu? More consommé, and nothing but consommé!

"Protests on all sides. No response. Doubtless the Company doesn't want to interrupt the reading of the great adventure novel *The Aerial Burglars* in the early chapters.[15]

"Very gripping, that novel. Let's listen...

"...Nocturnal raid on a house, breaking in from the roof...dramatic abduction of an heiress. Pursuit of burglars by a police aero... Heavens! The heroine has just been stabbed! Will anyone come to her aid?

"Bang! Electrical breakdown in the tube...and we have to follow the agonizing ups and downs of the crime, with frightful details, in complete darkness! I'm shivering with horror...

"The tele interrupts the reading at the most dramatic moment and tells us: 'To be continued after dinner'. To table, then! A manner of speaking, for we have no table.

"Let's see the menu...more soup! The Company's cooks are decidedly lacking in imagination. We protest. No response. We'll see about that tomorrow. Quickly, the continuation of *The Aerial Burglars*! What has become of the poor young heiress, so pretty and sympathetic? Will they have murdered her? No one knows...the corpse can't be found... A mystery!

"Third day. Breakfast: soup. Reading of newspapers. Too much politics. I'm in a hurry to get back to *The Aerial Burglars*.

---

[15] Although there does not seem to be a French novel entitled *Les Cambrioleurs aériens*, there is an English novel called *The Aerial Burglars* (by James Blyth), which had been published in 1906 some years before Robida wrote this piece. It is doubtful that Robida knew of its existence, though, and its plot is markedly different from the one described by Colette.

"Lunch: soup!!! Reading. The plot thickens. The heroine is almost recovered and the bandit aircraft trapped…it's exciting, but the tele tells us: 'To be continued after dinner.'

"Dinner: soup. Always soup! It's exasperating."

Colette's notes are becoming briefer; one senses that the poor child is discouraged.

"Fourth day: soup. Reading of newspapers. Soup. Reading: final chapters of *The Aerial Burglars*. All ends well for the charming heiress. I'm very happy for her. Will we be as lucky as her?

"Fifth day: soup. Reading. Soup. Another novel. Boring, this one…we play games. Soup…

"Sixth, seventh, eighth, ninth days: soup. Reading. Soup. Reading. Lecture. Subject: 'The industrial development of the south-western region of Australia and its repercussions on world commerce.'

"I'll try to go to sleep.

"16th day: soup, reading, soup…ah! Something new… I daren't say… yes… it seems to me… I'm not mistaken…the train moved…. Unstuck! We're unstuck! Saved! Thank God! It's high time—I don't even have the strength any longer to put exclamation marks in my notes…"

X. Reception of the Villennes survivors. The Duffers' Club.

Yes, it was only on the 16th day, at 1:45 p.m., that the rescue work came to a successful conclusion. Unfortunate travelers! A triumphant dispatch announced the deliverance:

"*After 16 days of work, beset by difficulties, the rescuers of the Paris-Naples tube have reached the trapped train. The tube, slightly distorted by a movement of the granite masses weighing upon it, 2595 meters beneath the summit of the perforated Alpine chain, has been, if not straightened, at least planed and polished inside, in order to permit sliding. The tube is free on the French side; work continues on the Italian side.*

"At 1:45 p.m. the train was released and compressed air recovered it at the normal speed of 500 kilometers an hour."

At 3 p.m., a considerable crowd was waiting at the Tube station for the arrival of the people who were being called "the survivors of the tube catastrophe."

Reporters, cinema cameramen and photographers were filling a vast reserved space, along with the relatives who had come running, among whom Monsieur and Madame Turbille were in the first row.

All hearts in the excited crowd beat rapidly. They wait. Telephone bells ring. A distant noise in the tube, increasing rapidly in intensity. The train arrives. General shiver of excitement. Cheers...

The first travelers appear on the platform; the elevator collects them and they descend. Exit.

They stop, dazzled by the sunlight, to which they have become unaccustomed after 16 days. Photographers and cinematographists go into action.

Parental embraces. Effusions. A great deal of noise. Reporters run from group to group, interrogating, asking for details, impressions, soliciting anecdotes...

"Oh! Oh! Oh! Of course! Oh, it's too much! Oh, not really! Yes! No! Oh! Oh! Ah!!!!"

All these exclamations are uttered by the Villennes pupils, who are jostling one another at the exit from the elevator.

"This is it—Italy! Come on then! We're in Naples? I can't see Vesuvius? We demand Vesuvius! And the blue sea? Where is it? Over there...yes, that's Montmartre! This isn't Naples—there's the Eiffel Tower!"

Vehement protests are soon mingled with the clamors of amazement; the pupils stamp their feet.

The enchanted cinematographists reload their cameras.

"What, Messieurs?" cries Colette Turbille, at the head of a protesting group, addressing the tube engineers who are greeting the "survivors." "You've brought us directly back to

Paris? That's monstrous! After our misfortune, after all our annoyances, after your eternal soup! We're arriving debilitated, Messieurs!"

"I'm suing the Tube Company!" says one furious gentleman. "A huge deal missed. 10,000 tons of Neapolitan macaroni, which I haven't been able to but—I must have compensation!"

"I'm suing too! Considerable damages!"

"Me too!"

"Me too! My life's dream stolen! Court! Indemnity! A fine voyage!"

"And me, then! My heart broken! Court! Indemnity!"

The last two protesters have exceedingly sad faces; their trip to Italy has not turned out well; they have become depressed during their 16 days in the tube."

The Villennes airship is waiting for the young tube-passengers. To cut short her pupils' irritation, the Headmistress, who has come to meet the in person, immediately gives the signal for embarkation.

"Come on, Mademoiselles—to Villennes, right away! People are waiting for you; you can chat to your heart's content there. What an event! What drama! And what a scare you gave us, unfortunate children! You'll have a great deal to tell us!"

At Villennes, cheers and applause greeted the dirigible's arrival. There was a crowd in front of the school, of parents, friends and all the Chambourcy pupils.

Gustave nearly dislocated his arms waving them joyfully. At the disembarkation, he hurled himself into the group of the "survivors of the tube catastrophe," elbowing others aside in order to embrace his sister and his cousin more rapidly.

"Bonjour! Bonjour! You've finally returned!"

He was interrupted by another push from behind. It was Labrouscade, who wanted to get past.

"Permit me, Mademoiselle Colette to solicit an interview for my magazine, the *Free Student*. You must give me details, tell me about your suffering—I'll write a thrilling article, something terrifying. You'll see—I intend to give my readers goose pimples. Then you can tell me your impressions of Italy—I like that—cheerful, picturesque notes, no?"

Irritated, Colette abruptly turned her back on him.

"No interview, then? You're refusing to tell me your impressions? Mademoiselle Valérie, you don't want to say anything either? It doesn't matter—I'm a generous fellow; I congratulate you all the same. You've had a stroke of luck, Mademoiselles! Your nice trip was only supposed to last a week, and you've had an entire fortnight—16 days, even! That's superb!"

Marcel Labrouscade was obliged to beat a hasty retreat, for the senior girls of the fifth and sixth were adopting offensive stances. He was about to have his eyes scratched out, or at least blacked—for some of the bigger girls had pretensions as boxers. As he was a stranger to rancor, as soon as he was back in school he ran to shut himself up in the library in order to write the sensational article designed to give his readers goose-pimples. He had learned enough, in any case, by listening to the travelers—who, in a sudden flood of words, had set about recounting their annoying adventure to the pupils who had remained at Villennes—and Gustave, to whom his sister had told the whole story, furnished him with the rest, adding a few lurid details and comico-dramatic amplifications.

The library—or rather, to give it its official name, the phonoclichotheque—was not generally crammed with students; it was very comfortable and one could take a nap there. Whenever he was in there, Labrouscade put a placard on the door:

THE FREE STUDENT
Editorial Office. Administration. Subscriptions.

He was rarely disturbed, especially in good weather, when the grounds offered much greater attractions. However, Alfred Koufra, who worked ardently, often came to the phonoclichotheque during the recreation period between the study-period and dinner, to get stuck into difficult authors and troublesome subjects. He and Labrouscade worked alongside one another. Today, more than once, the overexcited Labrouscade made Koufra get up to try out the effect of a particularly terrifying passage of his article on him.

"Perhaps these communications are not entirely regular," he said. "Let's not forget that we're adversaries; the affair hasn't been settled and our duel with lances will take place one of these days, but...bah! Between loyal enemies who respect one another...I can continue. Listen to this!"

Koufra consented to declare himself overwhelmed by horror and frozen with fear; then he plunged back into his difficult author.

Thus pestered, having read or consulted a dozen volumes and filled a notebook, Koufra felt that he was getting dizzy. His head was spinning somewhat, and when Labrouscade read him the finished article, and few more lines of verse—only 18 feet long, still on the tube catastrophe—Koufra briefly confused times and events, the tube-journey with Hannibal's crossing of the Alps, and asked why the Carthaginian elephants had not collaborated in the rescue.

Finally, Koufra remained alone with his books and notebooks. It was pleasant in the phonoclichotheque. The shouting, the calling, the whole turbulent racket of the footballers and other sportsmen only reached him, muffled, as a feeble murmur. The autumn sunlight, which was completing the gilding and reddening of the foliage in the grounds, was nevertheless quite attractive, and it would be delightfully pleasant dreaming under the trees along the Seine, or even aboard the *Old Homer*, the little yacht in which Gustave went out every day for an hour's sailing, running along the banks outside the school's harbor.

That was very tempting, but there was the work, the authors to consult on points about which he still felt confused. And Koufra, stopping up his ears so as not to hear the calls from outside, plunged back into personal encounters with the historians of antiquity, mingled with the *littérateurs* or illustrious scientists of recent centuries.

In the drawers of the phonoclichotheque, it is all ready to hand: antiquity—all of antiquity—as well as modern times; all the authors, condensed and simplified to varying degrees. All the ages are to be found there, with all the sciences and all philosophies—condensed and abridged, naturally, in the appropriate proportion, prepared to be assimilated easily and rapidly, on phonographic disks classified and arranged in the most perfect order.

A little phonograph is activated, and, without delay, the old master or the antique author to be consulted comes to clarify the subject. If it is a matter of another author, a modern one, that is better still, for it is the voice of the author himself, deigning, via the phono, to give you any necessary explanation, and repeat it as often as might be required.

It's admirable and so convenient! A decidedly agreeable place, that school phonoclichotheque: quiet solitude; a silent hermitage, much more tranquil than the football field and much less crowded.

The time passes; Koufra ends up going to sleep. It's Gustave's fault; he was supposed to come and meet Koufra here, and hasn't come—but Gustave has an excuse.

At the school, alongside pupils who work, like Koufra, there are those who don't. The latter have formed an association for the defense of their assumed right to tranquility; they have founded the Dunces' Association, or the Duffers' Club.

Turbille is not a member of the Duffers' Club. He has considerable sympathy for it, but he is not in it; as a worker, he is a fantasist, but he is a worker nevertheless. He is, in fact, working at this very moment on the Club's behalf; he has promised to make known his meditations on a very important subject.

A delegation of the Club has come to grab him at the end of the study-period, as he was about to go to meet Koufra, and dragged him mysteriously into a corner.

"The Club, old chap," said the leader of the delegation, his friend Pipard, a second-former—an old one, of course, but who nevertheless shows a certain amount of deference to Turbille—"has proclaimed with one voice that only you can alleviate or annoyance. When we require advice from anyone, the response is unanimous: we must see Turbille."

"That's flattering," Gustave replied, "but what is it about?"

"You know," said Pipard, sadly, "that times are getting hard; we're overwhelmed by bad reports and impositions. Truly, that's excessive, for a few distractions. With the best will in the world, all the students in a class can't be in the top four—they don't seem to understand that! At the school, we represent fantasy, and also modesty, and we ought to get some credit for that."

"That seems fair enough to me."

"Isn't it? On the contrary, we're overwhelmed with work! And then we can't profit from pleasant hours devoted to various sports. For us, there's no tennis, no football, no cricket, hockey, golf, yachting, etc. So the open air school is deliberately failing to live up to its prospectus: muscle and brain, physical culture, and so on. What will become of our muscles, which are at risk of atrophy? It's worrying!"

"Indeed—quite distressing. You're melting my heart."

"So much the better—that encourages me with respect to what I have to ask of you on behalf of the poor Duffers' Club. You can save us, if you'll consent to take a interest in us. Here goes! We're weighed down by impositions, which take up our precious time; well, it's well-known and much appreciated, that you're very strong in mechanics—I only say *very strong* to avoid sounding like a vile flatterer."

"Oh," said Gustave, modestly, "just because I can repair an aero, because I know how, I don't call myself an inventor—I really can't, since that's the fact—but because I can, if necessary, make a few improvements to a machine…"

"Genius! I say that squarely, since I've come to make an appeal to your genius for invention. So, to conclude, I'm placing an order..."

"An order for what?"

"Listen!" The Duffers' delegate leaned close to Turbille's ear. "A machine! A machine for finding, for creating...a machine for..."

"For what?"

"*A machine for doing impositions!* Well, old chap, can you glimpse the magnificent invention, the enormous discovery? No one has dared to think of it until now, since there have been schools and impositions.[16] Students have been annoyed, have suffered, have moaned in a cowardly fashion, without seeking the means of..."

"Yes, that's a denial of Progress," said Turbille thoughtfully.

"It required our Duffers' Club, with a clear-sighted committee, to think of it. What glory, eh, for Chambourcy School, my dear Turbille, if you were to discover *the machine for doing impositions!*"

"I'll devote myself to it!" exclaimed Gustave, getting carried away. "Yes, I promise you, I'll work seriously on the question! I can already glimpse some possibilities, but I'll require time, reflection, study..."

"That's understood: seek, work—we'll continue to suffer with patience...but don't take too long."

The promise sealed with a firm handshake, the delegates of the Duffers' Club went way radiantly to take the good news to their electors.

Thus, Gustave forgot Koufra in the phonoclichotheque, and forgot the drama of the Tubes—and for a week or two, in the intervals of sports sessions, study-periods or lying on the

---

[16] In fact, one of the staple story-devices of the school story was the fabrication and use of mechanical means of reproducing "lines," usually involving multiple pens. Robida was obviously aware of the fact, and is dutifully updating the motif.

grass, Gustave Turbille was to be seen daydreaming, with furrowed brow, in front of blank sheets of paper. He made notes, scrawled diagrams, rubbed them out and started again....

"What are you trying to do?" Koufra asked him, when he saw him so absorbed.

"Something quite serious...and difficult."

"What?"

"You wouldn't understand—at least, not yet! When it's ripe, as you're a friend, you'll be the first to be informed...and even to profit from...hang on, yes, that's an idea—you can help me with the experiments!"

Perhaps for the first time, Gustave performed badly at tennis, and had to be severely called to order by his partners. At the school, there were a few class receptions, with tea, cigars, refreshments and items of unpublished verse; the third form had the honor of being invited to one such soirée by the fifth form science students. It was a good party, but Gustave, the star pupil of the third, lacked enthusiasm during the joyous occasion, appearing more than distracted.

Koufra, forsaken, had to console himself by spending more time in the phonoclichotheque, where he interviewed ancient authors in long consultations, for he was not always content with authors sagely condensed and short phonograph rolls—a filtration process which the best minds had nevertheless judged quite sufficient for our overloaded generations.

"Something's amiss with Turbille," Monsieur Virgile Radoux said to him one day. "He was first a fortnight ago, now he's 42nd. And his assignments are full of scribbles and scrawls—designs for machines. The authorization for the hammock will be withdrawn!"

XI. Rugby Football in the Greek Grammar Course.

A few days later, when Koufra was getting ready to take a solitary walk in the shade of the grounds, in order to bring a little order to his ideas and notes, he was suddenly accosted by Labrouscade, who surged out of a clump of bushes, requisitioned him and dragged him away at high speed to the phonoclichotheque in order to polygraph an issue of the *Free Student* there.

"You've had the first look at the articles, as a literary judge—today you'll become a collaborator!"

"But we're enemies," said Koufra, in a cowardly attempt to avoid conscription. "It's still not appropriate—our affair of honor...."

"Bah—when the time comes, we'll meet one another, weapons in hand; until then, you can collaborate..."

Resigned, Koufra was following Labrouscade when his friend Gustave appeared unexpectedly in his turn, running in a state of high excitement and calling out.

"Hey, over there! Hey! Stop! Wait! Complications!"

"Eh? What? What's getting complicated?" Labrouscade asked.

"The Paris-Naples Tube affair!" said Gustave, out of breath. "I've just come from Villennes—it's odious! It's revolting! An abominable injustice! Let me catch my breath."

"What is it?"

"Well, it concerns the poor Villennes girls—the victims of the tube and the school! Oh, it goes without saying that the pupils cannot bow down before the administration ukase, bend their necks beneath the yoke. 'I see no alternative but revolution!' Colette roared. When she puts her mind to it, you know, she's serious—she'd get her claws into the minister himself! Valérie is with her, resolved to brave anything to obtain satisfaction."

"But what's it all about?"

"You know very well. The missed voyage, the tour of Italy won in the competition, which consisted of 16 days of forced seclusion in the depths of the tube. The failed voyage ought not to count—it should begin again..."

"Naturally."

"Well, the administration has decided that the failed voyage counted, and it won't begin again, under the pretext that it would disrupt the regular progress of studies. So, general discontent, agitation....Colette and Valérie fuming like volcanoes. Unfortunately, the others are wet chickens; the ferment isn't taking hold. We have to do something—Chambourcy must support Villennes!"

"We must!" said Labrouscade, resolutely. "And you were right to come to me. The *Free Student*, forgetting past polemics, will fight for Villennes. I'll add something to my article—an energetic protest—and you'll help me to get the issue out."

"I can't, myself," said Gustave, "being required elsewhere...another affair, important for Chambourcy, and I've promised...but I'm counting on you!"

Gustave had cares and worries; he was beset by them. Troubled by preoccupations on the subject of the tube catastrophe, he was unable to get his machine for doing impositions up and running. He, Gustave Turbille, universally considered as an inventor of genius, had not yet found anything! O misery!

He had been spending all his recreation time on his boat, the *Old Homer*, in solitary thought, or with Koufra, silent by order, drifting slowly on the Seine near Chambourcy—but nothing came to him! Koufra maneuvered the sail at random; Gustave, at the tiller, sometimes forgot to steer. It was pleasant sailing all the same. One day, they passed distractedly through a squadron of canoes, which caused at least two dozen duckings and raised a squall of furious cries—for the water of the Seine, as Labrouscade knew very well, was beginning to seem chilly, especially for unexpected baths. On another occasion, the *Old Homer* came into slightly-too-sharp contact with the hydroplane of a student in the upper sixth. The result of the collision was a double bath and damage on both sides. Monsieur Turbille had to send a check for the repairs.

Gustave continued his meditations, on land now, in outdoor classes or in study periods. He collected impositions on several occasions for falling asleep in his hammock during lectures, even interesting ones.

"So much the better," he said to the delegates of the Duffers' Club, who were pressing him for results. "I have a personal interest in pursuing my research; that will spur me on...besides, I'm on the track."

Autumn drew on. The weather was still so fine that classes continued to be held in the arbors, now yellow and red. A few pupils, desirous of taking further advantage of the last fine days, had proposed to Monsieur Radoux that classes be held on the water. Why not? By bringing together a few vessels, it would be easy—and so delightful!

The form-master, however, being truly old-fashioned, did not much like changes and innovations. He made objections and refused to ask the headmaster for authorization. In consequence, they stuck to the arbors.

That day, in spite of the fine weather, it was a little cooler; Monsieur Radoux assumed that that would only make them keener to get to grips with the difficulties of Greek grammar, which a stern and erudite professor was explaining over the phonograph loudspeaker. Besides, it was necessary to work seriously, for Greek had to be finished in four lessons.

They worked—at least, the entire class sincerely intended to work; but they had reckoned without the great and solemn rugby football match between the pupils of the Classical and Modern sixth forms, who had been doing battle for two hours, amid an enormous tumult of shouting, punctuated by whistle-blasts—which was slightly troubling, both to the third form's ardor for work and Monsieur Radoux's poetic inspiration, which was too often disposed to take flight at the slightest disturbance.

"Oh, Monsieur," a student said, at frequent intervals, "it's difficult to grasp, and we can't hear very well with the footballers—could you begin the passage again?"

The form-master went to the phonograph loudspeaker, in order to put it back a little, and the professor, suddenly interrupted, jabbered a little, then recommenced the poorly-understood passage in his firm voice.

"Louder! Louder! We can't hear anything…"

The grave professor shouted his lesson thunderously, while he was seen on the telephonoscope, cool and serious, buried in his detachable collar, gently turning pages and making delicate and measured gestures.

"Louder still, please!"

But the phonograph loudspeaker, out of breath, could not give any more voice without bursting.

A further explosion of loud shouting suddenly died away, and the football crowd clustered together. Suddenly, the football fell right on top of the phono, rebounded, and shot through two rows of pupils like a bullet, banging heads and carrying away books and notebooks. The entire class was on its feet. At the same time, a whirlwind of older boys, smashing through clumps of trees and bushes, raced after the ball, knocking everything over—pupils, benches and rocking-chairs. Gustave's hammock, abruptly unhooked, fell down, and Gustave with it, furious at suddenly finding himself on the ground, enveloped in his canvas.

"I had the idea!" he cried. "I had it, and *bang!* It's gone!"

In spite of the form master's calls to order and energetic objurgations, it was the end of the Greek class. Everyone was in the air, or on the ground, in the general chaos. The ball ran on, dispatched by kicks, projected and borne away. All of 3A joined the crowd, with no regard for the rules, and took part in the match.

Monsieur Virgile Radoux raised his arms in the air, despairingly.

Through the furious cries, the exclamations and the laughter, the voice of the phono loudspeaker could still be heard; the professor recited his lecture imperturbably, continuing his earnest gestures on the screen of the telephonoscope— but the game-players and the pupils of 3A were far away, the rule-bound rugby football degenerating into a chaotic game of *soule*—or *choule*, as it is pronounced in Picardy.[17]

Monsieur Radoux continued to protest, although he had every reason to be proud of his class, for the pupils of 3A seemed to be on the point of winning a victory over the two sixth forms, partly thanks to the vigor and experience of G. Turbille—who, having been disencumbered of his hammock, had leapt on to the ball like a first-class *forward*.

Sixth-formers, fifth-formers and the pupils of 3A were no longer anything but a confused mass, a swarm of heads, arms and legs agitating vertiginously. That confused mass rolled in the bushes and tumbled over grassy banks. Now it came back again, by virtue of a shift in the bustle, into the third form's classroom. Monsieur Radoux's pupils were no longer as victorious, but still as animated and joyful; they continued the game with enthusiasm.

As well as the Greek lesson, they had forgotten something else—which was that the telephonoscope, as well as being seen, could also see, and that the Headmaster, once alerted, could observe the disorder of the class from his office.

The Greek professor suddenly disappeared from the tele screen. The Headmaster replaced him, and spoke.

He was scarcely heard at first; only Koufra noticed his presence. Terrified, he withdrew from the mêlée and ran to his bench to hide his head in a heap of discarded notebooks.

---

[17] *Soule*, a sport popular in France under the *ancien régime*, is presumed to be the ancestor of all kinds of modern football; its principal focus was on the scrum rather than kicking the ball and there was no limit to the number of players on either side, as is the case with the version of "Rugby football" featured in *Tom Brown's Schooldays* and the infamous "Eton Wall Game," as well as the kind of football vaguely described here. English public schools were not the only inheritors of the tradition, however; the *choule* played in Normandy and Picardy remained popular long after the popularization of the more rule-bound versions of the game.

On the screen, the Headmaster tired himself out making indignant gestures; he folded his arms or thumped his fist on his desk. The phonograph loudspeaker thundered.

Gradually, the pupils of 3A, decisively beaten, abandoned the game. They could hear now...

"Intolerable disorder...exemplary severity...considerable imposition...for the whole class, tale note, Monsieur Radoux...the whole class...with the exception, nevertheless, of that young pupil over there, Koufra, easily recognized..."

He shouts of the footballers drew away. Void game; match to begin again. The classes in the arbors, somewhat disturbed everywhere, albeit a little less than 3A's, resumed calmly.

3A breathed hard, dusted itself down, rubbed ribs and shins. Monsieur Radoux searched for his papers; he had lost a sonnet that only lacked a line and a half, carried off during the brawl.

"To work, Messieurs; let us resume where we were," the form master said, sternly.

Where had they been at the moment of the players' irruption? No one knew any longer. There was nothing to do but begin the lesson again. The professor reappeared; the phono loudspeaker resumed in a louder voice.

The phonograph seemed to be angry, but minds were no longer on Geek grammar; the entire class was thinking about other things: the exciting match that was coming to a conclusion in the distance, and the terrible imposition suspended over all their heads. Little notes were passed to Turbille.

Hurry up and find it! The time has come! The whole of 3A is counting on you!!!—with 15 exclamation marks. *If you don't find it by tomorrow morning, my poor old chap, you're dishonored!*

Gustave, scratching his head and feverishly tearing at his hair, replied with a simple statement, which circulated from bench to bench. "It will be found tomorrow morning—I pledge my word and my head."

XII. The Aero-Moto-Mechano Driving Test.
A Breakdown on a Bell-tower.

The members of 3A, gathered in the refectory for breakfast the following morning, were anxiously awaiting Gustave—but Gustave was not very prompt. When he finally appeared, followed by the inseparable Koufra, all gazes turned toward him. He seemed distracted, detached from worldly matters, indifferent to everything that was not the morning chocolate. The entire class shivered.

"Well? Well?" said the class-members, all at once.

"Well, what? It's very hot, the chocolate."

"Yes! Yes! No! No! That doesn't matter…the machine?"

"Oh, the little invention? Yes? Good! Good! It's done, of course—didn't I promise?"

Oof! They could think about the exam, in tranquility.

Gustave was the third form champion at every sport; he gave sound advice to Koufra. The latter, while drinking the chocolate that arrived scalding hot through the pipes, appeared to be executing all the movements recommended by Gustave for tennis, golf, running or the high jump on his chair, and he continued to do so in the corridors, stretching the muscles of his arms and flexing his legs.

Luckily, the Sun was still shining superbly. The proofs of the exam would have been disagreeable in rainy weather, for the sky had to be dispensing diluvian downpours for the exam to be postponed. In real life, does one not go out routinely in an airplane in downpours and squalls? It is necessary to become accustomed to ignoring the atmosphere's little whims.

In spite of the advice and example of his mentor, Koufra did not shine much in the morning's tests. Weak at tennis, he recovered a little in the 100 meters flat race, but was only passable in the 100 meter hurdles, passable in discus-throwing passable in the long jump, passable in boxing—in spite of a copious nose-bleed sustained by poor defense of that delicate organ—and, alas, utterly useless at the high jump, which cost him a fall and another nose-bleed.

"What would have happened," said Gustave, to console him, "if you'd had a white person's nose, more fragile and more exposed by virtue of its dimensions?"

A god siesta in the Sun in Gustave's hammock sufficed to relieve poor Koufra of his fatigue and his emotion.

After lunch, 3A rested, lying blissfully on the grass of the lawns or on the grassy banks of the study-halls. They were no longer thinking about the terrible imposition. Peril averted. It was sorted: Gustave's invention gave them tranquility for the present and also for the impositions of the future. A seductive prospect! O marvels of science!

At half past two, Gustave Turbille, getting up with one bound, called on his friend. He had to shake him and threaten to unhook the hammock to convince him to wake up. Koufra had indulged in a complete siesta—so, when he had rubbed his eyes thoroughly, he declared himself to be in good form and ready to confront further proofs.

It was now the most difficult part of the exam, for him, at least: aero-moto-mecano piloting.

In addition to the lessons of the special professors—which professors, along with those of the other sports, were alone in giving their courses at the school other than via the phono loudspeaker—Koufra had had the lessons and advice of G. Turbille, a clever fellow whose superiority in aero-moto-mecano, etc. was recognized by the entire third form, and was considered as well up on those delicate matters as the professionals.

Gradually, by dint of listening to and meditating upon Gustave's advice, Koufra—initially full of anxiety when confronted with the engine of an aeroclette—had ended up familiarizing himself with that disquieting machine, always flexible and obedient in expert hands, but slyly restive or madly capricious in others, the inexperienced and the timid. With Gustave beside him, he had learned to control the apparatus, and had now begun to undertake short solo flights over the school's aviation-field.

All went well. Self-confidence grew. He no longer made errors. Anyway, the machines were safe and easy to manage. A cab-driver or tram conductor of ancient times would have completed his apprenticeship in three quarters of an hour.

"So, my dear Koufra, how are you now? To catch up, are you going to distinguish yourself in piloting?"

"I'll do my best."

"You're my pupil—it's a matter of doing me honor! One has one's self-respect!"

Gustave took out a large package, which he had gone to fetch from his room. "You see this?" he said. "It's a little invention of my own, my latest little discovery..."

"The machine for impositions?"

"No, stupid—the machine for impositions is more complicated! This is something very simple—an accessory for air trips: a parachute-hat, in case of accident, serious damage or a landing in difficult terrain. With the parachute-hat on one's head, one is calm; there's nothing to fear. The apparatus opens automatically; one has only to let oneself descend, quite gently. I even think that, with some kind of oar yet to be discovered, one might float and direct one's descent...we'll have to see. A good opportunity to conduct the experiment, eh?"

"You haven't tried it yet?"

"No, I haven't had time. Today's the right moment—I thought of you for that...."

Koufra seemed lacking in enthusiasm. "Perhaps it will be even more difficult for me," he said, hesitantly.

"Bah! Take my parachute-hat anyway; with that you'll have perfect security."

The exam began. First there were the take-offs, the circuits of the field, then the grand tour of the grounds, the courses with various obstacles, which it was necessary to go around, over or under, and the descent on to a roof specially fitted with numerous chimneys.

It was amusing to watch. For Gustave, it was child's play. Koufra manifested less assurance; nevertheless, he came through the first tests without much difficulty.

"You'll have more than a passable report!" Turbille shouted to him, when he saw him land on the roof, only knocking over two chimney-pots. "It's going very well!"

Now came the biggest test: Rambouillet and back. They made the trip in the school's aeroclettes, excellent and carefully-checked machines.

Koufra was gaining in confidence; he was content. They departed in alphabetical order; Turbille would be some way behind him. No matter—he had had his final advice.

"In any case," Turbille said to him, taping him on the shoulder as he set out, "haven't you got my parachute-hat?"

A good take-off. The aeroclette lifts off smoothly, describes an elegant curve over the grounds and gains height. Koufra is slightly anxious, but the weather is still calm, only a few small fleecy clouds are to be seen rolling along, floating unhurriedly, very high, drifting in the blue of the immense celestial ocean.

Koufra steers very well; he perceives his comrades flying ahead of him, crossing the paths of trippers, tourists, and even a wedding party, which is making a tour of Versailles.

He proceeds at low altitude, following the itinerary mapped out, above small towns and graceful villages distributed along the roads, large farms and sumptuous villas. The park of Versailles and its water features are amusing, seen from above.

Now the change of course over Rambouillet. Suddenly, there is a slight rocking and hesitation on the part of the apparatus. Something is wrong! One might think that the engine is seizing up…or that there's a fault in the controls….

It is probably quite simple, and Gustave would get himself out of trouble promptly and easily, but Koufra loses his head slightly. What should he do? He has forgotten the maneuver; his friend's instructions have fled…

This definitely won't do! Let's go down! And he prepares, somewhat feverishly, for a landing, searching with anxious eyes for suitable ground. Over there, a nice field, behind that church...

Two minutes later, the aeroclette, still pitching slightly, has arrived, not in the field, but on the bell-tower of the church; Koufra, severely shaken, switches off the engine and clutches the old Gothic balustrade.

Oof! He is on the bell-tower; thank God! But it's a genuine breakdown. With the apparatus well-secured, Koufra gets ready to descend. Good—the door to the internal stairway is locked. He must stay where he is. He has been seen from the village, and someone will come to free him. Let's be patient.

But he is hailed from below. What are they shouting?

"It's the bell-ringer who has the keys to the bell-tower; he's gone to the market in Limours; he won't be back until 6 p.m.!"

And it's scarcely four. A disastrous hitch. What should he do? There's still the parachute-hat. Koufra does not hesitate for a moment: he will not make use of it. Better to be patient, it's not bad up here on the bell-tower. It's a Gothic bell-tower; one doesn't find those on the banks of the Oubangui. The landscape is lovely, seen from up here—50 kilometers of horizon to study. And his comrades can be seen in the distance, flying over Rambouillet.

Time passes. Fortunately, his friend Gustave has seen the apparatus on the bell-tower from afar, and he makes a detour in that direction.

"You haven't tried the parachute-hat? But this is the ideal opportunity!"

"I don't think of it..."

"Silly duffer!"

In two minutes, Gustave has found the cause of the breakdown—something trivial—and put things back in order. He makes Koufra take off, and flies behind him.

Journey to Rambouillet and return without any other incident than volleys of jeering whistle-blasts on flying over

Villennes at low altitude. It is the pupils of the school, who, under Colette's direction, are saluting all the Chambourcians in the piloting competition with that flattering music, without seeking to distinguish between the strong and the weak.

Koufra assumes that the whistling is aimed at him and his humiliation increases. To cap it all, he is told that he has only been marked "almost passable."

XIII. The Machine for Manufacturing Impositions.

After that emotional day, Koufra slept well, as did the entire class.

Everyone had joked about Alfred Koufra hooking up to all the chimneys and bell-towers that he flew over during his trip in the sky. What an idea, to stop and visit monuments in the course of such an important exam! Gustave had taken back his parachute-hat, with the vexed expression of an inventor scorned, but that had not prevented Koufra from sleeping.

On awakening, however, the memory of the terrible imposition—the imposition that was monstrous for the entire class, except Koufra—returned to everyone. It would be necessary to do it. They talked about nothing else as they jostled one another on the staircases, while eating breakfast, and yawning in the first study-period. In the general anxiety, there was also much curiosity.

"Come on, my dear Turbille, where's your invention? What have you found?"

"It'll be necessary to put it to work, you know. With ordinary means, we'd be at it for at least six hours! How many will we need with your invention?"

"Let me be—we have time; it'll be done painlessly. I've promised; I've sworn!"

"But how much time? It will be hard anyway today...the Sun's still shining; we mustn't waste it—the end of the fine weather is imminent."

"When are we going to get started on the wretched impo-sition?"

"When I choose—that's my business."

"Ours too!"

"Not at all—I've taken it all on me! This formidable im-position that terrifies you will require exactly ten minutes of work!"

"Oh! Admirable! Marvelous! Turbille is a great man."

"Not yet," said Gustave, bowing modestly, "but it will come! Exactly ten minutes of work, for me...but for you..."

"Ah! For us?"

"For you, not an eighth of a second! You shall see that I alone will work: while you go to daydream, lying on the grass, or to exert yourself in sports, I shall work, all alone; I shall manufacture this famous imposition for you!"

"Thank you, illustrious Turbille; we venerate you, O be-nefactor of humankind!"

"Wait! I shall, however, require one willing assistant. Ten minutes of work for me, the rest for my collaborator... Come on, who'll volunteer?"

Profound silence. A chill passes through the whole of 3A.

"No one says a word? But when the moment eventually comes, a good and devoted fellow will have to be found...that's understood! Break!"

At the end of the midday meal, Gustave passed the word around: "All typewriters in good condition, and all ready on the desks—and quickly!"

As one man, the members of 3A rose to their feet and headed for the study.

Monsieur Virgile Radoux followed them with his eyes. "They're setting off for the famous imposition without ill grace. No hesitation; general determination—I'm content with my class. For me, the muse and a cigarette beneath the last red and yellow foliage in the grounds!"

In 3A's study-room, all the typewriters were already on the desks, and the intrigued pupils were following Gustave's movements as he ran a slender copper thread from one to another. When all the machines were thus connected, Gustave looked at his watch.

"Eh? I said ten minutes of work—only nine!"

"What now? How does it work?"

"Watch!"

Gustave set a little electric motor, less voluminous than his Quicherat,[18] down on his desk.

The class applauded. "Very simple," said two or three envious rascals.

"Genius! Genius! Turbille for the Pantheon! Long live Turbille!"

Already tranquil and eager to make their way into the grounds, the members of 3A set off to rush down the stairs amid a great rumor of joy, but Gustave called them back.

"Wait, dash it! You're forgetting the volunteer I asked for. Come on, one volunteer, who will sacrifice himself for the others? One of those devoted beings that history always shows us in tragic hours! Come on! Come on! Don't all speak at once—but someone speak! A hero? We need a hero? What, there are 46 of us, and not one of the 46 has a heroic and devoted heart? A quarter, an eighth of a hero?"

Moving noiselessly, a number of pupils were already at the bottom of the stairs; the others were also trying to reach the door.

"Halt!" cried Gustave. "Shall we be obliged, then, to select the hero by drawing straws?"

"The idea of genius came to you—there's only you who can comfortably see things through to the end!"

"And the two nights of meditation and research—you don't think that counts for anything? My intellect is fatigued, almost crushed to a pulp; I need a reparatory rest. I've furnished the flash of genius; someone else must carry out the

---

[18] A Latin dictionary, as compiled by Louis Quicherat (1779-1884).

material task. If you don't want to draw straws, then, I propose an election; we'll elect the victim. Put it to the vote!"

Four or five pupils remained in front of Trubille—those whom he held by the arm. All the others had fled shamelessly and were running to the tennis courts or elsewhere, seeking a way to occupy their time more pleasantly than the monstrous imposition.

Turbille looked behind him. When he turned back again, the remaining five had disappeared, having vanished into thin air as if by magic.

"No one left!" he said. "But after having the idea, I'm not supplying the rest—that wouldn't be fair!"

Nothing remained of the class but the faithful Koufra, full of admiration for Gustave's brilliant idea and for his friend's mastery of the art of resourcefulness.

"My dear Koufra," Gustave declared, resolutely, "in the name of the whole of 3A, I requisition you—it's you who must operate the machine! I'm counting on you! Your entire class is counting on you! You must show yourself worthy of that honor and politely bash out our 46 impositions!"

"But I didn't get one—an imposition," stammered Koufra, who bitterly regretted having lingered in the study hall. "The Headmaster said so—you know very well…"

"That's true, you didn't—there are only 45 impositions. But, that only makes your devotion finer—much greater! You're sacrificing yourself for your comrades—that's an admirable trait, as Monsieur Radoux will tell you, worthy of a Roman of the great era! Come on, my dear Koufra—to the imposition, and swiftly!"

Koufra no longer tried to protest—Gustave was so persuasive! Come on, let's get on with the sacrifice with a good grace! He darted a glance over the grounds, seething with a joyful animation, and sat down at his desk. "What do I have to do?" he asked his tyrannical friend.

"Almost nothing: you're going to hammer out the 15 pages of imposition on the machine; my motor is working very well; the other machines will follow suit. At the end of each page, you get up, make a tour of the 45 machines, and put in a fresh sheet of paper. When you reach the end, you stop; then we'll all come, in a procession, to clasp you to our emotional hearts and cover you with flowers…do you understand?"

"Perfectly," said Koufra, still with a certain bitterness.

"Then get moving—and good luck, old man."

Resignedly, Koufra set to work. The *tap tap* of the machine was repeated on all the other benches.

Gustave listened for two minutes, darted one last glance at the 45 machines, and then, reassured, went downstairs with a sensation of duty accomplished.

A superb afternoon: an excellent Thursday. What delightful games on the sports field! Well-organized football, hotly-disputed tennis matches, boat-races on the Seine, etc. Pleasant reveries and sweet idleness almost everywhere.

Every time that he went to his machines to change the sheets, Koufra gazed out over the grounds. Sometimes, he was able to recognize third-form comrades in the animated groups, and then he sighed as he sat down to resume tapping out the lines.

All went well, however; the imposition drew to an end, as did the joyful games down below in the grounds. In sum, instead of five hours, as Gustave had said, it only took four and three-quarters: conscientious work, well-executed, thanks to the admirable regulated march of the motor and the determination of the self-sacrificing hero.

Alfred Koufra was about to tap out the final period when Monsieur Radoux came in, attracted by the regular noise of the 45 machines in the silence of the study hall.

"What!" he said, astonished. "It's you alone making all that noise!"

"Yes, Monsieur, I was doing my imposition."

"But you didn't have to do it—the imposition. You've inflicted it upon yourself voluntarily, then? And what's this? These wires? That box is a little electric motor…oh! Oh! Hang on! Oh! Oh! I get it—I've guessed, I understand. Very good, my friend, very good! Admirable! Are you the one who arranged all this?"

Koufra hesitated, not wishing to adorn himself with peacock plumage, nor to betray anyone.

"Good, good," said Monsieur Radoux. "I see—I can guess. It's the audacious Turbille, of course. A fellow with a future! Go tell him to come and speak to me; it's necessary that he also search for something on my behalf—a machine of capital interest which is still lacking: *a machine for correcting impositions!*"

XIV. The Villennes Revolt.
A Terrible Duel with Lances.

Since the Paris-Naples Tube accident there had been discontent at Villennes. The pupils had been unable to obtain satisfaction for the famous failed voyage, in spite of their protests.

A few of the girls, angrier than the others, threatened to raise the flag of revolt, and, supported by the *Free Student*, maintained a certain agitation in the upper school—but the majority of the pupils were much more preoccupied with mixed competitions in tennis and hockey, for which they were training seriously. Some time before, Colette Turbille had told her brother that the victory of the champions of Villennes was certain, but Gustave did not show the least terror, declaring that the champions of Chambourcy were unbeatable.

When the day came, those champions of Chambourcy presented themselves in on the tennis court with attitudes of tranquil superiority that were rather irritating. They offered their adversaries a 30-point handicap, and almost shrugged their shoulders in response to the indignant refusal of Villennes. They threw themselves into it as soon as the first shots were exchanged, as if they were about to eat their opponents alive; they sniggered among themselves and permitted themselves to give advice to the champions of Villennes, as if to beginners.

Villennes dug its heels in and played a tight game. The first round was hotly disputed. The honor of Villennes was at stake; if they had to go down to defeat, it would not be without a valiant defense.

Then the insolent champions of Chambourcy, those braggarts of the tennis court, started playing like duffers. Games followed one another; Chambourcy was beaten, thrashed, crushed, shamefully routed.

Both colleges were there, following the contest, but Villennes no longer dared applaud, while Chambourcy affected to beat the drums at every victory of the rival college.

The hockey match that followed went the same way as the tennis. Chambourcy, insolent at first, was outrageously flattened in less than half an hour. Its 11 champions, however, struck poses of brutal superiority, brandishing their sticks like athletes deigning to condescend to pit themselves against little children, and, as soon as the contest had begun, they accumulated foul after foul, committed so clumsily that they were soon sent off by the referee.

At a stroke, Villennes became annoyed. It was obvious. Chambourcy was deliberately losing, in order to humiliate the female college of Villennes. That could not be tolerated.

"You did that deliberately! It's an insult! Apologize immediately—we require an apology! And an honest game in compensation!"

Colette called attention to herself by virtue of her indignation; she summoned Gustave to her aid, and, when he refused, threatened to come and tear off his ears. Gustave, an unnatural brother, contented himself with laughing.

"Begin again? Never. We admit defeat, completely—trounced."

"Vanquished! Flattened! Demolished! Chambourcy capitulates! Villennes school is first rate! Strong courses in tennis! Crushing superiority!"

"We throw ourselves on your mercy," said Gustave. "I prose that a delegation from Chambourcy follow you to Villennes, to the Headmistresss, trailing on all fours…"

"And a rope around the neck!" added Labrouscade. "Is that enough, though, to disarm your wrath? Hold on, a rhyme…

"Is that enough, just Heaven, or would you like
"All our throats cut and our heads on a spike…"

"Pipe down!"[19] cried Colette, sending half a dozen tennis balls into the mass of Chambourcians. Gustave caught two of them in flight, but Labrouscade and Koufra each received one in the face. That was the signal for a thrilling battle—a tennis match liberated from all inhibiting rules. There was no lack of ammunition. Chambourcy, carried away by the ardor of combat, took its revenge, perhaps rather too vigorously, for it seemed momentarily to be on the part of driving its adversaries all the way back to their school under the rain of balls.

The form-masters of Chambourcy, who were taking the air along the Seine, heard the clamor distinctly, but they refrained from coming back, thinking that it was the hockey match that had become exciting. As for the Villennes formmistresses, they tried in vain to cover their pupils' retreat.

Several window-panes were broken in Villennes' concierge's lodge by sharpshooters running forward. It was getting serious. The Administration, advised of the tumult, came running.

To cut matters short, Gustave proposed to settle the difference immediately, with a vast bridge tournament on the sports field—but the senior staff of Villennes opposed it, and set about ushering the pupils inside.

---

[19] Colette actually says *flûte*, which has a far greater range of possible meanings than its English equivalent, thanks to which she might also be insulting Labrouscade by referring to his stature (likening him to a thin loaf of bread) and telling him to hop it.

The day finished badly, the disorder continuing inside the school. Cleverly taking advantage of the ferment, the victims of the Paris-Naples Tube renewed their protests, and all the rooms resounded with the cry: "The voyage! The voyage!" sung to the tune of *Lampions*.[20]

Things were under way. Dinner only restored a momentary calm. As soon as dessert was over, the noise resumed. A procession was organized in the grounds; when night had fallen, it set off on the march, crossed the courtyard and circled the headmistress's house, chanting: "Down with the Administration! Down with the Administration!"

Colette, carried away, marched at the head of the procession, carrying a Japanese lantern on the end of a pole. "At the head" is not entirely accurate, because she was pushing Valérie Mérindol in front of her, fully lit by the lantern. The other pupils in the procession were able to shout seditious cries at the top of their voice; they were indistinguishable— only Valérie was visible, evidently the instigator and director of the insurrectional movement.

In the following days the ferment was not entirely quieted. At the end of every lesson, the most turbulent of the pupils tried to re-form processions. As the form-mistresses remained powerless to re-establish order, the most influential or most energetic professors intervened via the tele screens; they made appeal to finer sentiments or distributed impositions—a total waste of time.

The administration threatened to punish the most indiscreet pupils—those who were setting a bad example and inciting their companions, like Colette Turbille and Valérie Mérindol—very severely.

While Villennes was on the boil, the temperature was also rising again. Gustave and Tony Lubin decided one morning that it was necessary to take advantage of that for the terrible

---

[20] Not so much a drinking song as a crudely repetitive three-syllable chant. A *lampion* is a Chinese lantern, but the verb *lamper* means to gulp down a drink.

duel with lances, too long delayed by circumstances. They set off immediately in search of the two adversaries, whom they found in the process of working side by side in the phonoclichotheque.

"Hey! On your feet!" cried Gustave. "25 degrees in the shade for a week, the Seine has warmed up again; it's time. To arms, Messieurs!"

"Eh?" said Labouscade and Koufra.

"The duel will take place today, at 4 p.m. precisely. We've organized everything; it will be fine. The boats are prepared, the lances polished—everything's ready! Have a good lunch, so as to be well set up, and full steam ahead!"

There was no reply to be made. Labrouscade looked out of the window; the Sun was shining. Nothing to object to. Koufra also looked at the sunlight, and sighed. Life was beautiful, and he was about to expose his breast to the lance of the terrible Labrouscade!

Between lunch and the time of the combat, Koufra tried to work—was it really worth the trouble?—while Labrouscade wrote his will, in verse.

Time passed. At 3:30 p.m., Gustave arrived with the other seconds. Valérie Mérindol was missing. They had telephoned Villennes repeatedly, in vain. A tyrannical order retained her at Villennes, where revolution was brooding. It was no more than a matter of hours, Gustave was informed by Colette.

Koufra required another second; Valérie was replaced by a comrade strong in all sports. In two groups, seconds and adversaries went to the Seine. Almost the whole school happened to be strolling on the bank, as if by chance, heads in the air, sniffing the breeze.

"There must have been indiscretions," said Gustave, who had personally advertised the duel in every class. "Rumor of the affair has leaked out."

"That changes nothing," said Béguinot. "The two combatants will only fight harder under the sympathetic gazes of their friends. It's regrettable that Villennes can't be here, but the unfortunates are groaning under the oppression of a pitiless Administration."

The adversaries lost no time. They were rapidly attired for combat, swathed in the colors of Chambourcy, as were their oarsmen. Soon, each of them, standing on a little platform in the bow of his boat, received from his seconds a light buckler and a long, heavy lance, with some advice as to how to hold it in the hand, well-balanced under the arm.

The preparations seemed long to Koufra, but on looking at the tip of his lance he saw that it was none too sharp—on the contrary, there was even a heavily quilted roundel there. Just as long as those roundels were solidly fixed—especially his adversary's!

Labrouscade, leaning on his lance, was standing up proudly in the prow of his boat, and had already declared himself ready.

When Gustave had given the final instructions to the oarsmen, the boats took to the field.

Gustave took out his watch and, at 4 p.m. precisely, gave the signal by means of a whistle-blast. "Let the combat begin!" he shouted.

In a hushed silence, the oarsmen set off vigorously. Koufra and Labrouscade lowered their lances. They were about to clash...

An immense cheer went up on the bank, the boats having crossed, the lances having struck the bucklers and the two adversaries, lifted from their platforms in less than a second, having performed a complete pirouette into the Seine...

The seconds' boat flew to their rescue. Labrouscade and Koufra were splashing around, both being rather poor swimmers. Splashing, with a good deal of glugging, they clung on to the boat desperately, both on the same side—a bad move on their part, and on the part of the seconds, who all went to render resistance at the same time. The boat tipped over and everyone, seconds and adversaries alike, was floundering in the Seine.

But the adversaries' oarsmen arrived, and soon brought them back to the bank. All saved, thank God! And the cheers were redoubled when Labrouscade and Koufra were seen, dripping like two mariners or gun-dogs, shaking hands as a sign of reconciliation.

Honor was satisfied!

The *Free Student*, which appeared at the end of that warm week, bore the flamboyant headlines:

DUEL AT CHAMBOURCY
REVOLT AT VILLENNES:
TO THE AID OF THE OPPRESSED!

Koufra, requisitioned again, had had to labor for long hours to polygraph, in addition to the official report of the duel, articles by Labrouscade and Gustave, who had turned journalist for the occasion. The valiant Labrouscade took up the cause of the oppressed unfortunates. He began by making apologies to Villennes, on behalf of the school, for the jokes that Chambourcy had played, without malice, on the day of the competition. Chambourcy would redeem its debt by fighting for Villennes!

The story of the insurrection, by G. Turbille, took up two pages filled with picturesque and thrilling details; it ended with this menacing sentence:

"Chambourcy is alert; we shall not allow the reconstruction of the Bastille!"

In the editorial, Labrouscade, after having exposed the particular protests of Villennes, had passed on to more general claims, and frankly proposed what he called "our Estates General"—which is to say, a meeting of the Congress of Schools and Colleges—to take responsibility for examining all the questions, to formulate the claims and to pass all the resolutions appropriate to bring about the triumph of the legitimate demands. The crisis was becoming grave!

"Elections! Elections! Immediately! Immediately!" That was the general cry at Chambourcy, as soon as the proud articles of the *Free Student* had carried Labrouscade's great idea into all the classes.

They did not hang around. Within half an hour, the elections were announced, prepared and held! Every class nominated two delegates, who met and chose four députés for the school. Gustave was at the head, elected unanimously; Labrouscade came next, then Koufra, and a fourth, a boxing champion.

"Labrouscade elected!" said one orator, announcing the result in the main drive of the grounds, filled with agitated groups. "Elected on one condition: he will not continue his *Amended Virgil*…"

"Understood!" cried Labrouscade, climbing on a portico of the gymnasium. "Citizens, I shall abandon literature temporarily; besides, I don't have time for my *New Georgics*…it will require a long and sustained campaign in the *Free Student* and all the other school magazines, and many preliminary negotiations, to arrive at the meeting of our Congress! That will take up a great deal of time, and—I won't hide it from you—we mustn't expect it to happen before next year!"

"Long live Labrouscade!"

XV. Winter Sports, Chilblains and Saint Charlemagne's Day.[21]

Turbille and Koufra had become the great men of 3A, and even of the school. The explosive success of the machine for fabricating impositions won them universal esteem. The stars of the sixth form paid them flattering attention. On sever-

---

[21] Saint Charlemagne was—and is—the patron saint of French schoolchildren; at the time when Robida was writing many French schools celebrated the saint's day (January 28, the anniversary of Charlemagne's death) with special dinners at which distinguished pupils were honored.

al occasions Turbille was asked to give a little lesson on his machine to a class that was in distress because of some rather serious imposition. Koufra was even asked, since he was accustomed to it, to do what he had done for 3A and work the apparatus—and Koufra, even on the pretext of urgent occupations, was not always able to decline the invitation.

The days passed; winter arrived with its fogs, its cold rain, its keen north winds and anticipated snow. A vile season for an open air school!

Gustave talked enthusiastically about winter sports, heavy snow, hurtling down specially-prepared slopes in the grounds on luges or bobsleighs. Koufra wondered anxiously whether classes would be held in the park when it was frozen. The idea itself was sufficient to give him chilblains.

But no, the arbors, in which the tall leafless trees were shivering in the north wind, were abandoned; they stayed in the buildings for lectures and study-periods. For outdoor recreations, the students put on thick pullovers, and gave preference to energetic and warming sports.

Gustave threw himself into them as much as possible, and, considering himself to be Koufra's trainer—the latter being somewhat numbed by the temperature—he jostled him to wake him up, to make him participate in the long jump, boxing, football, discus-throwing, golf, hockey, etc. There were cross-country runs held over a certain number of kilometers, and the painting Koufra had to follow his friend, who was always well-placed.

What an appetite they brought back to the school's dinner-tables! "Athletic sports," Gustave said, emphatically, attacking the dishes vigorously, "athletic appetites! Muscles, brain, stomach! It's as necessary to be first in beefsteak as in Latin dissertation, boxing or sciences!"

Besides which, the meals were good. There were no kitchens in the school, only a few emergency stoves in case of a breakdown at the Central Kitchen of Paris—a breakdown that never happened, or almost never. Everything traveled from the Central Kitchen to the school and colleges of Paris via a rather complicated system of pipes. It was remarkably well-equipped, with huge stoves and expert cooks under the direction of a first-class engineer: bourgeois cuisine, healthy and abundant, served every day, by way of a quality check, to a panel of chefs in service at the ministry.

Student critics, however, claimed to have found the formulas by which all the aliments scientifically produced and served by the enterprise were manufactured: peptogelatinophospine (soup); defibrinated panhetamine (polony); ovonutrine (egg), ichthyosyntonine (fish); phospholecithin and oxymargarine (brains in black butter); diamylofecukline (flour); glycofermenolactine (sugared white cheese); malafructose hydrate (apple ice cream), and so on.

When Saint Charlemagne's Day arrived, practical jokers even went so far as to translate the menu for the banquet into chemical formulas. It was, however, a remarkable menu, carefully-planned:

Consommé: $H_2O + C_8H_{15}NO_2$;

Turbot: $C_{14}H_{27}N_2O_4 + H_2$, etc, etc.

Coffee: $H_2O + C_{24}H_{32}NO_3$;

Champagne: $H_2O + CO_2H\ CH_2\ CHOH\ CO_2H + 18\ CO_2S + KOH$.[22]

---

[22] Apart from substituting the modern N for Az to signify nitrogen, I have rendered these formulas exactly as Robida does, although the subsequent sophistication of chemistry and education have undermined his joke somewhat. His punch-line reflects the fact that, in the early days of organic chemistry, long before *appellation contrôlée*, bad French wines—including poor "champagne"—were sometimes given considerable chemical assistance in an attempt to render them drinkable; alkalis were often used to neutralize excess acid, although washing soda was a more likely additive than caustic potash. If anything similar happened today (perish the thought!), we can be reasonably sure that it would only be done to wine intended for export.

Turbille and Koufra having both been first or second in something—Latin, sciences or sports—several times over, were at the banquet, and did honor to the menu. There was no suggestion at all of chemistry; the haunch of venison came from a roe deer, the *foie gras* was authentic, the iced *bombe* perfect and the champagne utterly sincere.

"Headmaster," cried Turbille, when the coffee was served, "I ask your permission to telephone congratulations to the chef via the delivery pipes."

The day after Saint Charlemagne's Day, an abundant snowfall permitted the pupils to devote themselves seriously to winter sports. Gustave dragged Koufra, who was not at all enthusiastic, on vertiginous runs in luges and bobsleighs; he rolled his friend over, turned him upside-down and buried him in the snow, while Koufra thrashed his arms and legs in vain. He made him go skiing. Poor Koufra would a 1000 times rather have been doing Latin composition, advanced math or even terrible Greek imposition, but he was obliged to follow Gustave's persuasive objurgations in support of a warming bout of boxing.

"Come on, come on, idler, sluggard—to the ski slope! To the luge! It's to harden you up; that way you'll never get chilblains in the African bush!"

"In the meantime, I've got them here," groaned Koufra, blowing on his fingers, which were clad in a double pair of fur-lined gloves.

And after somersaults in the snow, there were skating sessions. Koufra, useless on skis, hopeless on a luge, skated more on his head than his skates, while Gustave distinguished himself by the purity of his figure eights and his elegant flourishes on the ice.

Koufra went back joyfully into the well-heated school buildings, without even waiting for the siren summons to class. He departed at a gallop, always first in the race to get back in, and far ahead of the others. He already had his nose in a book when Monsieur Virgile Radoux arrived, even though the latter did not much appreciate winter sports either.

O sweetness of Latin composition! O joy of Greek translation! Koufra thought, his spirits revived by the central heating but still blowing on his fingers.

"You're a good student, Koufra," Monsieur Radoux said to him, on one of these occasions. "Not brilliant, but willing. You'll get there! But your comrade Turbille is disillusioning me—I expected better of him. He's definitely too sporty; he cultivates his muscles too intensively and too exclusively."

"Me, Monsieur?" said Gustave, having just come in after coming up the stairs with the other third-formers like a whirlwind. "On the contrary, I'm very intellectual, and it's to restrain the pressure of intellectuality slightly that I precipitate myself into vigorous games from time to time."

"In the meantime, my friend, you're falling behind! It seems to me that you're slacking in your scientific studies. I believed you to have a questing mind, avid for discoveries and new applications. You know, since a certain execution by unprecedented scientific means of a considerable imposition, in which I was able to observe a remarkable ingenuity…"

"Yes, Monsieur."

"You'll recall that I suggested a little idea to you then—I asked you, in order to encourage your scientific disposition, to find a means of realizing another machine that would be genuinely useful, and would render great service…"

"Yes, Monsieur."

"A machine for correcting assignments! But you don't appear to have given it much thought yet…"

"On the contrary, Monsieur, I've been dreaming about it! It's difficult to realize. It's complicated. I've been working, planning, racking my brains—but I haven't yet found…"

"Come on—don't get discouraged, my friend. Carry on racking! In that respect, Koufra isn't doing badly. Is there good news of your father, the African monarch? Yes? Very good! He must have some nice little administrative sinecures in his nice warm kingdom…tee hee! In these icy months, that's tempting…a nice little position out there!"

The legend of Koufra's father, a monarch on the banks of the Oubangui in the Congo, was now accepted by everyone at the school. When people talked to Koufra about his father's court, he seemed quite embarrassed, but that all-too-visible embarrassment was reckoned as diplomatic reserve.

In the absence of a machine to correct assignments, Monsieur Virgile Radoux would have been quite content with one of those little sinecures in the hot Congo Sun to which he had just made allusion, which would have permitted him to warm up his Muse, who seemed to have as many chilblains as poor Koufra.

Winter approached its end, however. To occupy the rather long evenings, the pupils—save for the dunces punished with extra work—could choose between the theater and concerts on the telephonoscope. From 8 until 10 p.m., in a large hall adapted for the purpose, they watched performances of French or English plays in Paris or London—always classics, of course.

Next door, in another room, there was an opera or a concert, vocal or instrumental music, still by telephonoscope. A third neighboring room was reserved for lectures at the Sorbonne or the *Hautes Écoles*, but we must admit that it was less crowded there than in the theater.

The cinematic history course had reached the fall of the Roman Empire and the Barbarian Invasions. It was still thrilling, but they waited impatiently for the fine days of spring, to set about the study of geography by modern methods—which is to say, from nature: geography on location.

XVI. The Course in Geography from Nature.
The Glacier Palace Famine.

For a fortnight Chambourcy school—which had become an open air school again, with courses in the grounds beneath the young, fresh greenery and among the new flowers—had been dreaming of nothing but geography.

Greek and Latin were done without enthusiasm; mathematics had palled, its joys being insufficiently savored. Mind turned toward geography. A beautiful science, geography: the study of our globe, which has become so easy and pleasant, thanks to the means at our disposal.

The fortnight went by, and the impatiently-awaited day arrived for the entire third form. The course was about to begin.

The siren, whistling to wake the school up, found all the pupils already out of bed, ready to leave, books and notebooks in little satchels slung over the shoulder. They still had two hours, however, before the anchor would be raised.

Breakfast dragged on. The phono on the table started speaking; it was the Headmaster giving his final instructions to the pupils, who were listening distractedly. They knew it all; they had already done the other years of the course in "geography from nature." Only Koufra was a newcomer, a pupil entirely new to the new method, and he gazed excitedly at the dirigible bobbing on its mooring-ropes above the grounds, ready to bear away the whole third form on the course in physical geography.

It was a fine dirigible, brand new, and larger than the airship-omnibus in service between Paris and the school for the benefit of pupils not flying by their own means. It was a neatly-designed airship, fitted with the latest improvements and offering all possible guarantees of safety.

"Follow me, old chap," said Gustave Turbille, when they embarked. "I went to inspect our places yesterday; they're at the front, to starboard, and will suit us very well. Besides, I'm on good terms with the chief mechanic, who sometimes asks my advice, and we can go on to the helmsman's gangway as often as we want."

The "physical geography course from nature" strongly resembled a vacation. A long trip, in a joyous troop, in a good and comfortable dirigible; a tour of France. In order to study from nature the coasts, the valleys, the rivers, the plateaux and the mountains. Superb and enjoyable! A week-long excursion! And the barometer stood at *Set Fair*!

Did one ever see, at the opening of a course, that universal expansiveness and urgency, even from the worst duffers? It seems unlikely. Today, the third form went to class uttering hurrahs, which the geography professor—a real one, this time, not a phonographic professor—tried to calm with appeals for order, in competition with the form-masters.

When the third form was aboard, gathered in the vast cabin beneath the helmsman's gangway, the professor arranged his papers and maps on a desk on the balcony at the rear, where he had the entire class under his gaze.

"Satchels and notebooks at the ready, Messieurs" said the form-masters. "We're taking off!"

The first phase was a mere stroll: the Seine valley, very familiar; the Norman and Breton coasts, also quite familiar. The day was spent reviewing long chalky cliffs, sandy beaches, steep-sided promontories beaten by the waves, jagged rocky coasts, groups of islands, isolated reefs, gulfs and bays.... Then the dirigible set a course for the open air school in Nantes, beneath the pines at the mouth of the Loire, for the evening meal and overnight stop.

"It's going very well," said Gustave. "I've already filled one notebook."

"And me two notebooks," replied Koufra, increasingly fascinated.

Things also went very well the following day and the days after that, when they studied the Loire valley and the Langres plateau, and started on mountains with the Massif Central, the Vosges and the Jura chain.

The Alps! A marvelous spectacle, the white tops of mountains, standing on one another's shoulders, filling the entire horizon around the dirigible *Chambourcy*. The professor gave the famous names of all the peaks and all the glaciers, from which avalanches crumbled and torrents sprang. He identified the valleys lost far below in the greenish blue or violet, and the celebrated rivers that were born amid the snows and bounded from crag to crag, and the great and small lakes formed in the hollows of the valleys...

After a rapid survey from the balcony of clouds of the whole vast Alpine panorama, and the inspection of Mont Blanc, they were supposed to stay the night at the open air school in Dijon, but fate decide otherwise.

"Breakdown!" Gustave suddenly cried, lending an ear to the engine, which was manifesting a certain agitation.

They were over the slopes of Mont Blanc, a few 100 meters above the Sea of Ice. As their speed slowed, it became easier to admire the landscape. Koufra rubbed his hands together, but the professor interrupted his explanation of the glacial phenomena.

"This is it," said Turbille, descending from the gangway. "A genuine breakdown. Listen—it's stopping! We're heading straight for the glacier. Sublime!"

"Oh," said Koufra, and a few others, abandoning their notebooks, "but..."

"Sublime!" said Monsieur Radoux. "But there are some exceedingly sharp rocks down there...let's not study them at too close a range! I don't trust them!"

Gustave, pleased with his effect, did not reply immediately. "Calm down" he said, eventually, "We're going down, but gently. I've pointed out a good place to land to the mechanics, down there on a tranquil Alp—and a hotel, Messieurs, a hotel! One couldn't have chosen a better spot for a comfortable breakdown, eh?"

The organ-pipe hum of the engine developed a jerky hoarseness, but the airship descended toward the indicated Alp quite smoothly. The professor, anxious at first, as reassured. A short stop, time to make repairs, and then they would be on their way again. If the worst came to the worst, there was a hotel.

The *Chambourcy* settled tranquilly on the grass in front of the hotel; it really was a comfortable breakdown. The me-

111

chanics immediately set about examining their machines. The third-formers stretched their legs on the ground.

"3000 meters!" the professor said to the mechanics. "It will get cold; we must try to leave again soon. I'm going to get a cup of hot coffee at the hotel…"

Gustave came back from the hotel. "Monsieur," he said, "the Glacier Palace is closed; I've knocked everywhere—there's no one here; the season hasn't started yet. There's no one in the chalet lower down, either."

"Oh!" said the professor and the form-masters, simultaneously. "We need to get going again right away. Let's see about this breakdown…"

"I know what it is, Monsieur," said the chief mechanic. "A little snag—nothing at all, easily repaired…but it's necessary to take the engine apart. That will be six hours' work, at least…and then to put it all back together again…"

"Ouch! In the cold, at 3000 meters!"

"Monsieur," Gustave returned to say, "I've found an unlocked shutter at the hotel. I've shoved Koufra inside, and he's going to open up the Glacier Palace for us…we'll be all right."

"Let's go—to the Glacier Palace, quickly!"

Five minutes later, the Glacier Palace was open and crammed with customers: the 500 pupils of the third form, with their teachers. A nice beginning for the season. Gustave and Koufra rummaged around everywhere, with Monsieur Radoux. It was a superb installation for a health cure: magnificent rooms, an immense dining-room, a splendid view, admirable kitchens, vast stoves—but solitude everywhere, and no food supplies at all! Nothing but the previous season's last menu, pinned up in the dining-room.

That discovery terrified everyone. The excursion in the clouds and the keen Alpine air had generated a good appetite, and the general emotion increased it considerably.

"Dash it!" exclaimed Gustave. "It's the sequel to the Paris-Naples Tube catastrophe…but down there, the passengers wedged in the tube still had soup whenever they wanted!"

"Villennes is going to make fun of us mercilessly."

"What are we going to do? Are we going to be forced to eat Koufra?"

"Eating a black boy might not be as great a crime as eating a white boy—me, I'm leaning toward Koufra…"

"No, no," said Gustave. "We have to think of something else."

"I've got it!" said Koufra, returning at a gallop, "We shan't die of hunger; in the chalet, there are five large balls of gruyère."

"Hurrah for Koufra! Let's go fetch the balls of gruyère!"

Gustave, feeling jealous, hurried down to the cellar of the hotel, which he had forgotten to explore. Nothing but six bottles of white wine, forgotten in a corner. There was still that. They would eat. In the meantime, he filled up the central-heating boiler, for the cold was becoming intense.

Dormitories were organized in the rooms and corridors. The table was set, two balls of gruyère sliced up—one slice for the soup, one slice for the roast and one slice for dessert for each guest, plus another in the guise of bread—and to table! For want of gypsies, Gustave succeeded in starting up a mechanical orchestra, which played all the fashionable opera tunes…

And to think that at that moment, a substantial hot dinner, now going cold, was waiting for them at Dijon school!

The meal was cheerful al the same. The excitement and fatigue were forgotten in god reparative sleep. Unfortunately, the dirigible as not as easily repaired. The chief engineer declared that it definitely did not work. The situation became grave. Monsieur Virgile Radoux wrote his will, in verse.

A second day of isolation. The Crusoes of the desert Alp blew on their fingers. The chief mechanic still said that they would be there for no longer than six hours, but another six hours were added to those…

And snow began to fall thick and fast. The unfortunate third form was besieged by snow and famine!

The professor heroically continued his course in the hotel's ballroom. At least the third-formers would come out of

113

the adventure quite strong in Alpine geography, the folding of the terrestrial crust and the formation and environment of glaciers.

Unfortunately, their attention was elsewhere, directed toward the balls of gruyère that were dwindling away before their eyes. The dirigible obstinately refused to move. What would become of them?

XVII. In which young Koufra makes sensational prehistoric discoveries.

In the ballroom of the Glacier Palace, during the professor's intentionally long-drawn-out lecture Koufra searched in vain for Gustave, who had already been put down for a severe imposition. Where was he? What was he doing?

Koufra imagined some accident, in the frightful precipices surrounding the hotel or one of the avalanches that the professor had mentioned. Gustave must have ventured out to search for a path through the icy chaos; Koufra could already see him lying frozen at the bottom of some crevasse when he reappeared, quite calmly.

"Monsieur," he said, "I've seen the machine. Nothing much, there's a silly little thing missing, which is quite important; it'll require at least five times six hours to sort it out—and the gruyère won't last that long!"

The entire class seemed as refrigerated as the nearby glacier. Monsieur Radoux immediately added another stanza to his will.

"But it will be fixed, all the same, Monsieur," Gustave added. "I've been working on something... The hotel's wireless telegraph station was dismantled, but I've improvised an antenna and I can communicate with the people down below. An airship will set off to bring us the missing component and..."

"Bravo! Bravo! Hurrah for Turbille!"

"…And something for dinner!"

Thus it was that Gustave saved the situation. He was definitely the great man of the third. The return was effected without any further breakdown. On arrival at Chambourcy the Headmaster congratulated him officially in front of the whole assembled school. Koufra was also highly praised, and was promoted to second great man for having discovered the balls of gruyère and relieved the entire class of the cruel necessity of resorting to cannibalism.

The third form produced some remarkable geography essays. Those judged the best were even published in academic journals. There were variations in different accounts of the incident. The duration of the Glacier Palace famine varied from one week to six weeks. In several of them, Koufra had already been put on the spit when help arrived, and it was not entirely clear whether or not bites had already been taken out of the unfortunate boy.

With these two resourceful individuals on hand, one could be tranquil everywhere, and the following week, when the time came to resume geography from nature, it was without apprehension that the third form took off again in the dirigible *Chambourcy*, repaired, checked and rechecked by Turbille and Koufra.

This time they were not going to any more mountains or doing any more climbing; on the contrary, they were going to descend into the bowels of the Earth—leaving he dirigible on the surface, of course. The program indicated: *physical geography; geology; study of mining centers.*

The *Chambourcy* set a course northwards, toward the region of the Somme: the oil wells of Béthune and Lens, the black country of French and Belgian Flanders. No more white summits, but black pits.

The professor of physical geography scarcely had time to begin his lecture before they were flying over mines, miners' cottages, factories and blast furnaces, amid swirls of black smoke.

115

Only Monsieur Virgile Radoux manifested a somewhat melancholy appearance when the airship stopped above an important mine, whose exploration and study featured in the program. He would have preferred to study an agricultural and virginal region with sunlight, flocks of sheep, or a shady forest of beech and oak trees—but he had instead to descend into the utmost depths of the Earth and plunge into pitch darkness!

With great animation, the third-formers put on miners' equipment, were given lamps, and were swallowed up, mounted in skips. They were counted as they went down, and counted again at the bottom. Then, with the professor in the lead and lamps attached to their shoulders, they set off in a long procession into the labyrinthine tunnels of the mine.

A few pupils felt the small packets of provisions in their pockets: croissants and chocolate, brought just in case. They certainly had nothing to fear, but it was necessary to be ready for anything.

Gustave made fun of these cowards; he had also packed his provisions, but he had eaten them already.

The professor began his lecture. He had interesting things to say, but could only be heard by the pupils at the front; the others passed on these interesting things and they arrived at the final rows somewhat distorted, amid laughter, jokes and jostling.

The professor searched for some traces of fossils; preserved in a block of coal, the imprint of the bones of a little fish were found, and that provided an opportunity for a fine dissertation on prehistoric fauna and flora.

Gradually, Turbille allowed himself to be overtaken, while holding Koufra back, under the pretext of having something curious to tell him.

"The bowels of the Earth, Messieurs!" he said. "Pay attention, you back there in the rear. Count ourselves and keep recounting yourselves! Don't let anyone leave the column! The professor has mentioned that a living dinotherium was found in one of the mines of Artois—perhaps it was this one!"

"Eh? What's that?" said the pupils of the rear-guard. "You've found a fossil dinotherium?"

"Not a fossil—alive, but a trifle torpid," Turbille replied, "with two plesiosaurs and three starving diplodocuses. Watch out! Oh, why didn't I bring a revolver? Look out! They're galloping through the tunnels—we mustn't allow ourselves to be devoured…"

"What's this?" asked Koufra, picking up a handful of mussel-shells.

"People claim that they're mussels of the modern era, recently eaten by some miner, but I maintain that they're mussels of the Tertiary, Secondary or perhaps Primary Era, cooked by the interior fire when, during the early days of our globe, the people of that epoch, who were more advanced than we supposed, first invented central heating. Quickly, pass these precious relics from hand to hand, in order to ask the professor's opinion. It's an interesting discovery, that—the third form of Chambourcy school will bring itself to the attention of the scientific societies."

"You don't say!" said young Béguinot, who had come to join his friends. "The central fire makes me think—one might perhaps light a cigarette. This would be the right moment; Monsieur Radoux won't notice…"

"What about the firedamp, idiot?"

"Dash it—I forgot about the firedamp…"

"Firedamp?" said a few pupils, falling back. "What? You're saying that there's firedamp?"

"The head of the column seems to me to be taking a big risk," said Gustave, in a voice that he strove to render lugubrious and tremulous.

But the visit to the mine was completed without encountering firedamp; the column returned via other tunnels toward the shaft in order to go back up into the daylight. There were no accidents, save for a few bumps sustained in the lower galleries.

They had the satisfaction of delivering a few pick-axe blows with the miners and detaching a few kilos of coal. As souvenirs, they brought back little pieces containing the bones of prehistoric fish.

They also brought back the mussels discovered by Koufra, although they had been declared to be of dubious antiquity by the professor. It did not matter; they would look good in a display case with the label:

Shells of the Tertiary Era
discovered at a depth of 375 meters in the Lens Mines

The skip brought the pupils up; only two dozen remained, along with Monsieur Radoux.

"Count yourselves! 145, 146, 147...one member of 3A is missing."

Monsieur Virgile Radoux frowned. A 3A pupil lost and abandoned in the depths of the mine, wandering endlessly through the tunnels!

"Count yourselves again!"

"No need, Monsieur," said Gustave. "It's Koufra who's missing; I haven't seen him for half an hour—we left him in the lower gallery where he was still searching for fossils... I lost sight of him in the darkness; we couldn't make him out against the background. We need to organize a rescue expedition. Come on—I need four brave volunteers to come with me..."

"Go! Run! Not so fast, though, in case you break anything. We'll wait for you here..."

With a crew of miners and four pupils, Gustave Turbille left in search of his friend, one astray in the bowels of the Earth. That took two long hours. Koufra was so difficult to see. Gustave finally found him and grabbed him by the collar.

Love of science and the desire to distinguish himself by some discovery had pushed Koufra from gallery to gallery, forgetting the time and his comrades, who were going back up to the daylight, and the dirigible waiting above the mine...

Fortunately, his research had been fruitful; triumphantly, he brought back a fine well-preserved fish-bone, which he invited his comrades to admire.

"That's not a Plesiosaurus!" Turbille exclaimed. "Nor a Brontosaurus, nor an Ichthyosaurus, nor a Stegosaurus—it's a Harengsaurus:[23] a superb specimen, a marvel, a new fossil hitherto unknown."

XVIII. The Industrial Geography Course. Gustave Turbille launches himself in Big Business.

The course in geography from nature had not concluded. There were still several excursions to go: the study of canals and rivers; the South; the Mediterranean; and the big attraction, the Côte d'Azur! But summer arrived, and it was very hot. Koufra declared that it was cooler on the banks of the Oubangui.

To combat the heat, the lecture was held under the pine-trees of a tranquil sheltered cove near Cannes, with the professor in a bathing-gown, the beach-huts gathered in a circle in the shallows and the pupils in swimming trunks, some almost chin-deep in the water—which made it a trifle difficult for them to take notes.

To refresh themselves they made the grand tour and came back via Brittany and Mont Saint-Michel, almost at wave-height. As they lingered for a while to see the marvel by moonlight, the dirigible, on turning around for the return journey, almost carried away the steeple of the abbey—or became impaled thereon—but a skilful thrust of the tiller permitted that inconvenience to be avoided. Gustave Turbille claimed

---

[23] This pun does not translate, alas. A *hareng saur* is a "red herring" in both the literal and metaphorical senses. Readers of *The Adventures of Saturnin Farandoul* will remember the crucial role played by herring in that narrative.

that he had saved the situation by warning the overly distracted helmsman.

After Physical Geography there was Industrial and Commercial Geography, another very important course, given by another professor, Monsieur Poujolas, a remarkable technologist and practical man. Along with introductory lessons at the school, the course comprised a four-day trip to England.

That four-day tour of the British Isles was another big attraction for the pupils, because every evening, after the day's work, they would be able to find shelter for the night in one of the famous colleges of England—Eton, Oxford and Cambridge—after a huge reception and dinner...practically a banquet, Turbille said.

When the dirigible *Chambourcy* appeared, lavishly decked with French and English flags, they embarkation was not long drawn out. Three cheers were uttered.

"Above all, try to beat Eton at football!" cried the pupils of the other classes, who had made the voyage the previous year, or would undertake it subsequently.

An hour later, the *Chambourcy* crossed the channel, scarcely 100 meters above the half-dozen tubes that crossed it, not far from the ancient tunnel. They went up the exceedingly busy Thames, which was sometimes difficult to make out, other than by the swarm of ships, barges and hydroplanes of every shape and size, and the immense city of London appeared, with its towers, its aerial platform, its tubes projecting in every direction like hundreds of arms, and its girdle of industrial chimneys belching swirls of smoke.

Launching themselves through the smoke so as to reach the region of clouds more rapidly, airships surged forth in their thousands. The song of aerial engines, celestial music, combined with the great orchestral hum of all the machines in the factories below, in a symphony that was more or less formidable, according to the vagaries of the atmosphere—a symphony that filled the ears, sometimes to the point at which it was necessary to plug them. It was beautiful, but a trifle violent.

To begin with, the Chambourcy described large circles at low speed above the British metropolis: a tour of London at 300 meters; rapid views of edifices important from the point of view of social institutions and organization; the quotation of statistics. The pupils stuffed their notebooks with long columns of figures.

"Now that you know London in broad terms, to the Docks!" said the professor.

A plunge into the thickest smoke and a descent to a cluttered landing-platform. The professor hurries the pupils along; the study of the docks is very important, and he recites more statistics, of the greatest interest. The visit is quite long, from one dock to the next and one warehouse to another, amid elevators, swing-bridges and ferry-boats, while the pupils think about Eton, where they are awaited.

They will arrive late; the reception will suffer in consequence.

"Messieurs," says the professor to the form-masters, would you care to inform the pupils of these impressive statistics, while I prepare the practical lesson."

"What's that?" Koufra asked Gustave, who was always well-informed.

"This: Monsieur Poujolas is negotiating a big rice deal with Anglo-Indian merchants."

"What?"

"The course in Industrial and Commercial Geography includes practical lessons. The professor uses his trip to make commercial representations, to sell articles of French manufacture or to occupy himself with imports. The form-masters are invited to do likewise; you see those little suitcases— they're samples...there's only Monsieur Virgile Radoux who isn't carrying any—he lacks the inclination."

The delay at the docks is prolonged. *Eton! Eton! The reception at Eton will be a washout!* the students are thinking, still inscribing figures in their notebooks.

Finally, the professor reappears, chatting with gentlemen and arranging papers in his briefcase.

121

"I shall summarize a practical lesson every day," he said to the students grouped around him. "A large consignment of imports has just been arranged: 50,000 tons of top quality rice, originating in Bombay...discussion of numbers, timetable, transportation and customs..."

Ten minutes of figures, explanations, and more figures...

"Take note all that—no errors in your figures, above all. Next we'll discuss the cost price to shops and the probable profits of the exporter and importer..."

Another ten minutes of explanations and arithmetic. The pupils' heads are ringing; the scheduled arrival-time at Eton has definitely been missed!

"Now that you've seen how it works, to the dirigible!"

Alas, it was almost nightfall when they arrived at the old and magnificent Eton College, on the bank of the Thames facing the enormous Windsor Castle. A delegation of Eton pupils in aeroclettes came to meet the *Chambourcy* and escort it to its landing in a field beside the Thames.

There was a fine reception in the great halls of the ancient college. Eton has also been greatly modernized, by all its adjoined buildings and annexes, but one would not know it from the central kitchen, Out of respect for tradition, there are no culinary engineers, but chefs in the old style, perhaps even bourgeois cooks! An excellent dinner, all the same: speeches in five or six languages; toasts; thanks, next year in Chambourcy, gentlemen of Eton!

Then Monsieur Poujolas revealed the program for the following day.

The dirigible will raise anchor at 8 a.m.

"Very good, Eton, fine reception—the football match is postponed until tomorrow morning," Gustave whispers mysteriously in Koufra's ear as they go into the dormitory.

"But what about the 8 a.m. departure?"

"The match is scheduled for 7:30 a.m.; the *Chambourcy* won't go without us!"

The matter has just been arranged with the pupils: an international match; honor at stake! Impossible to shirk it!

"The practical lesson at the docks has excited me," Gustave says to his friend. "I can definitely feel a taste for big business awakening within me, and I'm going propose something to Papa involving Manchester of Birmingham."

At 8 a.m., the professor and the form-masters arrived at the *Chambourcy* for the departure, but the pupils were not there. A tumult of loud cheering some distance away, on the sports field, allowed the reason for the delay to be deduced. The dirigible would have to be patient. The contest was long, but Chambourcy triumphed. Hurrahs, speeches, refreshments. Eton would seek its revenge the following year.

Finally, the departure took place at 11 a.m.

Second day: Birmingham. Study of industries. Metallurgy, iron, smelting, steel, machine tools, blast furnaces, cyclopean machinery, Babylonian factories fuming like Vesuvius multiplied a hundredfold. The pupils were soon all as black as Koufra. That evening, Oxford college. General face-washing; reception as warm as Eton's.

Third day: Football. Manchester. Different industries, but almost as much smoke. Insufficient time to visit the coal-mines of Northumberland. Evening, Cambridge. General face-washing, reception as warm as Oxford's.

Fourth day: London. Lesson in practical commerce. They have been able to follow the professor doing a few little deals in the foundries of Birmingham and the cotton-mills of Manchester. Now Monsieur Poujolas makes representations of behalf of the silk-factories of Lyon.

Gustave's father, glad to see his son launching himself into big business, has instructed him by telephone to negotiate the purchase of half a dozen top-quality pocket-knives in Birmingham. But Gustave is launched, and to the paternal commission he has added a larger item of personal business: 500 dozen razor-blades, on which, if his calculations are accurate, he can make a considerable profit. At any rate, Chambourcy has beaten Eton, and Cambridge too. Oxford won, but not by much. It's a fine result; everyone aboard congratulates one another when the dirigible reaches France again.

XIX. The Great Treason of the Pocket Phono-Whisperer.

Considerable annoyances are overwhelming Gustave, exerting a lamentable influence on his habitual good humor, and also on the fine ardor for work that distinguishes him—not always, admittedly, but often enough—on occasion, when he has reason.

To begin with, the magnificent deal involving 500 dozen razor-blades has turned out badly. Gustave has felt his confidence in the commercial geography course dwindling away; the professor must have neglected some important point.

Instead of being warmly congratulated by his father for that revelation of his commercial genius, Gustave obtained nothing but a vigorous reprimand and a considerable diminution of his pocket money. Disaster and humiliation. Utter gloom.

While awaiting the liquidation, Gustave drew on his stock of razor-blades to offer souvenirs to his comrades—souvenirs received with a cruel indifference. Moustaches were not yet inconveniencing anyone in the third form, who were, in any case, opposed in principle to the fashion for clean-shaven chins.

And the critical period of the end-of-year exams was imminent. Koufra rejoiced, in that he would soon be able to see his family again, his native river-banks and Villeneuve-sur-Oubangui.

"My dear Koufra," said Gustave to his friend, who was interrogating him about his low spirits, "what worries me most isn't the business with the razor-blades, plagued by the intrigues of competing houses. In the vacation, I shall take away part of my stock, if I'm to spend the holiday with you, in your parents' home at Villeneuve-sur-Oubangui…"

"Yes, that's agreed, isn't it?"

"Yes, but only with me—who is, of course, the interested party! Here's the snag: it's necessary to take into account the demands of parents. Papa has declared that I have to obtain universal mark of *very good* in the exams in order for him to consent to my spending the vacation out there. Therefore, I need that *very good* mark. I'll struggle hard—I must."

Koufra's only response was to plunge into his books and the reproductions of authors in the phonoclichotheque.

On returning to the school on Monday, the first day of the terrible exams, Koufra found his friend's attitude both mysterious and radiant.

"Victory!" Gustave eventually deigned to say, as he put away his aeroclette. "I have that *very good* mark—it's within my grasp!" In response to Koufra's surprised and interrogative expression, he added: "As good as, at least. This is the rule, my boy: never to give up on myself. I needed the means: absolute urgency; ineluctable necessity! I searched, and—naturally—I've found it! Victory! I have them all, my *very good*s! *More than perfect!*"

For the important end-of-year exams, with a view to taking account of the timidity that troubles some students and sometimes prevents them from showing their true merit in their answers, the Administration had long since adopted a simple custom: the exams were to take place, not in the classrooms, but in the rooms that the pupils occupied in groups of two to four, at the most. Examination in one's own surroundings, by telephonoscope: hence, no reason to feel inhibited or intimidated.

At 2 p.m., after a good game of cricket, Gustave, now tranquil, was whistling in his room while arranging various small items among the books and papers on his desk. Koufra, seeing him repeatedly fiddling with thin wires leading to the slightly-inflated left-hand pocket of his jacket, asked him a few questions.

Gustave made him wait for a reply. In the end, he said: "There! I'm ready. The *very goods* will rain down. You see this little gem?" He took a little box about as big as two fists from his left-hand pocket, and another, almost identical, from his right-hand pocket. "This, my friend, is a little pocket phono-whisperer, manufactured to my specifications—I'll take out a patent when I have the time. It works very well—I've tested it. I install myself tranquilly at my desk, the phono-whisperer in my pocket, connected to my ear by a wire, like this, and when the examiner asks a question, my phono-whisperer murmurs the answer in my ear. Good! I speak entirely at my ease, and I secure, at a stroke, a mark of *very good...more than good*. Aren't the answers there, in the box? I have a wide choice of them—an immense choice, for all possible questions, in the little disks carefully prepared by me. And that, my friend, is how one disentangles oneself, with a little ingenuity, from the difficulties of life!"

The telephonoscope bell rang.

"The moment has come!" said Gustave. "I shall begin—watch my movements carefully, and when I've finished, I'll pass you the apparatus."

The examiner's silhouette appeared on the telephonoscope screen and rapidly came into focus. He was a gentleman of a certain age, rather plump, of jovial appearance, with a casual smile that reassured Koufra in advance and gave him confidence.

Gustave continued whistling as he arranged his disks in series, classified according to subject-matter, with clearly visible numbers.

"Nothing forgotten? All is well!" said Gustave, manipulating his answer-disks with the skillful dexterity of a conjuror.

And the exam began.

At first, it looked as if things would turn out as well as expected; the phono-whisperer' first answers, without being absolutely brilliant, were not bad. The questions, in any case, related to simple matters and had been anticipated. Gustave smiled triumphantly. Suddenly, however, everything changed.

The examiner's physiognomy became less relaxed; he leaned forward, his fingers tapping his papers impatiently.

Koufra saw that his spectacles were throwing off sparks, and very softly, without making any noise, he escaped into the corridor.

Of noise, there was now enough in the room! It was becoming an authentic duel, a heated battle between the examiner and the examinee: questions posed and repeated in a dry and severe voice; answers form at first, then suddenly hesitant and woolly...excited exclamations and interjections succeeding sudden silences...renewals of bursts of speech...

Decidedly, it was going wrong. In the corridor, Koufra waited anxiously to hear the telephonoscope explode.

And the inflexible voice of the examiner continued, utterly dominating, crushing the patient...

"I'm giving you a zero, Monsieur, and that's not all! Another zero! Zero! Zero! Zero! Zero!"

Nothing more: abrupt silence. Koufra listened, astounded.

Gustave knocked him over as he came out, as red as a tomato, with his hair in a mess. "Go on," he said, "it's you—your turn. Go on! I don't recommend that you use my phono-whisperer; it's come unstuck. The invention isn't perfected—I'll have to go back to work. Good luck, old chap!"

Gustave went away, furious. That wasn't playing the game! The examiner must have planned in advance to trouble him with insidious and difficult questions, deliberately prepared. Everything had gone wrong—and how!

As he ran into the grounds to catch his breath and calm down, poor Gustave tripped over the legs of Monsieur Radoux, who was daydreaming under the tall trees.

"Well, Turbille," said the form-master, emerging from his reverie. "What about that invention? That discovery?"

"Failed!" Gustave replied, thinking about the phono-whisperer.

"This would have been the ideal time to succeed, though! Heaps of assignments to correct—one doesn't even have the time to shape a quarter of a sonnet!"

"Oh yes! The machine for correcting assignments. I wasn't thinking about that any longer. Excuse me, Monsieur, but with all these exams to prepare for, I'd forgotten the commission. Alas, alas, I've made no more progress in that matter; I believed that has failed too. Failed! Failed!"

Monsieur Virgile Radoux seemed so put out that Gustave ran away, promising to continue searching.

In the grounds, the examined pupils were circulating in little groups; those who had succeeded were hurrying off to play football, the others wandering around in a melancholy fashion.

Gustave was given a rather cold welcome by the latter. Some were old comrades to whom, as a good fellow devoid of egotism, he had communicated the secret of the phonowhisperer, who had been as badly served as him.

"Inventor of shoddy gods! A machine to manufacture zeros!"

Gustave flinched under the bitter reproaches with which they overwhelmed the vanquished warrior.

"I see it now! I understand everything! They were your stupidities that annoyed the examiner, and it's rebounded on me!"

XX. Gustave Turbille decides to hand over his career as an inventor after misfortunes and catastrophe.

"Discouraged, me?" said Gustave to his friend Koufra, who was lavishing consolations upon him. "Get away! I'm never discouraged! All is not lost—I still have the sports and I'll try to catch up."

"I'm glad to see you so valiant in adversity."

"There, I'm certain to be marked *very good*, without any trouble! Then, with, *very good, very good* and *better than good* in all the branches of athleticism, I'll still have a chance, which is that Papa will be very busy. I hope that he'll have some big deal in progress on the day that the report from the school arrives, which will put him in a difficult position. What luck that would be! You can see it from here—he runs over my report with a distracted eye, thinking about his big business deal, perceives the *very good, very good*, etc, and skips the rest!"

"I hope so, for your sake, my poor Gustave"

"And then, after all, if you've got excellent marks, it by meekly falling in with the old routine, without seeking something better. Me, I'm one of those who isn't content with the old routine; I wanted to innovate; I found an ingenious and truly modern method…unfortunately, I didn't have time to perfect it…and it rained zeros. So be it, I'm an unfortunate inventor—there've been many others before me, and I may justly say: *all is lost save honor!*"[24]

Alfred Koufra could only bow down in admiration.

In fact, Gustave did distinguish himself in the grand sporting competitions, and obtained all the *very goods* he desired.

The school year concluded gently. All trace of fatigue had to disappear; there was no overwork as Chambourcy. The program of work in the final days was designed to restore the spirits of even the most depressed students after the fastidious exit exams: literary lectures by phonograph loudspeaker, to which they listened while lying in the shade on the grass in the arbors, Gustave swaying in his hammock, alongside several others that had recently been authorized. In that too he had been an innovator, a precursor; the introduction of the hammock to scholarly furniture was due to him.

The cinema repeated the entire courses in history and geography: antiquity; modern times; the mores and customs of all peoples, ancient and modern; great spectacles of nature; literary history, the heroes and heroines of books and the thea-

---

[24] "*Tout est perdu fors l'honneur*" is what François I is reputed to have said in 1525 after losing the battle of Pavie and being taken prisoner by the Spaniards.

ter; world commercial news and images of industrial life, etc. Very agreeable and marvelously restful, those last days at the school before the great departure. It was necessary to ease the transition between the intensive work of the weeks of exams and the good weather of the vacation.

In the evening, an hour or two of concert or theater by telephonoscope. Not classics; the time for serious studies had passed; relaxation now, a little fantasy, laughter and tears; vaudeville, operettas and melodramas—all carefully selected, of course.

The distribution of prizes took place very calmly, on the vast central lawn in the shade of the large trees: an entirely familial ceremony, brightened by a orchestra of phonos operating in a distant clump of bushes. The traditional speeches—which is to say, a short allocution by the Minister of Public Education, by phonograph, then the Headmaster's speech, not spoken aloud but put into the hands of each student on a phonographic disk, to be savored at leisure on the return to the family, and even resavored from time to time, if one were in the mood: an excellent fashion of getting the sage advice of experience to penetrate those young intelligences.

Immediately after the speeches, with the distribution of palms illustrated with photographs—a souvenir that each student received in an elegant parcel—the prizes: superb volumes or phonographic editions of good authors.

Then there was the great departure! The school dirigibles, whose hum, more joyous than ever, seemed to manifest a hint of impatience, floating majestically in the air, surrounded by a cloud of small aircraft. Handshakes, appeals, clamors, recommendations, warm congratulations. Embarkation and take-off.

Chambourcy School will remain silent for two months.

Before leaving, Gustave Turbille and Koufra wish Monsieur Virgile Radoux a happy holiday.

"You know, Turbille," the form-master says, "you're going study the little machine that I mentioned to you...that's understood, isn't it? It's a vacation assignment, as in days of old, that will release you from stagnant idleness!"

The aeroclette carrying Turbille and Koufra away was saluted by cheers from their friends in 3A. Koufra had inherited Gustave's celebrity, which had fallen somewhat into decline since his last scientific failure. The son of an African king of the most central Africa, already so remarkable in Classics!

The rumor had got around, however, that Koufra's father was merely a notary in the brand new and very modern little city of Villeneuve-sur-Oubangui. A sixth-former had heard it from an uncle who was a sub-prefect in the Congo. Koufra, put in the dock and interrogated, had admitted it, but no one believed either the sixth-former or Koufra, who was thought to be dissimulating for political reasons. It would be certain when they came back, since Turbille was still talking about his holiday in the Congo and big game hunting in Koufra's kingdom.

"Good luck in the African bush!" cried the comrades. "Bring me back a pair of elephant tusks! A living gorilla for me! A lion-pelt to put on in winter for me!"

Koufra, whose parents were awaiting him impatiently out there, was due to take the next Bordeaux Tube, and then the Great Central African. Would Gustave be accompanying him? Alas, nothing was less certain.

"That depends on Papa's business," Gustave repeated to his friend. "If he turns out to have a few exceedingly complicated deals in progress, all will be well. I'll find out in the offices—we'll see to that right way."

Gustave saw to it immediately. In the offices, he was told that all was calm; no preoccupations, all business progressing routinely.

"Damn! Damn! No, I mean: Perfect! Perfect!"

On leaving the offices, Gustave, unusually anxious and melancholy, found Colette and cousin Valérie already returned from Villennes with palms and a respectable collection of large volumes that the men on the Villennes dirigible were having some difficulty unloading.

The pitiless tele had already summoned Valérie, and voices more numerous than usual could be heard in the next room, *yes uncle*s succeeding one another more rapidly.

"What's up?" asked Gustave, glad to be able to hide his preoccupation.

"Oh, they're all on the tele today," said Colette. "Uncle Pierre, Uncle Georges, Uncle Florentin and Uncle Lucien, to congratulate Valérie…"

"Congratulate? You don't say—it doesn't sound like it!"

"Yes, one could say that the four uncles aren't very happy…"

Despite all their discretion, Gustave and Koufra were obliged to overhear and to follow the conversation, which was a little more animated than usual.

"But Valérie, you told me that our greatest desire was to go to the bar, that you wanted to be an advocate, didn't you?"

"No, my dear chap—she's always sworn to me that she felt impelled by an irresistible vocation toward medicine!"

"Pardon me, not medicine—let's see, Valérie, you've been dreaming of practical sciences, an industrial career, absolutely determined to go to the Centrale?"

"You're wrong! Valerie has always talked to me about the École des Chartes…that must be understood. Well, Valérie!"

The *yes uncle*s were more widely-spaced, and scarcely audible. Valérie sighed, and sighed again, surely about to burst into tears.

"I'll tell you…hold on…yes, uncle…I don't know…I'd like…"

"We shall know everything," said Gustave. "She's about to declare her true vocation!"

"She won't get out of it," said Colette. "I'm going in myself!"

Colette had closed the door, but she could be heard explaining to the uncles.

"Hang on, cousin, look: first prize, the gentle arts, Mademoiselle Valérie Mérindol; embroidery and lacework, first prize, Valérie Mérindol...here, look at these samples of her school-work: Venetian stitch; English embroidery; Bruges; Richelieu lace...that's not for the École Centrale, all that, nor for the École de Médecine... So?"

The uncles uttered stupefied exclamations. Gustave could not hear any more.

"It's not going well for Valérie," he said. "My turn now!" And he headed for his father's study with the expression of a condemned man marching to the scaffold.

The next day, in Koufra's room, as the lucky fellow was buckling his suitcase, the mournful Gustave related his troubles to his friend.

"Papa had time; his eye wasn't distracted; he read the entire report...of my defeats! He's annoyed, seriously annoyed! I shan't be going to the Oubangui—no hunting in the bush. You can tell your rhinoceroses, your hippopotamuses and your lions that they can still sleep easy during this vacation. Do you know what I'll be doing, old chap? Do you know? I'll be spending my vacation here, in Paris, with the Universal Phono-Repeater, and working! Well, I'll work! That's a promise!"

Koufra squeezed his friend's hand sympathetically.

"I renounce inventions, for the moment," Gustave went on. "I've thought about it; I really can't launch myself into large-scale industry to exploit the ideas that I might have, nor enter the Académie des Sciences for a number of years yet, so there's no urgency; I have all the time I need for a little learning. I'm returning to old-fashioned work—it's decided! And I'm handing over my career as an inventor to you. You can already look after yourself a little; you'll do very well out of it. Think about it under the baobabs of the Oubangui.

"To begin with, here's a rather extensive program of scientific research; it's a matter of finding, if not by the start of next term, then as soon as possible, firstly the machine for correcting assignments that will give so much pleasure to Monsieur Radoux, then an automatic machine for rich rhymes, a machine for shortening winter, a machine for extending vacation time, etc., etc.

"Go on, my dear Koufra—happy holidays, and see you again next term!"

CHALET IN THE SKY

I. The Great Resurfacing of the World.

Seated between his nephews Andoche and Moderan on the balcony of the villa that he had just bought, with a view to a fairly long stay, the well-known scholar Monsieur Cabrol seemed thoughtful, his brows slightly furrowed.

"Aren't you pleased with the arrangements, Uncle?" asked Moderan.

"Yes, yes, they'll do," said Monsieur Cabrol. "The first floor is quite well organized: four rooms...one for you, two for me, and we still have one for guests—that's enough. That will do very well. What worries me a little is...but no, no...it will do. I was thinking about my work, my dear Moderan—I don't want it to suffer from our move. No, no, it won't suffer...on the contrary, with the tranquility, the calm, the silence...nor will our studies, my lads, for you'll be working too!"

"Oh, certainly, Uncle!" exclaimed Andoche and Moderan, with one voice.

At that moment, the balcony shifted abruptly. Andoche almost slid off the divan. Behind them, the villa oscillated.

"Come on—one last look at the furniture," said Monsieur Cabrol, pushing the French windows. "My bedroom is fine, my bedstead, my desk and filing-cabinet. There are only 40 drawers and pigeon-holes for my 42 works in progress—it's inconvenient, but, well, I need order; it's a matter of not confusing my archives! 42, my lads! I know that many don't yet have any more than a title written down, but they'll make progress!"

135

"Look down there, Uncle," said Andoche, going back on to the balcony.

"Oh yes—the swirls of dust and smoke above the elevators and winches of the Great Northern Works, which became active a fortnight ago. We should have left already."

Monsieur Cabrol turned his back on the Great Northern Works, muttering: "The world is becoming uninhabitable, alas. Our planet is being sabotaged. No solidity anywhere, in Europe and America, or in the scarcely-tranquil hidden corners of Central Africa. The perforated, worn-out soil, creviced in all directions by quakes, subsidence, shocks and slippages, former mines collapsed or invaded by subterranean seas, forests destroyed... I'm not making recriminations; doubtless the imprudence of our ancestors is to blame, but our globe is getting old as well, and it's aging terribly badly."

"Oh yes!" said Moderan.

"Then again, it must be admitted that the work of the first great consolidation undertaken in the 22nd century, rather meanly, with the simple resources that the state of Science could furnish in that distant era, didn't do a lot of good. It's necessary now to resume work on a vast coordinated plan."

"And here's the first part getting started!" said Moderan, pointing northwards at new vortices of vapor and smoke, which accompanied a frightful racket of rattlings, whistlings and explosions."

"Yes, there it is, as it has to be! The pyramids sank further three months ago, you know. The former summit of the great pyramid is no more than 72 centimeters above ground now; the others have completely disappeared! It's time to decide on a general reconstruction of our planet. But how long will this vast resurfacing that has become so very necessary take? How vexatious it's going to be, before a brand new and perfectly solid globe is restored! Far-sighted men, friends of tranquility, have already gone, flown away hastily, to go and live in remote spots preserved by chance or in sectors that won't be disturbed straight away..."

"Let's go, Uncle, let's go!"

"Personally, I'd rather see the commencement of the upheaval, to give more savor to our tranquility elsewhere. The egotism of a sybarite—it's very naughty, and I've already been punished for it, since I'm told that all of these fortunate and rather rare *Elsewheres* are already full—overfull—of fugitives like us."

"But what about the sixth continent, Uncle?"

"The sixth continent? But your sixth continent is already old, my boy, since it was constructed at the end of the 20th century."

"Yes, that's true, you showed me an old atlas from 1975 in which it wasn't yet depicted."

"Don't worry, though—I hope I can still find a few nice little corners for us near the South American pleasure-cities, in the Chilean Switzerland or the Patagonian Riviera, or the islands constructed in the Pacific—they're said to be very successful."

In spite of his uncle's explanations, however, Andoche's lips visibly formed a sort of moue.

"Well, what now?" said Monsieur Cabrol.

"Why not another world?" Andoche objected, eventually.

"Oh!" said Moderan.

"You'd prefer another word, imprudent youth"

"Not me!" said Moderan.

"Yes, you're more reasonable; I've always said that you resemble me, physically and intellectually, and I was paying you a compliment! Personally, I detest adventures, as you do—that's very good, but this Andoche is a risk-taker. When you were little, by virtue of crazy imprudence, he was always setting off over the ground or into the air with his aeroclettes, getting into dangerous situations from which you, his junior, had to extract him. I wouldn't have taken responsibility for him if you weren't with him to put a brake on his high spirits."

"I'll put the brake on, Uncle!"

Bursting into laughter Moderan and Andoche exchanged a few friendly punches.

"Calm down, calm down!" said Cabrol. "Both of you put the brakes on."

"There are some other worlds that are very nice!" Andoche protested, again. "I've read about interesting communications by the Geographical Society."

"I've read them too. I'll even say that it's been reported that the conditions of life there are truly delightful for our Earth-dwellers...and that acclimatization is easy, even in the worlds newly arrived in our skies, diverted from their routes by ZZZ rays and imprudently captured by distant planets."

"Oh!" said Andoche.

"Come on, young fellow! You must know very well that the voyage presents a few difficulties, all the same. You find those great difficulties tempting, with your daredevil mentality, but you'll see...."

"No trouble," said Moderan.

"Firstly, you need a special apparatus, very carefully constructed, of guaranteed solidity, almost invulnerable, with internal equipment—and it's extremely delicate, the internal equipment of such apparatus. Then one sets off, launching into the blue—that's all well and good, but does one ever know what one will find out there? Listen—as I've told you many a time, I to, in my youth, was adventurous, like Andoche, and I didn't have a younger brother to put a brake on me. I allowed myself to be tempted by the travel agencies' advertisements. I made a great voyage to the Moon. It was expensive: 80,000 francs all-included: hotels, meals, excursions, guides, etc. Except that I didn't see anything! We arrived in the middle of a flu epidemic and fell victim to it as soon as we tried to put our noses outside! We followed the entire program, of course, but from one quarantine to the next, all the travelers in bed..."

"Not enjoyable," said Moderan.

"Yes, yes!" said Andoche.

"My dear Andoche, don't pull that face again—we're going to offer ourselves good weather and places to see, without difficulty and without fatigue, as comfortably as possible. Come on, one last tour of the house where we're going to live for seven or eight years—perhaps ten, for it's always necessary to expect delays in huge, enormous enterprises like that of the reconstruction of our dusty old planet, disfigured in an abominable fashion by preceding generations: careless people, tenants, simple occupiers like us, but who have used and abused the place instead of living like the parents of families, as was their duty, and have left us a heritage in an awful state!"

"We're made a complete tour of the house, Uncle," said Andoche. "Everything's perfect. It's genteel, elegant, the furniture well-made, the beds and armchairs comfortable."

"It's a little expensive—out of our price range, under normal circumstances, but I've told the constructor that your father recommended me. Needless to say, he's furnished us with the latest model aerochalet, state-of-the-art, carefully finished, with a proven intra-atomic-energy motor, carefully checked in running, able to go anywhere, with no fear of squalls or tempests. In sum, an all-purpose aerial caravan, for air, sea and land! In case of a mid-Ocean breakdown—improbable, but it's necessary to be prepared for any accident—we can sail, and get ourselves out of trouble by our own means..."

"Of course!" said Andoche, smiling with pleasure.

"And if I'm content and satisfied, I'll have given my constructor a further payment in five years and an additional premium in ten—and I ask nothing more than to pay him that additional premium. For the moment, I declare myself quite content with our chalet, a floating villa that will carry us far away from that colossal Reconstruction Works, flying from country to country in search, not of a single pleasant place to live, but ten or 20 in succession! When we've studied the local people and horizons sufficiently, and want a change, we'll change them!"

"Bravo!" cried Andoche. "I like variety!"

"Me too," said Andoche.

"And me, just as much as you!" concluded Monsieur Cabrol. "So, you've seen everything. There's your room, with its two beds in front of one large window, from which you won't miss any of the landscape. My bedroom's next door; I'll have you close by; we'll each work in our own rooms. Meals will be taken in a corner of my study, at the customary hours, in order not to change our routines at all. Instead of staying rooted to the spot in our earthbound domicile, my flying villa will carry us wherever we wish, as we wish, at top speed when it's a matter of gaining ground, or very gently when the landscape is worth the trouble of being savored in every detail, without missing anything. That's real tourism! And then, in nice places, descent to Earth and rest; we'll moor the house with a good view for a few days or a few months, in some proud promontory, gentle hill or Alp-like peak, or even in an air-garden, close to some interesting city. Are you content?"

"Content? Joyful! Let's get going right away."

"Ah! First, we have to give a name to our flying villa, where we'll be so comfortable. I propose…"

"The Villa Beauséjour."

"No, the Beauséjour Family Aero-Boarding-House! Tomorrow, the opening of our family boarding-house, the house-warming and leaving party."

Monsieur Cabrol rubbed his hands together and his face took on a jovial expression; his eyes seemed to be laughing through his spectacles, the creases in his slightly-hollow cheeks quivering.

He was a man of average height, but rather thin and very stiff. He was, as always, dressed in a long doublet—a sort of overcoat, as they used to say in olden times—with a broad belt, with a hood folded down over the shoulders and a broad upturned collar. That collar framed a long neck, a narrow, sharply-outlined face hollowed out beneath the cheekbones, and spectacles set over other hollows sheltered by black bushy eyebrows. A long moustache hung down in two lovely black curls. As for his hair, that was reduced to a single thick tuft at the rear of a majestic skull, which seemed to be full of thoughts, whose seething kept his wrinkles perpetually in motion.

His nephew Andoche resembled him, perhaps, but rather vaguely, being more filled-out. He was young, and life, with all its exigencies, studies and formidable brain-work, had not yet sculpted his face and his rounded pink cheeks, nor traced the slightest wrinkle on his forehead. Let us note that he was behind other young folk of his generation in that respect. His lips laughed easily and, when they were not smiling, had an audacious expression that accentuated the gaze of his keen, alert eyes.

Moderan was also good-looking, with pink cheeks, but he had a soft gaze, and gentler features. The resemblance between the two brothers was in the legs, nervously agitated in perpetual motion—the legs of young sportsmen, avid to run and jump.

"Let's go—tomorrow, we escape!" concluded Monsieur Cabrol, after a last circular glance around the aerochalet's drawing-room.

The two brothers leapt into action. Moderan took the floating stairway, while Andoche launched himself on to the airstrip hanging on to a wire.

II. A Party. The Train lost for 800 Years.

The great day has arrived: the house-warming and leaving party. A lovely little aircraft has just moored at the Saint-German-en-Laye airstrip, disgorging the owner of the Villa Beauséjour and his two nephews, and the latter's parents: Madame des Ormettes, the member of parliament for the Seine, and Monsieur des Ormettes, the director of the famous Interplanetary Travel Agency, both well-known in political and scientific circles. Monsieur des Ormettes is a very round man, a ball surmounted by another, smaller ball. Madame des Ormettes is a trifle...slender, like her brother Monsieur Cabrol. Each of them has a stout portfolio laden with papers under one arm; both of them stride over the ground of the airstrip with the hasty gait of people in a hurry, their eyes vague and heads overburdened with preoccupations and projects.

"Ah, let's see—so that's the aerovilla! Well, well, I recognize it—that's definitely it. I've seen all the blueprints. I've just ordered six of them for clients. Hang on—just making a note so as not to forget... There! I'm all yours..."

"Come in," said Cabrol.

While Madame des Ormettes was searching distractedly for the villa's doorbell, Andoche and Moderan were already on the first-floor balcony, laughing uproariously.

"Come up, come up—or we'll raise the anchor and set off on our own, Mama, Papa! Come in, quickly."

Monsieur des Ormettes made another little note, and came up last.

"The proprietor's tour!" said Monsieur Cabrol. "Vestibule, service-room, store-rooms and drawing-room—it's quite large, as you see. In font, here's the steering-compartment... Andoche, please don't touch the wheel or the directional switches, you'll have us leaping up into the air and carrying off your parents at 200 kilometers an hour."

"Wretched boy!" cried Madame des Ormettes, getting up precipitately. "I'm chairing the Budget Committee of the joint Chambers at 5 p.m.!"

"No silliness!" cried Monsieur des Ormettes. "I have business meetings his evening..."

Andoche burst out laughing.

"It would be as well to come with us, though, Mama," said Moderan. "We have a shared room on the first floor."

"I'd love to, my boys, but what about the time? How shall I find the time?"

"You're lucky, my dear Cabrol, to be able to escape all the inconveniences of this turbulent period of reconstruction, but you'll lose something by it. Think of all the archeological discoveries that might be made in the course of these immense labors, which will turn over and lay bare almost all of the surface of the globe. Discoveries of all sorts—geological, historic, artistic and others. Who can tell what we might learn. It's already begun…"

"Yes, yes, all that Gallo-roman or Batignolaise pottery."

"No, better than that. Yesterday, someone stumbled on something fascinating, at least for people of the 22nd century. An old mystery cleared up! This morning's phonocinetelegazette gave us the news. I'd been woken up at 6 a.m. by the whistle advertizing a special edition. When I opened my eyes, the phono was already functioning. Didn't you hear it?"

"Yes, but I hit the stop button so that I could snooze for another half hour. What was it about?"

"In brief, this: you must be vaguely aware that in the 22nd century, about 2123 or 2125, a Metro train on the second network, the last of the night, disappeared completely on the Châtelet-Longchamps line, between Saint-Cloud and Puteaux stations. The train was crowded with people leaving the Grand Opera de Longchamps, to which the Paris Opera had been removed about 25 years before, into the nicest part of the former Bois, facing the large airport established on Mont Valérien. The Bois de Boulogne was searched; the Seine was searched; all the branches of the Metro were searched, in vain. In spite of all the searches, no trace or vestige of the train was ever found, nor any of the passengers. An incomprehensible enigma! A fearful mystery! People still talk about it, like the Man in the Iron Mask or…"

"Yes, yes…"

"Are we're holding this house-warming?" Madame des Ormettes put in, consulting her watch.

"Here it is; sit down. While we eat, our friend can demystify this troubling enigma for us…"

Everything was set out for the meal: flowers on the tablecloth, a few saucers and a few little bottles of pills. Monsieur Cabrol deposited a pill in a saucer in front of each guest. "Enjoy!" he said.

"Well," des Ormettes went on, "This is what happened. Yesterday… you know that they're digging into the part of the catacombs that the Metro didn't use. They're clearing material, replacing supporting pillars; so, in the Vaugirard sector, the excavators suddenly came across the train that had gone astray 800 years ago. Amazement at first, but it really was the same one. They found newspapers of the period: May 2124. Once the first wagon came to light, the engineers pressed on with the work, and they were able to see the drill slide all the way to the end of the train—the carriages were all there."

"What about the passengers?" asked Moderan.

"Them too!"

"Damn!"

"The inquest has begun—legally and, informally, in the newspapers. We'll know the details later—crimes like that make a lot of noise, for it was a matter of an enormous crime! Today, we can affirm that the train, diverted from its track into the catacombs by the audacious malefactors at the intersection of a line under construction on the second level of the second network, plunged into the tunnels under Vaugirard. Then…"

"Oh no—no sensational details," said Madame des Ormettes.

"No, I'll cut it short. Their work done, the frightful bandits blew up a part of the vaults, covering the unfortunate train and the space behind with debris 150 meters long and 15 meters thick, plus a few houses that collapsed on top. The Metro track ran alongside that mass burial for centuries, and it required the world-wide resurfacing to provide the key to the mystery. Brrr!"

Monsieur des Ormettes solemnly placed a little pink pill on a spoon and raised his hand.

"I've seen the label on the bottle—it's a synthetic extract of Clos-Vougeot. I raise my spoon to your health, Cabrol, and to the Villa Beauséjour, wishing you a pleasant and peaceful trip through tranquil skies! I wish you all the good luck in the word! Work hard, all of you! Come back, Andoche and Moderan, my dear boys, ready to claim your diplomas in all subjects, and you, Cabrol, with your 42 volumes finished."

"Oh no," said Cabrol, laughing. "Not all of them—that's too much. I'll be content with my two great works, which are already well advanced."

"Which ones?"

"You know very well!"

"The ones that the scientific world has been awaiting so impatiently for…is it necessary to say it?" said Monsieur des Ormettes. "For 25 or 30 years?"

"The work conceived in the first bloom of my literary life, deepened and caressed throughout my mature years. I've devoted myself to perfecting it and bringing it to a conclusion. Shh! Don't reproach me for the excessive conscientiousness of my labors! First and foremost, there's my *History of the Lunatic Civilizations, according to the documents brought back by travelers and the works of the Selenites*, and then, *The Prehistoric Populations of our Globe and their political institutions…*"

"Very good!"

"Yes, as one can't always be flying around, I shall have enough to occupy myself! We'll sometimes be disturbed, but I shan't complain about that…friends to receive, visits to make…and then, too, won't I have to supervise my nephews' studies? We have the complete apparatus of the Cinephono University; it will function regularly, I assure you, and the boys will come back to you armed for life, equipped for whatever career they may choose…"

"With you, we are tranquil, my dear Cabrol."

"Our program is concluded—let's get back to our house-warming. Another pill of Chambertin…let's be merry! But what has happened to my housekeeper, Melanie? She was here a moment ago, but I can no longer see or hear her. Melanie! Melanie!"

"Delicious, this pill…"

"Wait until Melanie brings us the gustatory capsules."

"But they're there, in front of you. Melanie has got everything ready."

"Oh yes—I can see the little box of capsules."

Indeed, a bottle and an oval box ten centimeters broad were standing in the middle of the table on a silver tray framed by flowers. Monsieur des Ormettes picked up the bottle, read: *Sauterne...Champagne*, and exclaimed: "Well, well! You'll make us overdo it!"

"Bah! There's no harm in tripping up once now and again. The Sauterne pill is to accompany that of the truffled pheasant, and then there's the capsule of synthetic glazed fruits for dessert, with the champagne pill—and that's all."

"What a feast!" said Madame des Ormettes. "I won't have any of the truffled pheasant myself; I'll be content with a champagne pill."

"Only one? No more? So you don't think it's very good, my champagne?"

"On the contrary—it's marvelous, a liquid flame. That pill has gone to my head; don't forget that I have my Finance Committee this evening; I'll be getting confused amid the numbers..."

"Dear old Cabrol has a well-established reputation as a gourmet; he's very partial to his gustatory pills. Truly, his house-warming is a success. What a feast! One might believe that we had returned to the times of our worthy ancestors!"

"Our gross ancestors, you might say," said Madame des Ormettes. "Can you believe it? For so many centuries they ate actual food—what horror! They swallowed food of every sort. Fattened, plump animals, game of every variety and vegetables of every species, which they forced down with liberal does of wine or liqueurs. They stuffed themselves with cakes and various pastries—I found a list of them in an old history: rum babas, coffee cakes, tartlets...ugh! And what an incredible waste of time! Two hours at table! After that, can we be astonished by their intellectual barbarity, the weakness of their sciences..."

"Our poor ancestors!" moaned Monsieur Cabrol.

"We, at least, have feasts lasting a minute and a half at most; we have alimentary syntheses free of all harmful ferment; we have essences concentrated in pills, which gently caress the taste-buds without dulling our intellect. What does our organism require to prosper? Nothing more—and we can therefore devote all our time to work, and our projects. Think about it! Imagine what fabulous delays the old modes of alimentation must have inflicted on Progress and Civilization!"

"It's very sad, I agree," Monsieur Cabrol went on, "but in the end, it's necessary to nourish oneself, and if possible, I want to bring you back two sturdy and healthy young fellows—replete, even. Would you like to see the larder? Come on, it's downstairs, in the cool—the big cupboard with double doors. Let's see, there'll be four of us, counting the pilot. But where is my housekeeper? Has she gone back to the house? I still have a host of instructions to give her."

"She has your instructions, and she knows perfectly well what she has to do," said Madame des Ormettes."

"Oh, I'll give her a good talking to by telephone...I know full well, of course, that she's furious that I'm not taking her along...but it's necessary for her to remain in the house, to look after it and keep watch on my collections."

"You can give her the final instructions by wireless."

"Yes, yes, Melanie be damned!" muttered Monsieur Cabrol. "We were saying, then, that I'm taking ten years' supply of food for four people. At two meals a day, that makes 730 meals per person per year, which is to say, 7300 meals over ten years. Multiplying by four, I'll need...30,000 pills. I'm taking 40,000—that leaves a small margin for a few occasional guests."

"That's prudent," said Monsieur des Ormettes.

"You approve? I'm delighted by that—you have experience of traveling. Thus, a ton of pills, that's the solid nourishment. What about the liquid provisions? Pills of concentrated liquid: 500 kilos of assorted droplets. Naturally, the whole gamut of wines, hydromels, beers, etc. In addition—it's necessary to anticipate everything—a box of pharmaceutical pills for every possible ailment, along with the handbook of the Académie de Médecine."

"Perfect!" said Madame des Ormettes. "With all that, I'll rest easy. I know that I can entrust my dear boys to you without anxiety."

"I shall bring you back men!"

"Oh, if I weren't so busy, if I didn't have to live up to my obligations to my electors, I'd go with you."

"As well as the Cinephono University, we have a little library. I'll make sure that my nephews work regularly."

"It's so convenient, that Cinephono University," said Madame des Ormettes, "but can you understand why they haven't yet found a machine to correct assignments?"

A bell rang. It was a signal from the pilot, who came out of his cockpit. It was time to go. The Beauséjour Family Aero-Boarding-House was about to take off.

"Monsieur," said the pilot, "it's three and a half minutes to 4 p.m.—which is the departure time you set."

Everyone got up. Andoche and Moderan leapt to their feet joyfully. The others did not seem overly excited.

"Yes, I left three minutes for effusions," said Cabrol. That's sufficient—life is so short! Come on, let's embrace. No emotion, since we'll see one another every evening on the Tele, and can tell one another calmly how we spent our day, quite at ease."

"When your aerovilla is installed somewhere—but what about when it's flying?"

"Well, what about the wireless? Come on, we've only got half a minute. Goodbye, and good luck to everyone! Until the Tele, tomorrow!"

"Good luck to the Villa Beauséjour!"

Monsieur and Madame des Ormettes were on the ground of the airstrip, Andoche and Moderan on the balcony of the villa, waving their handkerchiefs.

The Villa Beauséjour trembled in all its limbs, rolled gently over the airstrip and took off, almost without a shock.

The constructor was worthy of his reputation; the flying villa was as well-balanced in full flight as at its mooring. It gleamed in the sunlight, with its enameled façade and its roof checkered with pink tiles, reminiscent of the roofs of terrestrial buildings.

On the ground floor there were three windows on each side, a large balcony in front, which extended like a beak with the cockpit at its tip, and a rounded balcony at the back. On the first floor, there were another three windows on each side. Elegance and simplicity.

The aerovilla described a broad circle above the airstrip and headed south, while Monsieur and Madame des Ormettes went back to their jobs in their flying car.

III. The Collapse of the Alps, the Rise of Venice, and Other Changes.

The Villa Beauséjour was flying at 500 or 600 meters, at a moderate speeds, in a pale blue sky strewn with little clouds that were heading northwards in more or less compact squadrons, interrupted by long thin trails. The tall buildings of Central Paris were already fading away in the distance, along with the interminable lines of the faubourgs, amid the green patches of parks or the tangles masses of iron, pylons and towers of the industrial districts.

It made a magnificent landscape—already significantly eroded, unfortunately, by the immense upheaval of the worldwide reconstruction.

"Settle down, boys," said Cabrol, who was now in a slightly bad mood, doubtless caused by the change in his domestic habits.

"But we're on our way, Uncle!" Andoche and Moderan replied, as one, running from one window to another, to the east or the west.

And for a quarter of an hour there was: "That's beautiful, don't you think? What's that down there? And that up in the sky? Look, the Loire! What's that smoke? A volcano? No, the entrance to a Works."

"Veer slightly eastwards," Monsieur Cabrol said to the pilot.

"Look—Switzerland!"

"And the sea-baths! Do you recognize them, Moderan? We were there last year, on the beaches of the Jungfrau. That subsidence of the crust last century, which caused the sinking of Switzerland and the invasion of the Adriatic through long corridors, has it finally stopped?"

"Work has been going on in that sector for 20 years— that's fortunate, but what work is it!"

Poor old Venice was not sinking—oh no! Like the movement of a balance, the sinking of the Gulf of Quarnero had been causing it to rise slowly, by eight or ten meters a year, for 50 years, and it had reached an altitude of 460 meters. What a job it was to reclaim and underpin the ground beneath it! How many pillars of reinforced concrete, and cross-pieces had been slid under the pilings of the Doge's palace!

Look at those modifications on old map, that chaplet of seaside resorts in competition with the Lido, instead of the ancient lakes, under the ex-Jungfrau, Cervin, Brunig or Simplon.

Leaving the panorama of transformed Switzerland, with its great sea-ports of Lucerne and Geneva, the Villa Beauséjour, having gained height, now set a course westwards and flew at top speed. To the left, Cabrol pointed out the heavy swirls of vapor, over which flashes of light were passing.

"The Auvergne!" he said. "The volcanoes have resumed their activity, fortunately regulated by the marvelous endeavors of our engineers, and used for the central heating of hot water for a good part of our ancient continent. The repair-work is quite advanced in that region because it was begun so long ago, when someone had the idea of stiffening the ground with gigantic girders of reinforced concrete—vast checkerboards through which the sea-water, carried in huge conduits descends to be heated by the volcanoes of Puy de Dôme and rises again, boiling, to the central heating factories.

"From here you can't see the new, quasi-tropical vegetation that has developed in this region, which has thus become an immense and marvelous hothouse. And the work has been imitated by every country lucky enough to possess torpid old volcanoes, or even active volcanoes, which have thus been rendered inoffensive by controlling their expansions and explosions."

"It's getting a little warm," said Moderan, going out on to the balcony.

"Yes, that's the breath of the Puy," said Monsieur Cabrol. Look at all that seething, and those jets of steam down there; the natural boilers of the central heating are blowing in our faces, but in a moment we'll find the good fresh wind of the Atlantic."

Monsieur Cabrol spoke to the pilot, an old airman accustomed to voyages, who did not seem to look at anything anymore, indifferent to everything happening down below. With his eyes half-closed and a little pipe in his mouth, the old cloud-dweller drowsed, while following the slight spirals of smoke from his pipe. He was not completely asleep, for he darted the occasional brief glance at his control-panel and his levers.

"Well, Barlotin?" said Monsieur Cabrol.

"On course," Barlotin replied. "South-south-west, altitude 745, headed for Arcachon Airport..."

"How long?"

"30 to 35 minutes. Should I increase speed?"

"No, there's no hurry. We'll bed down at the airport."

The little pipe, which had never stopped working, projected a large smoke-ring, and the pilot became somnolent again..

"Not talkative, Père Barlotin," Andoche murmured, returning to the balcony.

"A trusty old pilot; your father vouched for him, having often employed him. Père Barlotin, always in the air, hasn't spent one week a year on the ground for years. He says that he's no longer used to it, and gets vertigo as soon as he sets foot on a terrestrial floor...he can no longer walk. When, by chance, he's in Paris, waiting for some big aircraft to fly, he doesn't leave the 300-meter lighthouse platform of the air-strip...no, he's not talkative...his little pipe is his only confi-dant."

The afternoon was coming to an end. Already, in the western sky, clouds were running over a broad yellow sheet, and the line of the horizon was sparkling with light mauve bands.

"The sea!" said Andoche, leaping from one side to the other.

"The open air has given us an appetite," said Monsieur Cabrol. "As soon as we're moored, we'll eat—then a little walk under the pines, to stretch our legs—then to bed."

Gently, softly, after having described two or three spirals above the long beach and pine-woods framing numerous sea-side châteaux, the Villa Beauséjour landed on the blue thistles of a sandy knoll, a dozen paces from the waves that were lan-guidly beating out the song of the evening tide.

Andoche and Moderan did not wait for the Villa to be secured and anchored to leap to the ground and run off over thistle-free sand into a clump of superb pine trees. They braced themselves, lay down, leapt up with one bound, and began again, jostling one another with joyful exclamations.

Monsieur Cabrol did not have so much ardor to expend; he got down carefully and walked around the Villa with his arms folded, rubbing his forehead with the tip of his finger.

"I don't understand it," he said to himself. "The Beauséjour's weight is greater than I thought. Yesterday, with all of us on board, the needle marked 2647 kilos and 125 grams; today we have 2739 kilos and 858 grams. What does the discrepancy signify? I know that I have a tendency to put on weight, but 90 kilos in a day! So what? It's not important, but I'll keep an eye on it all the same. I'll only take half-pills."

He went to join his nephews under the pines and sat down beside them to admire the fiery Sun at his leisure. Its rays were reaching out across the sky as if in preparation for the dive into the sparkling waves in the distance.

"Listen!" said Moderan. "You'd think we could hear Phanor."

"That's true—the voice bears a strong resemblance to poor Phanor's," said Monsieur Cabrol, having cocked an ear. "It's some dog belonging to the castle behind us. Or that little air-caravan that's poised over the nearby waves, adrift on its anchors."

"Poor Phanor looked very sad when he saw our luggage; he understood that we were leaving and weren't taking him with us."

"Poor Phanor—we were wrong to leave him behind, Uncle."

"Yes, we were wrong—I regret it now."

"Can't we send for him?"

"Yes, but not before we're installed somewhere."

"Let's hurry, then."

"Not so fast—ah! Look at Phoebus sinking; we'll go back for dinner and then, at 9:35 p.m., a word to the family over the Tele; then bed, sleep, and wake up tomorrow at 6 a.m."

Monsieur Cabrol got to his feet slowly and effortfully. It was so pleasant under the caresses of that gentle breeze, in the calm of that lovely evening! Oh, how well one felt, far from Paris and the infernal upheaval of the worldwide resurfacing! This part of maritime Aquitaine was scarcely affected, in the direction of Bordeaux.

The meal on the Beauséjour's balcony was rapidly concluded. One pill and one synthetic droplet—which is to say, two pills each to swallow, or, if one is something of a gourmand, to allow to melt while slowly drinking a glass of cold water—doesn't take very long. The three diners chatted, sprawling in sturdy wicker armchairs.

"Yes, I'm something of a gourmand," said Monsieur Cabrol.

"Me too," said Andoche!

"So, in our provision of pills and gustatory capsules, I've set aside some nice little dishes for Sundays and holidays: roast chicken, ducks Rouen-style, lamb cutlets, roe venison, jugged hare, chitterling sausages and salmon trout; for vegetables: stuffed cabbages, sauté potatoes, peas, snipe pâté etc., to make a change from ordinary boiled beef pills…"

Andoche and Moderan exchanged smiles of satisfaction..

"Very pleasant…and very economical, the pills, my lads! Whereas, with chicken consumed with the aid of one's teeth…do we still need teeth now, except for decoration?"

Andoche and Moderan smiled, displaying natural teeth in the old style, but not very shiny, while their uncle allowed a glimpse of two rows of admirable teeth, in gold in the upper jaw and silvered enamel in the lower.

"Nothing better has been found, as yet, to complete a face. Yes, as I was saying, how many people can one nourish with a chicken brutally consumed, in the fashion of our primitive ancestors? Two at the most. Well, the factories, by combining it with a little sea-wrack, essences and various condiments can get 50 pills out of one—which is to say, 50 complete meals. You can see the enormous advantage! How else could we feed the overpopulated Earth, I ask you? Thus Paris wanted to pay the tribute of recognition due from the entire world by erecting a great monument to the four chemists of genius who invented the synthetic pills! A colossal group, in which they are represented in the midst of their retorts, their ovens and their saucepans, receiving the long procession of all the animals useful for nutrition: livestock, game, poultry, fish, etc.—a pure masterpiece! But watch out! It's 9 p.m. Quickly, go to the Tele, to say goodnight to your exceedingly busy Papa and your dear Mama, if she hasn't been held up at the Budget Committee."

The Telespeaker, a marvelous instrument that truly suppresses absence by wireless, since, with a relay to a regular mast, one can recover on the screen of the apparatus, no matter where, the presence and the voice of dear individuals 1000 kilometers away.

Monsieur Cabrol's first concern, on landing, had been to plant a terrestrial antenna in the ground, to link up with the Arcachon mast.

Art the agreed time, Monsieur and Madame des Ormettes were due to be at the rendezvous in front of their screen in Paris. Scarcely was he on the balcony of the Aero-Beauséjour when Cabrol heard the sound of raised voices in his room.

"Come on! Your father's getting impatient. Seeing that no one's replying to him, he's switched on the amplifier."

Andoche and Moderan were already upstairs, replying to the thunderous summons.

"Well, well," said Monsieur des Ormettes. "What were you doing, then?"

"Admirable sunset! We were admiring it," said Cabrol.

"It's just that I'm in a hurry."

"And we were idling before the panorama—but here we are. All going well, first day perfect…"

"Where's Mama?" asked Moderan.

"Not back from the Chamber. Hold on, see for yourself."

The screen suddenly sparkled. Monsieur des Ormettes disappeared; then a big green table appeared, laden with papers, around which some 20 people—seven or eight of which were women—were arguing. Madame des Ormettes was there, reading a report. A few words and figures were heard; then the apparatus sparkled again, and Monsieur des Ormettes reappeared.

"Everything's going well. Good. Perfect…"

"We're setting off tomorrow at 6 a.m.," said Monsieur Cabrol.

"Goodnight, then. See you soon, children."

The screen went dark.

"Now, boys, you've seen Papa and Mama; it's time for bed. Sleep well. I'll stay here—I have a few last things to say to Melanie—a list of important things to remember. For safety's sake, I'm going to repeat my instructions in written form..."

IV. Supplementary Voyagers

Andoche and Moderan were still sleeping profoundly when a rather strong lurch of the Villa Beauséjour caused them to pen their eyelids slightly; the rocking continued for a few seconds, gradually dying away.

"Hey, we're off!" said Moderan, yawning and stretching his arms.

"We're leaving," said Andoche. "Quickly—let's not miss any of the countryside. Then again, I'm very hungry this morning."

The two youngsters were dressed in less than five minutes. Monsieur Cabrol, also up, was shaving in his room. "Good morning, good morning!" he said. "But what's all that barking? Arcachon's drawing away, but we can still hear it. Am I hearing things?"

"But it's still Phanor's voice," said Andoche. "And who's scratching like that?"

Moderan had already opened the door. A little dog leapt forward, ran around the two boys several times, yapping, and tried to jump into Monsieur Cabrol's arms. Mouth agape with astonishment, with his cheeks still lathered with soap, he brandished his razor.

"Down, Phanor, down!" said Monsieur Cabrol. "You'll make me cut myself. Down! It's nice to see you, but where have you sprung from?"

The door opened again. "Good morning, Monsieur. Did you sleep well?"

This time, Cabrol dropped his razor. "Melanie! Melanie, here! But how?"

"Well, yes, Monsieur, I'm here. Not being able to bear the idea of staying in the house all alone, far from Monsieur, who might have need of me…and the young gentlemen too…I was going out of my mind with anxiety. So, at the last moment, I stayed in the aero…at the back of the wardrobe in the guest-room…and not all alone, Monsieur."

Phanor yapped and bounded around Melanie. "Yes, yes, not all alone…yes, yes, Phanor!"

Melanie, who was clutching a sort of basket-suitcase against her chest, opened her arms. Miaowing was coming from the basket and the head of a large white cat emerged from a blanket, along with two lazily-extended paws,

"Babylas too!" exclaimed Monsieur Cabrol. "The whole household, then?"

"Phanor and Babylas would have died of boredom away from Monsieur…"

"What about my collections?"

"I've warned the insurance company! After all, it's Monsieur who must be looked after rather than the knick-knacks, old debris of wood or stone that can't fall ill, or get any worse than they are. So, my duty…"

"We're at an altitude of 7000 or 8000 meters, Melanie; I don't want to send you back…"

"Monsieur wouldn't do that…"

"No. You tyrannize me in the house, so you might as well continue here. Come on, Phanor, down! You, Babylas, come sit on my knees."

The cat, undulating the white arch of his back, leapt on to his master's knees, curled up into a ball and closed his eyes, purring, without paying any apparent heed to Phanor's barking. The latter came to sink his muzzle into the cat's soft fur.

"It's all right—install yourself upstairs, in the room, not the wardrobe. But what about your luggage? I expect that the works will be rather well-advanced before Paris becomes habitable again, you know. We'll be staying here as long as necessary, perhaps eight or ten years."

"My luggage is here."

"I get it! All those packages I didn't recognize, scattered through all the wardrobes…"

Melanie smiled.

She was a slightly plump woman, a strong woman, physically and mentally. Her calm eye and the tranquil assurance of her full face clearly showed that no doubt ever crossed her mind regarding the excellence of her intentions and the legitimacy of her decisions.

Monsieur Cabrol had already made his decision. Leaving Melanie to get on with her unpacking, he took his nephews on to the forward balcony. They all savored their morning pills, an extract of chocolate and banana, and were able to concentrate all their attention on the route.

"Well, Barlotin," said Monsieur Cabrol. "A fine day in prospect, eh? Beautiful sunrise...we need to cover a lot of ground in order to get to the truly interesting part of the trajectory tomorrow."

The pilot opened an eye; he had already raised his little pipe to his mouth, and released a few spirals of smoke before putting it back in. "I know the route well, Monsieur," he said. "Going smoothly, without any inconvenience, we'll be half way between Dakar and Panama this evening. I know the exact itinerary you've given me, with changes of course at the marked points. Besides, they're the usual points of diversion on the Dakar-South America line."

"Are we working this morning?" Monsieur Cabrol asked his nephews.

"Oh, Uncle, let us off again today—we'll start tomorrow."

"All right—me too, then."

Andoche and Moderan installed themselves beside the pilot, pretending to take a lesson in navigation. To be ready for any eventuality, a young man of today must know how to maneuver any wheeled or flying vehicle—which is, in any case, very simple—on land or in the air, be it a small aircraft, a hydroplane, an autoplane or any other. They did not yet have their qualifications, but expected to take the tests within a matter of months.

Nothing more was heard within the cockpit, save for the words *stabilizer, tube, lever, radioetherogoniometer, radioloxodromogoniometer...*

Monsieur Cabrol, who was striding back and forth, suddenly announced, in the tone of a steward on a great airship: "Toledo dead ahead! Aleazar! Puente d'Aleantara! Puente San Martino..."

Andoche and Moderan leaned over the balcony, binoculars in hand.

"Look out! Don't fall on to the bridges of Toledo from this height—you'll break them. At their age, they can no longer be very solid. Pilot, spiral around for a better view."

In the Sierras, the great restoration had begun; they were old, those mountains; their crumbling carcass, baked and worn, stood out on high like a long skeleton with blanched sides, lying on a bald terrain. The Villa Beauséjour flew over it, accelerating its speed, attracted by a brilliant dot that the pilot had pointed out, on the side of another sierra, this one snowy.

"Grenada! The Alhambra!"

Andoche and Moderan leaned over again.

"What's that shining?"

"The pilot told you—the Alhambra."

"But it's made of glass!" Moderan exclaimed, after a brief pause.

"A glass case, in fact, to preserve the old Alhambra from any accident and prolong its old age. The Alhambra attracts a lot of visitors—you can see the dirigibles of every sort circling above it—and those visitors aren't always very careful. They drop litter and bottles, and even erode bits of the architecture as they move around. Then there are indelicate tourists who descend on to the patios by night to carry off little souvenirs—sculptures, pottery or whatever. With a thick glass cover in a strong steel framework, these dangers are averted."

The Aero-Villa Beauséjour continued on its way, gaining altitude. The Alhambra was now sparkling in the distance behind them, becoming confused with the snows of the Sierra Nevada.

Ahead, at the extreme tip of Spain, well above the Rock of Gibraltar, so famous in the distant past, which had collapsed in a war, the work of world repair consisted of the enlargement of the great maritime canal of Cadiz, excavated a few centuries before to double the ancient strait. A broad white zigzag line cut across the peninsula, extending from Cadiz to the Atlantic.

"We've made good progress with the wind," said Monsieur Cabrol. "In fine weather, it won't cause us any inconvenience, the Sun of that Africa you can see down there, yellow and ink, to our left. We'll get to the landing-ground early."

There was nothing more to see but blue; they were able to have lunch in the dining room listening to the phonogazettes on the Tele—nothing interesting, just news of major reconstruction projects, complaints coming from every direction about the inconvenience and unprecedented hindrance to life and business.

Then there was a siesta in the comfortable armchairs, a few hours of good rest.

"A little concert?" Moderan suggested.

"No, a little theater. What? Nothing sad, or...or..."

"All right! I'll choose," said Monsieur Cabrol.

A troop of clowns appeared on the screen of the Tele, capering hilariously, jumping over one another and doing tricks.

Melanie had run to see the circus. Phanor almost leap on to the Tele, barking at the clowns and the clever animals— donkeys of remarkable intelligence and geese that followed them. Slightly alarmed by the drumming, Babylas took fright and came to wind herself round, without wanting to watch what was happening on the Tele, simply accompanying the actors and the music who a purr of disdainful well-being.

After half an hour, Andoche and Moderan being drowsy, Monsieur Cabrol switched off the Tele and picked up his notebook in order to jot down a few ideas that had occurred to him, with regard to the lunatic civilizations.

The ringing of a little bell awoke all three of them. The pilot was signaling something.

"Good!" said Monsieur Cabrol, looking at the clock. "We must be getting close."

"The Caucasian Archipelago in view, Monsieur!" the pilot shouted into the telephone.

"There! There! Get up, boys—we're arriving…"

"Already!" said Andoche and Moderan, yawning. "It was so comfortable!"

"Well, you mustn't miss anything. The Caucasus is new to you—I've already visited it myself."

The Caucasus in mid-Atlantic? Yes, the Caucasus, or very nearly. The Caucasus was the archipelago constructed 100 years before, mid-way between Dakar and Panama, when the great work of the amelioration of the Caucasus began.

The Caucasus was then a country encumbered by its mountains, a confused network of narrow gorges between formidable rocky peaks, which considerably hindered communications between Europe and southern Asia. Tunnels had been bored through the blocks, but it was costly and dangerous; inundations of oil and collapses of rock as trains passed through rendered the exploitations of the tunnels precarious. A speculator of genius had had a good idea: all these pebbles are inconvenient; let's remove them, clearing the Caucasus, and exploit them as an inexhaustible quarry of concrete.

The work began. The inconvenient peaks were attacked with drills and electric crushing mills, transformed into concrete and pebble pudding or preserved in enormous blocks, which were loaded on to ships and taken away, not over short distances but via the canals of the Black Sea, the Sea of Marmora, the regularized Mediterranean and Gibraltar, into the open Atlantic, over the shallow depths of the Sargasso Sea. The double operation was a success. A practicable Caucasus was left behind, and the Caucasian Archipelago emerged from the waves.

Here the constructors had paid attention to the picturesque, and the structure of the islands and been carefully designed and carefully contrived, with a view to making something fine out of the isles, which were surrendered to engineers, foresters and landscapers as soon as they were constructed.

The result had been marvelous: jagged coastlines, bristling with beautiful rocks and cliffs, punctuated by promontories, fringed with white surf, with beaches of fine sand beneath admirable woodlands—a mixed African and European flora of palms, umbrella pines, oaks and olive-trees—springs tumbling down to the sea in cascades or majestic falls; rivers descending in cataracts from a great lake-reservoir accommodate at the highest point of each island...in brief, everything necessary to make the islands a pleasant holiday-resort and air-cure, frequented by the aristocracy of six continents.

The archipelago, in the middle of the ocean, beneath an ardent Sun but refreshed by the currents of the returning gulf stream and the breezes and gusty sea-winds, enjoyed a delightful climate.

There was no governor or administrator. The promoter of the enterprise, the owner of more than half the shares, governed his archipelago himself, to the satisfaction of all, for a full third of a century, and founded a prosperous dynasty. There was, therefore, a completely happy people somewhere. The sedentary population, living in the towns and villages disseminated through the paradise, was not very numerous; the first arrivals had been carefully selected in their countries of origin, physically and morally; they offered every guarantee as laborers in fields and towns, tradesmen, intellectuals or magistrates: all people in good order, protected against any intrusion from outside by a civil guard.

As soon as the aero-villa had touched down in a charming cove, superbly shaded, Monsieur Cabrol and his nephews leapt down on to the sand.

"To the woods over there, above the rocks, quickly!" cried Andoche. "From there well be able to see the entire layout of the coast."

"Not yet," said Monsieur Cabrol. "First, the medical customs—we have to pass the admission exam. If we're admitted, the certificate will enable us to go anywhere we want in the archipelago."

"Where are they, these customs?"

"That building up there, under the big trees," the pilot replied. "I know—I've been here before."

"Good," said Andoche, launching himself into the climb.

"Would you like to wait for us?" shouted Monsieur Cabrol. "And Melanie, whom we've forgotten. She must come too. Melanie! Melanie!"

"Do we need to bring Phanor and Babylas too?"

"Don't joke—these rigorous measures have preserved the archipelago from many diseases, preventing the spread of epidemics."

Melanie came running, anxiously. Following the pilot, all the tenants of the Aero-Beauséjour set off along the path, with was pretty but a trifle primitive. The youngsters soon went on ahead, but Melanie, a little out of breath, called: "Gently! Gently!"

It took ten full minutes to arrive at the top, in front of the medical customs, which overlooked a truly splendid horizon.

"Quickly! Quickly!" said Monsieur Cabrol, tearing his nephews from their contemplation in order to go into the office. "The examination, quickly! Provided that the doctor's here. And silence! No protests, so as not to waste time—let's do as we're told."

The doctor was there. The examination did not take long, save for the housekeeper, whose excessive breathlessness required a more rigorous auscultation. In half an hour, though, they were all issued with permits.

Andoche, disdaining the beaten paths, bounded joyfully through the countryside, but they soon caught him up, standing in the greenery in front of a clump of unfamiliar trees.

"Isn't all this beautiful!" he exclaimed. "The ground, the rocks, the trees…and what trees!"

"They're banyan fig-trees, crouched on their sheaves of roots. They're still young—come back and look at them in 50 years."

"I couldn't ask for anything better! And those, extremely tangled?"

"Baobabs! And those candle-cacti, grouped in candelabras five meters high…and those agaves, spiny all over. Don't get impaled on those spikes! That's what we're exchanging for unhealthy plane-trees, eaten away by all the chemical exhalations of our factories and industrial vehicles, and the wave-currents of every sort that intersect in our poor atmosphere! Let's breathe, breathe deeply of this unpolluted air."

"I like this place!" exclaimed Moderan.

"Me too!"

"A trifle steep for my legs," said Melanie. "Personally, I'm going back to the villa. I'll look at it from down below."

"Above all, Melanie," said Monsieur Cabrol, "don't touch anything—we're not yet anchored. Don't go into the cockpit; imagine what would happen if you touched some item of apparatus inadvertently—you might take off with the Villa."

"No danger, Monsieur," said the pilot. "Before leaving, I switched off the intra-atomic energy; the motor won't budge. Besides, I'll go back down with Melanie. I know the country—and I've forgotten my pipe."

"Good! That reassures me. We can continue—we'll return to the house later."

The three voyagers resumed their march, in order to clamber through the arborescent ferns and the bushy clumps of cotton-trees toward a summit neatly divided by a rocky promontory, the base of which was beaten by the sea-waves.

They passed beneath cedars brought from the Caucasus or Lebanon and 120-meter-tall sequoias originating from the Congo; they filed between the roots of Hindu banyans beside such beautifully-constructed banks, through a landscape so admirably composed.

"I'm enchanted by the walk and furious at the same time," said the uncle.

"Why's that?"

"Look...you find this country superbly splendid, don't you? Superior in its construction. Well, elsewhere, here, well-hidden in the depths so as not to jar with the landscape, there's a triangulation-point that is a descent into the lower reaches for both surveillance and for internal maintenance work. Let's go this way...look, you can see the tips of reinforced concrete girders sticking out in that ravine, and higher up, in those black holes, one can glimpse the carcass, the skeleton of the giant cliffs and the whole of that superb promontory topped with greenery."

Andoche and Moderan scrambled down to the bottom of the ravine, through a tangle of brushwood.

"Watch out for wild animals!" Monsieur Cabrol shouted after them. "The Caucasian Archipelago has no dangerous animals; they only imported those recommended as quite safe—but after all, one never knows."

Down below, Monsieur Cabrol found the disappointed youngsters sitting on a heap of stones in front of the triangulation-post: a little rotunda sheltering the head of a stairway, closed by a grille.

"Nothing, of course! With the door closed, you can only see a black well—but when your eyes get used to the darkness, and you can vaguely make out the enormous pillars of reinforced concrete that support the entire cape. Oh, it's very cleverly planned—perfect work."

Still preceded by his nephews, Monsieur Cabrol climbed back up, talking all the while.

"Yes, perfect. The Caucasian Archipelago has lived up to all the promises of the enterprise, realized all its plans. It's incredible—all that vegetation in half a century—for the gross work, the rocky carcass, required an enormous time for its completion."

The enthusiasm of his nephews gripped him as soon as they arrived at the ridge, along which they moved over a sufficiently comfortable carpet of grass, in the shadow of a cedar, confronted by the immense panorama stretching away in a blue-tinted semi-circle.

"Magnificent! Look at those green inlets down there, those indentations carved in the rock, which seem to be supporting the massive towers attached to the mountain-side and pockmarked with caves. Oh, very successful, very successful. Do you see those islets out to sea? Proud and luxuriant landscapes to the right and the left, everywhere! And those villages down there, that little harbor directly below us, those large villas strung out along the beaches, with a host of aeros of every sort floating above them—aircraft or aerocottages—and those flying over the open sea, taking a gentle stroll or fishing for fun."

"Very chic!" said Andoche. "Super-chic!"

"Delightful! Utterly delightful!" Moderan corrected him.

"Yes, super-chic and delightful!" declared Monsieur Cabrol. "I'm delighted, arch-delighted, and quite furious at the same time."

"Furious? Why, uncle?"

"It's a marvelously successful work of art, this archipelago in mid-Atlantic, this magnificent continental morsel added to a revised and corrected creation, a land of pleasure and the ideal, planned, fabricated and shaped to serve as the sumptuous frame for a dream-like existence, but..."

"But what, Uncle? What can you find to say against these marvels?"

"Nothing at all, since you see me plunged in admiration of them...but I'm furious...wait, furious with myself! This was an industrial enterprise, to begin with, this very successful Caucasian Archipelago, a great enterprise mounted by means of shares. Well, I inherited a dozen shares from my great-uncle. In my youthful inexperience, I didn't foresee the immense future of the business, and I sold those shares on the stock exchange one day, at a small profit, instead of waiting for the era of fabulous dividends! Look, let's not think about it anymore, and walk on."

"What about lunch, Uncle?"

"Yes, that's an idea—we've already walked a long way. What do you say to a little picnic?"

"Right away!"

"Not so fast. Let's go down to the beach; we'll be better able to breathe in the sea breeze and the foam of the waves."

Immediately below them there was a little round cove bordered with coconut palms. Our three hikers were soon installed beneath a coconut palm, their heads in the shade, in a warm atmosphere refreshed by the breeze and the regular beating of the waves, which sent fine droplets of water scented by algae into their faces.

"I'm a man who takes precautions," said Monsieur Cabrol, taking a little box from his pocket. "Before leaving the villa, I loaded myself up with victuals. Here's a pill for each of us, of which you'll give me your impressions. Lobster salad with pineapple—entirely appropriate for a maritime feast. We'll wash it down with a pill of wine from the Canaries. That's not all, of course—a third pill of fine Mocha!"

V. The Caucasian Archipelago, Pleasure Resort.

At sunset, the excursionists returned to the Aero-Beauséjour, enchanted by their trip. They were warm, their expansive expressions testifying to their satisfaction.

"What if we were to stay here?" said Moderan. "As a tranquil and delightful place to stay, the Caucasian Archipelago seems to me to be the dream location. What do you say, Uncle?"

"Yes, but…there is a *but*: the sojourn tax. It's a little dear, that tax, for a prolonged stay. As I've said, as a pleasure resort, the Archipelago is marvelously successful; one can't find a better one. The enterprise has brought together all the natural attractions and added artistic, sporting and other attractions—but all those fine things are costly! Then again, I still have many ideas in my program for the agreeable employment of our ten years, no shortage of projects. We'll talk about all that later. We're here for a nice little interval, of course—time to sate ourselves on blue sky and tranquility."

"Have you seen the pilot, Monsieur?" Melanie asked her master in a low voice.

"No, why?"

"Look at him, Monsieur, look at him! Fortunately, we're no more than 700 or 800 meters up in the air. Personally, I lunched wisely on an ordinary pill of concentrated fresh water; he washed his pill of I don't know what beefsteakade down with at least four pills of Burgundy and Bordeaux, taken from the store cupboard, which I'd forgotten to lock. Then he went all red and started to sing—and now he's snoring on the balcony."

"Ah! Pilots, of wheeled vehicles or aircraft, are almost all like that. They gladly take pills in superalimentary quantity and wash them down with well-chosen strong synthetic droplets...but don't alarm yourself, Melanie, there's no inconvenience today, and tomorrow..."

"Tomorrow?" asked Moderan, who had overheard. "What about tomorrow?"

"You know very well that he had to leave us after bringing us to the Caucasian Archipelago. The Panama-Dakar-Paris dirigible touches down here tomorrow, and he'll take it...but I'll say a few words to your father, who gave him to us as an entirely reliable pilot; he needs to be warned. It's possible that this lapse of sobriety is quite exceptional, but one never knows.... Unfortunately, it appears that people fall prey to temptation—it's so easy and so comfortable! And repeated abuse of these wines in pill form leads to alcoholism. Physicians have told me that the Académie de Médecine is worried about it. Three or four pills of Bordeaux and Burgundy! Damn it! And I thought his only fault was his pipe!"

"What about excursions, then?" asked Andoche, anxiously. "Who's going to pilot the Aero-Beauséjour."

"You, me or Moderan—or Melanie, if need be."

"Uh-oh!"

"First of all, you've taken a few lessons from Barlotin; secondly, I know how to do it—I have my little mini-airplane for personal excursions. Then again, you know that, so that we might be free in our movements, and, in case of need, dispense with a pilot, I've had our Villa Beauséjour fitted with a radioloxodromogoniometer, which steers automatically near the Earth's surface, and by excess of precaution, a radioetherogoniometer for interplanetary space. With all that, we're ready for anything."

"Hear hear!" said Andoche.

"Uh-oh!" repeated Moderan.

"Once the heading is selected, it's just a matter of letting it run. You've seen Barlotin, in his cockpit, asleep at his instruments. He only had to cast an eye over the route-recorder from time to time. It's child's play."

"Of course!" said Andoche.

"The route ahead is cleared by the waves we transmit, which cause any apparatus that might get in our way to change course, just as the waves transmitted by another apparatus in our path would gently alter our course. On the next excursion, tomorrow, I'll take charge of the steering; I'll complete your education. Besides, you're used to autoplanes—it'll be simple and easy."

"Especially as the sky is almost empty at 500 meters," said Andoche, "Which isn't the case in the vicinity of Paris, where traffic jams at every height are an incessant nuisance."

"And with our safety apparatus, I'll bet you that I can drive the Aero-Beauséjour without the slightest difficulty, while reciting a chapter of my *History of Civilizations*, or even improvising rhyming verse…"

"No, no, Uncle—no difficulties!" exclaimed Moderan. "I won't raise any more objections. No rhyming, no rhyming—there's no need."

"Understood—I won't bring the lyre on our excursions. Now, we're going to work for a while. Come on, to your desk. Before getting to work on my *History of Lunatic Civilizations*, I want to see whether the Universal Cinephono University is working properly."

The Cine-University apparatus, a large light box about 80 centimeters wide by a meter tall, was fixed to the wall above a table-desk. There was nothing monumental about it, but it contained a summary of all the human sciences: general history, ancient and modern; specific histories; geography, sciences, properly speaking, including the most recent; languages; literary history, the first year of law; mathematics, etc.—the entire syllabus of the three baccalaureates in letters, sciences and arts, more than 300 carefully-selected lectures, plus 1500 homework exercises, essays and translations. The fully-qualified apparatus displayed in its prospectus the approbations and eulogies of all the faculties and universities of the six continents; one could rest easy—it was simple and easy to operate, never broke down, and, in case of an accident, any clockmaker could get it back in working order.

On pulling a handle, the cupboard opened, displaying four sets of little drawers, one on top of another, each bearing a dial. It only remained to choose the drawer of the human knowledge required and to turn the needle on the dial, then press the telephone button—and the masters spoke!

"A College in one's own home," said Monsieur Cabrol, "even while traveling, distantly displaced, deep in the woods or the mountains—it's so convenient! Sit down boys, and work! Take notes, write, do the homework or the advised essays conscientiously."

"We'll get stuck into it, Uncle—what a fine walk we had this morning!"

"We'll have others, tomorrow…come on, a little bit of work today, eh? Don't neglect the assignments. And to think that we haven't yet been able to devise a machine for correcting assignments that works properly. It's so necessary! What a fortune the scientist who invents one would make! Truly, it makes one doubt the genius of our inventors. Come on, I'm going to work for a while too. Then, well-rested, we'll go to pay the sojourn tax."

In the well-lit and cheerful room in which the light and blue of the sky penetrated and sparkled everywhere, where the pleasant odors of the waves and seaweeds swaying under the rocks came to vivify their breasts, they worked joyfully.

Andoche and Moderan put themselves into it without enthusiasm at first, their minds wandering over the rocks bathed by the waves, into the picturesque creeks or caves opening under the pines, over the spangled sand where families of crabs and gigantic lobsters were roaming amid the wrack and the long, decorative, tangled sheets of blue, green and yellow algae.

Soon, explanatory diagrams appeared on a great central disk, and the phono spoke. Abandoning the beach, the foamy waves and the clouds racing through the blue, Andoche and Moderan took notes dutifully.

In the next room, with the door closed so as not to hear the phono, Monsieur Cabrol, sprawled in a wicker armchair, reviewed the first pages of his book, thoughtfully. He took notes too. Nothing is better for intellectual labor than exercise in the open air, excursions over uneven ground, which shakes up the intellect and caused ideas to spring forth. It seems that the legs pull the strings of the slumbering meninges.

"Come on, lads," he said, arriving after an hour of solid work, "time to eat now, and then to take a walk. Ah, we'll settle up with the Administration and pay the sojourn tax."

The professor's voice in the phono fell silent, and the youngsters leapt up joyfully. A pill swallowed by way of a meal, and they left the aerovilla to visit the charming village, half-terrestrial and half-aerial, in which elegant buildings in every style lined up on the shore almost at the tide-line, where, set on the rocks, surrounding gardens exceedingly shady gardens, clumps of palms or sprays of large bright flowers were swaying. Behind almost all of the terrestrial houses, aeros were sheltering in garages formed simply of a roof shape like a flowery parasol. And always, between each pair of houses, there was the blue sea, the sparkling sand, groups of cabins and stalls, with bathers floating in the water or curled up in the Sun in dressing-gowns of every color.

Phanor bounded ahead; although he had not been working, he had been sleeping in the Sun, having swallowed his pill like a civilized dog, and wanted nothing but to stretch his legs, barking at the little creatures encountered on the sand, and at the waves that came to surround him and sprinkle him with foam.

A placard saying *Office* on the door of a pavilion in the Chinese style reminded Monsieur Cabrol about the sojourn tax. He went in momentarily and paid the tax for four people. It was expensive, but it was necessary to remunerate the capital expended and pay for the work of maintaining the Archipelago, the various attractions, general expenses, dividends, etc, etc.

Monsieur Cabrol explained it to the youngsters.

"Then again," he said, "there's the politicians."

"Are there politicians?"

"Undoubtedly! The Caucasian Archipelago, pleasure resort, is an independent State; it is self-governing, so it has politicians, an administrative council and diplomats."

"Diplomats who don't have a great deal to do," said Moderan.

"Perhaps…in the beginning, things didn't work automatically. As soon as the construction-work was finished, England generously offered to take the Archipelago under its protection. The administration declined the protectorate, which gave rise to long and difficult negotiations. Albion said: 'This new archipelago, constructed with your own materials, belongs to you, that's understood—but I feel that I'm the natural mother of all islands, and I open my arms to you…you don't want that? So be it! But these islands, which you've brought into my shipping-routes, inconvenience the passage of those ships somewhat. The ground on which you've constructed your Archipelago isn't yours, you realize. Well, to regularize

172

the situation, you're going to pay me for the location in the form of a port of call for my ships and an airport for my dirigibles.' And the negotiations are still going on…"

"Look!" said Andoche. "What's that?"

To the west, at the edge of a circle framed by high cliffs, at the base of which snaked an uneven little path, a new coastline had just appeared, which unfolded like the other coast, with the same inlets and the same rocks. Pleasure villages in their verdant tresses were perceptible in the distance, but, closer to the obscured point, the terrain broadened out to form a plateau ten meters above the sand.

On this plateau, a slender tower with a iron framework rise up 30 or 40 meters, circled by large airstrips ten meters square, above long iron hangars lined up among the pallets of the offices and the personnel. On the ground, a large dirigible had just moored; travelers and luggage were moving on to the first airstrip. A few little mini-planes were circling the dirigible, doubtless carrying other travelers or friends come to greet the passengers, the dirigible remaining in the port for three-quarters of an hour before continuing on its way.

"It's the airstrip of the Panama-Dakar-Paris and Paris-Australia-Mexico lines—and the Madrid-Paris, etc."

"Then that's the airship that will pick up our pilot for its return journey. He must already be aboard…"

"He's never in a hurry—he'll arrive at the last minute."

"Good, god! It's a good spot here—we'll have a very good view of the departure. That won't be long delayed—the elevators are operating. Here, Phanor! Would you care to refrain from deafening us with your displays of enthusiasm? Or I'll send you back to Paris!"

At the tip of the airstrip, a flame had just gone up. The dirigible emitted a strident whistle-blast. A loudspeaker on board howled interjections in various languages, even Latin, toward all points of the horizon. The airship shuddered, and seemed to sway.

"Look out—it's taking off!" said Monsieur Cabrol, stopping up his ears.

A new explosion of howling, and the elevators came down again. Half a minute of howling, and everything suddenly fell silent. The dirigible rose up, jet-fashion, as if breathed in by the sky; having arrived at 500 or 600 meters, it turned its prow eastwards, and plunged toward the horizon.

"We'll have another sunset in fireworks," said Monsieur Cabrol, cutting through a wood of coconut-date-palms. "Let's get back to the villa. Here, Phanor!"

"A nice place to stay—I've already spotted I don't know how many places to roll on the sand, or in the grass, when the sand's too hot."

"Uncle, can the Phono University be unscrewed? I'd love to bring it to a nice little corner under the trees, or into one of those caves on the shore, to do my homework in the midst of nature."

"We'll see about that…"

As they arrived at the villa, Phanor bounded on ahead.

"What's up with him?" said Moderan, also breaking into a run.

With his nose in the air, in front of the Beauséjour, Phanor was barking plaintively.

"Ah!" said Moderan. "It's for Babylas, who's on the roof."

Up above, the cat Babylas also had his nose in the air. He miaowed, launched himself up the slippery slope, and tried to grasp the stem of the weathervane, fell back, and miaowed more plaintively, shivering and tensing as cats do when on the lookout for little birds.

The fine weathervane was a bird cut out in aluminum, which oscillated at the slightest breath of air, and poor Babylas was completely fooled by it. Oh, that one could not get used to alimentary pills, and could think of nothing but crunching the bird that was insolently stirring on its iron perch, seemingly mocking him.

At Phanor's barking, the pilot's head appeared on the cockpit balcony. Monsieur Cabrol climbed the ladder and went back into the villa. "What? You haven't taken the dirigible?" he said

"My word, no," Barlotin replied. "I didn't feel well. I'll take the one tomorrow."

"You are a little red-faced, in fact. It's a bit warm here. Is it the climate that doesn't suit you?"

"It must be something of that sort."

"I'll go look in our little pharmacy and give you as pill to relieve the congestion."

Melanie had a coughing fit, which terminated in broad silent laughter.

Monsieur Cabrol went into his room and gestured to Melanie. "What is it?"

"Don't worry, Monsieur," Melanie said, ending up with a smile. "I know all about Monsieur Barlotin's congestion; he has his own little private pharmacy and looks after himself. His appetite's not bad: he lunched on three or four pills, beefsteak with apples, bacon omelet, veal escalope and I don't know what else, which he washed down with Bordeaux *grand ordinaire*, followed by a coffee pill and a liqueur coffee…the kind one reads about in old books."

"Ah! You've set my mind at rest, Melanie."

VI. The Stadium of Violent and Other Sports.

The pleasant existence of rest and pure air continued for the inhabitants of the Aero-Beauséjour. Truly, the pleasure Archipelago had not stolen its reputation. There one led the existence of the ultra-perfected Earthly Paradise, provided with all the natural attractions borrowed from the Nature of the three or four best-provided continents, and further attractions of every sort added to the pleasantness of the countryside; it really was the Archipelago of the Prospectus.

The aerovilla was no longer parked on the beach where it had landed. After having explored the entirety of that section of coast in the course of long walks, it had moved to another part of the Archipelago, the Central Isle, the archipelagian capital, from which one could radiate outwards to all the rest.

Oh, it was not difficult to find things to occupy one's time. The first day, after a short walk in the town, which was nothing but an immense park, with a scattering of palaces and splendid villas, perched in every possible fashion on an extremely uneven terrain, they went to visit the sports grounds.

Everyone was very sporty there; it was necessary to struggle against the temptation to idle in hammocks suspended from the branches of the baobabs, and to take somnolent siestas to which the mildness of the climate was so conducive.

That first day, after lunch, in front of the principal government building, which the architects of the enterprise had given the appearance of a Tartar Aul,[25] hooked on to a rocky spur, as forbidding as those which studded the old far-away Caucasus, Monsieur Cabrol and his nephews, accompanied by the housekeeper Melanie, and followed reluctantly by Phanor, came to a halt before a huge advertisement for the Sports Ground, a long wall decorated with images depicting all the kinds of sports practiced by the Archipelagians.

They were all there: bridge, roulette, dancing, boxing, wrestling, various kinds of fencing, skating, sledding—luge and bobsleigh—etc. etc. It was rather surprising to encounter the latter sports in that tropical climate, mildly tempered by the breath of the ocean; accustomed to scientific miracles, however, Andoche and Moderan accepted the affirmations of the advertisement without protest. It was necessary to go see it immediately.

Every three minutes, a train composed of mini-aircraft cabins suspended from a long cable left for the sports ground. It was an old procedure of the Middle Ages, revived to avoid aerial crowding in the area and the inevitable accidents.

---

[25] An aul (Robida spells it *aoul*) is a kind of fortified village found in the Caucasus.

Andoche and Moderan were already seated in a cabin. "Quickly, Uncle—I want to try the luge!"

"Quickly, quickly!"

Monsieur Cabrol pushed Melanie forward. The train was about to leave. It left, moving in a delightful air-current.

Four exclamations rang out: "What about Phanor?"

They had forgotten Phanor—but a joyful barking resounded in the foremost cabin; it was Phanor replying. Also a sports fan, he had got aboard before his masters, and, being installed in the front cabin, was watching the countryside, almost on the back of the driver, without paying any heed to his protests.

Anyway, there was not enough time to get annoyed; the journey only lasted three minutes. They left; they arrived.

At first sight, Andoche and Moderan found the sports ground bizarrely designed—very large, to be sure, as was appropriate, but all in gently undulations, covered with thick soft grass, a veritable vegetal fleece, which was knee-high almost everywhere.

There were a few small stalls—almost tents—here and there and, in the center, a large, perfectly oval construction: a little two-meter wall surmounted by ten meters of glass, forming a brilliant ring, without any kind of partition or framework.

"It's in there—let's go," said Andoche.

Melanie took Phanor in her arms and hid him under her mantle. "I won't be forced to take part in exercises?" she said, a little anxious.

"No, no—me neither," said Monsieur Cabrol. "My favorite sport is the rocking chair."

"Exactly!" said Andoche. "They have them here, as you see…"

On the inside, the construction formed a vast open air semicircle, whose center was marked by a slender tower like a minaret, terminating in a balcony bearing a bizarre apparatus, whose wheels obviously allowed it to rotate in every sense.

On the ground, all around the minaret, rows of rocking chairs were aligned, occupied by a noisy crowd, their backs turned to the tower.

"Let's sit down to get a better view," said Monsieur Cabrol. making the chairs rock while waiting for the other sports.

They had only been sitting down for five minutes when the blast of a whistle pierced their ears. On top of the tower, a phono loudspeaker announced: "Winter sports in Savoy!"

Cabrol and his nephews looked at one another in alarm.

Abruptly, the great circular glass wall, dull and colorless until then, went white—lighting up, so to speak—and formed around the lined-up sportsmen an immense horizon of immaculate snow, with steep slopes, opening over blue-tinted gulfs, and mountain ridges between which glaciers poured forth—and behind the glaciers, peaks projected their white needles into a sky almost as blue as the one suspended a little while before over the date-palms and cacti of the Archipelago.

"I haven't brought a coat—I'm afraid of getting cold," the housekeeper said to Monsieur Cabrol.

Suddenly, on one of the snowy plateaux, something appeared in the distance: little dots moving and growing in size very rapidly. Leaning forward, arms folded or raised in the air, cutting through the snow with their skis, they flew over the slopes, or plunged into the abysses.

Behind them, in every direction, other amateurs surged forth, gliding, whirling, tumbling, plunging thigh-deep into thick layers of snow, and luge-riders lying on their little sleds were running, always head-first, between the legs of the skiers; toboggans and bobsleighs followed, making up a multicolored, fluttering swarm amid all that white.

The Cabrol family missed none of the ups and down of the session; no one around them said very much, which permitted the laughter and shouts of the skiers to be heard, and even the sound of crashes, and the quarrels of luge-riders who had collided. At one moment, in the background, there was a thunderous din, followed by a long rumble. It was an avalanche, which could be seen in the distance collapsing from a high white wall.

For three hours, Monsieur Cabrol and his nephews, as well as the housekeeper, watched winter spots in this manner. It was not too tiring. There was a ski-jump at the top of one snowy slope, a luge track, and one for toboggans and bob-sleighs, which excited the spectators seated in their rocking chairs almost as much as the people out there, whose cheers could be heard.

Suddenly, a mist spread over the entire alpine landscape; the mountains and glaciers, luges, toboggans, skiers in brightly colored woollens, all gradually disappeared; then the mist dissipated in its turn and the snows reappeared. But it was another landscape—an immense forest of large trees, all white, dressed in a carapace of frozen snow.

"Canada!" cried the loudspeaker.

Phanor growled. A family of white-coated bears passed by, prancing heavily; the parents and the cubs plunged into the trees on all fours.

The Canadian landscape also faded away, replaced almost immediately by another, just as white.

"Greenland!" howled the loudspeaker.

The wind was whistling and howling in a sinister manner, blowing in gusts and sweeping up whirlwinds of snow.

Black rocks stuck up here and there. A few black trees raised their lugubrious carcasses over white plains, soon lost in the fog. A sleigh leapt forward, pulled by a team of dogs.

This time, Phanor burst out into volleys of barking—which, in spite of Monsieur Cabrol's efforts, lasted until the sleigh disappeared into the mist.

"A sinister excursion! Are we going to plant our Villa Beauséjour out there?"

After that there was nothing but snow; there was a crush of enormous fractured glaciers, lifted up by waves—an ice-sheet with icebergs drifting away.

"Oof! Let's get out of here!" said Monsieur Cabrol, finally.

"We'll end up falling ill in all that snow, Monsieur," said Melanie. "I can already feel myself getting a chill."

"You can take a borage and quatrefoil pill when we get back," said Monsieur Cabrol. "Let's get back to the 30 degrees and perfumed atmosphere of our graceful archipelago. At this moment, I'd like to climb into the coconut palms or the baobabs and try myself in the sports of our little brothers the monkeys."

They left the sports ground, not without first informing themselves what was going on in the brightly-ornamented colored pavilions around the arena of rough and difficult sports.

"Here, there's fencing, over there, rugby football, baseball, etc. Let's go in and see.... Very fine fencing—I've done a little in my time, on doctor's orders, to rest my brain."

In the fencing pavilion, however, as in the larger stadium, the fencers were on a cine-phono screen. In the boxing pavilion, the boxers were not boxing themselves. Installed in nice armchairs, they were following the ups and downs of black or white boxers on the cine-phono. It was the same for the rugby. No kicking or scrimmaging, other than on the vast cine-phono, which gave the people comfortably seated in the tent the illusion of being on the pitch, in the brutal mêlée, exposed to dangerous tackles.

"Oof! Let's get away!" said Monsieur Cabrol. "I can't take any more of this."

"There are many others," said Andoche. "Look at that pavilion: Bridge…"

"And that other one," said Moderan. "Roulette…a tranquil sport, this time."

"Good. We'll come back."

And they gladly climbed back into the train-carriage.

VII. Airstrip 148, New York.

The aerovilla stayed in the Caucasian Archipelago for more than three months, drifting from island to island, sometimes installing itself on top of a mountain, sometimes beneath the green dome of an oak forest, sometimes in spa towns among bathers from all the countries of the world, nabobs from India and billionaires from America who had met in the richest casinos of old Europe. Sometimes—and most frequently, anchored on the marvelous beaches—they anchored on the marvelous beaches of the Sargasso Sea, where the waves sometimes bought the scents of marine vegetation, mountains of algae swarming with marine insects, hunted by crabs, hunted in their turn by myriads of lobsters emerging from all the holes in the rocks.

And while they led this gentle existence, the great work of repairing the world was entering a period of intense activity out there in the Parisian region. Oh, how much better it was here, breathing the pure Atlantic air beneath the noisy forests.

Every evening, Moderan said to his mother or father, in the Tele: "Leave those Reconstruction Works, those engineers repairing the world who might succeed in precipitating Paris into the third underworld…come here, where everything is so nice…."

"But what about business?" said Monsieur des Ormettes.

"And the Chamber?" said Madame. "I'm glad to tell you that I've been promised a portfolio in the next ministry."

"Yes, it's very pleasant here in the climate of the pleasure Archipelago," said Monsieur Cabrol. "I might even say too cozy—let's not linger! In this excessively agreeable environment, I'm not working. My great work hasn't advanced by six pages since we got here. We raise anchor tomorrow. Bah! We'll come back. Let's not forget that we have many things to see. Listen—there's one extraordinary item in our program:

Astra Island, the fragment of an unknown world that fell in the Atlantic[26] only 30 years ago."

"Oh yes!" exclaimed Andoche and Moderan. "Astra Island—the morsel of a world that nearly shattered our poor planet!"

The joyful prospect of going to the island fallen from the sky consoled them for leaving the Caucasian Archipelago. That was something genuinely new.

"And it isn't far," Monsieur Cabrol added. "900 kilometers to the south."

"We'll be there tomorrow evening, then?"

"No, it's necessary to measure out sensations. We'll go to America first. Oh, just to pass through—time to see the contrast between this happy archipelago that we're about t leave, this excessively comfortable life beneath the caresses of the Sun and softening breezes, and America, brutal industrial civilization taken to its apogee, America, where the reign of technology is the most powerful imaginable."

Andoche and Moderan dreamed about Astra all night, burning with impatience. They were up at dawn, waking their uncle.

Monsieur Cabrol had warned Melanie, who was already regretting the Archipelago, where everything was so pleasant. There were no preparations to make, since they were taking their house with them.

"What about the pilot?" she asked.

"Oh, that's true…Barlotin's still here, since he's missed all the Dakar-Paris airships. Call him, then."

---

[26] The text subsequently places Astra in the Pacific Ocean, but that must have been a change of mind, since there is a supplementary reference here to it being south of the Caucasian Archipelago. Given the double reference, I thought it best to leave the contradiction in place rather than changing it for the sake of consistency.

Barlotin took three quarters of an hour to wake up; he was heard moaning and yawning in his room. He arrived still half-asleep.

"Well, Barlotin, you missed the dirigible again two days ago. Are you going to take today's?"

"My word, I don't really know. I still feel very ill, and the climate here suits me quite well."

"You don't look as ill as all that, Barlotin—you seem well enough."

Melanie, who was setting the table—which is to say, putting out a few saucers—smiled and winked.

In fact, Barlotin's face was slightly red, and he seemed to have put on a lot of weight since arriving in the Archipelago. "I often feel weak," he said. "I need to get my strength back. Perhaps I ought to take the waters here—Vichy, Bourboule or something like that. They have them all here. I'll ask, or even try them all."

"But we're leaving soon, for a brief visit to America."

"Oh! In that case, I'll leave with the villa."

"As you wish—come with us. Get ready for departure, then. We'll take off at 9 a.m. exactly."

"Understood, Monsieur."

"Yes," whispered Melanie, "he has a red nose and he's getting a bit too fat. He has four or five meals a day and he isn't content with one or two pills—he takes three or four, well washed-down, I assure you, with refreshing Burgundy or Bordeaux, hardly moistened at all. It'll do him no good. I keep telling him, and I refuse to give him the pills, but he has his own personal supply."

"Let's keep him anyway, to maintain and man the apparatus."

While Barlotin prepared his apparatus and tidied up the cockpit, which was a little dusty, Monsieur Cabrol went to the customs-house to have his papers stamped. He soon came back and made a rapid tour of inspection.

Everything was ready. Seated in the cockpit, Barlotin got ready to press the starter button.

"Is everyone here?" asked Monsieur Cabrol. "Melanie hasn't gone out? Nor Phanor? Nor Babylas? Good—let's get going."

The Villa Beauséjour was detached from the bushes and swayed momentarily as if it could not quite decide to quit the soil of the Archipelago, then rose gently into the radiant sky.

"Head north-west, and set a course for New York," said Monsieur Cabrol, "not too fast to begin with."

Below the villa, the landscape changed. They flow over the capital, Archipelia. All around the large island, like chicks around a mother hen, the islets waved their greenery, changing position with the perspective, and they all looked as if they were on the march, heading for the open sea to escort the Villa Beauséjour. Soon, however, they all became confused, the mass blurring and fading away into the blue of the sea, reflecting the blue of the sky.

Phanor barked on the balcony. Moderan sighed. The Archipelago was far away. Monsieur Cabrol went back and forth, but his eyes never strayed from the cockpit. He no longer had any confidence in the pilot that had been supplied to him with such fine guarantees. Only the cat Babylas remained indifferent; curled up in a ball, he was asleep in an armchair.

"So we're going directly to New York?" Andoche asked his uncle. "What time will we arrive?"

"Oh, it's a matter or five or six hours. We could have aimed for Panama and then headed north, but we'll take that route when we go to Astra…"

What a change there was in the afternoon, long before America came into view! Less blue above and below: a slightly turbulent sky; a greener sea. On the sea there were many long, broad and heavy cargo-ships heading in all directions; in the sky, innumerable dirigibles, aircraft of every kind and size, gigantic or minuscule, swarming at all altitudes.

Without allowing himself an instant's distraction, Monsieur Cabrol kept watch on the protective apparatus vitally necessary to avoid all possible accidents in the midst of the heavy traffic, which became increasingly accentuated the further they went into the skies of New York. At 4:35, Monsieur Cabrol uttered an *oof!* of satisfaction; the Villa Beauséjour arrived safely in harbor, moored on the rather cluttered terrain of Airstrip 148, south of New York, in the district that had seem to them from above as the most practicable.

"Well?" he asked his nephews, when they had taken their places in comfortable armchairs at the dining-table, "are you delighted, overwhelmed, seduced by the beauty of the land-scape, the tranquility of the location?"

The howling of sirens, rumblings and explosions punc-tuated his speech.

"Hmm! Interesting…terribly interesting, Uncle…"

"What did you say? Speak louder… Yes, we're in the quiet district, the quietest—the Airstrip attendant has just con-firmed that."

What a landscape! As far as the eye could see and pene-trate through the thick vapors or swirling clouds of smoke, colossal superimpositions of edifices of every shape, heaps of factory buildings, extended in every direction, all tangled up, branches sticking out like tentacles beneath scaffolding. There were aerial bridges and iron towers carrying more iron build-ings upwards on large platforms, moving elevators, and vari-ous kinds of mighty cranes rotating and rumbling. Further away, lines of skyscrapers 40 or 60 stories high, were stacked pyramid-fashion on top of one another, mounting an assault on the clouds, succeeding one another and melting into one another, extending to all four corners of the horizon.

And what a concert the vertiginous rumor of that indus-trial Pandemonium was! What an infernal concert! Gasps, groans, roars and whistles, regularly punctuated by muffled explosions! Strange music escaped from every one of those immense factories, rising in crescendos and tremolos, accom-panied without by the frightful tumult of the traffic: the howl-ing, miaowing and bellowing of wheeled or flying vehicles; the noisy rumbling of millions of trucks.

Monsieur Cabrol took stock of that landscape, the huge agglomerations of factories, each as vast as a large town, and closed his eyes in terror as he thought about the frightful internal machinery of those colossal constructions, and the populations attached to those gigantic machines in operation.

"The birdsong doesn't sound promising to me; even so, it's necessary to see it at closer range. Since we're here, let's venture outside."

Monsieur Cabrol and his nephews went out on foot, setting off prudently along 255th Street, their eyes alert to avoid any collision with some small truck, only weighing 25 tons and launched into the battle at a speed of 40 kilometers an hour.

It was necessary to risk crossing crowded intersections at a trot, to pass over footbridges from one sidewalk to the other, to take elevators to be lifted up and carried over islets of factory buildings, or pedestrian tunnels to go underneath them. After half an hour they emerged, completely lost. They had forgotten to take a compass.

They were in a district of skyscrapers: immobile giants in the form of towers or pyramids, extending stiffly into the clouds, with exterior elevators and platforms at the summit bearing gardens, statues and fountains, with huge iron airstrips projecting into the void on audacious iron arabesques.

After letting himself fall on to a bench in the vestibule of one of the skyscrapers, in order to catch his breath, Monsieur Cabrol declared frankly that there was no need to take things to excess, and that it would be prudent to go home, close the windows firmly and have a rest from the accumulation of slightly terrifying visions and impressions in the tranquility of their home.

"Yes, but how are we to get back? I can't see any possible vehicle for us in this place!"

The resourceful Andoche stood up, selected an elevator at random and climbed into it. In the elevator, on a console bearing 30 buttons with explanatory labels, he read: *Janitor 12th Floor*. He pressed the button; the elevator rose, as if sucked upwards. Two minutes later, it came down again.

"Come on," he said, "it's up top."

"What?"

"The means of getting back. The janitor just ordered a taxiplane by wireless telephone. We'll find it up there."

A further two minutes later, they were climbing into their taxiplane and setting off for the Villa Beauséjour's mooring-strip.

"This little stroll has worn me out," said Monsieur Cabrol. "I've got a headache."

"Me too!" said Moderan.

"And me!" said Andoche. "I must have a klaxon in my head; I can feel my poor brain shaking."

"We had to see that. This evening we'll see what effect the night has on us…and tomorrow…."

"Tomorrow?"

"Tomorrow, we leave…"

"For the Pleasure Archipelago?"

"No, to follow the program: head for Panama and the Pacific Ocean, for Astra Island…but we're arriving at the Airstrip."

"Hang on," said Andoche. "I don't see the Villa. This isn't the right place, then? But it is…there's the elevator and the kiosk down there…so where's the Beauséjour?"

Monsieur Cabrol jumped down on to the platform and looked around for a few moments, rubbing his eyes. "No—the Villa is no longer here!"

Andoche and Moderan had run behind a group of stout aircraft, behind which the Villa had been anchored to the landing-strip.

"No, it's no longer here!"

"I'll give the pilot a good ticking off when he gets back," said Monsieur Cabrol. "He too must have wanted to go and cast an eye over the skyscrapers, but I don't want him taking the Villa away when we're not there."

"Monsieur! Monsieur!" shouted a voice behind them.

It was the housekeeper, who was running and waving her arms, and seemed very upset. Phanor was bounding behind her, obviously no less upset, for he was punctuating and drowning out Melanie's voice with his barking, sometimes furious and sometimes joyful—furious when she pronounced the name Barlotin and joyous when, on jumping up, he recognized the hand or face of Andoche, his master, which he wetted with his effusions of amity.

"Well, Melanie?" said Monsieur Cabrol, when Phanor let him get a word in. "We come back and find the house no longer here! Has Barlotin taken it on a little trip?"

"No Monsieur," said Melanie, "not a trip—he's stolen your house! I've just run to make a complaint, but I don't know whether the police sergeant understood me. First, he was annoyed with Phanor, who had followed me, and with me, because I wasn't speaking American; then I got annoyed too and I said some silly things in Limousin,[27] so that he wouldn't understand at all."

"Explain yourself calmly, now, Melanie. What's happened?"

"This: when you had gone, Barlotin went out on the pretext of sorting out something that was wrong with the mooring. He called to me for help, then climbed back up and made Phanor jump down. Then, all of a sudden, the Villa Beauséjour took off, turned around a little, then gained height and disappeared within five minutes…"

"That animal of a pilot is mad! Where has he gone with the house? He'll come back soon, I hope!"

"No, Monsieur, he won't come back. When I called to him to come back and told him that you wouldn't be happy, he answered me by thumbing his nose and he went back into his cockpit. Thumbing his nose—him, who was always so polite to me, and everyone else! Hypocrite! Nasty fellow! And the Villa set off at speed. He's stolen it from you, Monsieur! It immediately went up very high and headed that way, Monsieur. It wouldn't have done any good to cry: "Stop, thief!" so I ran to the police station.

"Strange, strange!"

---

[27] Limousin is the dialect of the region around Limoges.

Perplexed, Monsieur Cabrol tugged at his moustache, gazing at the clouds strewn with aircraft of all kinds. Andoche and Moderan, shading their eyes with their hands, tried to discover the Villa Beauséjour among the swarm of aerial vehicles of every caliber, from great airships to minuscule miniplanes.

"Nothing, nothing!" they repeated. "And he's taken our binoculars along with the house."

"If only that were all he's taken," moaned Melanie, raising her handkerchief to her eyes.

"What else?"

"What! Think about poor Babylas, Monsieur! Our cat, who loves us so much, poor plump darling—such a nice animal! He's taken him along with the house, the villain! Where are they now? Where are they?"

Melanie wept. Monsieur Cabrol felt upset. Andoche and Moderan were walking around nervously, shaking their fists.

"Animal! Villain! Scoundrel! Thief!"

"But it's not impossible," Monsieur Cabrol said, "that he's gone to run an errand—I don't know where. He'll explain everything when he comes back—because he will come back!"

"No, no, I'm certain he won't—that's why I went to the police station without waiting for you."

"You did the right thing, Melanie."

"That's what the police sergeant told me when he finally understood. He told me that it happens quite often, thefts like that. Aircraft are sometimes stolen from the Airstrip, or aircraft parked in quiet spots, ill-guarded camping aircraft, which the thieves disguise right away and sell 10,000 kilometers away—unless they make use of them in robberies. The sergeant told me that, but he reassured me. *The police are alert*, he told me, *and they catch these thieves!* They'll catch ours, that Barlotin who's carried off poor innocent Babylas! Not, Phanor, who would have escaped!"

"It's necessary to catch him as soon as possible. I'll run to the police station to hasten the pursuit. Keep a tight hold of Phanor, so that he doesn't get mixed up in the conversation."

Monsieur Cabrol ran to the Airstrip office and raced to the Tele, while his nephews ran this way and that, searching for the Villa down below, on the ground beneath the Airstrip, behind the nearest group of factories or in the sky, behind the skyscrapers. Nothing! Nothing at all! The Villa was nowhere on high, and nothing came back to the Airstrip.

They went around the office-kiosk, where bells were ringing.

Finally, Monsieur Cabrol came out.

"I've seen the superintendent of the fourth district and I've lodged a complaint of misappropriation. He immediately telephoned a description of the Villa and the thief everywhere. All the brigades of mounted police circulating in aircraft, describing arcs of a circle at different heights around the city, have been put on alert, as well as the coastguard brigades patrolling the gulf. There's a good chance, the Villa Beauséjour having a rather distinctive profile, that the aeropolice have noted its passing. The superintendent advised me to go to the pound tomorrow. If he learns anything this evening, he'll call me immediately. What an annoyance that trusted pilot is causing us! My God! As long as he doesn't touch my great work, which I left on my desk…tell me, Melanie, you didn't notice anything before he took off? Not the slightest suspicion?"

"Nothing at all. He was complaining, as usual, about feeling ill, this country not being to his liking…too much agitation, too much movement, he said."

"I can understand that—but we're only passing thorough!"

"*Me, I like a quiet life*, he said, *watching little birds, fishing with a line in the shade, in a nice spot…that's what I need!* I'd heard him say it before, it was his obsession. This morning, he was walking on the balcony, saying: 'Ontario or Vésinet?[28] Vésinet or Ontario?' And he kept repeating 'Vésinet or Ontario?' while looking at the maps in the cockpit."

---

[28] La Vésinet is a commune in the suburbs of Paris.

"He mentioned Ontario? That's a clue—I'll go speak to the superintendent on the Tele."

"In the meantime, Monsieur, he's carried off the provisions. I don't have anything for dinner…"

"We'll see about that in a little while—the nearest pharmacist."

Walking around the Airstrip had become monotonous. Nothing was seen coming; the familiar outline of the Villa Beauséjour did not appear in the sky, among the crowd of aircraft of every sort that were touching down on the Airstrip or disappearing into the clouds, rose-tinted by the setting Sun.

"And where are we going to sleep tonight? Moderan asked, sadly.

"Yes, where?" said Melanie, seemingly overwhelmed. "We haven't any shelter."

"I'll take care of that; first, I'm going to see the superintendent."

VIII. The Stolen Aerovilla Beauséjour

They had dinner, however. Monsieur Cabrol brought back the necessary provisions, and he also found a hotel of tranquil appearance, rising up a mere 38 stories into a sky traversed by fiery streaks of all colors, intersecting one another repeatedly in all directions, like rays of light escaped from the mouth of hell. Moving gleams burst out overhead: luminous sentences written in the black holes of the clouds; or advertising slogans seeming gigantic amid the stars. They hardly slept at all, thanks to the racket outside, the factory sirens, strident enough to tear through the most solid drumming, howling like demonic banshees. Thus, one nightmare after another, they arrived with difficulty at the morning.

Andoche, scarcely awake, ran to the window then looked out in the direction of the Airstrip, with the hope of finding the

Villa Beauséjour returned to its berth. There was still no sign of it.

After dressing hurriedly and taking his morning pill, Monsieur Cabrol went to the pound to see if his villa had been recovered.

The pound was immense. At ground level, interminable store-rooms and hangars described a great circle, in the middle of which iron pylons supported the landing-ground 50 meters above.

Monsieur Cabrol went aloft immediately, and was transfixed. No Villa Beauséjour. A few aeroclettes here and there, a damaged dirigible, and that was all. He was already going away, dejected, when the attendant out to called him.

"Don't despair, sir—have you looked down below?"

"Why down below? I didn't see anything of interest to me?"

"This is the whole pound—look in the scrap-yard. It's not very cheerful, but you need to search there all the same. Your house might be in pieces there."

Monsieur Cabrol went pale; he had not thought about the scrap-yard. The descent in the elevator, which only took 12 seconds seemed long to him.

"Where's the scrap-yard?"

"Not here, sir," said an employee. "Only stray dogs. Next door's the department of stolen hats, umbrellas, handbags and so on. It's over there, on the other side of the department of children lost on buses…"

"Thank you!"

The scrap yard was huge. Gripped by terror, Monsieur Cabrol hesitated before going in. Finally, he plucked up courage and went through the gate. It was a vast enclosure filled with debris of every sort: cabins that were warped, torn open or crushed; little aircraft folded up like broken umbrellas, amid bristling spikes of twisted steel, dismantled machines, muddy engines…but nothing, still no sign of the Villa Beauséjour—fortunately!

Extremely discomfited, Monsieur Cabrol returned to the Airstrip, where he saw the superintendent once again on the Tele. No news there either—no message had come in, no police station had observed the passing of the stolen flying villa. The coastguard patrols had seen nothing.

What should he do? Wait. There was no cause for despair, though.

"Unless the thief immediately headed for Europe," said the superintendent, "and flew over the bay before the coastguard had been alerted—but that's scarcely probable, since the theft was discovered almost immediately."

Monsieur Cabrol then asked for Paris on the Tele and gave Monsieur des Ormettes' number. It took time, because it was night-time in Paris. Monsieur des Ormettes was asleep; he did not hear the phone; it was necessary to ring more loudly. Finally, Monsieur des Ormettes awoke and ran to the Tele. He uttered loud cries on learning what had happened.

"The Villa stolen! And stolen by Barlotin, a reliable man, a trustworthy pilot! It's not possible. I recommend him to all my clients for tranquil little trips in the sky: no vices, no faults…except one, line-fishing, as in olden times. But that calm and blissful passion is another recommendation."

"What does he do with his fish?"

"I don't know anything about that. Do they catch fish, then, line-fishermen?"

"Sometimes, it's said. They doubtless take them to a food-factory, where they're made into extracts and pills. Anyway, it doesn't matter. Listen. Cabrol, keep us up to date. Can you come to the Tele tomorrow morning—which is to say, this evening, for you. I'm going back to sleep. I'm not worried—all will be explained."

Monsieur Cabrol was about to leave the Tele to go back to the hotel when another bell rang. The superintendent reappeared.

"Villa recovered!" he said. "You see, my poor fellow, that one mustn't become anxious too quickly. A message from Buffalo in Michigan…

"A Villa closely answering the description spotted this morning, proceeding at a very modest speed, flying low and tacking back and forth as if searching for something, along the shore of the lake. Summoned by wireless to stop, your house rapidly gained height to hide in a large cumulus cloud heading north-east. Police aircraft immediately gave chase, following the trail into the cumulus, where it lost it, but quickly found it again by means of its detector. The Villa attempted a rapid descent into a mountain gorge, hoping to find a hiding place in a pine-forest, but it was futile. After a quarter of an hour, the police were on to it. Hands up!—but no resistance. There was only one man aboard, who hid under a table, terrified. The man, interrogated, said his name is Barlotin, in the service of Monsieur Cabrol of Paris...

"I immediately ordered that the Villa and the thief be brought back here."

"Thank you!" cried Monsieur Cabrol, relieved. "My compliments to the aeropolice, Monsieur Superintendent. When do you expect the Villa to arrive?"

"Oh, not more than half an hour."

"Very good!"

Andoche and Moderan were just arriving at the Airstrip, with long faces. "Nothing, nothing—there's no sign of it in the sky," they said, looking down at the ground in discouragement.

"Good!" said their uncle. "Don't worry—I've found our Villa Beauséjour myself. She's coming from Buffalo, along with our thieving pilot. We have only to wait, while walking around the Airstrip."

Monsieur Cabrol rubbed his hands together joyfully, but a sudden thought caused him to frown.

"So long as he hasn't damaged our domain! Anyway, we'll soon find out..."

They walked around the Airstrip, impatiently searching the swarm of airborne vehicles whose paths were crossing incessantly in the north-west, at every height, seeking to distinguish the familiar silhouette.

Finally, Andoche, who had good eyesight, called attention to a bright dot in the background of the sky. Gradually, the dot grew in size. A host of large air-freight dirigibles went past, masking the white dot. Then there were swirls of smoke melting into brown mist; the mist brightened and the Villa Beauséjour appeared quite clearly, with nothing changed. Three minutes later, it landed on the Airstrip. Andoche and Moderan each seized a mooring-rope.

"Hold tight, Andoche," cried Moderan. "Don't let it take off again!"

At the same moment, the elevator disgorged the police superintendent who had alerted Monsieur Cabrol, and a few employees of the Airstrip also came running up.

"Well," said the superintendent, "We've recaptured your house very quickly, as you see. There's so much surveillance up there to prevent malefactors from falling from the sky upon isolated wealthy towns or the upper stories of skyscrapers. We're going to interrogate your thief—you can serve as my interpreter."

The door of the Beauséjour opened; the air detective responsible for bringing the villa back appeared at the top of the ladder. The detective was a strong fellow with sturdy arms, armed with two revolvers and an immobilizer pistol in his belt; it would not have been a good idea for the pilot to attempt any resistance.

Monsieur Cabrol quickly climbed up, with his nephews and the superintendent.

Behind Monsieur Cabrol and the superintendent, Melanie rushed forward. With a single glance she glimpsed Barlotin, guarded by the detective, but that was not what she was looking for, and she went rapidly into the other rooms.

"Babylas! Babylas!" she shouted. "Where are you, Babylas? What has he done with Babylas, the scoundrel!"

Collapsed in a chair in a corner of the drawing-room, with cuffs on his hands, Barlotin, his head lowered so far that it seems to have retreated into his shoulders, did not dare to raise his eyes or open his mouth.

"Wretch!" said Monsieur Cabrol. "To abuse my trust in this fashion! What were you going to do? Where were you going?"

The pilot remained mute.

In a severe voice, the superintendent asked a few questions, which obtained no more response.

Melanie reappeared in a gust of wind, followed by Phanor, who was bounding and barking.

"I can't find Babylas, Monsieur Superintendent. What has he done with him? He's thrown him in the lake, Monsieur, or simply let him fall—he has to tell us!"

"No, no," Barlotin moaned.

"When he saw that he was captured," said the detective, "stricken by surprise and emotion, he talked. He confessed everything—the theft planned from the first moment of the arrival at the Airstrip, its premeditation during the sojourn in the Caucasian Archipelago; he'd been thinking about it for a long time."

"That why he missed all the airships departing for Europe," said Monsieur Cabrol. "Everything's explained—but where was he going?"

"When I arrested him," the detective said, "he was searching for a quiet little cove on the banks of the Ontario."

"Don't go to any trouble, Monsieur Superintendent," Melanie put in, arriving unexpectedly once again. "He's been found—look, here he is. Babylas had hidden in my wardrobe, for fear of all the upheaval yesterday. It's Phanor who found him. Wasn't it, Phanor?"

Delighted with his triumph, Phanor redoubled his barking.

"I'm all right now—you can continue, Monsieur Superintendent." Her face blooming, the housekeeper lightly passed one hand over the backs of the chairs, as if caressing the recovered house, and pressed Babylas to her heart with the other. "I beg your pardon!" she said. "That's what he was always saying, as if to himself: Vésinet or Ontario."

The thieving pilot muttered into his beard without raising his head. "I confess! I confess!" he said, hoarsely. "I hesitated between the two. I didn't dare go back to Paris, and I looked for the Ontario for want of the Vésinet. Besides, the fish must be more varied in the Ontario. Oh, a nice little house like the Villa Beauséjour, on the shore of a lake, a well-shaded spot—that's the dream! That's why I wanted to take her away—she pleased me so much! Lake Ontario also pleased me a great deal; I barely glimpsed it, but I miss it…I have tranquil tastes. I've had enough of traveling; a Villa Beauséjour, that's what I really needed. I landed it on a little stony substratum, shut off all the machinery, and it made me a nice country house—my dream, exactly! But it's finished, my dream!"

The man was standing up now. He extended his bound hands and punctuated his confession with heavy sighs.

"Poor devil!" said Monsieur Cabrol.

"Oh, I've had it with voyages! I've globe-trotted at all altitudes, under all skies…I'm entitled to be thirsty for a little rest, you understand, Monsieur? Oh to fish with a line, comfortably installed in my little corner…in my own little house. It was a golden opportunity—I let myself be tempted—that's it! What are they going to do with me? Let me go back to Paris, Monsieur—I promise not to do it again."

"After all," said Monsieur Cabrol, hesitantly, "the house has been recovered…"

"One moment!" said the superintendent. "The law has caught him; there's been an established theft; the police had to be mobilized, to carry out a search to catch the malefactor; the district attorney has been notified; the process can't be stopped. The law is severe, particularly in cases of aerial theft. It's necessary, Monsieur—you must understand that."

"Yes, yes, I know," said Monsieur Cabrol, "there's been a misappropriation; but as I've got my property back, I'm leaning toward indulgence…"

"Impossible, Monsieur. The case will follow the usual course; it will doubtless be presented at the next assizes."

It was now Monsieur Cabrol's turn to stand before the police with a long face—almost as long as Barlotin's.

"Oh, Uncle," said Moderan, in a low voice, "as long as they don't want to keep the Villa until the trial, as an item of evidence."

"Damn it!" whispered Monsieur Cabrol. "Yes, so long as..."

"That would be a bit of bad luck!" exclaimed Andoche. "But then, are we going to escape right away and take the superintendent with us?"

"Monsieur Superintendent," Cabrol went on, "I'll send you the registration papers and give you all the necessary explanations; then, recommending the guilty party to your indulgence, we'll resume our interrupted voyage. Serious matters require my presence 1000 kilometers from here. We wanted to pay a flying visit to New York; that's done. Very nice, very interesting—we're charmed—but I have to leave."

"Very well, Monsieur."

"I shall therefore leave you the aforementioned Barlotin, and take off again in my aerovilla."

"One moment!" said the superintendent, stopping him with a gesture. "If urgent business requires your presence, you may go—but the aerovilla must remain here; that's indispensable. Evidence, Monsieur, indispensable for the depositions, for the preparation of the case for the prosecution...."

"But I'll be able to communicate as much as the prosecuting attorneys need by Tele."

"Impossible, Monsieur—that's not admissible."

"But..."

"Don't worry, though; the case is quite straightforward— it won't take more than five or six weeks, two months at the most. You can answer us from wherever you might be by Tele, but the principal item of evidence in the case must remain here, at the disposition of the judge. You can stay, or leave someone here, as guardian of the item of evidence."

Andoche and Moderan let themselves fall into chairs, sighing, discouraged and distressed.

"What a predicament!" murmured Monsieur Cabrol, no less discomfited than they were. "Oh, that Barlotin!"

"Now, let's continue our investigation," said the superintendent. "Let's see—let's make a tour of the house to see if anything is missing, and whether there's any damage…"

"Oh yes, that's true!" exclaimed Monsieur Cabrol. "I forgot to check! My great work in progress, my *History of the Lunatic Civilizations*…that would be serious. Great God! It's very important to me. Quickly, let's take a look at my room, my work-desk…"

He was already in his room; the superintendent followed him, jostled slightly by the youngsters.

"It's there, Monsieur Superintendent. Would you care to go in?"

The key of the item of furniture in which each drawer was consecrated to a particular work was still in it. Monsieur Cabrol swiftly made a tour of it, and lifted up his papers, but nothing had been touched—neither the precious manuscript nor the documents. Barlotin had disdained the opportunity to obtain cognizance of his employer's great scholarly work.

"He didn't have time to disturb anything," said the superintendent, "and that's thanks to the vigilance of or police aircraft, it should be said, for he was spotted very quickly and pursued immediately. Let's look at the other rooms…"

"Nothing's missing," said Monsieur Cabrol. "I assure you that the unfortunate fellow isn't a professional thief, like your pirates of the clouds or your aerial burglars. It was the opportunity that awoke an evil impulse in him."

"Yes, he seemed very sincere in his confessions and protestations of repentance. He can explain that to the judge; he can say that his desire for a quiet life on the shore of a lovely lake, and his dreams of line-fishing, suddenly turned his head. His advocate can plead a fit of madness."

"Ah! Yes, we'll have to find the poor wretch a lawyer, to get him out of the affair as cheaply as possible…"

"You're very good. You'll need one too, for the civil action."

"What a bother!"

"I'll try to hurry the affair along," the superintendent said, finishing taking a few notes. "Don't worry, see the lawyers. It's possible to make arrangements for a raid or extra-rapid solution."

The superintendent made a tour of the house. "Ah!" he said, pointing at the plaque above the balcony bearing the name of the villa. "Your thief has begun to camouflage the inscription of your flying home."

"Look, Uncle, it's true!" said Andoche. "We didn't notice it, in our joy at recovering our home, you see! He'd begun to change 'Villa Beauséjour' into 'Villa B...ien le bonjour.' That's his paint-pot on the balcony."

"It was the pursuit by the police aircraft that interrupted him," said the superintendent.

Barlotin tried to bury his head in his waistcoat. "A fruit of madness—you said it! An aberration. I was too content, I put on airs—it brought me misfortune!"

"There we are," aid the superintendent. "Crystal clear—we should be able to settle it for you as quickly as possible. I'll let you have the addresses of a few lawyers. See them right away, since you're in such a hurry."

Monsieur Cabrol escorted the superintendent to the elevator. Behind them marched the air policeman and his prisoner, who darted a lamentable glance at the Villa Beauséjour as he left.

"The prison is close by," the superintendent was generous enough to say, "and it's comfortable, of course—every modern comfort. Don't worry about your thief; he'll be fine."

X. The Barlotin Case.

"Now we're in a pretty pickle," said Monsieur Cabrol, letting himself fall into a rocking-chair. "Oof! Oof! All this excitement's breaking my arms and legs; I feel faint."

He lowered his head and closed his eyes, uttering long sighs. A joyful purring along with a gentle silky friction on his face made him open his eyes again; it was Babylas, who had jumped on to his lap and was testifying to his delight by means of that music.

"You're very sweet, my brave Babylas, but you're pricking my eyes with your whiskers. That's all right—you're family! Go see Moderan. As for you, Phanor, don't bark any more, you've already told us...go see Andoche and let me think."

"Yes," said Andoche, "but what about the lunch we're forgetting?"

"Soon, when I've had a moment to think about the situation...but your appetite is making demands. So be it! I'll think afterwards. First we'll go..."

A bell rang on the villa's Tele.

"Again!" groaned Monsieur Cabrol, getting up painfully from his armchair.

The screen of the Tele lit up. Monsieur and Madame des Ormettes appeared. It was morning in Paris. They had only just got up and had come in search of information.

"Good morning, Cabrol. How are things aboard? Everyone's health is good? Good morning, my dear Moderan. You're still keeping your big brother on the end of a none-too-long string? Keep him firmly in hand—don't let him bolt, the daredevil, the excitable young fellow!"

"No fear, Papa, I'm watching him. Good morning, Mama!"

"Good morning, good morning, children. What excitement, eh? Well, what's new? I see that the Villa Beauséjour has returned to its berth after a little excursion, eh? Everything has been explained, hasn't it? Your pilot left in search of tobacco and forgot the number of your garage?"

Andoche and Moderan burst out laughing, at the sight of which Monsieur and Madame des Ormettes joined in.

"In search of tobacco...not exactly. In brief, here it is: he really did steal our house and left, leaving us in the lurch. But

I set the police in motion without delay, and they caught the thief after a lively pursuit, and brought back our house, as you can see…"

"Nothing broken, I see—that's perfect. I suppose you've given that Barlotin a slight reprimand. Tell him to come and talk to me!"

"I can't—he's in prison. Jailhouse No.18, for those caught in the act."

"What? You've had him locked up?"

"Not me—the superintendent! A very serious case, prosecution in hand; it will go to the criminal court."

"Really? Quite remarkable. There's a little adventure for your travel diary."

"An amusing adventure? Rather say misadventure! These days, alas, there are only misadventures!"

"You seem rather annoyed."

"To say the least!"

"Oh yes, definitely!" exclaimed Andoche and Moderan, nodding their heads with conviction.

"We too, are in prison, here at the Airstrip! The poor Villa Beauséjour has been retained as a piece of evidence, of which we will be the guardians until the trial."

"What?" said Monsieur des Ormettes. "How long will it be until this trial—three or four days?"

"Six weeks or two months," the superintendent told me, "but I'm not confident about that."

"My dear chap," said Monsieur des Ormettes, "don't get too upset: you left to escape all the annoyance of our great resurfacing of the terrestrial globe, and God knows we're in the midst of it now, amid the great disemboweling of the world's carcass in the Parisian region. Things must be quieter in New York—the great work began there 20 years ago."

"Wait a minute before judging our tranquility. I'll take you through our neighborhood of the Chicago-New York sector in the Tele."

"No, no, don't do that—I believe you."

"Yes, the Chicago-New York sector is advanced enough as far as the resurfacing of the carcass goes, but I'm only talking about the infernal daily routine. Oh, when one leaves the Caucasian Archipelago, and its delightful shores, the diabolical din every day, here, has nothing cheerful about it. My brain has already turned to marmalade in my head. And to think that we'll have to remain here for some time! I'm going to see a lawyer, to take every possible step to hasten the moment of our liberation as much as possible…"

"Come on, don't get so upset. Be brave! We're going to leave you now…go to your lawyer right away, hurry!"

"Not right away—only tomorrow; you're forgetting that it's evening here. We'll try to sleep, and tomorrow morning, the fight! *Au revoir*."

The evening was short. They had had enough of discussing the annoying consequences of the theft of the Villa. Andoche and Moderan had already made up their minds—too bad; everything would work out. Then again, they were sleepy.

Phanor and Babylas were already asleep. Brave Phanor was barking in his dream, but Babylas, curled up in a ball on an armchair, had already forgotten the risks he had run.

Before going to her room, Melanie made a circuit of the vicinity. From the balcony of the Airstrip her anxious eyes tried to pierce the ocean of darkness streaked with long searchlight beams, punctuated by gleams of every color bursting like bombs. The entire nocturnal landscape was humming with a rumor compounded out of 100,000 noises. She shook the balustrade as if to assure herself of its solidity. "As long as the Airstrip doesn't fly away!" she said, shaking her head.

She went back in, and locked all the doors carefully. "Well, we'll see tomorrow morning whether we're still here."

No one got up early the next morning. After so many fatiguing incidents and emotions, they were entitled to lie in, in spite of the buzz of the 100,000 noises.

It was nearly 11 a.m. when Monsieur Cabrol went out, having consulted the notes and addresses that he police superintendent had given to him.

"Let's see: the lawyers Mr. and Mrs. Bloomfield, number 1235, 738th Avenue—that's a long way from here, at least a quarter of an hour by taxi-plane."

A little taxi-plane that had just brought some passengers to the Airstrip was just preparing to plunge down below. Monsieur Cabrol hailed it and gave the address.

A quarter of an hour later, indeed, he got down on 738th Avenue, in front of a three-step pyramid of three-story houses in the form of square towers stacked one on top of another, seven or eight at the bottom, five on the first platform, three on the second platform and a single one on top. The edifice was exactly similar to those built by children with their construction kits.

Mr. and Mrs. Bloomfield lived on the third stage of the building at the very top of the pyramid. Monsieur Cabrol took the elevator and ran the bell n the third stage. He was immediately introduced into the lawyer's office, where two people were swaying in rocking-chairs, each studying files placed in front of them on the armchair's desk-top.

Which of the two people, identically dressed in long morning-coats, both clean-shaven—or so it seemed—with their long hair similarly plastered down over their foreheads and descending as far as the silk scarves around their necks, was Mr. Bloomfield and which was Mrs. Bloomfield? At first glance, it was hard to tell.

With a beard one is always certain, but this happened to be a period in which beards had been proscribed for 90 years. It was taken for granted that those absurd, uncomfortable and unaesthetic chin-fleeces were intolerable. In another 90 years the wheel would turn again. Every century has its particular aesthetic; people would find those shaved chins ridiculous, those stripped lips quite ugly, those plump hairless faces overly comical, and beards would flourish once more.

In the meantime, with respect to Monsieur Cabrol—who was from Europe, where beards had been worn again for some time—this gave rise to a certain unpleasant scorn.

He addressed himself to the first armchair and asked: "Please, is it to Mr. Bloomfield that I have the honor of speaking?"

"No," the first armchair replied, its swaying ceasing. "Mr. Bloomfield is over there."

"*Excusez-moi...scusate mi...*I beg your pardon—I meant Mrs. Bloomfield."

"Then yes, I'm Mrs. Bloomfield."

On leaving the Villa Beauséjour, Monsieur Cabrol had intended to hire Mr. Bloomfield as his lawyer, but so be it—it would be Madame. That was unimportant, since both had the same reputation for eloquence and the same expertise in legal matters.

"Madame," he said, "I'm a foreigner; I have been told, with a recommendation of our great ability, that you might perhaps consent to attend to a very disagreeable matter in which I have become involved."

"Would you care to explain, Monsieur?"

Monsieur Cabrol had a gift for languages; he therefore recounted rapidly, in almost pure American, a salad of Anglo-French-German, Russian, Italian and even Chinese terms, the tale of the theft of the Villa Beauséjour by its treacherous pilot, the rapid pursuit, the capture and the return of the house, along with the thief, who was to be brought before a judge in the criminal court.

He explained that he was in a hurry to leave New York to continue his journey, and that he would be glad to see the case reach count as soon as possible. The thief, giving the lie to an entire life of honesty and hard work, had had a moment of madness, he was now conscience-stricken and merited every indulgence.

"If you consent, Madame, to undertake the defense of this unfortunate man, I will ask Mr. Bloomfield to act for me, as the injured party. I will ask him to put all the blame on us;

he may say whatever he wishes; he will be able to let his imagination run wild, etc. The essential thing for me is to take off again with my aerovilla."

"Perfectly understood," said Mrs. Bloomfield. "And you, Will, understand equally?"

"Entirely, Arabella."

"Then you'll become the injured party and I the defender of that poor man, the pilot, the innocent victim of a culpable obsession, who might perhaps have the right to clam damages. That's understood. And an extra-rapid resolution, if possible."

Things did not drag on with the two Bloomfields. Monsieur Cabrol thought that boded well. After a few supplementary explanations, the final arrangements were soon made, and Monsieur Cabrol was able to return to his taxi-plane, which was waiting for him on the terrace.

He went back to the villas, a little more serene.

"Well, my lads, the ball is now rolling—everything is in hand. Don't give it another thought, since Mr. and Mrs. Bloomfield have promised me an imminent departure. In the meantime, we shall work or relax, and also go on excursions—but not with the Villa, which must remain in its berth while the investigation continues and the prosecution is prepared...."

X. The Escape of the Evidence.

The prospect of an early resumption of the interrupted voyage brought a hint of gaiety to the Villa. Andoche and Moderan seemed to find some charm in the spectacle of American life considered from the 300-meter height of the Airstrip. They amused themselves in riding the elevator up and down and running around the aircraft that landed with passengers: Westerners coming from 'Frisco; tanned families from the South; men in sombreros whose faces seemed to be fashioned in brown leather, black and curly-haired families with broad red and white smiles; mixed families of every shade, ladies and gentlemen in yellow ocher, neutral tint, Sienna earth, reddish brown or burnt sepia, forming an entire range of water-colors. The vehicles were no less varied: old aero-coaches and, coming from long distances, flying cars from Louisiana, light and open-topped; Canadian avionettes, veritable flying boxes hermetically sealed and padded for defense against the cold; large aerobuses bringing local wedding-parties for the day; and the host of businessmen's taxi-planes, some of which only remained on the platform for a few hours, while others, after depositing their passengers, were taken down to garages on the ground; and the dirigibles of the innumerable American or transoceanic lines, which touched down in order to drop passengers off or pick them up.

There was an incessant movement around the immobile aerovilla, suspended, by virtue of slow-moving justice, in the middle of a whirlwind that carried everything away—people and objects, buildings and smoke—in that vertiginous America.

They also worked—without enthusiasm, but it was necessary to do something. Monsieur Cabrol tried, at least, but inspiration was lacking. Every day he went to 738th Avenue; Mr. and Mrs. Bloomfield were very busy lawyers, overwhelmed by cases. When, by chance, he did not find them at their office, plunged in their files, facing one another in their rocking-chairs, rocking more or less rapidly in proportion to the arduousness of the case under consideration, it was because they were in court in Chicago, Cincinnati or somewhere else.

Monsieur Cabrol came back from these visits furious one day and discouraged the next. As distractions, they had the visits and interrogations of state attorneys and, from time to time, flights in the Villa Beauséjour to study the working of the machine in order to see whether, by chance, the accused Barlotin might have been taken away and abducted by the engine involuntarily.

They went in this fashion to Lake Erie, Lake Michigan, and to the former Niagara Falls, which had been eroded and flattened by the waters a long time ago, and was now a tranquil little cascade.

There was a reconstruction of the crime, with Barlotin removed from prison for a day, strictly guarded on the balcony of the Villa by two policemen. For hours the Villa flew over river-banks that were nothing but an uninterrupted series of rumbling factories, with widely-spaced little pine woods on crags, scarcely visible in an atmosphere darkened by vapors of every hue.

Barlotin seemed disenchanted. It was here that he had searched for his cheerful oasis of coolness and quiet!

Six months had already gone by and the promised extra-rapid solution did not materialize. Monsieur Cabrol was depressed. Mr. and Mrs. Bloomfield no longer heard anything about the progress of the case and the probability of an imminent denouement. Mrs. Bloomfield no longer promised anything. For one thing, she was too busy and no longer had the time; she was often absent, summoned to Chicago, where she was representing a group of financiers in a very big trial, leaving her husband to look after minor current cases.

Mr. Bloomfield, alone in his rocking-chair, was not in a good mood and replied evasively to Monsieur Cabrol's objurgations. One morning, the latter found Bloomfield extremely surly. Mrs. Bloomfield, increasingly busy, had just left for Chicago and, as he had refused to accompany her, she had left instructions for the trifling research and formalities necessitated by her important case.

"I congratulate you on Mrs. A. Bloomfield's success," the distressed Cabrol said to him, "but can't you…"

Mr. W. Bloomfield leapt out of his armchair. "Ah! Yes! Wait: Mrs. Bloomfield is defending your thief; I'm representing you, as the civil party. You want to go away with your Villa? Good! You'll leave this evening." He picked up his hat and leapt into Monsieur Cabrol's taxi-plane. "Drop me off at the district court, then go back to the Villa and expect me at about 3 p.m."

Never before had Mr. W. Bloomfield demonstrated such activity; he told the driver to hurry; he kneaded his briefcase nervously, rolled official documents into a ball and threw them overboard. At the Courthouse, Monsieur Cabrol would have liked to follow him to ensure that the fever of goodwill did not cool down, but Mr. Bloomfield stopped him, saying: 'Impossible! Many formalities to take care of, people to see, clerk of the court to hustle, papers to obtain, legalizations…over there, then, at 3 p.m."

Cabrol returned to the Airstrip at top speed. He was very excited. So then…but no, it wasn't possible, it was a false dawn; tomorrow, he would find the Bloomfields in their office, swaying with their files in their rocking-chairs. He and his nephews were the Latudes[29] of the Airstrip, in for 35 years of captivity, like the prisoner of the old Bastille, where the view had debtless been more agreeable than the one over these volcanic heaps of factories.

Andoche and Moderan saw that their uncle was preoccupied but dared not ask him any questions. It was necessary to force down the pills of his lunch; he was not hungry. While serving the lunch, Melanie began to complain; Bablyas and Phanor were getting bored on the Airstrip, and finding their

---

[29] Jean-Henri Latude (1725-1805) was a con man who tried unsuccessfully to put one over on Madame de Pompadour, the king's mistress, and was imprisoned in the Bastille in 1749. After being transferred to Vincennes, he escaped in 1750 but was soon recaptured. He escaped again, this time from the Bastille, in 1756, and also escaped a second time from Vincennes in 1765, but kept getting caught, until he was eventually released in 1784. His escapes made him something of a folk hero, and called attention to the length of his imprisonment for an exceedingly trivial offense—which might have played some part in the inspiration of Victor Hugo's *Les Misérables*.

life very monotonous. And the horrible dust that covered everything!

Suddenly, a bell rang on the Tele. Monsieur Cabrol leapt up. It was Mr. Bloomfield, brandishing a piece of paper.

"It's done. Here's the order, with all the signatures and stamps. I'm on my way to the Airstrip."

Monsieur Cabrol did not say anything else, but he ran to the balustrade, binoculars in hand, searching the horizon feverishly. Andoche and Moderan, followed by Melanie, were soon by his side, searching the sky like him, while wondering what they were looking for.

Five minutes, ten minutes, went by. Monsieur Cabrol wiped the lenses of the binoculars, quivering with impatience.

Suddenly, he said; "Ah! Over there! Yes! Yes...that must be him. Aren't they slow in this country? Finally!"

A taxiplane was heading straight for the Airstrip. It was indeed Mr. W. Bloomfield, whom Cabrol seized by the arm as soon as he was on the platform, and rapidly took up to the Villa's drawing-room.

"Here's the paper!" said W. Bloomfield. "Aerovilla Beauséjour is no longer necessary as an item of evidence; the seizure is lifted; you can leave. The trial of Arthur Jean Baptiste Édouard Barlotin will follow its course; it will be permissible for you to come back, if you wish, to witness the arguments and hear the sentence."

"Thank you, thank you!" said Cabrol. "We can really go, then?"

"Whenever you wish."

Everything was soon settled: the garage expenses at the Airstrip and the fees of Mr. W. Bloomfield and Mrs. Arabella Bloomfield; handshakes and thanks. Mr. W. Bloomfield took charge of a small provision of pills to comfort the treacherous pilot in his prison, and took off again in his taxi-plane.

Free! Free at last!

"Lock up Phanor and Babylas, Melanie—we're leaving right away."

"For good, Uncle?" asked Andoche and Moderan, who dared not believe their ears.

"For good, and immediately. Don't jump for joy."

"I've other things to do, Monsieur," said Melanie, coming down rapidly from her room. "I have to bring back…"

"Nothing at all—we're escaping, as you can see. Is everything in order? Good. I'll set the course. You two, Andoche and Moderan, keep an eye on everything; look out to port and starboard; it's a matter of not breaking anything of our neighbors', or our own…no damage here, above all!"

Phanor had undoubtedly understood; he jumped on to the balcony yapping with joyful fury, and Babylas, locked in Melanie's room as a precaution, answered him with plaintive miaows.

"Silence, now."

Already, the Aerovilla Beauséjour was moving off. Monsieur Cabrol maneuvered carefully; the attendants, put in a good mood by generous tips, had cleared the way. The Aerovilla rose a few feet into the air, left the platform with a majestic slowness, and described an ascending spiral around the Airstrip.

"Everything's in order," said Monsieur Cabrol. "Due South now, flying over the coast!"

The joyous afternoon! After the gentle progress and precautions of the departure, the Villa put on speed. They floated in the blue above the sea, the horizons appeared distinctly, the heavy vapors of the industrial regions having gradually been left behind, disappearing in the distance. To the right, the Allegheny mountains designed a vague blue line; then came the forests and greenery of Carolina[30] and Louisiana.

Soon the sea took on violet tints, which turned to red, seemingly wishing to catch fire, like an immense brazier, the Pacific Ocean that was divinable down below, the glare of which the eyes could not support.

---

[30] Robida has *Californie* (California) but that has to be a misprint.

"The Mexican coast!" said Monsieur Cabrol. "We'll look for a nice tranquil little spot to land. We'd be able to find a garage for the night in a town, but I like the countryside better."

"So do we!"

Half an hour later, as the darkness was becoming total, Andoche pointed out an area on the verdant bank of a river, in the depths of a wooded valley somewhat reminiscent of those of the Caucasian Archipelago, that was easy of access. There was nothing there but a group of small houses, hardly a village. Further away, they could make out a little white and pink town, huddled around a church with a bell-tower, whose bells were ringing as if to welcome the voyagers from above.

Monsieur Cabrol opted for the village, and the Villa Beauséjour descended slowly to touch down in a sufficiently flat and bush-free field.

The entire population was there: people of a general Indian type, a few displaying to varying degrees a mixture of Spanish blood.

Andoche looked at them sadly. He had expected Guatemalan, Indian or Mexican costumes, decorated with feathered head-dresses, necklaces and ear-rings, but he found the universal costume of Europe, America and Asia, the sole and unique fashion of Paris, London or Peking, for men as for women, with only a few small modifications imposed by the climate, such as lighter fabrics.

These Guatemalans seemed to be good people; they would have liked to assist with the maneuvers, but there was no need for their help; the Villa Beauséjour had gently stabilized on the ground by itself. They pushed one another, groups of señors and señoritas, with the children in front, and moved around under the balcony, welcoming their guests with a hum of admiring guttural voices in which the syllables of a terrible Aztec Spanish buzzed and overlapped.

Only one person took hold of the ladder to climb aboard, doubtless for some formality. Monsieur Cabrol greeted him and tried to seize something within the flux of words that rolled over the balcony and made the walls of the house vibrate as they echoed therefrom. The tone was benevolent though, and the gestures welcoming.

"Good, good" said Monsieur Cabrol. "I get it; it's the local policeman who is wishing us good evening on behalf of the Mayor and the population. Very good!"

He took a card from his wallet and the vessel's papers, which the policeman signed with a flourish of the pen. The functionary made a tour of the balcony with an admiring expression, then bowed with a refined politeness, offered a few more friendly interjections, and took his leave.

"It's very nice here. I can only see three or four factory chimneys, over there in the distance; that doesn't spoil the landscape. They're doubtless simple culinary factories, where the local produce is processed and a few alimentary pills produced. Come on! We're installed; it's time for dinner."

Everyone having admired the sunset sufficiently, night fell and the indigenes returned to their homes.

"To the table, on the balcony, and quickly—it's no longer light."

"Bah! Just to swallow two or three pills!" said Andoche.

"Pat attention! You mustn't take the wrong pill by mistake, in the dark. Let's see—are you very hungry? Very well—this evening, by reason of the fatigue caused by the excitement, we'll offer ourselves a stimulating, even Pantagruelesque meal—a Belshazzar's feast!"

"Bravo! Bravo!"

"Here's to joy! Melanie, here's the menu. Four pills each: a hors-d'oeuvre variety pill no. 1; a truffled turkey pill; a banana fritter pill; a Chasselas de Fontainebleau pill.[31] Drinks:

---

[31] Chasselas is a variety of grape used in making desert wines. It is possible that the pill in question is made directly from the grape, but it is more likely that Robida is mischievously classifying a dessert wine as food rather than drink, and that the citation is continuing his tongue-in-cheek celebration of the effects of alcohol.

Burgundy, one pill each; a carafe of *agua fresca*...and let's celebrate our escape joyfully!"

They had no more worries, they were no longer in a hurry. Sprawling limply in their armchairs, they drew out the meal; they took three quarters of an hour to consume the truffled turkey, the banana fritters and the warming Burgundy. It was absolutely dark when they got up from the table. No light was shining in the Guatemalan village; the people were probably sleeping in the open, beneath the fan-palms sprouting in the gardens.

"Serious business tomorrow!"

"Look!" said Moderan, who had just gone over to the other side of the house. Look this way—one Moon, two Moons, ten Moons...50 Moons!"

It was, indeed, a matter of Moons; the darkness on the other side was scattered with large gleams that looked almost exactly like constellations of Moons—but they were not Moons, for they were various in shape, and also in hue, varying from bright red to dark red, some of them fiery, extended in scarlet-tinted vapors or emitting incandescent jets.

"Volcanoes of course!" said Monsieur Cabrol. All the land over there, the plateaux of the ancient isthmus of Panama, was turned upside-down and torn apart by the formidable earthquake that twisted and broke the isthmus into several fragments a few centuries ago, and opened three or four wide breaches through which the waters of the two oceans flowed into one another. All of the ground—the entire bedrock, in fact—is pierced by holes, through which fire, lava, hot mud and boiling water flow from the depths, and it's all those various volcanoes that you're mistaking for Moons. We shall see all that, my boys; it's on our route. We'll pass over it, high enough, at least, not to set our hair on fire."

"O! Yes—high; very high!"

"Just as long as that seething Earth doesn't play any dirty tricks on us tonight!"

"Bah! We can sleep easy; those mountains only tremble five or six times a year, on average. Let's hope the annual quota has been used up."

The night was quite calm; at least, the inhabitants of the Villa Beauséjour did not perceive any shocks, and awoke hale and hearty at dawn the following morning. The sunrise was very pretty, behind a myriad of little clouds that rose into the sky like a advance guard of little herald angels. What was about to appear in the soft and tender blue behind those clouds? It was His Majesty the Sun, who was coming from the lands beyond the Atlantic, beginning to launch his rays toward the zenith, to graze and decorate the crests of the waves.

Moderan was not fully awake, and rubbed his eyes at first. No more airstrip, no more of those huge carcasses of iron cutting out squares and triangles from Heaven and Earth alike, no atmosphere swirling turbulently with yellow or black vapors. They were no longer back there, tied down to the Airstrip, impounded in New York. He jumped for joy.

People from the village were working here and there in the fields; the Angelus was sounding in the bell-tower of the distant church. No more volcanoes either! They had melted into the profound blue of the Occidental mountains.

A group of Guatemalan youths, male and female, clad in long robes deeply cleft at the neck and decorated with bizarre embroidery, was circling the Villa, holding hands, wide-eyed with admiration.

"I vote for a short stay here, before continuing," said Andoche.

"We'll stay for a few days," said Monsieur Cabrol. We ought to alternate our sensations, the sweet and pleasant with the severe! So, a week of utter peace in this pleasant landscape; then, after the idyll, we'll go on to something rougher, for the next thing on our program now is Astra, the great island that fell from the sky 30 years ago, as you know, having given the world a famous scare. I'll tell you all about that, with authentic details, one of these days, since I was a young man when the terrible event occurred, and lived through those days of terror and anguish. There was quite a stir, in fact."

"Tell us the story now, Uncle."

"No, no, we ought to save that for the departure—you'll want to fly to Astra straight away."

"Let's remain in the idyll for a while."

XI. Astra's Fall

A bell from the Tele cut short Andoche's demands.

"All right! All right! I'm coming. Who's this, so early?"

It was Monsieur des Ormettes arriving by wireless; he appeared on the screen, a trifle excited.

"Well, well, where are you, then? You've left the New York Airstrip? The case had ended sooner than you thought? What sentence did Barlotin receive?"

"The case hasn't yet got to court. He hasn't been sentenced; we're the ones who've escaped."

"Really!"

"Yes, with the complicity of Mr. William Bloomfield. The case isn't over. Mrs. Arabella let it drag on. Our case was a mere trifle for the dear lady, such a busy lawyer! She was caught up in something more important, a big trial in which to appear before the Chicago bench. Her husband William Bloomfield, annoyed at being preferred to her for that, left behind to clear up trifling matters, cut through the formalities somewhat and had the seizure order on the evidential Villa lifted…and we took off immediately, much regretted by the garage but well content to fly away at top speed."

"Very good! Very good!"

"Barlotin will get himself out of it as best he can. I've recommended the poor devil to the indulgence of the court…just so long as Mrs. Bloomfield doesn't get him condemned to life imprisonment—but no, Bloomfield is his lawyer; he'll get him out of it, we hope. We'll know the outcome soon. William Bloomfield will telephonoscope us."

"Now," said Monsieur des Ormettes, "I like the tropical landscape in which you've set down. Very pretty! Dry and luxuriant at the same time. What rocks, and what vegetation! Jeanne, come and see—scorched rocks here, a nest of exuberant vegetation there…"

"Good morning, good morning," said Madame des Ormettes. "All's well, then? The dear children's health is good, and yours too—keep it up! We're fine too. Oh, if you'd heard my speech in the Chamber yesterday, on the budget! What a success, my dear! I'll let you hear it—I'll send it by Tele right away. Where are you, then? Yes, an environment fit for that old romance of the Middle Ages—you know the one…*Paul et…Stéphanie*?...no, *Paul et Virginie*. Exactly like that!"

"We're in Guatemala, near the great breach of Panama. We've only just arrived, and we haven't seen anything much yet. Last night, 100 volcanoes were flaming in the distance, which promises some excitement when we pass over them in a week's time, after a rest cure. My dear des Ormettes, you must come and see us—a holiday beach could be created here, with a big hotel and a fine advertising campaign. And how is the great work progressing where you are?"

"Oh, I try to think about that as little as possible. But I have the infernal rumble of 100,000 machines in my head all day long. Then again, there's a danger of delays in the region—a lack of materials to remake the subsoil sufficiently solidly. They're going to cut a slice off the former Mont-Blanc as soon as possible, but it takes time, all the same, and we're in a hurry. They're carefully hiding it from us, my dear chap, but I've learned from one of my friends who's an engineer…I've been told under a seal of secrecy, you understand—above all, don't repeat it anyone…"

"What? You've been warned…"

"That our quarter has been sinking steadily at a rate of a millimeter a day for nearly two years. Above all, don't say anything! Absolute secrecy!"

"Of course! I've known that for more than three years. I noticed something, and followed the work of excavation with exceedingly sensitive instruments; its slowness reassured me slightly."

"Oh yes—those bizarre instruments that you have at home. I wondered what use they could be to you, a scholar and literary man."

"Yes—I didn't say anything about it, so as not to worry you. Since you know, get the instruments from my house and follow the process. I repeat, there's no immediate danger, merely a supplement of prospective annoyances."

"I'll keep watch, but I'm not a man of science—I get lost in all calculations."

"Talk to your friend the engineer—he'll set up the apparatus for you. You'll only have to look at it every morning."

"So long as we don't go the way of Montmartre 20 years ago…"

"No, the hill of Montmartre, which was still 85 meters above sea level 100 years ago, began its slow descent without anyone noticing—a few centimeters a year at first…a somewhat neglected quarter, evidently; an old Airstrip for a few major airship lines, not very busy. Then the descent accelerated and people at the Airstrip noticed something."

"I know, I know."

"Errors in calculation! The arithmetic was wrong—sea level had declined following the oceanic perturbations…."

"Exactly! Produced by the fall of Astra, the island fallen into the Pacific, which we'll go to see one of these days…"

"As I was saying…errors in calculation, so to speak, inevitable given all the upheavals, and on day, the 150-meter Airstrip found itself at ground level, and…"

"And today the former summit of the hill, so famous in the Middle Ages, is nearly 60 meters lower down, and forms a small mound in a large cavity."

"In sum, since they're working flat out to complete the solidification in your neighborhood, I don't think there's any immediate danger to fear…"

"I'm assuming that too," said Monsieur des Ormettes. "I'll keep an eye on it, with my friend the engineer."

"Try to take a vacation, then, and come and join us in the Panamanian region, or even in Astra!"

"A little break would certainly do us a lot of good, in the midst of all this upheaval. I'll do everything I can to but a few projects in order, and when you get to Astra, perhaps we'll be able to spend two or three weeks with you to roll in the grass, dream, sleep or think at our ease…and perhaps find a little business to do out there…a new land, with a wide-open future…we'll see."

Madame des Ormettes returned, still in a hurry, her eternal briefcase under her arm, stuffed with papers. Family effusions. Complaints about the frightful racket of the great Resurfacing; headaches, no longer any way to organize one's thoughts and he arguments of a speech, etc.

The Tele vibrated. Monsieur and Madame des Ormettes seemed to have brought with them all the noise of Parisian life. When they had disappeared, Monsieur Cabrol, fatigued, treated himself to a little siesta in the shelter of a thicket of cacti and agaves, while Andoche and Moderan, reinvigorated by the sea breeze, set to work with the Cine-Tele University.

In the curse of a stroll, after a late-afternoon bath, Andoche restarted the conversation about Astra, the island fallen from the sky, with which he was in such a great hurry to become acquainted.

Monsieur Cabrol was still thinking about the hill of Montmartre, descended from its former rank of Parisian mountain.

"Yes," he said, "two or three centimeters a year, at first, then…."

"What's that? Astra, two or three centimeters?"

"No, the former Butte Montmartre.

"No, we were talking about Astra, the island we're going to see; we know it well thanks to the course in geography, but you were going to tell us details of its fall into the Pacific…"

"Oh yes. Well, you know that, in the course of the last century, someone at the Observatory noticed a perturbation in the sky one day, which had not yet been noticed by anyone else—and a most extraordinary perturbation. Something had to be happening somewhere in space, in the vast emptiness beyond the limits of observation, at a distance that could only be recorded with the aid of several 100 digits. But numbers aren't my business, as you know; beyond ten or 12 zeros, I'm finished. So, the Observatory observed a very tiny thing that had to be an explosion of suns, a tremor of worlds...

"Yes," said Andoche, "a jostling among a crowd of stars."

"Probably! The little thing that emerged from the jostle, scarcely visible, divined rather than perceived, took ten years—you can see how far away it was—to reach our atmosphere and become something like a tiny, very tiny planet. It insinuated itself into the company of larger ones, the more or less distant cousins of the Earth, the jolly family that Papa Sun draws in his wake through the immeasurable immensities of the sky—Jupiter, Venus, Mars—with whom we've been traveling through the ether for such a long time without even giving one another a few signs of amity, or even politeness. It was necessary to wait for our era to begin to send very vague and short messages over long distances and to try to understand the replies."

"But I have high hopes that we'll soon see them at close range, Uncle," said Andoche.

"Yes, yes, if you like—your father says so, at least, since he's entitled his company The Interastral Travel Agency, but his interastral airships have only got as far as the Moon as yet."

"Progress, Uncle!"

"Yes, Progress with three capital letters, if you like: PPProgress! But..."

"You're definitely behind the times, Uncle!"

"I'd like to think so."

Andoche and Moderan uttered scandalized exclamations.

"Then we're not going…"

"Perhaps! Setting all difficulties aside, though, by traveling with one's nurse, from the age of six months on, one might hope to disembark in one's ninetieth year or thereabouts, with a respectable white beard. That would be very nice, truly…but to get back to the little thing that the astronomers, already a little anxious, were following with their telescopes, at first it followed a very irregular course; it was as if it were performing waltz steps amid the large planets and their satellites, leaping here and there—I'm not an astronomer, so I can't attempt to describe its motion more accurately—but it was as if the large planets were playing ball with it and throwing it back and forth. That lasted for some time; then the little thing, rebuffed by the others, gave us its preference, headed toward us, and started rotating around us, behind the Moon…"

"I know: attracted into the orbit of the Moon," said Moderan gravely. "I read about that."

"Attraction, satellites…spout scientific terms," said Andoche. "Show that you can get your baccalaureate in science whenever you wish."

"If I wish!"

"I'll give it to you—but let the story continue…"

"Come on, no arguments. Listen: I'm not only concerned with the picturesque aspect of facts, myself, in my research on the political and social institutions of the Lunatics; I've taken note of some curious facts. I know that the poor Lunatics were much more annoyed than the Terrans when the indiscreet little morsel of a plant penetrated our system and started following the Moon in its orbit around us like a little dog, a satellite of our satellite. But that phase of the little thing's progress was only apparent. Subject to the attraction of the Earth, undoubtedly, the little thing finally adopted a regular path that brought it gradually closer to our terraqueous globe. To begin with, uninitiated Terrans were not overly worried; only the astronomers got excited and devoted themselves to studies and calculations regarding the intruder's trajectory. It was gaining speed perceptibly, and becoming more visible with every pass-

221

ing month. At first a simple point of light in the heavenly plains, the little new Moon gradually increased in intensity and in size. People unversed in astronomy were easily able to see that it was visibly closer, and everyone became anxious.

"The new Moon was still getting larger. The observatories were calculating. Ten years had already gone by since the appearance of the insignificant 'little thing.' It was not describing a regular orbit, however, like the old familiar Moon, but an ellipse, a spiral that would...no one dared say it, but they thought it—hurl it upon us, after an indeterminate, but perhaps not very long, interval.

"Drawn at a speed that was accelerating day by day, it was approaching with increasing rapidity,

"Another ten years passed; the little thing had grown considerably and took up more space in our sky than the Moon; its dimensions seemed to be doubling every month, an enormous Moon traveling toward us. It began to be visible during the day, suddenly appearing in gaps in the clouds, at points where one did not expect to find anything, very high or very low in the sky. Then the great panic began!"

"There was reason enough," said Andoche. "We, the young, know what happened; we accept the event without thinking about all the emotion, the extreme terror with which people must have gone through before the denouement. Brrr!"

"What happened next?" asked Moderan

"Oh, let me breathe—the weather's so good! The sky's so blue! It's hard to go back to those evil moments in thought!"

XII. A Planetary Fragment in the Pacific

A very restful day, sweet and beautiful. Sunlight to make colors vibrate; the yellow-tinged bright pink of the rocky soil; the cinnabar or emerald green of the vegetation—agaves pointing all their blades and giant cacti, palm trees swaying their fans—the darker green of gigantic mahogany trees, garlanded with lianas and plumed with flowers; thickets defended by 1000 thorns, inhabited by hundreds of birds of every color, adding shrill notes to the grating music of insects of every sort, swarming on all sides.

Phanor galloped everywhere, raising small game-birds; he danced with delight, already in rank amity with the children of the village. Babylas, more careful in his gait, glided through the foliage, prudently exploring the interior of bushes, swinging indolently on lianas or climbing trees in pursuit of birds that jeered at him and mocked him, perched in rows on the low branches. In her anxious solicitude, Melanie called him back continually; Babylas shut his eyes and continued to sniff the powerful aromas of the flowers and the scent of the chattering prey frolicking in the foliage.

When Babylas went to sleep in the heart of a palm tree, Melanie finally decided to go back inside, in order to start hunting herself, waving napkins at the insects that permitted themselves to invade the rooms, filling them with a hum of trombones and fifes. For the tranquility of the imminent night, it was necessary to get all the little creatures outside before dusk.

Monsieur Cabrol had started work, but it was very hot! After ten minutes of attention his eyes close of their own accord, and he slumped in his armchair without thinking about it. It seemed to him that the music was a lullaby; he sighed with contentment, stretched himself out and went to sleep voluptuously.

What a fine siesta! It lasted at least three hours, which went by too rapidly, and would probably have been prolonged if his nephews had not suddenly come in, rather noisily.

"Uncle, uncle! The Moons are rising!"

"Eh? What?" said Monsieur Cabrol, with a start.

"The Moons, Uncle—you know, the Moons of the mountain, out there!"

"It's already dark—how did that happen? I'd hardly dropped off…"

Indeed, dusk had arrived very quietly; the Sun had finished taking its invariable evening bath on the other side of
the mountains, in the immensity of the Pacific, and, as they
did every evening, the volcanoes were becoming visible, some
mere fumaroles and others little gleams or fiery projections.

"Us too, Uncle! As it's no longer very bright, our eyes
are beginning to close. It's rather elegant, that illumination
over there. What if we were to go and see it at closer range?"

"We'll go, but not this evening; it's too far, we wouldn't
have enough time to make the trip. Let's see—we have to go
northwards toward Yucatan and come back down to Panama.
Tomorrow, perhaps, if the weather seems favorable."

"And what about the story of Astra, Uncle?" Andoche
said. "The planetary fragment fallen into the Pacific? You left
it at the moment when the people of Earth were beginning to
dread something. I'd like to have been there."

"Damn it! I was there, a little later, when it actually
fell—and I shivered like everyone else in the world!"

"I would have shivered with you—I like violent emotions...when everything comes out well, naturally."

"Let's go up to the top floor, to contemplate the volcanoes. I'll finish my story for you."

They went up into a little upstairs room equipped with a
large window, and installed themselves on the balcony. It was
a trifle cramped, but they discovered such a broad section of
horizon there that it recompensed them somewhat for the seats
being too close together. The sunset had been less incandescent than the previous one; now it was completely extin-
guished, darkened into a violet ultramarine, almost black, over
which the volcanoes loosed their flames and red smoke.

"Yes," said Monsieur Cabrol, "When it was evident to
everyone that the little thing wandering in the sky was getting
closer to the Earth with every rotation, and that it was bound
to fall on the surface, everyone shivered with fear. Where
would it fall? What country would receive the impact? What
part of the world would be struck by the frightful projectile,
and undoubtedly crushed, pulverized? Would it be the old

continent, the cradle of civilization, or another? Naturally, everyone thought: 'Just so long as it's not on us that the sky falls!'

"I was there; I remember. I was your age, and like everyone else I followed the preparatory phases of the immense catastrophe suspended over our heads passionately. The fate of our entire planet was at stake!

"And that accursed morsel of broken planet that threatened to destroy everything was still growing! It was clearly visible by day now, and I don't whether it was more terrifying for us then than by night. It arrived in a corner of the sky, sailed through violently disturbed clouds and traversed a part of our horizon. The astronomers were lost in their calculations; they were trying to measure its exact orbit in order to try to discover the threatened location, and the discussions were never-ending. The scientists did not understand the nature of the bolide. What was it, exactly? What was its composition? A solid body, a fragment of a planet, or a nascent planet? Molten matter? Brrr!

"Everything stopped, all business abandoned in almost every country. People became more insane as time went by. The suspense became unbearable.

"The spiral followed by the monstrous projectile shrank. Soon, binoculars could distinguish its exact form. The frightful bolide was not a sphere, but an elongated, irregular mass, sharpened by its progress, which plunged into the atmosphere, crumbling slightly, for it scattered small fragments of its surface, aeroliths of all sizes, some of which were received in Europe.

"Their analysis removed the doubts as to the composition of the body; it was very similar in nature to our Earth. The projectile was known, it had been measured and weighed; it was a considerable morsel, almost equal to France and Spain amalgamated, perhaps with Switzerland added on.

"The point of impact remained to be determined; that was more difficult.

"It was necessary to see the anguished populations gathering in the evenings in the grand plazas of cities or on hills to watch the monster rise over the horizon. The people bent down beneath the terrible menace, huddled against one another, some lying flat on the ground hiding their heads in their hands, eyes closed. People spoke in whispers. News items circulated, all causing greater anguish to some than others; there was talk of earthquakes, volcanic eruptions and the antipodes and everywhere...eruptions that were doubtless only the first sparks of a general explosion of our unfortunate condemned world!

"And when the bolide, lit up by a sinister flame, began to rise over the horizon, a great cry went up above the crowds, who, standing up abruptly, started to flee in all directions in search of illusory refuges, no matter where—in the depths of woods, behind some molehill, or even in the cellars of houses.

"And by day, the sinister shadow of the formidable bolide arrived over us, covering the countryside and the cities—a terrifying eclipse that lasted for long minutes and augmented the panic. A few more upheavals were produced on the surface, for we saw jets of vapor shooting up from various places and swirling for a long time in heavy cloudy masses.

"That final phase of the event lasted for months on end; it was soon evident to the scientists, resigned to everything, and the people who had conserved a little calm, that the denouement was near. Finally!

"For all those who were still resisting the universal panic, it was a veritable relief; it was the end of the torture.

"The monstrous bolide was orbiting ever more closely, and closer still; the details of its surface were discernible, the bristling of mountains and hollows where shiny threads ran, which had to be rivers or streams. It arrived amid a frightful rumbling of hurricanes and storms which went on for weeks, incessantly...

"And suddenly, the end came. One morning, I remember, the Sun didn't rise—or, rather, couldn't pierce the thick layer of black cloud that covered all of nature! In that Stygian obscurity, we waited. The Earth seemed to be holding its breath beneath our feet. For hours on end there were earthquakes, the rumbling and growling of storms without end; then the release; the noise diminished slowly; it seemed that nature was uttering long sighs. Gradually, everyone raised their heads; we looked at one another, pale and trembling, without daring to ask questions, but with the sensation that the peril had passed.

"Where had the event taken place? How? What region of the world had been crushed by the impact?

"For a day and a night, we knew nothing. Communication by wireless radio and other means was totally disrupted, confused in crazy currents of rays and waves. It was necessary to wait, to be patient! But we were safe, that was the main thing. Egotistical reasoning, but natural to everyone....

"The observatories already knew; eventually, the news arrived and was spread!"

XIII. The Great Tidal Wave

"There it was! The morsel of an unknown planet, projected toward us by some unknown fabulous explosion from the extremity of the solar world, had not grazed any continental region or pulverized any capital. The great terror was over!

"It had fallen into the middle of the Pacific Ocean, in the place where it would do the least harm. That was providential! What a stroke of luck!

"Before having the details, we feared for the sixth continent; we were quickly reassured. The point of impact had been south of the equator, between the Marquesas, the little Hawaiian archipelago and the sixth continent constructed in the 20th century.

"A few islets in the dust of islands scattered in that region undoubtedly disappeared beneath the enormous mass, along with ships and indigenous canoes, unless everything that had been at sea had fled from the menace much earlier. A large island was born, 400 kilometers long and 300 kilometers broad—a considerable island, rocky and mountainous, as much so and more than any mountainous corner of our old Earth bristling with peaks torn to shreds, pitted with holes and difficult of access.

"The bolide's fall led to frightful catastrophes, which disturbed a large part of the world. Terrifying tidal waves ravaged the coasts of North and South America; the waters broke through all the weak points the isthmus of Panama, Yucatan and Costa Rica, devastating regions, causing all the volcanic cauldrons of the coast to explode and ruining hundreds of towns, from the coasts of China and Japan on the Asian side to the glacial seas of the North, where Kamchatka suffered particularly badly. It was the same for the Australian coasts and the regions of the South Pole.

"That fantastic tidal wave, a fury of waves, was propagated by successive shocks as far as the coasts of Normandy and Brittany. Fortunately, people didn't go sea bathing much during the great menace, otherwise there would have been many more casualties.

"The great wave did not reach us until three days after the fall. What a mess! The formidable wave turned everything upside-down, lifting up and bearing away boats, beach cabins and the roofs of collapsed villas—and hurling all of that far inland, over jetties, cliffs and dykes. The tidal wave made the rivers and streams that emptied into the sea around our coasts flow backwards.

"I have a little personal souvenir of the effect of the tidal wave on us—perhaps I've told you about it already. Three or four days after the event, my parents were leaving for the seaside to calm their emotions and recover a taste for life after such a threat, for we, like everyone else, were both joyful and worn out, like convalescents going out for the first time after a serious illness.

"We were entitled to a little vacation anyway; it was the right time—the beginning of August. My father judged that the bank could do without him for another five or six weeks; it was necessary to give business the time to wake up from its deep torpor. We were in our nice little villa in Poulingen; your mother was playing with her dolls or her friends on the beach. As for me, I began to find existence delightful again, and rolled in the sand in front of the house without a care.

"Although the weather as fine and very warm, the sea was rough away from the shore, but I was finally able to try out my hydroplane and my little rowing canoe in an inlet. I had finished with the hydroplane; the weather became duller, and I was rowing slowly when the foaming wave suddenly arrived, without warning, with the noise of a hurricane, scaling and breaking everything. I was on the crest of it before I could say *oof!* I was lifted up, carried off and thrown over I don't know what—walls, sheds, beach huts—and hurled with a pell-mell of little pieces of broken objects on to a clump of flowering bushes at the back of a garden...without sustaining any damage, fortunately, splashing in a tide of foam, bewildered, beneath torrents of dirty water that continued to pour from the open sea over my head, with bunches of algae torn from the sea-bed.

"What a shower! Around me, plunged in the tide, beach-huts arrived by way of the air, with loungers, deck-chairs, ladies and gentlemen who had taken a similar route, children and nurses, a donkey, legs in the air, and geese even more bewildered than me.

"A violent bore swept up the Loire, carrying away all the boats; ships in port were dragged away with their anchors and followed the boats they met or ran aground on the bank, in the grass, when they did not end up in the riverside houses, where the water rose as far as the upper floors. Bridges cracked under the pressure of the water and were also carried away.

"During this time, I shook myself, rubbed myself and, as I definitely had not broken anything, watched the phenomenon open-mouthed while waiting for the next phase. Nearby, women and children bearded with foam were still splashing around; I helped them to get out of the lake and climb into the house, where the water as cascading down the stairs. The women were weeping and crying that it was another bolide, a second one, raining from the sky. It was the end; the universe was coming apart; the worlds, their foundations having been worn away for such a long time, were being demolished and the pieces were falling on our heads!

"You can imagine what I went through, emotionally! Finally, observing that nothing more was coming, that the sea was continuing the racket it made in bad weather but no longer seemed to be thinking of overflowing, I reassured myself conclusively and set forth to make sure that my parents were safe and that the house hadn't suffered serious damage.

"As for my boats, I could be proud of them; they had both made the voyage to Nantes in the state of bits of wood, for the stern of the canoe was recovered a little while later on the old Quai de la Fosse and the prow of my little hydroplane in the Île Feydeau.

"That wasn't all. The following day, at the same time, there was a further tidal wave, a little less violent; the day after that, another, further diminished, and every day for three weeks there was a similar palpitation of the Atlantic, of decreasing strength, until the Ocean too recovered from its great shock."

"I wish I'd been there!" said Moderan.

"Me too!" said Andoche, looking at his uncle with envious eyes.

"Do you think I've finished with the more or less serious consequences of the arrival of the traveling island?" Monsieur Cabrol continued. "Oh no! The voyager through interplanetary space, taking its abrupt dive into the middle of the Pacific, caused many other perturbations. Oh, at first, I didn't even catch cold, in spite of my unexpected bath and the showers that subsequently fell upon my head—nor did anyone else, I believe, for the water was warm; the tidal wave gratified us all with showers that were sometimes even too hot; there were doubtless a few cold billows, but immediately followed by volumes of overheated seawater in which half-cooked fish were dying. Oh, the poor fish!—they were found all along the coast, trying to swim in the fields: shoals of rays, sole or whiting heaped up in the estates, where the peasants, delighted with the windfall, hastened to gather them up. I saw two living seals, jumping, flexing themselves and jumping again, with great difficulty, along the road, trying to get back to the sea, uttering plaintive cries at every hop, like the whimpering of dogs or the wailing of children: the lamentations of innocent animals who had no understanding at all of what had so brutally afflicted their native element."

"Poor seals! Did they succeed in getting home?" asked Moderan.

"Alas, in the main square of Poulingen, when they thought they were almost safe, there was a circus tent that the water was threatening to carry away. The people were working to consolidate its moorings during the final wave; the two joyful seals, barking more loudly, were engulfed by the canvas; there, splashing around, entangled with ropes, chairs and musical instruments, they were easily captured by the acrobats and imprisoned in large basins."

"Poor seals!!" the good-hearted Moderan groaned, again.

"Bah!" said Andoche. "They enjoyed a more agreeable existence thereafter than the depths of the Greenland sea from which they came would have been able to give them. They made their tour of France with the circus and friendly clowns, more amusing than the polar bears of the ice-sheet…"

"Poor polar bears!" said Monsieur Cabrol.

"What? Poor polar bears, uncle?"

"But yes! You don't know. I can't tell you about all the repercussions of that formidable tidal wave, which turned all the world's seas upside down, but there were particularly disagreeable consequences for the polar bears of the North, inhabiting the snowbound countries or the polar ice-cap. Poor beasts!"

"Nice little animals!" said Andoche.

"Imagine them, our polar bears, accustomed to their immutable white plains, their icebergs, the solidity of their oceans of ice, shaken up by the first explosions of the ice-sheet, when the waves of the tropical seas arrived in scalding waterspouts! The depths of whole oceans disturbed by the fall of Astra, warm seas thrown over the coasts, awakening volcanoes, creating crazy currents—which, overflowing the old habitual routes, went to assail the barrier ice of the Pole, in the vicinity of Kamchatka, where dozens of volcanoes erupted in flames in their turn, and even reached the shores of Europe through the Panama breaches and went to attack the ice-sheets of Spitzbergen.

"And there goes the North Pole, heated up by warm squalls above and seething billows below—it was the right time to visit it, but no one thought of it. There goes the ice-cap, bursting and shattering, torrents of warm water spouting from every hole, icebergs melting like sorbets...

"Can you imagine the distress of the polar bears, or other game-animals of the white solitudes, surprised by the catastrophe? 50 degrees below freezing turning to 40 degrees above, or more, volcanic eruptions under the ice, the boiling of the waves, the vortices of scalding vapor, the geysers of hot water! And the poor polar bears, the seals, the walruses, the penguins, the entire animal population of barely habitable countries, frightened, overheated, burned, cooked, fleeing the hot water for the melting ice—perishing, for the most part!

"It was like that for a month or two after the event—so many corpses of animals unknown in our country washing up on our coasts. For our part, one morning, we found a half-dead penguin in our garden, and 20 polar bear corpses were collected on the beach at Pornichet, parboiled or drowned!"

XIV. Here, once, was the Moon.

The Villa Beauséjour spent a very pleasant week in that little corner of Guatemala: a week of complete tranquility, with the weather set fair; no more worries. There was nothing to do but let themselves live, descending every morning by a rapid path to the beach, in order to bathe, and climbing back up in the afternoon for a siesta in the shade of a mahogany tree whose tumbling lianas made a sort of flowery and moving bower, like a great aviary in which hundreds of variously-plumaged birds lived, fluttered and sang.

They were so happy there, and yet they thought of nothing but getting away from it.

Andoche and Moderan were dreaming of the island of Astra, a little piece of the planet Mars, fallen so luckily in the great emptiness of the Pacific 30 years before. They were so close to it now—scarcely 1000 kilometers away! Impatience also took hold of Monsieur Cabrol.

The departure date was finally fixed; one last stroll through the Guatemalan village and the pleasant neighboring town, which felt so distant from the oppressive industrial machinery of the North, and the following day, at the earliest opportunity, they would leave.

A fine day, a good siesta, a tranquil night. Morning has come. The clearing up for the departure is soon done. The apparatus is checked. Babylas is shut in so that he will not go astray in the exuberant surrounding vegetation in pursuit of small birds. Phanor, more reasonable, watches the preparations from the balcony. He has understood, and seems quite melancholy at the thought of abandoning such a tranquil abode.

It is 9 a.m. The Villa Beauséjour oscillates on its foundations, stirs, turns round, then gently rises into the air; it surpasses the fans of the highest palms and begins to describe a great circle in the sky in order to review all the details of the landscape.

All the indigenes of the surrounding area are down below, waving and shouting, bidding them farewell. Signs of amity are made in response, and joyful *au revoirs*, with which the brave Phanor joins in, capering on the balcony and barking hoarsely. The Aerovilla heads eastwards and gradually gains speed.

"We have time; it's sufficient to arrive at Astra in daylight, so we can make a little detour in the direction of the volcanoes; if that's interesting, we can stay there for a day or two..."

"No, no, Uncle, I beg you," said Andoche. "You've told us too much about Astra!"

In less than half an hour the Villa Beauséjour reached the line of volcanoes scattered along the Pacific coast, on the mountain peaks of Guatemala and the isthmus of Tehuantepec. In the daylight, the volcanoes are less imposing. Here and there, smoke rises up in swirls, fumaroles escaping from dark holes with fiery dots at the bottom of profound craters, in a frame of scorched rocks, often devoid of vegetation—and that is all.

To the south, all the fractures of the former isthmus of Panama were visible: great breaches opened up by the terrible fury of the waves kicked up at the moment of Astra's fall. They could make out the immense works undertaken to rectify the irregular fractures, consolidate the debris of the isthmus and remodel the bedrock between the two Americas, according to carefully-drawn-up plans.

This region of the world had suffered an abrupt ruination that was purely accidental; it was not, as it was at home in old Europe, an exhaustion produced by centuries of intensive wear and tear. Here there had been populations that were by no means numerous, in a rich and prodigal nature—the Aztecs the Toltecs, or less well-known Indian tribes. In Europe, so many generations of tenants had succeeded on another, using and abusing the old Earth.

The Villa Beauséjour, veering deliberately eastwards, gained a few 100 meters in height. A splendid Sun illuminated the atmosphere, where they were fortunate to encounter a light breeze, after the dull heat of the overheated rocks of the mountains.

Ahead, the entire immensity of the Pacific seemed to be striped by long white waves. To the north and south there was the same immense emptiness. They seemed to be going into space. There was not the slightest interruption: a complete void above and below; not the slightest cloud or any little aircraft in a pure sky; not the smallest island in view in the liquid infinity below.

Andoche and Moderan stood open-mouthed with admiration, and Monsieur Cabrol no longer breathed a word. It was too vast, too beautiful. Into that infinity they plunged at 50 kilometers an hour, without perceiving the slightest dot moving in the depths of the sky or on the surface of the waves. Monsieur Cabrol, however, suddenly recovered the power of movement and speech. He straightened up, and his arm, describing a great circle, made a tour of the horizon.

"Well, my boys," he said, "you can grasp all of this in a single glance—the famous violet hole of the Pacific."

"What violet hole, Uncle?"

"That immensity filled by the sea, the enormous void without a single islet since Mexico and Panama, since the long chain of mountains bordering the coasts without interruption—you can see it clearly." His gesture embraced the entire horizon. "Here, my boys, is where the Moon used to be!"

"What did you say, Uncle?"

"I said that here, once, a very long time ago—perhaps hundreds of thousands of years—, and well before the birth of humankind, before all the cave-dwellers and our remote prehistoric ancestors—was the Moon…"

Andoche and Moderan looked at one another. "Our Moon? The true one?"

"It's not me who affirms it, it's the scientists. Oh, that must have been an upheaval greater than the arrival of Astra, the departure of a fragment of our globe at the moment of a dislocation of the terrestrial carcass, caused by some explosion of the central fire. Try to imagine that! Explosions, eruptions, upheavals, more explosions…suddenly the Earth bursts, a fragment is separates and sets off into space, a monstrous projectile, which cannot escape terrestrial gravitational attraction and, having become a satellite of the Earth, begins to follow it in its course, rotating around it. And there you are! The Earth has lost a large part of itself, but it has gained a faithful companion for its eternal journey through space."

"The night-star so precious to poets!" said Andoche.

"And what economy of lighting, for so many centuries!" said Moderan. "Try to calculate it!"

"Yes, but let's not forget Astra, uncle!" said Andoche. "It's very empty, immensely empty, here—there are no reference-points. Aren't we going to get lost over these infinite waves? Have you made sure of our course, Uncle?"

"Now that we've admired it properly and our eyes are sufficiently drunk on space, we can go back to our apparatus."

Melanie, who had been listening with Babylas in her arms, looked alternately at the sky and the sea, frowning anxiously, hugging and caressing the cat and groaning in a whisper: "My poor Babylas! My poor Babylas!"

"What's wrong, Melanie?" asked Monsieur Cabrol.

"Nothing, Monsieur. I'm talking to Babylas to reassure him. Poor plump beast! Perhaps I was wrong to bring him. You said, Monsieur, that the Moon was going to come out of that big hole down there below us—or that it was going to fall into it...I don't know; I didn't quite grasp it..."

"No, Melanie—reassure yourself and reassure Babylas; it happened a long time ago, so long that scientists can't specify the number of centuries, not knowing how to count so high!"

"Oh, good!" said Melanie, uttering a sigh of relief. "I don't trust scientists...I'm afraid of them. But I'm tranquil again if it's as old as that, and I can go and prepare my lunch. In five minutes, Monsieur, the pills will be served..."

"Very good! The pure fresh air has given us an appetite."

Monsieur Cabrol was already at the controls; he made a note of the heading shown by the indicator, rectified the course slightly, and checked the speed. Everything was going well; it was half an hour after noon; by 2 p.m., they would be flying over Astra—and they were able to go to table in total tranquility, idling at length after the coffee pills while awaiting their arrival.

The sky remained limpid, still a cloudless azure, but the sea as no longer so empty. A few islands were perceptible in the distance, minuscule green patches that had to be part of the Marquesas archipelago. Andoche jumped for joy; they were getting nearer. The needle of the indicator was turning rapidly. Another quarter of an hour of fidgeting n the balcony, wearing out the eyes searching the brightness.

Finally, three exclamations resounded, answered by Melanie's squeal and Babylas' miaow. Astra was in view. Phanor, who had been sleeping in perfect serenity, rolled between his master's legs, jumped to his feet and barked. Like all dogs accustomed to traveling, or trips in aircraft, he barked at the sky, running on the balcony, looking to see whether some visitor might be arriving by air.

They were beginning to make out Astra: an indistinct patch, at first, which grew larger and became gradually clearer, until a light and vaporous silhouette was outlined. Finally, the whole ensemble appeared: a large mountainous island, long and irregular, with extraordinarily uneven shores, rapidly elevating sheer slopes furrowed by undulating or zigzagging ravines, then bare Sun-burned plateaux, rust-colored rocks surging forth in the midst of hick forests, and, looming over everything in the center of the island, an enormous mountain surrounded by a girdle of bizarrely-shaped reddish peaks.

"It's even better than the Caucasian Archipelago!" Andoche exclaimed. "Let's land right away."

XV. Arrival on Astra Island.

Monsieur Cabrol moderated their speed, however, and descended to 500 meters, in order not to miss any details of the architecture of the extraordinary island, and to carry out a preliminary reconnaissance before touching down on the mysterious soil.

"My dear Andoche, one doesn't venture forth in such a place without first looking where one's putting one's feet. What do we know about it? Nothing very certain. What is this traveling island? Where did it me from? According to the most up-to-date opinion of the scientists, it's a fragment of the planet Mars. I'd like to...."

"That's been known for 20 years," said the impatient Andoche.

"I'd like to...but what shall we find among these rocks, in these ravines, in the depths of these wild-seeming woods? I'd like to study it for a while before taking any risks. What will we encounter?"

"Fossils," said Andoche, bursting into laughter.

"With you, at the Museum," said Moderan, "I've seen skeletons of animals as extraordinary in shape as in size."

"Fabulous livestock which came from here."

"Yes, but if, by chance, in one of these jolly corners riddled with caves and holes that don't bode well to me, we suddenly come across nose to muzzle, or nose to trunk, with one of those pretty creatures with frightful mouths and the horns of a super-rhinoceros, beneath its fangs and claws, what will you say to excuse the indiscretion of your visit?"

"You're joking, Uncle."

"I'm not laughing at all. I'm only remembering what happened to the first visitors, a few days after Astra's fall. You don't know? What does one learn at school these days? What does your Tele-Universal University teach you?"

"Everything, but in order."

"We haven't reached modern history yet, and Astra is only 20 years old."

"Then you don't know what happened. Listen—it's a stirring little adventure. At the first news of Astra's arrival, England hastened to send a large airship to take possession of it. Its men disembarked, and their first concern was to erect a mast on a high cliff, with a flag flying as high as possible, while they sent radio messages to announce that they had taken possession. All went well; there was nothing more to do but await a governor and people.

"What happened? No one knows. That very night, the entire crew was devoured by ferocious beasts and the dirigible moored on the beach was ripped apart. That was observed by a second dirigible, this one American, which arrived in the early hours of the morning, also to take possession. Seized with horror at the sight of the debris of the English expedition, the Americans had started searching for possible survivors, when they were attacked in their turn by all the ferocious beasts of the entire region, which had converged on the landing-ground."

"Uh-oh!"

"And without a doubt, there was no one left. No one knows anything about that, because the American expedition was also devoured in its entirety, as a third airship was able to observe, which flew over the battleground that same evening, just as the ferocious beasts, satiated, were beginning to go to sleep on the remains of the feast. That third expedition was Japanese; it had, therefore, the good fortune to be warned before disembarking, as to what awaited it. It was immediately embroiled in conflict.

The dirigible stayed 25 meters above the ground; the battlefield was a terrible sight, swarming with unknown beasts crawling or fluttering over the bones, howling and yapping with the voices of cracked trumpets, quarrelling over the horrible debris; there were long bodies armored with large scales, massive beasts half-cayman and half-rhinoceros, armed with enormous clawed feet, and serpents with short legs and the membranous wings of bats. All that terrifying swarm of filthy beasts woke up at the sight of the Japanese dirigible; the horned muzzles were raised in the air and began a concert of covetous howling; paws stretched out toward the new prey that had arrived, and long scaly bodies uncoiled, ready to attack. A few pterodactyls took off, trying to fly up to the dirigible.

"Damn!" said Andoche. "Fortunately, the Japanese were on their guard."

"And also ready to attack! They had electric machine-guns and two cannons firing paralyzing shells, and when they opened fire on the swarming mass of monsters, it must have been a fine spectacle."

"I'd like to have seen that!" said Andoche.

"The pterodactyls, which were beating their wings furiously to climb, and some of which succeeded in catching hold of the dirigible by the nails of their membranes, were also struck down, and fell back among the hideous monsters that were writhing desperately on the ground."

"And what became of the Japanese dirigible?"

"The men, full of ardor, joyful at their triumph, took stock of the infernal game they had shot, finishing off those which, in their last spasms, were trying to bite a leg or unleash a thrust of a horn, or one last kick of their powerfully-armed feet. A few of the monsters had been hit by the paralyzing projectiles; they made haste to separate those out and photograph them from every angle before carefully chaining them up, according to the instructions they had been given.

"A few of the monsters had been able to escape the slaughter—mainly reptiles, which had taken refuge in holes in the rocks. A contingent of the crew gave chase.

"How do you know that, Uncle?"

"From the report of the Japanese expedition itself. It caused a sensation 20 years ago. Many curiosity-seekers were preparing to make excursions to the new isle at that time; the report cooled them down somewhat. Only lovers of big game hunting, deprived of violent cynegetic delights since the extinction of the last ferocious beasts in Africa, and scientists ardently inflamed by the idea of a fragment of an unknown plant to study, solicited authorization from the Japanese government to land on the dangerous ground—for Japan had immediately taken possession and sent colonists with a governor and a commission of scientists. After occupying Astra, the Japanese strove to clear the island of game, to purge it, in the manner of Hercules, of its monsters, which were as dangerous as they were interesting—but the island is large, and it has a very extensive coastline, with rocky fissures extending into and becoming confused with the gorges of shattered mountains: all conditions favorable to the survival of those nightmare beasts. So…"

"So, Uncle, we're going to select a little treeless spot, tranquil in appearance, to moor our Villa Beauséjour?"

"No, first we're going to Astraville, the capital, to get our papers stamped and obtain a license to stay. There, we'll find all the necessary information, plus a certain amount of advice that won't be useless to us."

"Look, Uncle—some houses down below!"

Moderan, who was searching the coast with his binoculars, pointed to white patches and red roofs, a few kilometers away at the most.

Monsieur Cabrol consulted a small map of the island, on which only a few locations were marked.

"We're arriving at the North-West coast, that's certain—that must be the island's capital. There aren't many inhabited places. We'll be there in five minutes."

The Villa veered slightly to the right and proceeded slowly, along a coast punctuated by narrow fjords, cliff-lined fissures and larger coves, strewn with sharp rocks, on beds of shingle or sand. Monsieur Cabrol sent a radio message, giving his name and his port of origin, to alert Astraville. A few minutes later, the Villa Beauséjour was hovering over a slightly larger cove, through which a little stream, winding through reeds, descended in cascades from a distant brush-covered mountain.

Monsieur Cabrol was struck by the Japanese appearance of the site: steep crags, bizarrely twisted small trees, a rivulet strewn with little rocks, describing its curves between tall reeds and clumps of flowers and lily-pads: an entire landscape extracted from Japanese albums of long ago; a Hokusai print.

"It's very pleasant!" said Monsieur Cabrol.

"And over there," said Moderan, "the central peak of the island—one might imagine it as Fujiyama, to complete the resemblance."

On one side of the main square they perceived a landing-ground where a few miniplanes were sheltering under a marquee.

The Villa Beauséjour came gently to rest. A few Japanese ran forward very obligingly to assist its maneuvering.

Monsieur Cabrol was flattered; they seemed to be looking at the Villa Beauséjour admiringly. These people, so far away from everything else, did not see many others apart from the rare airships of the South American lines, and they were glad to receive unexpected visitors.

As soon as he was on the ground, Monsieur Cabrol sought information, without the need for an interpreter, using the international dialect—a mixture of French, Italian, English, Spanish, Japanese, and even Latin.

"Are we in Astraville? Good! I need to ask for a permit for a short stay. Will I be able to see the governor?"

"Certainly, Monsieur—there's the Governor's palace, the red house over there, where the flag is flying."

It was only a short walk away. Leaving the Villa in Melanie's care, Monsieur Cabrol went to ring the doorbell of the governor's house. The latter was contemplating the Villa Beauséjour from his balcony.

The radio had given forewarning of the arrival; he received the visitors amiably.

"We don't often have visitors in Astra, my dear Monsieur," the governor said, "And I'm delighted to welcome you. Your first impression is good?"

"Very good—your island seems to me to be extremely picturesque, and I hope you will oblige me with some advice as to our excursions. We've come from Paris, with the intention of traveling for a few years, in order to escape the annoyance and the noise of the immense works undertaken for the great resurfacing of old Europe, which is in much need of it. In your refuge, so tranquil in the middle of the Pacific, you

242

can have no suspicion, Monsieur le Gouverneur, of the noise of the upheaval…

"Our intention is to stay here for a while, time to study the unknown nature of this traveling island, which, after having orbited our Earth for 60 years, came to settle—so to speak—on the deep bed of the Pacific, beneath this magnificent sky."

"Magnificent," the governor repeated.

"First of all, Monsieur le Gouverneur, have you any idea of where Astra came from, to set down here? Do you think that it is a fragment of the planet Mars, as certain astronomers have suggested?"

"It's quite probable; Mars is our nearest neighbor."

"We're very glad to be on the soil of another planet, and we're going to take some long walks. Is there any danger, Monsieur le Gouverneur?"

The governor became serious. "I'll indicate to you, Monsieur, the regions of the island where you can go abroad without danger…while always remaining on guard, however. They're not very numerous, as you can see this map that we've drawn up. I'll also point out the regions where the risk of unfortunate encounters is great, then the parts marked 'considerable danger' and those which are absolutely forbidden, because no one ever comes back from them."

"We shan't go there!" exclaimed Moderan.

The governor smiled. "We've posted notices: *Entry forbidden*, without adding, *on pain of a fine*—a futile penalty, since no one comes back to pay it."

"Then there are still ferocious beasts on Astra?" said Monsieur Cabrol. "That's very interesting, from a scientific viewpoint. Wild beasts very different, no doubt, from those of our old world?"

"Very!" said the governor. "A jolly collection—a wide variety of species heavily armed for combat; we know something about them, because for 15 years, since the first day of our arrival m Astra, we've been trying to get rid of them. A huge task, Monsieur, but interesting, from a scientific viewpoint…

"In the 15 years that our scientific commissions, our geologists and naturalists, have been exploring Astra in all direction—guarded by solid escorts, of course—we've been able to establish a few facts. Firstly, the isle was detached from a planet less advanced in its evolution than our old Earth; that planet was only in a period corresponding approximately to our Secondary Era. It has therefore brought us a Secondary Era fauna. It transported through the ether, very much alive, all the strange beasts that we only know as more or less complete skeletons discovered in excavations of the successive strata of the ground. Those enormous fantastic animals, whose restored skeletons you have seen in Museums: armored or scaly beasts, armed with long sharp claws, with horns on the end of the nose, backs bristling with spikes, membranous wings…"

"More and more interesting," said Monsieur Cabrol.

"Well, if those beasts interest you, it will be easy for you to encounter them in a complete state, alive—all too alive—by straying into the mountains. But I don't advise it, for you'll be able acquaint yourselves with them without risk soon enough, in a little zoological garden established behind my house, where we keep the results of our hunts, the animals caught in our traps, and dead animals dissected and mounted by our employees. Those are destined to be sent to Tokyo, after which they'll be generously redistributed. We're supplying them to all the Museums n the world."

"I know," said Monsieur Cabrol.

"But dusk is falling. Stay in the garage for now and tomorrow morning, while giving you your temporary residence permit, I'll be glad to show you the little Astraville Museum…"

XVI. The Governor's Collections.

Monsieur Cabrol returned to the Villa rubbing his hands and frowning, anxious and delighted at the same time. He had scarcely expected to encounter, in the mid-30th century, living specimens of the fabulous animals of prehistoric eras! He had expected to bring back a few little souvenirs of Astra, the new island still so little-known, for his collections—but what good luck and what promises!

Let's wait and see how it comes out before rejoicing, he immediately thought, *the advertised game is a little on the large side and too powerfully-armed.*

The night was superb, but a trifle warm; it was necessary to keep the windows open. After two hours of sound sleep he woke up. All was calm; the gilded crescent of the Moon was rising into the blue above the somber outline of the mountains. He could not help thinking about all the animals he had once studied in courses in paleontology. There was more to them than their fangs and claws; some of those animals also possessed wings. Damn it! What if some great pterodactyl, avoiding traps and barriers, were to fall from the sky upon the Villa Beauséjour?

He shrugged his shoulders, calling himself a coward, and tried to go back to sleep. But just then, Phanor, sleeping in the open, growled dully in a dream. Sleep fled. Monsieur Cabrol got up and went to look out of the window. The bright Moon illuminated the course of the clouds. No, no nasty beasts in sight, on the ground or in the sky.

As he closed his eyes again, Phanor, in his turn, stood up and bounded toward the window, snarling and growling. Roaring burst forth in the darkness, followed by strangely-modulated yapping and ferocious barking, sharp enough to hurt the eardrums. Phanor, no longer able to hold back, leapt into the room, frightened, growling furiously at the sinister yapping. It was an authentic Stone Age concert, interesting as

245

music by virtue of its strange accents—but how could anyone sleep, now?

The Moon, drifting through the clouds, cast suspicious shadows on the floor. Monsieur Cabrol thought about the particularly redoubtable reptiles of the Secondary Epoch. Utterly resigned, he plumped up his pillow with blows of his fist and buried his head underneath it to force himself to sleep—but it was the same all night long. Phanor continued to sniff at the window with muffled growls.

Of course! Monsieur Cabrol said to himself. *It's those wretched beasts in the governor's Museum.*

Finally, dawn arrived. Monsieur Cabrol was finally about to go to sleep when he heard his nephews get down from to the balcony and go out of the Villa to take a short walk around the garage in the fresh morning air.

"Well," said their uncle, when they reappeared three quarters of an hour later, "did you sleep well?"

"Perfectly. We've just taken a look around; we were impatient to see something. Astraville isn't much of a capital—two dozen houses, two large barracks built, like the houses, on colonnades of reinforced concrete, in order to allow free circulation beneath....bizarre constructions."

I know why that is, Monsieur Cabrol thought. *It's in case vile little beasts try to come and eat the inhabitants.*

"Oh, and there's the Museum enclosure," said Andoche, "surrounded by a triple barrier and formidable grilles. I don't know what goes on behind them, but strange noises can be heard there."

"Good—we'll see soon enough; I have the governor's promise."

But Monsieur Cabrol was as impatient as his nephews. As soon as breakfast was over, he went out with them to take a walk around the town. The Governor's Palace was not at all sumptuous, but it was constructed in the old Japanese style and was not lacking in picturesque qualities, prudently perched as it was, like the other houses, on stout reinforced concrete pillars. A dragon sculpted in wood was mounting guard in front of the flagpole. Monsieur Cabrol thought that the old dragon, with its red tongue and large round eyes, was an artistic scarecrow, and must have seen many others, just as spiky but more real, better armed and more dangerous than itself.

A stroke of a gong announced that the governor was waiting for the visitors in his study. Very amicably, he gave Monsieur Cabrol the temporary residence permit, along with a detailed map of the island to facilitate the travelers' excursions.

"Before anything else," he said, "you must see our little beasts; I intend to introduce them myself to the distinguished scientist who has come so far to study the zoological curiosities of our little Astra. A pretty country, Monsieur, but a little strange, as you'll see!"

His Excellency had a few large-screen films of extremely picturesque Astralian landscapes displayed on the Tele, then a more dramatic film, taken after the arrival of the first Japanese dirigible, on the first day, amid the debris of the English and American expeditions.

Andoche, extremely interested, declared that he would have liked to have been there.

The governor smiled. "I was there," he said. "It was a bit lively, but I'm proud to have witnessed the first encounter between modern man and those fantastic animals, those revenants of ancient eras! They have rude jaws, those fabulous monsters; I know something about that."

The governor lifted his left arm and tapped the leg on the same side.

"Oh!" said the visitors. The left arm and leg were nothing but successful specimens of surgical technology.

"They work very well," said the governor, "but I preferred the others. The arm had the honor of being bitten off by a plesiosaur of enormous size. As for the leg, it must have disappeared into the belly of an iguanodon, but I didn't have time to notice—I was too busy."

Andoche and Moderan opened their eyes wide.

The governor smiled. "Let's go see my farmyard," he continued. "You'll see a few of our gluttonous beasts. They must have made it difficult for you to sleep last night?"

"A little," said Monsieur Cabrol.

Andoche and Moderan declared that they had heard something vaguely, but had not been very certain. Monsieur Cabrol did not tell them that he had found Melanie ill because of the nightmarish night, which she had spent behind barricaded doors and windows.

The governor's farmyard was well-guarded; poultry-thieves would have found it difficult to get inside. Narrow and solid grilles, lined with thick threads of barbed wire, strong fences and cages also rendered any escape by the inmates impossible.

In the enclosure that as so well-protected, there was an extraordinary swarm of monstrous heads, horns, long necks bristling with spikes, large paws with formidable spurs and nails, heavy hairy spines, and scale-clad muzzles in which horrible mouths opened—with teeth going all the way back to the throat.

A few animals reminiscent of toad-lizards were asleep, their open mouths resting on their paws; others were crawling between the scaly legs and carcasses clad in large plates bristling with upright spikes. In a corner, the heads of large-eyed batrachian heads with hairy necks were protruding from the shadows of cages. One strange animal attracted the attention of the youngsters more than the others: it was a sort of crocodile with a long birdlike neck, bearing a head with a stupid and ferocious expression. The massive body, with several rows of spurs starting at the shoulders and extending to the end of the long tail, stood erect, supported on thick legs armed with huge nails.

"Ugly beast!" said Andoche.

"A Dinosaur," said the governor. "And over there, in that pool you can see, there's a Plesiosaur."

"I recognize that one," said Monsieur Cabrol. "I've seen restored skeletons in the Museum."

"This one's alive, as you'll see!"

The governor made a sign to a man in the enclosure, out of range of the claws, armed with a long rake. The employee took a few large fish from a basket and threw them toward the pool.

The Plesiosaur's head came up rapidly, opening a serpentine maw with sharp teeth, and fell upon a fish that had fallen beside the pool. The heavy Dinosaur suddenly heaved itself clear, stood up on its hind legs and caught another fish in mid-air.

The sleeping beasts immediately woke up, their horrible mouths grimacing and grating, each opening in a frightful rictus; the entire swarm launched itself forward, with thrusting horns, snapping teeth, swiping claws, toward the food distributed y the employee, all twisting, convulsing, jostling their neighbors and knocking them aside with blows of horns of horny beaks.

"Infernal dragons and serpents!" said Monsieur Cabrol. "One searches for the Archangel Michael pricking them with his lance, or Hercules trying to strike the multitudinous hydra with great hammer-blows! What models for a painter!"

"Personally," said Andoche, "I hope to see them at liberty in the Astran countryside; it's too good an opportunity to miss. When I go back, I want to be able to tell tales of interesting hunts and say: one day, at a turning on a mountain path, I found myself face to face with an iguanodon of the Stone Age, which came out of its cave, and…"

"And what?" asked the governor.

"And I ran away at top speed!" Moderan replied.

"That's the safest course."

"Or," said Andoche, vexed, "here's the head of a Plesiosaur that I shot one night from a hide. I can already see people rolling their wide eyes, and hear the flattering murmur."

"Perhaps you'll realize your desire," said the governor.

"I don't have so much ambition," said Monsieur Cabrol. "What I want, myself, is simply to complete the paleontological studies of our scientists on the skeletons of antediluvian animas discovered in the deep layers of our soil, with a few observations made *de visu* of animals encountered alive and full of appetite, roaring and clearly manifesting a desire to swallow the indiscreet naturalist."

The governor gave them a few further details regarding the island on which he had lived since its fall into the Pacific. Immediately after Japan had taken possession of it, the government had sent a small garrison and a commission of scientists, which had been joined by others sent by the majority of the civilized nations, to carry out a complete exploration of the island fallen from the sky. Naturally, the exploration had started with the coasts; it was a matter of making exact measurements, of noting all the particularities of the shore and the ground, the rocks and cliffs that had only been washed by the waves for a few weeks, and which had come so far, having gravitated through our atmosphere for years and caused Terrans such keen apprehensions; and, finally, to study the flora and fauna of the far-traveled island, which might furnish us with a few ideas as to the nature and life of the unknown planet from which Astra had originated.

"In the beginning," said the governor, "insufficient precautions were taken in these explorations, in spite of the warnings furnished by the two devoured expeditions. From time to time, in extricable thickets, certain worrying traces were perceived, and the rumps of beasts disappearing into the undergrowth. A few explorers vanished, carried off by wild animals; others were fund half-eaten. The terrain was beaten, tracks were followed, and caves filled with animal remains found. Then, big game hunters were enlisted, to come and purge the island of those ferocious beasts; but they were too numerous, in spite of the massacres that were inflicted on them, especially in the early years."

"Do you have the large carnivores of our tropical regions?"

"No—no lions or tigers, or any big cats; no animals that are known on Earth today. Astra comes from a world less advanced than the Earth, which has not yet reached its present era, but only an epoch corresponding to our Secondary or Tertiary Era, and the only animals that can be und there are quite similar to those of our prehistoric times. There are no big birds on our island; they probably disappeared at the moment when Astra escaped its native planet in the curse of some cataclysm; we've seen nothing of the family of our vultures."

"And no creature remotely approaching the first representatives of the human family in the age of caverns?" said Cabrol.

"None."

"And our pithecoid species, our great apes?"

"Almost nothing—a few flying creatures with something of the monkey and bird about them, a sort of monkey-bat; a few specimens of another very characteristic species, intermediate between a monkey and a cat. I'll show you some, carefully stuffed."

XVII. Unfortunate Encounters in the Dead Forest.

The Villa Beauséjour took off slowly for an initial trip. The governor was standing at a window of the Palace, waving in a friendly manner. In the radiant weather, the Sun was very hot, but they expected that they would soon find a breeze higher up.

When Melanie had complained of a bad migraine, due to the anguish of the night, Moderan had taken her, before the departure, to the fences and grilles of the Museum, and had made her feel the strength of the iron bars, in order to calm her down. The migraine had eased immediately. Reassured, Melanie, was able to enjoy the trip.

At an altitude of 500 meters, the Villa Beauséjour encountered a pleasant little air current. They breathed more freely. The capital Astraville seemed a very small matter from there, but the island was outlined as a whole, with all its indentations and its crown of rocky peaks around the central summit.

The volcanic constitution of Astra was clearly evident. The rocks and subsidiary peaks around the central one bordered an immense crater from the middle of which the central peak surged. The entire middle of the island, devoid of vegetation, was nothing but a stony chaos, an aggregation of blocks that had fallen into ravines, beneath the edges of sharp crests.

"It's the crater of an ancient volcano," Monsieur Cabrol explained.

"And is it about to erupt suddenly?" asked Moderan, anxiously.

"It no longer can; its base is resting on the Ocean bed, so there's no more lava underneath, nothing but water and perhaps a few fish in the depths of the crater."

"That's true—I like that better."

The Villa descended again and began to follow the shoreline, entering into all the clefts and tacking in order to go and look at everything that seemed interesting at closer range—ravines in the depths of inlets, encumbered by landslides, which were nothing but the beds of former torrents and dried-up cascades.

What pretty creeks they discovered in this way while flying over the shore: neatly excised coves, bordered with high cliffs or rocky crags. There was no lack of handsome pines torn up and lying in the waves, as in Provençal creeks. They saw a few trunks pointing this way and that on the slopes, amid the young vegetation; the governor had mentioned plantations, started five or six years before along the shore, but they would need time.

"It will be better in a few years," said Monsieur Cabrol, "and it will pass from dry picturesque to verdant picturesque, embalmed with the perfume of the Japanese islands. That's in the program, the governor told me: rid the island of its nasty prehistoric beasts, which no longer have any place in our era, then reforestation."

As they went along a slightly wider valley, which emerged into an inlet on the southern coast, the Villa Beauséjour was allowed to gain speed slightly. There were tangles of brushwood there that did not originate from Japanese plantations; it was an ancient and unknown vegetation. Although he was a rather inexpert botanist, Monsieur Cabrol recognized vegetal species distantly related to terrestrial species.

"Look out!" said Moderan, consulting the map of the island. "We're in a region advertised as hazardous by the governor!"

"At 25 meters above the rocks we have nothing to fear," said Monsieur Cabrol. "I'll keep an eye on the route; we won't go any lower down…"

Andoche, leaning over the balcony, searched the hollow of the valley with his binoculars. He made a sign to Monsieur Cabrol and murmured, as if he were afraid to scare away some game: "Look behind that bush—something moved."

"I can't see anything."

"Yes! I can see…oh, it's gone. It was a reptile; it's gone back into its hole."

"I can see something else down there," said Moderan, approaching in his turn. "Near the glittering water…"

"Yes, a little pool."

"Well, there's something on the edge, to the right…"

"Mere toads—I can see them too!"

"Mere toads, you say," said Monsieur Cabrol, "seen from this height—but they're a meter wide, your toads. Let's go down a little. Can you see them more clearly? Swollen and pustulant, with horns…and even reptilian wings. A snapshot, Andoche, quickly!"

"Look out!" said Moderan.

The Villa had descended too far; they were about to skim the bushes and drive into the pool—but the photograph was taken; they were able to go up again.

"Penguins!" cried Moderan.

On a rocky crest, penguins were lined up, holding council, seemingly looking at the Villa in bewilderment. They covered their heads with their thick, heavy wings, and clicked their formidable moustached beaks, displaying pointed teeth.

"Another photo!"

"It's done!"

Phanor, who could not see the game, nevertheless started barking in a room—but the Villa rose up again. The landscape really was becoming fantastically picturesque. After all, while maintaining a height of 25 or 30 meters, they could not have anything to fear.

The binoculars continued to search the extraordinarily dense brushwood, or penetrated the holes in rocks that might have served as lairs for wild beasts. The latter, if there were any, did not allow themselves to be seen; they could clearly make out, among the lianas, beneath the arborescent ferns, ripples where the vegetation was stirred by the passage of some animal, but nothing more.

By following the coast in this fashion they arrived in a region of a very different character. There were still gorges and landslides of large boulders, but the slopes of the ravines were bristling with broken trees, which climbed in serried ranks up the mountain-slopes, their trunks dry and white, with no greenery—the mighty trunks of centenarian trees extending twisted and withered arms in despairing gestures, long gnarled branches or broken stumps: a nightmarish landscape.

There was no trace of green on any branch; it was truly a Dead Forest.

On passing over to the far side of the wooded ravines, however, they found brambles and ferns again, and saw undulations in the grass once again. There were also reptiles sliding silently through the grass. Monsieur Cabrol perceived that they were arriving in the region marked on the map as dangerous.

Andoche was pleased; he had his camera in one hand and a machine-pistol in the other. "It would be so nice to take back a little souvenir!"

Monsieur Cabrol wanted to go up to 50 meters, for the sake of his peace of mind, but he agreed to fly over a shiny little pool beforehand, where suspect dots were moving amid thick clumps of reeds.

Andoche exclaimed joyfully; entrusting the camera to Moderan, he showered the suspect dots with gunfire. Still nothing: more or less giant frogs and hideous toads. The Villa Beauséjour gained height in order to search a little further on.

"Come on," said Monsieur Cabrol. "A very agreeable day—one more little tour and we can go back to offer our compliments to the governor on the tranquility of his island."

The Villa described a large circle in order to get a better view of the central peak; then, having set a course for the return journey, Monsieur Cabrol stretched himself out in his armchair beneath the disk of the apparatus, the buttons and switches within arm's reach.

"Oof! It's going to be hot this evening."

An exclamation from Moderan made him jump. "Beware beasts!" the latter said. "Look out!"

"Bah! We're 50 meters above them," said Monsieur Cabrol.

"They're coming up!" cried Moderan. "Look out behind!"

Camera in hand, Andoche ran to the balcony, wanting a thrilling prehistoric photograph.

"What? They're coming up?" repeated Monsieur Cabrol, heading for the rear balcony. "They've got wings, then? Oh, damn it! Yes, they have—it's really them…there was mention of pterodactyls!"

Down below, above the dead forest, bizarre creatures were moving among the branches, shaking their long limbs and ponderously unfurling large membranous wings. Heads in the air, the hideous beasts were clicking their long crocodile-like jaws greedily.

"Don't worry! Before the beasts are able to free their wings in all that brushwood, we'll be far away—I'll increase speed."

"Quickly, Uncle!" Moderan shouted. "There's one coming up!"

Without pausing to look, Monsieur Cabrol pressed a button and the Aerovilla fled in the direction of Astraville. Two of the pterodactyls, suspended from the rear of the Villa by their claws, were trying to hoist themselves up to the window, which Moderan and Melanie were in the process of barricading.. Melanie was uttering exclamations, Phanor was barking and Babylas, with his tail bristling, was leaping on chairs, spitting and cursing.

"Dirty beasts!" cried Melanie. "Is that a bird's beak or a crocodile's head? You shan't get in!"

On the balcony, Andoche was trying to take aim with his machine-pistol, but he could not lean over far enough. Fortunately, a cluster of pterodactyls, gripping one another at the rear, putting all their weight on the claws of the first, caused it to let go. The entire group whirled around, without falling right away. They peeled off one by one and resumed the pursuit—but the liberated Villa Beauséjour was now flying at high speed.

Monsieur Cabrol mopped his brow and uttered a sigh of relief. "No more immediate danger, but let's go back! Those vile birds have impressive jaws."

At the rear, Andoche kept a lookout for the pursuers; he wanted his photograph and was waiting for an opportunity. Monsieur Cabrol made the concession of pausing slightly before accelerating to top speed.

The pterodactyls did not lack intelligence; they wheeled around in order to try to attack the Villa from the side, where the balconies might facilitate boarding. The huge wings were beating furiously, the ferocious beasts showing their powerful and avid teeth. Raucous cries and whistles were heard.

When Andoche saw that they were within range he succeeded in taking two snapshots.

"A flock of pterodactyls hunting—a rare picture," he said. "Now let's get away from them!"

The Aerovilla flew directly to Astraville, whose pink roofs were visible in the distance. The pursuit continued, but the pursuers soon began to show signs of fatigue. They gradually became spaced out in a long line, like a flock of wild ducks, and some, abandoning the pursuit, let themselves drift down to the ground.

Finally, they arrived. There was movement below; Astraville had perceived the pterodactyls and armed men were climbing a rocky point close to which the chase had to pass. Now the Villa descended slowly to resume its place on the grass. Andoche and Moderan followed the rout of their enemies with binoculars, joyfully.

As soon as they had landed, the Governor arrived in front of the Villa. "Well," he said, as Monsieur Cabrol hastened to lower the boarding ladder for him, "you encountered something, then?"

"Yes, Monsieur le Gouverneur, we've been attacked by a flock of nasty beasts, caymans with the long wings of giant bats—ferocious poultry, at any rate—which nearly caught us by surprise in the air and invaded the villa."

"Pterodactyls," said the governor. "The last on the island, six dozen at the most. I made the concession of keeping them, in case a scientific commission came. Two of the ones pursuing you have just been shot, but, to recompense you for the anxiety they caused you, I'll give the order to capture a certain number for stuffing."

"But we're very glad of the adventure, Excellency! A nice souvenir of the voyage…"

"And we have two photographs, Monsieur le Gouverneur!" said Andoche.

"You'll let me see them? You're content with the excursion, then?"

"We're delighted! Superb landscapes, bearing in all their contours, the clefts in the rocks and the ravines, something quite different from anything that the Earth can offer. They're not Terrestrial landscapes; we no longer have them here on our terraqueous globe. And in the somber gorges, beneath the thick vegetation in the depths of ravines, one divines so much that is disquietingly unknown—it must be swarming with so many strange animals."

"Yes, there are still interesting discoveries to be made there: curious little animals not yet described, inoffensive or very ferocious: little carnivores combining the features of rats and serpents, chickens and lizards; beasts of all shapes slithering on 30 agile feet or galloping with shells on their backs, like those of our dawdling snails; insects armed with mandibles, poison darts, drills, shears and pointed beaks. You'll see all that—it's interesting—but you mustn't touch! I'm expecting a scientific mission before long: botanists, zoologists, entomologists. You might have an opportunity to join them, and in total safety, for the mission will only be exploring under a strong escort."

"Gladly, Monsieur le Gouverneur."

The residents of the Villa Beauséjour were delighted with their excursion. Melanie, having recovered from her excitement, swore that she had never been afraid at all, and regretted not having been able to break her broom over the muzzle of one of those huge ridiculous chickens, because she had not been given time. On other excursions, she would always have that weapon close to hand, with the sole aim of defending Babylas if required—poor Babylas, who was sleeping peacefully, having already forgotten his recent terror.

As for Phanor, he went on to the balcony from time to time to look up in the air, barking insults addressed to the vile birds of the locality.

XVIII. On Astra's Central Peak.

Communication with Paris was renewed. Everything was going well over there, except that the resurfacing work—this was a constant refrain—was dragging on by reason of the immense difficulties that had to be overcome to avoid further collapses in the deep excavations and borings, for the removal of rubble before the construction of definitive underpinnings.

Monsieur des Ormettes laughed heartily when Andoche told him about the flock of pterodactyls chasing he Villa Beauséjour. As he gave evidence of a hint of incredulity, Andoche had his photographs put on the Tele. Monsieur des Ormettes was obliged to give in and admit that it was, at any rate, difficult and uncommon game.

"What about this?" asked Moderan, putting on the flying toads, larger than Phanor, enormous beasts dragging swollen belies along on four feet, their backs covered with spiky plates with long pointed wing-tips: a genre of pleasant beauty completed by a flat horned head split by an immense mouth and large round eyes with a haggard expression.

"Very pretty, as nightmare beasts," said Monsieur des Ormettes.

"And these?" said Monsieur Cabrol, putting on a photo of penguins perched on a rocky crest, near the dramatically-gesturing trees of the Dead Forest.

"What's that? A conference of penguins?"

"Yes, a tribe of old penguins in lively and animated conversation—oh, very animated, believe me! We heard the charming concert they gave by clicking their thickly-moustached beaks and beating their bony wings. I think they were expressing their amazement—or their admiration—at the sight of our Villa exploring the ravines of Astra, but the governor has promised us much more; we're delighted, awaiting the results of our next excursion."

"There's not too much danger, though?"

"Don't worry—we'll be prudent."

A few charming and interesting weeks passed on the extraordinary island. They were on the best possible terms with the Governor, who often came to have lunch at the Villa, and they also went to refresh themselves on the terraces of the Palace in the evenings.

His Excellency's wife, a very charming lady, had a great liking for the island where she had lived since the early months of Astra's fall. Having arrived quite reluctantly, solely to be with her husband, she had known the difficulties and dangers of the early years. Now that the island had almost been purged of its monsters, she found life there pleasant, and only complained of the lack of social intercourse and the rarity of visitors, annoyances due to Astra's bad reputation.

"Oh, the difficulties of the early days!" she said. "The first explorations into the unknown! It was necessary to live under guard, everywhere and at all times. With what was one going to be confronted in those profound mountain gorges, in all those caves, those dark holes serving as the lairs of huge unknown wild beasts? The first governor was only here six months before being devoured by a giant saurian; my husband succeeded him, and you've been able to observe the accidents that overcame his left arm and leg...unfortunate encounters with plesiosaurs of a sort, I think. But today, serious accidents are rare; the island and its surprises are familiar. Since the early days, my husband has undertaken its complete exploration. Above all, it's necessary to get to know this little gift fallen from the sky, isn't it?"

"Naturally," said Monsieur Cabrol. "And it must have been exciting—that step-by-step march toward discovery, on this planetary fragment, which had not yet been seen by anyone!"

"Indeed—and my husband devoted himself to it with a passion that he always wanted me to share, but I was truly fearful of too many unfortunate encounters in all that unknown! My husband organized great beatings with big game hunters sent from Tokyo. The first explorations had revealed amazing things: the existence of an extraordinary fauna that no

260

region of our own planet now possessed, fantastic beasts that the first ages of the Earth had known, but which no longer existed except as fragments of skeletons found by excavating the deep layers of the ground. Well, we have all those beasts here, alert and very much alive, some of mediocre size, others gigantic, but all endowed with an excessively hearty appetite! Annoying and troublesome neighbors! Our hunters beat the plains and mountains, woods and ravines; ditches were dug and traps set..."

"It caused me some distress," the Governor said, in a desolate voice, "to destroy all the animals that had come so far to find us in that fashion. I would rather have been able to preserve the ones that were not too nasty. I studied the character and mores of the game, which was abundant enough in the early days, in the hope of encountering a few species new to us and suitable for adaptation to the Earth—useful species, or merely harmless ones. I haven't despaired; I have a few animals that I'm caring for with a view to acclimatization—I'll introduce them to you. There's a kind of giant fowl with very pretty plumage, which can talk like our parrots, repeating what it hears, human voices or animal cries. Can you imagine that? A chicken-run chattering away at full volume, replying to the farmer's voice? There's a furry tortoise that trots over the meadows, where it feeds on a shelled rabbit that has no need of a hutch, carrying its house on its back..."

"Very interesting species," said Monsieur Cabrol.

"My dream," the Governor continued, "has been to discover some species of prehistoric horse among our large-footed quadrupeds, the members of which gallop almost upright on their hind legs, lifting up a small head on the end of a long neck—a kind of horse-bird, sometimes with wings of a sort—or even some large pack-animal, solid and docile, to compete with the dromedary or the llama. Can you imagine? What a gift to make to our planet! But I've only found ferocious beasts, stupidly greedy, which only think about chewing and swallowing everything they encounter...nothing but dangerous animals to shoot and stuff for zoological museums!

Our hunters have destroyed a great many of them. Of those that aren't too malevolent or stupid, we take fine specimens that we keep locked up, or raise in our park in order to attempt their domestication. We also supply curious and unknown animas to menageries and circuses. The important thing is to eliminate all the dangerous or harmful species and thus ensure the complete security of our island, but we can't yet guarantee that security everywhere…"

"Yes," said Monsieur Cabrol.

"We're getting there! Killing all those fantastic beasts, those apocalyptic animals, makes me very melancholy! If we don't want to be spitted by their horns, disemboweled by their terrible claws or crunched by their teeth, though, it's necessary to clear them out of our forests! Our hunters are working on it—but it causes me a great deal of grief, Monsieur."

"You must console yourself, Monsieur le Gouverneur, since you are conserving living or naturalized specimens of them."

"Alas! But you've come to study the inmates in my menagerie and farmyard. In the course of our early explorations we discovered, lying in ambush in a cave, a kind of gigantic plesiosaur, which we had to kill and which did us a great deal of harm. It had consumed a vast number of animals of every sort, large beasts as well as small game; its cave was full of bones, as was the lugubrious gorge into the depths of which it opened. Perhaps we have lost a few interesting animals to its gluttony. The monster's vast carcass—18 meters from head to tail—is in Tokyo."

Andoche and Moderan were enchanted; when the Aerovilla was not taking them on excursions, often with the Governor or Madame Kirosita, they were at the Governor's house—or, rather, with his prehistoric prisoners.

"We're going hunting," said Andoche, who never put down his camera any longer, "hunting for photographs, while awaiting more serious hunts—for I don't want to go back without some glorious trophy, the head of some abundantly horned, toothed and clawed mastodon that I've shot myself!"

"I'll watch over you!" said Moderan.

"We already have the feathery frog, which fills a lacuna, as Monsieur Kirosita says, between birds and fishes…"

"And the winged salamander, a near relative of lizards and bats."

"And the furry tortoise, which runs on four legs along the bottom of its pool in the menagerie to catch little fish!"

"Yes, and we'll have others still."

In the Menagerie—not in the section of dangerous beasts, of course, but in that of mild, inoffensive animals— Andoche and Moderan were watching a couple of shelled rabbits, which were calmly grazing the grass, face to face, with their shells on their backs. All that emerged from each shell was the head, the long ears and the forelimbs, with the tips of the rear feet.

Moderan was trying to attract them further out of their shells with cabbage-leaves, and Andoche was quietly taking their portrait, when a furry tortoise suddenly slipped tortuously through a gap in the fence directly behind the framed scene and leapt on the rabbits, clicking its teeth in a ferocious manner. Moderan abruptly stretched out a leg, however, and interrupted its leap.

The two rabbits, uttering shrill squeals, withdrew their heads and feet into their shells and hunkered down. The tortoise leapt on top of the shells, one after another, trampling them and attempting to turn them over, but the shells remained glued to the ground.

It was a nice picture, much enlivened; Andoche was pleased. At the cost of a few scratches, the benevolent Moderan saved the two animals; he shoved the furious tortoise toward a cage and shut it in.

Monsieur Cabrol did not remain inactive, in spite of all the charms of a siesta in the shade of the rocks on the beach, or pleasant conversations in the Governor's garden. He was taking notes too. Alas, no clue had been discovered on the island that revealed the identity of the planet from which it had been torn away. Was it Mars, or some other, more distant planet? They would never know. It would have been so interesting to venture, on the basis of a few archeological fragments, hypotheses regarding the political institutions of the planet Mars, or the mores of the Martians!

Nothing remained, therefore, but zoology and botany. The amiable Governor, inexhaustibly obliging, supplied him with as much information as possibly, and gave him access to his collections.

Afterwards, they often talked about an excursion. The Governor wanted to make an ascent of Astra's central peak, in company with Madame Kirosita. She had not yet climbed that beautiful mountain, which reminded her of Fujiyama in her native Japan. Monsieur Cabrol seized the opportunity to please the Governor, and one morning, the Villa Beauséjour took Monsieur and Madame Kirosita to the mountain. It was an excellent way to go mountain-climbing in one's own home. The climb was undertaken slowly, spiraling around the peak so as to get a better view of all its faces and all its details.

That took scarcely an hour. There were no trees, even after the fashion of those in the Dead Forest; not the slightest hint of vegetation. It was a desert of stones, nothing but rock and landslides on top of ancient lava-streams.

The summit was nothing but a narrow ridge above the crater, half-filled with heaps of fallen boulders, crumbling lumps of charred stone—but what a view! The island seemed immense from that perch, at an elevation of 800 meters. From above, they searched all the ravines tumbling from the peak, all the valleys ramifying from it, with slender threads of water sparkling on the slopes, and a few pools, almost dry at present, which would become small lakes in the rainy season.

When the Villa Beauséjour was solidly anchored, they got down on to the rocks.

"A nice place for a picnic!" said Monsieur Cabrol.

"Bah! Nothing but stone today. Tomorrow, if you wish, we'll go over there, into that green and mauve region on the horizon, and loose ourselves in 50 kilometers of arborescent ferns."

It was a very agreeable little trip, which was renewed several times.

One day, Monsieur Kirosita arrived at the Villa early. "I've been notified of the location of some pterodactyl nests," he said. "Probably the ones that grave chase to your Villa, for there are hardly any others on Astra now. And there are chicks in the nests! We're going to hunt them to destruction—would you like to be there?"

"What? Nests with chicks—oh, but we must see that! To bring back a baby pterodactyl—that would be excellent!"

Andoche and Moderan could not restrain their joy; they were already preparing cameras and machine-pistols.

The hunt was very exciting; the Villa Beauséjour avenged itself for the earlier scare. Andoche and Moderan, alongside His Excellency Monsieur Kirosita, machine-gunned their former enemies from the balcony.

The nests were nothing but tangles of branches in holes in the rocks. When the large pterodactyls had been shot or put to flight, not without risk, it was still not very easy for the hunters to take possession of the five little ones, which struggled madly, lashing out with their tails, their wings and their claws, and dug their already-long and sharp teeth into the leather of their boots.

Andoche got a few scratches in the process, but he brought back some fine photographs of the battle.

The weeks and months passed, very pleasantly, spent in excursions and studies. Perhaps Andoche and Moderan were neglecting the Universal Cine-Phono University slightly, but there was no hurry. They had time before their return to Europe, and since the period of rest was also a period of study, that was compensation.

They had thrilling things to recount in their conversations with the family over the Tele, and every time, Monsieur des Ormettes exclaimed and declared that he was going to take the Paris-Buenos-Aires airship, which called at Astraville, in order to join his sons in such an interesting place; they should expect him—but time went by, and business continue to retain him in Paris.

Andoche had his harvest of photos, as well as other souvenirs: a Dinoceros horn; Ichthyosaurus teeth; an Iguanodon skull; the terribly-armed paw of a Megalosaurus. That was something, those little souvenirs of ferocious beasts driven from cover while alive, then fought and massacred! In addition, Monsieur Kirosita had made him a gift of one of the baby pterodactyls—the very one that had bitten or scratched him, but which could no longer bite, having been carefully stuffed.

Monsieur Cabrol had brought back so many souvenirs that he no longer knew where to put them; he had filled the guest-room with them. It was necessary to send them to Paris at the first opportunity. He had been obliged to refuse, for lack of space, an enormous and very peculiar serpent with legs, which was 15 meters long.

After so many fine days, however, the weather was beginning to deteriorate; storms succeeded one another, drowning the shore under deluges of warm rain. Astra's Fujiyama disappeared into the mist, or appeared in total isolation, raising a menacing point above the dark clouds. Monsieur Kirosita had his Menagerie covered with large conical thatched roofs to protect his animals.

Monsieur Cabrol and his nephews went to the Palace to say goodbye and thank His Excellency and Kirosita, who displayed considerable sorrow at the departure of the Aerovilla.

"We'll come back," said Monsieur Cabrol. "Thanks to your friendliness we've spent a charming season—two charming seasons—here! We're going to continue our journey by heading for the Argentine coast, but in six months time, the Villa Beauséjour will come back to take shelter again beneath the walls of the Palace where we have been so well-received…"

"And then, said the Governor, "I shall doubtless be able to acquaint you with further discoveries—and perhaps I will have succeeded in my attempts to bred useful animals. I have some hope for my hybrids….look, I didn't want to tell you before having succeeded, but I think I've got there. In the streams of our planetary morsel we've found a large and handsome species of crayfish, and an idea occurred to me: I've had large breeding-pools prepared in the sea, in which the crayfish has developed so well that it's in the process of being transformed into a sort of giant lobster! A little while longer…and you shall see it when you return!"

XIX. Oceanian Paradise.

The Villa Beauséjour has been flying through the rain for five or six hours. It is a trifle monotonous; there is not much to be seen. Astra Island has disappeared, vanished; everything—land and sea—has melted, there is no longer anything but warm rain that is coming down in bucketfuls.

Altitude: 100 meters. Speed: 60 kilometers an hour. Heading: South. Very prudently, Monsieur Cabrol is thinking about finding a port before nightfall. The excellent Kirosita has told him about a little coral island which might furnish the Villa Beauséjour with a pleasant watering-place for a few days. The word *watering*[32] makes his nephews grimace; have they not been watered enough since morning—or, rather, for several days.

The sky is becoming clearer, though; toward the south, where they are headed, there is a gap in the clouds, a little blue window; there is less water in the ocean of the sky. Monsieur Cabrol sighs with satisfaction and picks up his binoculars to interrogate the horizon. Something is distinguishable in the distance: a small grey blur. After a quarter of an hour, the grey patch has clearly taken on the form of a wooded island sur-

---

[32] This pun does not translate, although I have improvised a half-hearted compromise; the French *mouillage* means both "anchorage" and "soaking."

rounded by reefs, accompanied by other, less clear-cut islets, scattered over some distance.

"We're now in the middle of Polynesia," said Monsieur Cabrol. "The rain is stopping; we're going to continue further south to take a look at the islands, in order to descend as soon as we spot a pleasant place to land."

"And here's the Sun again!" said Andoche, joyfully.

The Villa Beauséjour passed slowly over an archipelago of minuscule islets and 50 meters. Some were simple clumps of vegetation in the midst of the waves; others rings of madreporic reefs surrounding central lagoons bordered with coconut palms.

"Atolls," said Monsieur Cabrol. "Islands fabricated by corals, the constructive animalcules of the Australian sea: a little reef, at first, which gradually becomes a habitable island. Look, here's one of the atolls with a rather engaging appearance—we'll ask it for hospitality this evening. Does the prospect of a night spent on a desert island please you?"

"Good idea, Uncle."

From the balcony of the Villa they were able to assure themselves that the island was absolutely uninhabited: nothing but coconut palms encircling a pretty beach surrounded by rocks, where the slow work of the corals continued.

No more rain: a golden red Sun was about to set in the violet-tinted azure of the waves. A magnificently blue night, in which thousands of stars were twinkling. What calm! No neighbors, no other sound than the murmur of the waves beating the shore and the breath of the wind in the coconut palms.

"Let's stay here for three weeks!" Moderan proposed.

"Why bother, since we can find a similar shelter every evening?"

And the following morning, the Villa Beauséjour, thoroughly dry, took off again in a mild heat.

Islands, islets, and more islands; a seed-bed of islands above which the Aerovilla flew at a modest speed, making detours, sometimes descending almost to skim the waves or rising up to look over the sea.

They landed to eat lunch on the sand of one island, and ate dinner on another, before going on to sleep on a third.

Now there were larger islands, which seemed from on high to be enormous bouquets of flowers and tangled verdure floating on the waves—and isles under construction, in which men and coral were collaborating to create islets on rocky foundations that could gradually be linked up into a single island.

Moving from archipelago to archipelago, the Villa Beauséjour went to pay a short visit to the sixth continent, constructed long before in the 20th century. Monsieur Cabrol did not intend to stay there long; there was nothing very interesting to see on that continent, which as in a very poor state. Fragments of various sizes had been detached from it in the wake of some tempest and drifted away, as floating islands that the winds and currents carried toward the happy Tahitian archipelago, or pushed into cold regions, toward the polar icecap.

It had then been overtaken by a much more serious accident. Important repair work had been started on the eastern side, opposite Valparaiso. Use was then beginning to be made of intra-atomic energy. As with all sciences at their inception, of course, there were miscalculations and accidents due to misuse as well as to the imprudence of overly audacious scientists launched at hazard into the new science. Thus it was that the imprudence of a researcher, suddenly developing an intra-atomic force 100,000 times to that which he needed, blew up at a stroke the entire eastern coast of the sixth continent, the most populous region—an enormous accident, which had curious consequences.

The part of the sixth continent thus projected to vertiginous heights entered into the gravitational zone of the Moon, and began rotating around it as a minuscule satellite of our satellite. Thus, that new light in our sky, that little firefly accompanying the Moon, is of human manufacture, since it is a fragment of the sixth continent constructed by humans 800 years ago to relieve the old continents of their surplus of humanity.

One evening, on quitting the sixth continent, the Aerovilla encountered an islet that was exceedingly pretty in appearance, with a charming little beach beneath bouquets of foliage and lianas. On descending, they perceived a troop of monkeys leaping and swinging amid the flowery lianas—hardly troublesome neighbors, perhaps even amusing ones, for a nocturnal stopover.

Indeed, when he Villa had dropped anchor, it was visited by the entire tribe inhabiting the greenery and the coconut palms. The monkeys arrived in families, holding little ones by the hand, leaping and frolicking around the Villa, holding noisy conferences in which the elders, nodding their heads, seemed to be giving explanations.

The Villa interested them greatly, and the sight of humans did not frighten them at all. Andoche set up his camera on the balcony, and soon had a few snapshots of remarkable individuals. Then the monkeys, familiarizing themselves very rapidly, became indiscreet. They were shoving one another, leaping about and hanging in groups from the balcony, in spite of the threats of Babylas, who was following their movements with amazement, clutched in Melanie's arms. Two or three young ones having climbed on to the roof and hoisting themselves up to the weathervane, others were about to come in through the windows.

It was at that point that Phanor, easy-going until then, became annoyed and leapt up, barking furious reproaches. That was sufficient. There was a general stampede, the indiscreet bumping into one another, jumping over one another, regaining their verdant refuge, climbing into the trees, from which they began to bombard the Villa with branches and coconuts.

It was a beautiful evening, enlivened by disputes with the monkey neighbors, their grimaces and resumptions of the bombardment, and when everyone went to bed they slept well. Phanor walked around the Villa for a long time, proud of his victory over the pithecoid tribe, determined to mount an effective guard.

In the morning, the monkeys were there again, still noisy and mocking. Held at bay by Phanor, they capered in their trees and bombarded the Villa from afar. When the Villa left, in the afternoon, its departure was saluted by further salvoes of coconuts, and the monkeys, believing that they had vanquished the invaders, performed a war-dance on the sand.

Monsieur Cabrol had not intended to devote more than a fortnight to the journey through Polynesia, and yet the Villa Beauséjour took nearly five months to complete it, punctuated by more-or-less prolonged sojourns on islands, according to the whim of the moment or the charm of the landscapes encountered in the little Edens lost in the depths of Oceanian solitudes.

Finally, Monsieur Cabrol set an easterly course, heading for the States of South America. He wanted to explore that part of the American continent for a while, to look for a place for a longer stay, perhaps in the seaside resorts of the Patagonian coast, so popular in the tourist season. After so many hot days in the tropical islands, the Villa Beauséjour might find a few months of mild and restful coolness there.

Melanie was making Monsieur Cabrol anxious; she was getting fat! A life of sweet idleness was the cause of it. When she had given a flick of the duster to the furniture and swept the floor, which did not take long—there is not much dust over the ocean—she had nothing to do but contemplate the landscape while rocking in an armchair on the starboard balcony and yawn, ready to go to sleep. Then she got up and went to sit on the port balcony, where she yawned again, struggled momentarily, and fell asleep.

Monsieur Cabrol lent her books; she nodded her head in her armchair and slowly closed her eyes. The books did not amuse her. Unfortunately, the Polynesian islands still lacked lending libraries.

There was the Tele. Monsieur Cabrol displayed the photos taken by his nephews there, as well as a little collection of

271

films brought for rainy days. Then he thought of his nephews' Cine-Phono University—but sad to say, Melanie went to sleep all the more rapidly.

Then Monsieur Cabrol decided that it was necessary to force Melanie to exercise—two hours of violent exercise per day. He instructed the two boys to make use of those two hours in taking turns to take Melanie out, watching over her in order that there should be no trickery, and thus save her from obesity. On little islands, Melanie had to make at least two circuits of the isle on the beach, leaping from rock to rock if necessary at certain places—and Melanie kept to that regime.

A few days after leaving the Polynesian islands and their delightful solitudes, the residents of the Villa Beauséjour re-discovered the vibrant and noisy life of the great commercial cities of the coast, the elegance and animation of towns.

Monsieur Cabrol had no intention of installing them in that noisy society; he only gave it a passing glance, time to make a few purchases—notably some hunting equipment to vary their distractions; instruments as far from modern as possible: prehistoric American bows, crossbows firing para-lyzing darts, lassoes, and even an old flintlock rifle.

There was an exploration cruise then, over the coast of Chile, all the way to the Bolivian frontier, and Monsieur Ca-brol was able to take note of several spots where all the condi-tions favorable for prolonged sojourns came together—all that one could desire by way of distraction. Monsieur Cabrol loved the picturesque; he needed busy landscapes: mountains, rocks, lakes and rivers flowing under vaults of inextricable foliage.

All of that seemed to be present in the region where the Villa landed one morning, in weather that was warm but not excessively so, on an escarpment alongside a rapid splashing rivulet, which descended in successive bounds from the moun-tainous background, the beautiful line of whose crests and peaks stood out against the sky, above a series of successive outcrops covered in a thick fleece of forest.

Behind the Villa, old tall trees scale the hill and extend their gesticulating branches into the clouds on high. The residents of the Villa are delighted with the landscape; they follow the mountain's changes of hue at different hours of the day, from the light morning mist to the dramatic sunsets in mauve and dark blue. They allow themselves to be lulled, on the balcony or in their rooms, by the murmur of water running over pebbles.

They have the forest outside their windows, the profound green-lit undergrowth, the bushy thickets in which an invisible life can be divined. Some distance away the buildings of a hacienda are perceptible, livestock in the fields, huts and smoking roofs. Life is good. It seems better and sweeter still when one has just passed through large breathless cities, and especially when one communicates by Tele with the family that has stayed behind in Paris, in the great whirlwind of business and the chaos of the world-wide resurfacing.

They will stay here for some time, making seasonal excursions into the mountains, to the heart of a scarcely-inhabited country—where, it is said, a few Araucanian tribes survive, camped in the ruins of unknown ancient cities. Then, in the warm months, the Villa will transport itself toward the Atlantic, to the luxurious beaches of the Patagonian Riviera, frequented by the upper classes of Argentina, Bolivia and Peru. They are beginning to see bathers from China and Japan, attracted by the casinos, the palaces, the race-courses and the gambling.

The Villa Beauséjour will surely find, well away from the high society beaches noisy with a fake and illusory life, the fine beach of family dreams.

In the meantime, the forest air cure, short strolls and hunting trips in the forest with Melanie, who has so much need of exercise, and Phanor, who turns round from time to time and barks to call to Babylas, left alone in the house.

In the wild forests of this mountainous country there is a great deal of game, large and small, of every species: deer and antelope are abundant, dangerous animals are rare. Numerous hunters are beating the thickets and leading the life of the ancient leatherstockings of North America. The animals killed are taken to the culinary factories of each region, which send them, well-refrigerated, to central factories to be transformed into alimentary pills.

Monsieur Cabrol and his nephews are able to devote themselves to pleasant cynegetic distractions. Monsieur Cabrol has always loved hunting—he is the author of a well-researched book, a *History of Hunting and Hunters Through the Ages*—but he has never hunted, for lack of opportunity. Now is definitely the moment to surrender himself to his passion for the ancient and savage sport.

He has brought his book along, by virtue of sage foresight, and he has just re-read it, in order to get the subject back into his head, with the different fashions of hunting from antiquity to our own day: hunting, shooting, hunting with a spear, a javelin, a bow, a rifle, beaters, ambushes, etc, etc.

Every day, after lunch, Monsieur Cabrol and his nephews set off into the forest, Monsieur Cabrol carrying a bow, with a leather sheath full of arrows in his belt, Andoche armed with a flintlock rifle and Moderan brandishing a crossbow and paralyzing darts. They have taken lessons in how to use them and march in single file. Phanor marches at the head, searching the bushes, and Melanie forms the rearguard, equipped with a lance in case of need and carrying a gourd of fresh water and a game-bag slung over her shoulder.

XX. The Last Savages

In spite of their preparations and good intentions, the initial results were not very brilliant. They did not come back empty-handed, though; Phanor always brought back at least a few young rabbits that he had caught on the run, or even an unfortunate lizard slain after a 45 minute pause in front of a bush, with Monsieur Cabrol holding his bow ready to fire, Moderan down on one knee, crossbow shouldered, and Andoche further away, arming his flintlock.

Monsieur Cabrol also collected a few curious plants, in order to compare them to the ones he had collected on Astra. Melanie brought back armfuls of flowers to renew the bouquets in the Villa.

After a few weeks of cynegetic excitement, Monsieur Cabrol judged the apprenticeship sufficient; they found themselves drawn toward a more difficult, and probably game-rich, terrain in the heart of the mountains. The Villa Beauséjour took off for a few preparatory excursions to the right and the left. While flying over the long mountain chain and the shorter chains branching from it, a veritable labyrinth of profound mysterious valleys and wooded ravines where torrents tumbled from rock to rock and cascade to cascade, Monsieur Cabrol formed designs upon a narrow plateau, well-exposed and, especially, well-framed by forests and gorges, where all the picturesque attractions seemed to have been brought together for the satisfaction of the most demanding tourists.

They found a marvelous place to moor the Villa on a projection of the plateau, which overlooked a vast horizon, permitting glimpses of some sort of distant ruin on a reddish spur above the summits of tall trees agitated by the wind, where regular openings could be discerned among lianas and brushwood—doubtless a temple or ruined palace of the ancient Araucans.

"Very good—one more objective for an excursion!" said Monsieur Cabrol. "There's a good chance that we shall be the discoverers of those ruins, which the guide-books have forgotten to mention."

Lower down, before leaving the first landing-place, Monsieur Cabrol had the opportunity to chat with the people of the nearby hacienda and others who had come to watch the Villa's departure. These worthy folk, agriculturalists or livestock herders in the lonely pampas, regretted seeing them leave; they all advised them to be prudent in their excursions.

The mountain, on that side, had a bad reputation; there was talk, they said, of Araucanian or Patagonian tribes beyond the reach of civilization, living in the manner of their ferocious ancestors in the heart of the Sierras, in the depths of impenetrable forests.

Monsieur Cabrol burst out laughing. "Savages! It's more than 800 years since the last savage disappeared! Dangerous savages? But the police aircraft that watch over the vast pampas and patrol the plains and mountains, would have spotted them a long time ago!"

The residents of the Villa Beauséjour can sleep without anxiety, go out on excursions or hunt as they pleased without worrying about such tales. The last Patagonians! Legends, idle chatter! All peaceful cultivators of the fields, or artisans in the towns—a few were known who were municipal councilors, lawyers or pharmacists...

A delightful week of complete solitude and perfect calm in the mountains.

The nights are marvelous. In the evening, when one sits dreamily on the balcony, watching the Moon rise majestically over the blue forest, one hears no sound—nothing but the chirping of birds in the nearby bushes, or the occasional slither of an animal in the tall ferns. The contours of the mountain dissolve into the sky; all nature is falling asleep.

After a few days of rest, and also of work, study-sessions at the Cine-Phono University, put in order of penciled notes, the walks and hunts are resumed.

It is very beautiful, but a little hard at first. The terrain is very uneven, nothing but enormous holes and steep escarpments, rocks to climb over or go around, ravines, torrents, streams and bluffs to cross.

One day, when they are wandering under the obscure vault of tall trees, piercing the thick curtains of branches and lianas with great difficulty, Monsieur Cabrol and his nephews, panting and breathless, fall into a clearing near a trickle of water, where they hope to refresh themselves somewhat and get their breath back. Until now they have not yet met anyone in the largely-unexplored forest, but suddenly, through the foliage of the nearby undergrowth, the sound of human voices reaches their ears.

A dozen men are lying on the ground, resting around a fire, and those men are Indians, wearing the traditional costume of savages, as in old books. They are armed, some having rifles within arm's reach, others hatchets or long knives in their belts.

"What have we stumbled upon?" says Monsieur Cabrol, holding Andoche back under the cover of the foliage.

One of the savages stirs up the fire, in front of which some sort of antelope is roasting; another cuts bloody slices from the roast and throws them to his comrades. Why are they doing it? Incredible! These men appear to be nourishing themselves in the ancient mode: they are eating the antelope!

Anxious, Monsieur Cabrol looks at his nephews in alarm and gives them an imperious signed instruction not to show themselves. Flat on the ground, faces in the grass, they hold council. This band of savages with wicked and ferocious faces, and that sanguinary appetite, suggest nothing good to Monsieur Cabrol.

"We have to try to keep low and crawl, and then, at a certain distance from the enemy, we'll start to run. Come on, then, retreat, slowly!"

Alas, however, a rustle in the branches has given them away; the savages have keen ears and rapid eyes. They have stood up and have perceived he legs in the long grass. Two or three of them give chase.

The fugitives stand up, anxiously; it will be necessary to defend themselves. The savages stop, as fearful as they are. They say a few raucous sentences in an unknown language. Monsieur Cabrol speaks too; no one understands, but there is still the resource of sign language. One savage extends a hand; another offers the slice of red meat out of which he took a bite a little while before, and beckons to the palefaces to come and join the feast by the bivouac fire.

It is necessary to accept in order not to risk offending the savages, so here are Monsieur Cabrol, Andoche and Moderan, after handshakes and other marks of politeness, sitting in the grass with these disquieting friends. The savages show their teeth, but without evil intent—on the contrary, with benevolence, and welcoming laughter.

Monsieur Cabrol smiles for the sake of politeness; Andoche and Moderan laugh, but they stay on their guard, grouped together, with their weapons within reach.

As the savages insistently offer large slices of their game, it is necessary to decide to try one of them. In fact, it is not as bad as one might think at first sight, that well-cooked roast, but it seems tough to teeth that are not used to it. The savages laugh once more at Monsieur Cabrol's efforts; his golden teeth are aching.

The ice is broken. Monsieur Cabrol, in his turn, takes his little box of pills from his pocket and offers it round. The savages have undoubtedly had some contact with civilized life, for they recognize the pills, but they do not look as if they like them very much. Some swallow them unenthusiastically, other flatly refuse them. But the refreshing pills—Saumur and Old Claret—are better appreciated. No more grimaces. Monsieur Cabrol makes a second, and then a third distribution. Everything is definitely going well; the savages are friendly.

Andoche has his camera slung over his shoulder. He would dearly like to take a photograph of the picnic lunch with the intimidating Redskins—the last representatives of races that have disappeared or fused with the universal and banal mass of civilized people. A nice photo would be an interesting souvenir to bring back. He aims the camera, attempting to operate it surreptitiously, but the savage Andoche thinks of as "the old chief"—one of the most picturesque of the band, a fellow with grey, shoulder-length hair, a thin face with a few tattoos, dressed in a worn poncho with holes and loose threads—signals to him that he is unconcerned and immediately strikes a pose.

So the savages are familiar with photography. Strange! One of them, doubtless in order to improve his looks, takes a pair of spectacles from his pocket. No matter; Andoche will try to mask the spectacles, and the photo will be fine.

Now there is mutual trust. The savages solicit a further distribution of refreshing pills. Monsieur Cabrol calculates. Three of four pills, each one equivalent to half a bottle of fine Bordeaux, might go to the head—but they insist, and it is necessary to comply. Two savages, one old and one young, are prompted to get up to begin a dance accompanied by jumps and slightly unsteady somersaults. Fortunately, it is not a matter of going on the warpath; it is a joyful entertainment, for the dancers are humming or whistling the tune of a jig.

The eyes of all the savage braves are fixed on the pocket in which Monsieur Cabrol has put the box of flavorsome pills. A few lie down in the grass to sleep; others roll their moist eyes, making protestations of friendship in gestures, giving handshakes, punches on the shoulder or even approaching their faces as if to rub noses with their guests—which, as everyone knows, was once the ultimate demonstration of politeness and firm friendship in the old tribes of the pampas, as with all the savages in the world.

Monsieur Cabrol thinks that it is time to leave the party and return to the Villa. Melanie must be astonished by their lateness; it is necessary not to worry her. He gets up, along with the two youngsters, and the polite gestures are resumed. Suddenly the sound of barking in the woods causes the savages to prick up their ears.

"That sounds like Phanor's voice," says Moderan.

"Here, Phanor! Here, Phanor!"

Bounding through the undergrowth, Phanor arrives, and joyously giving voice, he precipitates himself into the arms of his masters, leaping from one to another. Then, coming into the clearing through the same gap as Phanor, Melanie appears herself, leaning on her umbrella.

At the sight of the bivouac and the band of savages, she stops, and seems to be making ready for a fight, but Monsieur Cabrol's voice reassures her.

"Don't worry, Melanie, come and take a closer look at them. They won't eat you—they're good people. But why have you come so far from the Villa?"

"So far? But it's quite close, Monsieur—scarcely five minutes away. I was taking a little walk to stretch my legs…"

"Five minutes? We've been walking for three hours."

"It's close by, on the other side of the wood. You've doubtless circled round and come back toward us."

"All right—we'll come back in."

"But who are these people, Monsieur? They're not cannibals, at least?"

"No, don't worry—you can come closer."

Seeing that their guests are about to leave, the savages also stood up, and the polite gestures are repeated. Monsieur Cabrol goes back into the wood, guided by Melanie and Phanor. The old chief follows, with Andoche and Moderan.

Indeed, in less than ten minutes they reach the Villa Beauséjour. The old chief utters admiring exclamations at the extraordinary dwelling sitting on the ground and attached to large isolated pine-trees.

"Come in, then," says Monsieur Cabrol, pushing him toward the ladder.

The old chief steeled himself in order to climb up into the drawing-room, where he was soon joined by three young men of the troop, who examined the furniture and unknown apparatus with immensely wide eyes.

The old man said many things in a language in which the occasional Spanish word seemed to be recognizable. He accompanied his speech with gestures and pointed over the balcony at the edge of the forest. Monsieur Cabrol thought he understood that he was being invited to come and see, in his dwelling, a part of the ruins that were perceptible in the distance over the treetops. Taking a chance, he acquiesced, by means of gestures, and promised to visit.

Just at that moment, the bell of the Tele rang, and Monsieur des Ormettes appeared on the screen, sitting in his study in Paris.

The old chief nearly fell over backwards in shock. The other three Araucans bounded on to the balcony and leapt to the ground. The old chief wanted to do likewise, but Monsieur

Cabrol held him back and succeeded in reassuring him. He established communication with Paris in order to introduce him to Monsieur des Ormettes. They chatted for a while, but, as the old chief still did not seem comfortable, Monsieur Cabrol let him go.

"Good! Don't worry, my old chief—there's no devilry in this. Go rejoin your friends, and we'll come to see you one of these days...."

That day, Monsieur des Ormettes was not in too much of a hurry. Madame des Ormettes had just got up, and they were going to spend the evening together—the evening, that is, for the Villa Beauséjour, since the morning had scarcely begun in Europe.

While it was still daylight, Monsieur Cabrol, as a simple precaution against unwanted visits, stabilized the Villa ten meters above the ground, solidly moored to robust branches of the large pine-trees. Then they all devoted themselves to family matters—to tales of Paris and impressions of the voyage.

All was well. Monsieur Cabrol, who had feared that he might be more than 300 kilometers from the relay station necessary to maintain Tele communications, was reassured. That had happened several times already, notably in the Polynesian islands, and he had been subjected to the reproaches of the family for the anxiety he had inflicted on them. Moreover, by virtue of that deafness, the Villa Beauséjour had been deprived for a few days of the daily Tele-Gazette, which had annoyed him considerably.

Monsieur des Ormettes talked about the global resurfacing projects in western Europe and told them that he would send a few films showing the progress of the works.

"It's not going very quickly," he said, "because they want to take advantage of the upheaval to make a few improvements to the original plans, rearranging coastlines that are too uneven, squaring off certain regions, straightening mountains chains—and even creating a few new ones to establish more definite frontiers. In brief, everything indicates that the anticipated timetable will be far surpassed..."

"I don't doubt it," said Monsieur Cabrol.

"And what about our boys' studies?" asked Madame des Ormettes. "There's no delay in the program? Interesting excursions and distractions are all very well, but are they working?"

"What?" cried Andoche and Moderan, simultaneously. "I'll say we've been working!"

"You must put your backs into it," said Monsieur des Ormettes. "I'm worried about Andoche's baccalaureate— you'll be taking your Tele exams soon, you know, Andoche...in exactly six months..."

"As soon as that?" said Andoche, with an alarmed expression.

"Well, you'll pass them!" said Moderan.

"Increase your efforts, then—I'm counting on you. Need I mention *flying colors*?"

"We shall have them, Papa, we shall have them!"

XXI. In the Heart of the Forest.

A few days later, Monsieur Cabrol thought that it would be polite to go to see the worthy folk—Redskins, Araucans or Patagonians—whose acquaintance they had made in the forest.

"It's an easy walk," said Monsieur Cabrol. "Three or four kilometers as the crow flies toward the village in the ruins, but it's necessary to find a route through the woods. The weather's good—we'll set off after lunch."

At lunch, Monsieur Cabrol and his nephews looked out of the window from which the ruins could be seen, and took a heading. The ruins positioned were directly north-north-east. They established a few reference-points to the right and the left, and took note of detours that had to be made to avoid ravines and cut through a rocky promontory that lay across the route.

"We shouldn't take that long," Monsieur Cabrol declared, "now that we've got a pretty good grasp of the topography."

It was not as easy as that, though. Monsieur Cabrol had to admit it: they had been marching through the woods in Indian file for a good three hours, battling their way through lianas in dense thickets, falling into holes, climbing over rocks and descending into ravines that they could not go round, and they had not yet seen any of the reference-points they had noted.

"We definitely won't arrive today," said Monsieur Cabrol, discouraged. "It would be better to return to the Villa."

"I should say so," said Andoche. "But which way is it?"

"Behind us, obviously."

Andoche coughed. "Let's try to retrace our steps…first re-cross the last ravine, then go around the big red rock, then…."

"No," said Moderan, "let's head for that big old pine with the broken branches…"

"That's a detour."

"A very short detour; we need to climb up as high as possible in the old pine…that's quite easy…"

"Not me," said Monsieur Cabrol.

"I'll do it," said Andoche, "and I'll find the right direction."

Fortunately, they were only five minutes from the old pine; Andoche did not have to climb very far to recognize the hill where the Villa Beauséjour was moored; there was no doubt—with his binoculars, he could even make out the Villa's roof. It was not far—a kilometer at the most; they had been turned around again in the thick woods.

"Get a move on, said Monsieur Cabrol, "or nightfall will catch us unawares."

"I'll find another old pine…"

One old pine? They had to find no less than 13, not counting the first, before getting back to the Villa Beauséjour.

At the second pine, when they had gone astray again, getting turned around in the dense wood, having confused the reference-points, it was Moderan who demanded to climb up as high as he could to discover the right direction.

"Forward march! It'll only take ten minutes!"

Five minutes later, they had gone wrong again.

Third pine. It is Andoche who wants to go up this time, so as to be quite sure of not making a mistake. He comes down joyfully.

"Less than a quarter of an hour, and this time, we're there!"

What devilry! All these thickets look alike!

Fourth pine. It is Moderan's turn. He has found it. In mid-descent, astride a branch, he cries out: "Ow! I've been bitten! Again! Again! In the neck, now. Ow!"

"What?" cries Monsieur Cabrol. "What is it, a snake?"

"No, I don't think so. Ah! Ants…big red ants. Oh—there are lots of them!"

"Come down—it's nothing."

Moderan descends as quickly as possible, shaking his hand and scratching his neck.

"Did you find the direction?"

"Yes—that way. It's easy, always straight ahead. Ow! That hurts…it's burning!"

"Let's march! I'll put something on your bites at the house. Straight ahead—that must be this way…"

"Yes, Uncle…oh, it's burning—and I've got ants running down my back. Thump me, Andoche! Wait, you're going wrong…straight ahead, that's the other way…"

Fifth pine. It is Monsieur Cabrol who climbs up in his turn, and finds it hard. When he arrives on high, painting somewhat, he is heard uttering exclamations.

"Have you found it, Uncle?"

He does not reply, but there is a noise in the high branches; broken branches fall, and Monsieur Cabrol clambers down rapidly.

"What is it, Uncle?"

The uncles seems upset. "Well! I got up there…fine! There are interleaved branches and leaves forming a platform. I take a look, prudently, and find myself face to face with a huge vulture in the process of feeding its chicks. Or it might have been hatching its chicks…I didn't stay long. Can you hear the birdsong up there?"

Another quarter of an hour lost in getting turned around. Sixth, seventh and eighth pines. Monsieur Cabrol begins the eighth climb. He is hoisting himself up into the lowest branches when suddenly, down below, Andoche and Moderan start shouting.

"Look out, Uncle—wild boar! A band of wild pigs!"

A galloping in heard in the thicket; it is a charge of wild beasts, which rush forward, breaking or tearing off branches and leaves. They arrive at the foot of the pine-tree, where Monsieur Cabrol, clinging to the trunk, throws pieces of wood at them.

"They aren't wild boar," Monsieur Cabrol shouts. "There aren't any here—it's a band of peccaries, I think."

Andoche and Moderan are also hastily climbing trees.

"What should we do, Uncle?"

"Nothing—no noise; let's keep calm, they'll go away…"

A quarter of an hour passes by, then 20 minutes, and the peccaries are still there, noses in the air, sniffing and rubbing themselves on the trees. Having grown impatient, Monsieur Cabrol shouts to his nephews: "I've left my pistol under the roots of my tree. You have yours—shoot at the brigands!"

Andoche and Moderan, sitting astride low branches, have their pistols, loaded with paralyzing bullets. They take careful aim and fire half a dozen bullets. The peccaries do not seem to notice them, and continue grunting and scratching at the foot of Monsieur Cabrol's tree.

There is a further detonation, at the very foot of the tree. A peccary has disturbed the pistol with its underbelly while rooting around among the roots. The peccary rolls on the ground. Having shaken its legs violently, it is no longer moving, but continued grunting angrily.

Andoche and Moderan fire again. This time, two peccaries are felled in the same way as the first; the others, gripped by panic, flee at a full-out gallop.

Monsieur Cabrol and Moderan have come down, and are contemplating their enemies fearfully. Andoche has leapt into the pine tree and is climbing up. He stays up there for two minutes, then comes down again triumphantly.

"I saw it," the aid. "It's not far away, to the left."

They have departed, without lingering to look at the injured peccaries, which will be unable to move a muscle for at least two days.

To the left? But where is the left, in this labyrinth of gaps and these thickets of brushwood. Ninth, tenth, etc...

Thirteenth climb. Where are we? No more reference-points; night has fallen...and fatigue is beginning to make itself felt. Monsieur Cabrol's arms are worn out by all that climbing. He sits down, discouraged. How are they going to get out of this?

Suddenly, Phanor's voice is heard in the distance—faithful Phanor is getting anxious and is calling out. Saved! Thank God!

Soon, Phanor, shooting through the undergrowth, arrives like a hurricane to throw himself into the arms of the poor strays. Understanding their distress, he takes the head of the column, and five minutes later, still yapping encouragements, leads them on to the plateau in front of the reattained Villa Beauséjour.

XXII. Culinary Reunions.

Naturally, it takes more than one day of rest to recover from the fatigue of that excursion in the forest. Monsieur Cabrol has decided that they will go to see the savages by air, with the Villa Beauséjour. That way, they are certain not to go astray.

And they will find another camp-site; this one is not sufficiently convenient as a center for excursions.

A few days later, the Villa Beauséjour takes off. Everyone is here? No one has been forgotten? Let's go!

Alas, they have been under way for a few minutes at an altitude of 100 meters when Melanie when Melanie cries out loudly: "Babylas! Where's Babylas!"

She thought he was sleeping peacefully in the room where she had shut him up for the departure, but he's no longer there. He must have gone out of the window, the reckless individual!

"Let's go back," says Monsieur Cabrol.

As long as we don't get lost, this time, Moderan thinks, anxiously.

The Villa Beauséjour veers to starboard and turns back. There is the plateau on which they camped.

"Babylas! Babylas!" Melanie calls from the balcony.

Babylas does not answer. No Babylas. Melanie is heartbroken, and blames herself. What will become of the unfortunate Babylas, lost in the woods?

Suddenly, a modulated miaowing is heard in the room, and Babylas, re-entering the dwelling at the rear, leaps on to Moderan's shoulders and rubs against his face, purring joyfully.

The Villa Beauséjour gets under way again. This time, it is impossible to go wrong; the hill with the Indian ruins appears above the somber mass of the forest, not far away. After a ten-minute flight, they are hovering over the ruins, and perceive little figures emerging from all the holes, who raise their arms to the sky, shouting.

Monsieur Cabrol spots a suitable place to land on one side; he makes a slow tour of the ruins to weigh up the ensemble, and then sets down gently on the ground. Immediately, the Villa is surrounded at a respectful distance by a noisy crowd, the members of which open astonished eyes and jostle one another to get a better view of the house that has fallen from the sky, and the people at the windows making gestures of friendship.

Monsieur Cabrol recognizes a few of the Indians from the other day in the crowd, busy giving the others explanations. The inhabitants of the lost village have occasionally—very rarely—caught distant glimpses of aircraft or dirigibles passing high in the clouds, without quite being able to imagine that such improbable birds might really exist. Today, here is one of these birds close at hand, on the ground—and the bird is a house, with residents! With wide open eyes, they draw nearer in order to touch it.

Here comes the old chief; he pushes through the crowd and comes to bow ceremoniously to Monsieur Cabrol and invite him to enter his domain.

People are still emerging from all the openings, the women dragging groups of children, pouring out on to the stony paths and the patches of grass growing in the rubble.

The whole thing is a sort of pyramid of superimposed terraces, pierced with irregular openings, with monolithic columns and the debris of sculptures among the tufts of vegetation, lianas hanging down from on high and brushwood climbing upwards. Following in the footsteps of the old chief, Monsieur Cabrol and his nephews have entered the ruin, somewhat complicated inside by virtue of collapses. It is evidently a former temple, all the corners of which are being used as habitations. All the galleries and rooms are occupied, down to the smallest hole.

"It's quite well-lit for a cellar," says Andoche, "but as a habitation, it's somewhat lacking in modern comforts. All the same, it's curious!"

Meanwhile, the old chief, who has not left Monsieur Cabrol's side, seems to have something to ask of him. He speaks, trying to explain. Finally, he taps Monsieur Cabrol's pockets, palpates them, and ends up putting a finger on something hard in one of the pockets. The old chief smiles, and Monsieur Cabrol understands.

It is the box of pills. The old chief has retained the memory of the refreshing pills. The visitors will offer them to him and show a little goodwill to these worthy people.

Monsieur Cabrol opens his box and, after having served the old chief, distributes a few well-chosen pills all round. They are synthetic pills of an excellent little Saumur. There are enough of them for the important individuals and the women of the tribe, who are suspicious at first but soon reassured, and who feed them to the children. Everyone is satisfied; a few ladies manifest an exuberant gaiety; the Saumur has gone to their heads and made them loquacious and noisily boisterous. Fortunately, the box is empty.

They have an excellent installation beside the ruins, slightly behind and to one side, in order to have a view of the whole site. They will be very comfortable there for a few days. What a fine opportunity to make a little trial of prehistoric life!

The afternoon is entirely devoted to a detailed tour of the troglodyte village, the shelters beneath the rocks and the caverns opening all around the old temple.

The furniture, which is very rudimentary, is composed of beds of dry grass in wooden frames in the most luxurious caverns or chambers, a few crudely-fabricated trunks, and earthenware pots with a few utensils. Monsieur Cabrol takes notes. The men of the tribe hunt in the woods, when they are not idling in the Sun; the women have more to do, with the housekeeping, the children, the fabrication of garments of animal-hide or fabrics they weave themselves.

Surprisingly enough, they catch a few Spanish, English, French and Italian words in the Indians, Araucan or Patagonian language.

As soon as night falls, there is silence around the ruined temple, all the inhabitants having gone inside. Only a few men remain outside, sitting in a circle amid the stones, watching the Moon rise over the mountains. When the biochemical lights go on in the Villa, the latter come to roam around the balconies in order to contemplate that interior moonlight, brighter than the other, admiringly.

A few fine days follow, employed in hunting-parties and excursions into the forest with the Indians. All day long, Melanie entertains visitors: the women of the tribe, curious and inquisitive. Unfortunately, they hardly understand one another at all, and have to converse in sign-language.

Phanor always goes out with his masters, but Babylas does not get bored; he hunts too, around the ruins, among the fallen stones, where rats and mice of different species are abundant, running or hopping everywhere. Babylas amuses himself greatly.

The Indian women cook, and Melanie begins to take an interest in it. It is a lost art, since the adoption of pills and synthetic extracts. Melanie only knows how to heat up tisanes, or a little milk when Monsieur Cabrol has a cold. The cave-women quickly perceive that culinary innocence, which makes them shrug their shoulders or burst into mocking laughter—and they show her the game that is gutted and butchered, the bloody slices of roasts, and the rabbits fricasseed in large earthenware pots. Melanie watches with such marked astonishment and mistrust that the Indian women almost have to force her to taste their cuisine.

Monsieur Cabrol heaps notes upon notes. He studies the tribe and its mores, its ideas, when he is able to discover them, its dwellings, its installation in caves...

The mores are mild, at any rate; the worthy people, living easily, understand one another very well.

He studies their language. Surprisingly enough, in their Araucan dialect he distinguishes even more strange locutions. He would dearly like to discover the origin of the tribe. Finally, pursuing his investigation, he discovers that the people are not all autochthons. There are among them people originating from different parts of America, and even Europe, who have escaped from industrial civilization and great cities, and taken up residence in these caves. Some are the descendants of people who arrived two or three generations ago; others have arrived here more recently, in search of tranquility, a primitive and placid life.

Everything begins to get clearer for Monsieur Cabrol; he has assembled numerous notes on the troglodyte village, with supportive photographs. He asks questions, tries to understand; he expects to discover, by pursuing his enquiries, interesting particularities regarding the ideas and habits of these people, lost in the depths of the deserted forest, about their costumes or their more-or-less strange superstitions...

And time passes, and the notes accumulate...

When they explore the immense forest, hunting with the savage braves, it is necessary to take part in their hunters' feasts. There are new experiences for Monsieur Cabrol and his nephews. It is necessary to eat game.

"Well, the old ways sometimes have something good in them, all the same!"

Andoche and Moderan proclaim that quite sincerely. In their turn, their savage companions disdain the nutritive ills; they only accord their esteem to the refreshing pills or extracts, to the pleasant little synthetic wines, with which they are increasingly pleased.

All goes well. Their health is perfect, they have pleasant communications with the family. Phanor and Babylas are in good health too.

Only one black spot: Melanie has begun to get fat again. Not enough exercise. She refuses to accompany Monsieur Cabrol when he goes hunting, and spends her time sitting on the grass, in long conversations with the Indian woman—in pidgin, of course. Then again, because, for lack of pills, they have to start making use of the produce of the hunt, as if by a strange backward leap, she has acquired a taste for that ancient cuisine, and is even getting ideas that have come down to her from distant grandmothers. She has started reinventing antique dishes and sauces, with which Monsieur Cabrol, Andoche and Moderan, far from protesting, seem to take pleasure in experimenting.

Monsieur Cabrol remembers having read in a rare and precious 20th century book entitled *La Cuisinière bour-*

geoise,[33] the names of dishes that come back to his memory: fillet of beef cooked in Madeira, Bresse capon with truffles; chicken casserole *à la Provençale*... These names make him dream—and what can "jacket potatoes" possibly be?

Malenie occupies herself with them too, and promises to reconstitute them.

After all, Monsieur Cabrol thinks, *it's still archaeology.*

More than three months have passed in the village in the forest. Monsieur Cabrol's exceedingly well-documented book is making progress; thanks to all the notes he has accumulated, it is going very well. They can, therefore, think about leaving; it is time to go to the Patagonian Riviera, whether the bathing season is beginning, to find he ideal beach, the little inexpensive spot where Monsieur and Madame des Ormettes will come to join the Villa Beauséjour and spend a little time as a family, before the traveling villa resumes is excursions and its stopovers in the places noted down during its adventurous vagabondage.

Moderan and Andoche—who will pass his baccalaureate by Tele in Patagonia City—are continuing to work. Monsieur Cabrol has nearly finished his book on *The Age of Caves*, while still working on his other books.

---

[33] This standard cookbook was actually a product of the 19th century; many of its recipes were plundered by Mrs. Beeton for her celebrated *Book of Household Management*.

SF & FANTASY

Guy d'Armen. *Doc Ardan: The City of Gold and Lepers*
G.-J. Arnaud. *The Ice Company*
Aloysius Bertrand. *Gaspard de la Nuit*
Richard Bessière. *The Gardens of the Apocalypse*
Félix Bodin. *The Novel of the Future*
André Caroff. *The Terror of Madame Atomos*
Didier de Chousy. *Ignis*
Captain Danrit. *Undersea Odyssey*
C. I. Defontenay. *Star (Psi Cassiopeia)*
Charles Derennes. *The People of the Pole*
Georges Dodds (anthologist). *The Missing Link*
Harry Dickson. *The Heir of Dracula*
Jules Dornay. *Lord Ruthven Begins*
Sâr Dubnotal *vs. Jack the Ripper*
Alexandre Dumas. *The Return of Lord Ruthven*
J.-C. Dunyach. *The Night Orchid; The Thieves of Silence*
Henri Duvernois. *The Man Who Found Himself*
Henri Falk. *The Age of Lead*
Paul Féval. *Anne of the Isles; Knightshade; Revenants; Vampire City; The Vampire Countess; The Wandering Jew's Daughter*
Paul Féval, *fils. Felifax, the Tiger-Man*
Arnould Galopin. *Doctor Omega*
G.L. Gick. *Harry Dickson and the Werewolf of Rutherford Grange*
Nathalie Henneberg. *The Green Gods*
V. Hugo, P. Foucher & P. Meurice. *The Hunchback of Notre-Dame*
Michel Jeury. *Chronolysis*
Octave Joncquel & Theo Varlet. *The Martian Epic*
Gérard Klein. *The Mote in Time's Eye*
Jean de La Hire. *Enter the Nyctalope; The Nyctalope on Mars; The Nyctalope vs. Lucifer*
André Laurie. *Spiridon*

Georges Le Faure & Henri de Graffigny. *The Extraordinary Adventures of a Russian Scientist Across the Solar System* (2 vols.)

Gustave Le Rouge. *The Vampires of Mars*

Jules Lermina. *Mysteryville; Panic in Paris; To-Ho and the Gold Destroyers; The Secret of Zippelius*

Jean-Marc & Randy Lofficier. *Edgar Allan Poe on Mars; The Katrina Protocol; Pacifica; Robonocchio; Tales of the Shadowmen* (anthologists; 7 vols.)

Xavier Mauméjean. *The League of Heroes*

John-Antoine Nau. *Enemy Force*

Marie Nizet. *Captain Vampire*

C. Nodier, A. Beraud & Toussaint-Merle. *Frankenstein*

Henri de Parville. *An Inhabitant of the Planet Mars*

J. Polidori, C. Nodier, E. Scribe. *Lord Ruthven the Vampire*

P.-A. Ponson du Terrail. *The Vampire and the Devil's Son*

Maurice Renard. *The Blue Peril; Doctor Lerne; The Doctored Man; A Man Among the Microbes; The Master of Light*

Albert Robida. *The Adventures of Saturnin Farandoul; The Clock of the Centuries; Chalet in the Sky*

J.-H. Rosny Aîné. *Helgvor of the Blue River; The Givreuse Enigma; The Mysterious Force; The Navigators of Space; Vamireh; The World of the Variants; The Young Vampire*

Han Ryner. *The Superhumans*

Brian Stableford. *The New Faust at the Tragicomique;The Empire of the Necromancers (The Shadow of Frankenstein; Frankenstein and the Vampire Countess; Frankenstein in London); Sherlock Holmes & The Vampires of Eternity; The Stones of Camelot; The Wayward Muse.* (anthologist) *The Germans on Venus; News from the Moon; The Supreme Progress*

Jacques Spitz. *The Eye of Purgatory*

Kurt Steiner. *Ortog*

Villiers de l'Isle-Adam. *The Scaffold; The Vampire Soul*

Philippe Ward. *Artahe*

Philippe Ward & Sylvie Miller. *The Song of Montségur*

MYSTERIES & THRILLERS

M. Allain & P. Souvestre. *The Daughter of Fantômas*
A. Anicet-Bourgeois, Lucien Dabril. *Rocambole*
A. Bisson & G. Livet. *Nick Carter vs. Fantômas*
V. Darlay & H. de Gorsse. *Lupin vs. Holmes: The Stage Play*
Paul Féval. *Gentlemen of the Night; John Devil; The Black Coats ('Salem Street; The Invisible Weapon; The Parisian Jungle; The Companions of the Treasure; Heart of Steel; The Cadet Gang)*
Emile Gaboriau. *Monsieur Lecoq*
Steve Leadley. *Sherlock Holmes: The Circle of Blood*
Maurice Leblanc. *Arsène Lupin vs. Countess Cagliostro; Lupin vs. Holmes (The Blonde Phantom; The Hollow Needle)*
Gaston Leroux. *Chéri-Bibi; The Phantom of the Opera; Rouletabille & the Mystery of the Yellow Room*
William Patrick Maynard. *The Terror of Fu Manchu*
Frank J. Morlock. *Sherlock Holmes: The Grand Horizontals*
P. de Wattyne & Y. Walter. *Sherlock Holmes vs. Fantômas*
David White. *Fantômas in America*

SCREENPLAYS

Mike Baron. *The Iron Triangle*
Emma Bull & Will Shetterly. *Nightspeeder; War for the Oaks*
Gerry Conway & Roy Thomas. *Doc Dynamo*
Steve Englehart. *Majorca*
James Hudnall. *The Devastator*
Jean-Marc & Randy Lofficier. *Royal Flush*
J.-M. & R. Lofficier & Marc Agapit. *Despair*
Andrew Paquette. *Peripheral Vision*
R. Thomas, J. Hendler & L. Sprague de Camp. *Rivers of Time*

NON-FICTION

Stephen R. Bissette. *Blur 1-5; Green Mountain Cinema 1; Teen Angels & New Mutants*

Win Scott Eckert. *Crossovers* (2 vols.)
Jean-Marc & Randy Lofficier. *Shadowmen* (2 vols.)
Randy Lofficier. *Over Here*

HEXAGON COMICS

Franco Frescura & Luciano Bernasconi. *Wampus*
Franco Frescura & Giorgio Trevisan. *CLASH*
L. Bernasconi, J.-M. Lofficier & Juan Roncagliolo Berger. *Phenix*
Claude Legrand, J.-M. Lofficier & L. Bernasconi. *Kabur*
Franco Oneta. *Zembla*
L. Buffolente, Lofficier & J.-J. Dzialowski. *Strangers: Homicron*
Danilo Grossi. *Strangers: Jaydee*
Claude Legrand & Luciano Bernasconi. *Strangers: Starlock*

ART BOOKS

Jean-Pierre Normand. *Science Fiction Illustrations*
Raven Okeefe. *Raven's L'il Critters*
Randy Lofficier & Raven OKeefe. *If Your Possum Go Daylight...*
Daniele Serra. *Illusions*